QUINCY ADAMS SAWYER

AND

MASON'S CORNER FOLKS

A PICTURE OF NEW
ENGLAND HOME LIFE

BY

CHAS. FELTON PIDGIN

BOSTON
C. M. CLARK
PUBLISHING COMPANY
1905

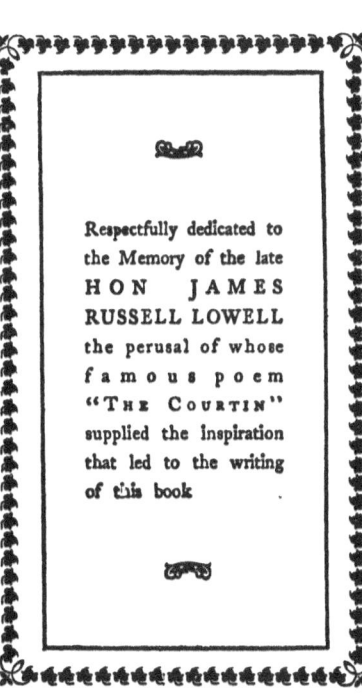

Respectfully dedicated to
the Memory of the late
H O N   J A M E S
RUSSELL LOWELL
the perusal of whose
f a m o u s   p o e m
"THE COURTIN"
supplied the inspiration
that led to the writing
of this book   .

AUTHOR'S PREFACE.

QUINCY ADAMS SAWYER'S only title was plain "Mr." His ancestors were tradesmen, merchants, lawyers, politicians, and Presidents. He, too, was proud of his honored ancestry, and I have endeavored in this book to have him live up to an ideal personification of gentlemanly qualities for which the New England standard should be fully as high as that of Old England ; in fact, I see no reason why the heroes of American novels, barring the single matter of hereditary titles, should not compare favorably as regards gentlemanly attributes with their English cousins across the seas.   C. F. P.

GRAY CHAMBERS,
BOSTON, October, 1902.

CHAPTERS

CHAPTERS

LIST OF ILLUSTRATIONS.

QUINCY ADAMS SAWYER.

CHAPTER I.

THE REHEARSAL.

IT was a little after seven o'clock on the evening of December 31, 186—. Inside, the little red schoolhouse
was ablaze with light. Sounds of voices and laughter came
from within and forms could be seen flitting back and forth
through the uncurtained windows. Outside, a heavy fall
of snow lay upon hill and vale, trees and house-tops, while
the rays of a full-orbed moon shone down upon the glistening, white expanse.

At a point upon the main road a short distance beyond
the square, where the grocery store was situated, stood a
young man. This young man was Ezekiel Pettengill, one
of the well-to-do young farmers of the village. His coat
collar was turned up and his cap pulled down over his ears,
for the air was piercing cold and a biting wind was blowing.
Now and then he would walk briskly back and forth for a
few minutes, clapping his hands, which were encased in
gray woollen mittens, in order to restore some warmth to
those almost frozen members. As he walked back and
forth, he said several times, half aloud to himself, "I don't
b'lieve she's comin' anyway. I s'pose she's goin' to stay

ter hum and spend the evenin' with him." Finally he resumed his old position near the corner and assumed his
previous expectant attitude.

As he looked down the road, a man came out of Mrs.
Hawkins's boarding house, crossed the road and walked
swiftly towards him.

As the new-comer neared him, he called out, "Hello, Pettengill! is that you? Confounded cold, ain't it? Who wuz
yer waitin' for? Been up to the schoolhouse yet?"

To these inquiries 'Zekiel responded: "No!" and added,
"I saw yer comin' out of the house and thought I'd walk up
with yer."

"Wall! they can't do nuthin' till I git thar," said Mr.
Obadiah Strout, the singing-master, "so we shall both be on
time. By the way," he continued, "I was up to Boston
to-day to git some things I wanted for the concert to-morrer
night, and the minister asked me to buy some new music
books for the church choir, and I'm goin' up there fust to
take 'em;" and 'Zekiel's attention was attracted to a package that Mr. Strout held under his arm. "Say, Pettengill!"
continued Mr. Strout, "when yet git up ter the schoolhouse,
tell them I'll be along in a few minutes;" and he started off,
apparently forgetful of 'Zekiel's declaration that he had
intended to walk up with him.

It is evident that 'Zekiel's statement was untruthful, for
his words have betrayed the fact that it was not the Professor of whom he had been thinking.

'Zekiel did not move from his position until he had seen
Strout turn into the yard that led to the front door of the
minister's house. Then he said to himself again, "I don't
believe she's comin', arter all."

As he spoke the words a deep, heavy sigh came from his
great, honest heart, heard only by the leafless trees through
which the winter wind moaned as if in sympathy.

What was going on in the little red schoolhouse? The

occasion was the last rehearsal of the Eastborough Singing Society, which had been studying vocal music assiduously for the last three months under the direction of Professor Obadiah Strout, and was to give its annual concert the following evening at the Town Hall at Eastborough.

A modest sum had been raised by subscription. A big barge had been hired in Cottonton, and after the rehearsal there was to be a sleigh ride to Eastborough Centre and return. It was evident from the clamor and confusion that the minds of those present were more intent upon the ride than the rehearsal, and when one girl remarked that the Professor was late, another quickly replied that, "if he didn't come at all 'twould be early enough."

There were about two score of young persons present, very nearly equally divided between the two sexes. Benjamin Bates was there and Robert Wood, Cobb's twins, Emmanuel Howe, and Samuel Hill. Among the girls were Lindy Putnam, the best dressed and richest girl in town, Mandy Skinner, Tilly James, who had more beaus than any other girl in the village; the Green sisters Samanthy and Betsy, and Miss Seraphina Cotton, the village school-teacher.

Evidently all the members of the society had not arrived, for constant inquiries were being made about Huldy Mason and 'Zekiel Pettengill. When Betsy Green asked Mandy Skinner if Hiram Maxwell wa'n't comin', the latter replied that he'd probably come up when Miss Huldy and the new boarder did.

News had reached the assemblage that Arthur Scates, the best tenor singer in the society, was sick. Lindy Putnam was to sing a duet with him at the concert, and so she asked if anybody had been to see him.

"I was up there this afternoon," said Ben Bates, "and he seemed powerful bad in the throat. Grandmother Scates tied an old stockin' 'round his throat and gin him a bowl of

catnip tea and he kinder thought he'd be all right to-
morrer. I told him you'd have a conniption fit if he didn't
show up, but Grandmother Scates shook her head kind o'
doubtful and said, 'The Lord's will be done. What can't
be cured must be endured;' and I guess that's about the
way it will be."

The outer door opened and 'Zekiel Pettengill entered.
The creaking of the opening door attracted the attention of
all. When the girls saw who it was, they ran and gathered
about him, a dozen voices crying out, "Where is Huldy?
We all thought she'd come with you."

'Zekiel shook his head.

"You don't know?" asked Tilly James, incredulously.
'Zekiel shook his head again. "Of course you do," said
Tilly contemptuously.

She turned away, followed by a number of the girls.
"He knows well enough," she observed in an undertone,
"but he won't tell. He's gone on Huldy, and when a
feller's gone on a girl he's pretty sure to keep the run of
her."

In the meantime Lindy Putnam had been using her most
persuasive powers of coaxing on 'Zekiel and with some success, for 'Zekiel told quite a long story, but with very little
information in it. He told the crowd of girls gathered
about him that he'd be twenty-eight on the third of January,
and that ever since he was a little boy, which was, of course,
before any of those present were born, he'd always followed
the rule of not saying anything unless he knew what he
was talking about.

"Now," said 'Zekiel, feeling that it was better to talk on
than to stand sheep-facedly before this crowd of eager, expectant faces, "I might tell yer that Huldy was ter hum
and wasn't comin' up to-night, but yer see, p'r'aps she's on
the road now and may pop in here any minute! Course
you all know Deacon Mason's got a boarder, a young feller

from the city. P'r'aps he'll come up with Huldy. But I heerd tell his health wa'n't very good and mebbe he went to bed right after supper."

"What's he down here for anyway?" asked Tilly James.

"Now you've got me," replied 'Zekiel. "I s'pose he had some purpose in view, but you see I ain't positive even of that. As I said before, I heerd he's come down here for his health. It's too late for rakin' hay, and as hard work's the best country doctor, p'r'aps he'll go to choppin' wood; but there's one point I feel kinder positive on."

"What is it? What is it?" cried the girls, as they looked into his face inquiringly.

"Wall, I think," drawled 'Zekiel, "that when he gits what he's come for, he'll be mighty apt to pull up stakes and go back to Boston."

Again the outer door creaked upon its hinges, and again every face was turned to see who the new-comer might be.

"Here she is," cried a dozen voices; and the owners thereof rushed forward to greet and embrace Miss Huldy Mason, the Deacon's daughter and the most popular girl in the village.

'Zekiel turned and saw that she was alone. Evidently the city fellow had not come with her.

Huldy was somewhat astonished at the warmth of her greeting, and was at a loss to understand the reason for it, until Lindy Putnam said:

"Didn't he come with you?"

"Who?" asked Huldy, with wide-open eyes.

"Oh, you can't fool us," cried Tilly James. " 'Zeke Pettengill told us all about that city feller that's boarding down to your house. We were just talking it over together, and he surmised that it might be the same one that you met down to your aunt's house, when you went to Boston last summer."

"As Mr. Pettengill seems to know so much about my

gentlemen friends, if you want any more information, n͡o
doubt he can supply it," said Huldy coldly.

" 'Zeke kinder thought," said Bob Wood, "that he
might be tired, and probably went to bed right after
supper."

"Well, he didn't," said Huldy, now thoroughly excited,
"he came with me, and he's outside now talking with
Hiram about the barge."

"Why don't he come in?" asked Bob Wood. "P'r'aps
he's bashful."

"If he didn't have no more common sense than you've
got," retorted Huldy, "he'd have to go to bed as soon as
he had eaten his supper."

The laugh that followed this remark so incensed Wood
that he answered coarsely, "I never saw one of those city
chaps who knew B from a bull's foot."

"Perhaps he'll teach you the difference some day," remarked Huldy, sarcastically.

"Well, I guess not," said Wood with a sneer; " 'less he
can put two b's in able."

Further altercation was stopped by the sudden entrance
of Mr. Strout, who quickly ascended the platform and
called the society to order. It must be acknowledged that
the Professor had a good knowledge of music and thoroughly understood the very difficult art of directing a
mixed chorus of uncultivated voices. With him enthusiasm was more important than a strict adherence to quavers
and semiquavers, and what was lost in fine touches was
more than made up in volume of tone.

Again, the Professor paid strict attention to business at
rehearsals, and the progress of the society in musical knowledge had been very marked. So it is not to be wondered
at that the various numbers allotted to the chorus on the
next evening's programme were gone through quickly and
to the evident satisfaction of the leader.

The last number to be taken up was an original composition, written and composed by the singing-master himself, and during its rehearsal his enthusiasm reached its
highest pitch. At the conclusion of the chorus, which had
been rendered with remarkable spirit, the Professor darted
from one end of the platform to the other, crying out,
"Bravo! Fust rate! Do it again! That'll fetch 'em!"

After several repetitions of the chorus, each one given
with increasing spirit and volume, the Professor threw down
his baton and said: "That'll do. You're excused until to-
morrow night, seven o'clock sharp at Eastborough Town
Hall. I guess the barge has just drove up and we'd better
be gittin' ready for our sleigh ride."

Miss Tilly James, who had acted as accompanist on the
tin-panny old piano, was putting up her music. The Professor, with his face wreathed in smiles, walked up to her
and said, "I tell you what, Miss James, that last composition
of mine is bang up. One of these days, when the 'Star
Spangled Banner,' 'Hail Columbia,' and 'Marching through
Georgia' are laid upon the top shelf and all covered with
dust, one hundred million American freemen will be singing Strout's great national anthem, 'Hark, and hear the
Eagle Scream.' What do you think of that prophecy?"

"I think," said Miss James, turning her pretty face
towards him, her black eyes snapping with fun, "that if
conceit was consumption, there'd be another little
green grave in the cemetery with O. Strout on the head-
stone."

The Professor never could take a joke. In his eye, jokes
were always insults to be resented accordingly. Turning
upon the young lady savagely, he retorted:

"If sass was butter, your folks wouldn't have to keep any
cows."

Then he walked quickly across the room to where 'Zekiel

Pettengill stood aloof from the rest, wrapped in some apparently not very pleasant thoughts.

At this juncture Hiram Maxwell dashed into the school-room, and judging from appearances his thoughts were of the pleasantest possible description.

"Say, fellers and girls," he cried, "I've got some news for yer, and when you hear it you'll think the day of judgment has come, and you're goin' to git your reward."

An astonished "Oh!" came up from the assemblage.

"Out with it," said Bob Wood, in his coarse, rough voice.

"Well, fust," said Hiram, his face glowing with anima-tion, "you know we got up a subscription to pay for the barge and made me treasurer, cuz I worked in a deacon's family. Wall, when I asked Bill Stalker to-night how much the bill would be, just to see if I'd got enough, he told me that a Mr. Sawyer, who said he boarded down to Deacon Mason's, had paid the hull bill and given him a dollar be-side for hisself." Cheers and the clapping of hands showed that the city fellow's liberality was appreciated by a major-ity, at least, of the singing society. "When we git on the barge I'll pay yer back yer money, and the ride won't cost any one on us a durn cent. That ain't all. Mr. Sawyer jest told me hisself that when he was over to Eastborough Centre yesterday he ordered a hot supper for the whole caboodle, and it'll be ready for us when we git over to the Eagle Hotel. So come along and git your seats in the barge." A wild rush was made for the door, but Hiram backed against it and screamed at the top of his voice: "No two girls must sit close together. Fust a girl, then a feller, next a girl, then a feller, next a girl, then a feller, that's the rule."

He opened the door and dashed out, followed by all the members of the society excepting the Professor and 'Zekiel, who were left alone in the room.

"See that flock of sheep," said the Professor to 'Zekiel,

with a strong touch of sarcasm in his tone. "That's what makes me so cussed mad. Brains and glorious achievement count for nothin' in this community. If a city swell comes along with a pocketful of money and just cries, 'Baa,' over the fence they all go after him."

"Hasn't it always been so?" asked 'Zekiel.

"Not a bit of it," said Strout. "In the old days, kings and queens and princes used to search for modest merit, and when found they rewarded it. Nowadays modest merit has to holler and yell and screech to make folks look at it."

Hiram again appeared in the room, beckoning to the two occupants.

"Say, ain't you two comin' along?" he cried. "We've saved good places for yer."

"Where's Mr. Sawyer?" asked 'Zekiel.

"Oh, he's goin' along with the crowd," said Hiram; "he's got a seat in between Miss Putnam and Miss Mason, and looks as snug as a bug in a rug. There's a place for you, Mr. Pettengill, between Miss Mason and Mandy, and I comes in between Mandy and Mrs. Hawkins. Mandy wanted her mother to go cuz she works so confounded hard and gits out of doors so seldom, and there's a seat 'tween Mrs. Hawkins and Tilly James for the Professor, and Sam Hill's t'other side of Tilly and nex' to S'frina Cotton."

"I guess I can't go," said 'Zekiel. "The house is all alone, and I'm kind of 'fraid thet thet last hoss I bought may get into trouble again as he did last night. So I guess I'd better go home and look arter things." Leaning over he whispered in Hiram's ear, "I reckon you'd better take the seat between Huldy and Mandy, you don't want ter separate a mother from her daughter, you know."

"All right," said Hiram, with a knowing wink, "I'm satisfied to obleege."

Hiram then turned to the Professor: "Ain't yer goin', Mr. Strout?"

"When this sleigh ride was projected," said the Professor with dignity, "I s'posed it was to be for the members of the singin' class and not for boardin' mistresses and city loafers."

"I guess it don't make much difference who goes," replied Hiram, "as long as we git a free ride and a free supper for nothing."

"Present my compliments to Mr. Sawyer," said the Professor, "and tell him I've had my supper, and as I don't belong to a fire company, I don't care for crackers and cheese and coffee so late in the evenin'."

"Oh, bosh!" cried Hiram, "it's goin' to be a turkey supper, with fried chicken and salery and cranberry juice, and each feller's to have a bottle of cider and each girl a bottle of ginger ale."

A horn was heard outside, it being the signal for the starting of the barge. Without stopping to say good-by, Hiram rushed out of the room, secured his seat in the barge, and with loud cheers the merry party started off on their journey.

The Professor extinguished the lights and accompanied by 'Zekiel left the building. He locked the door and hung the key in its accustomed place, for no one at Mason's Corner ever imagined that a thief could be so bad as to steal anything from a schoolhouse. And it was once argued in town meeting that if a tramp got into it and thus escaped freezing, that was better than to have the town pay for burying him.

Both men walked along silently until they reached Mrs. Hawkins' boarding house; here the Professor stopped and bade 'Zekiel good night. After doing so he added:

"Pettengill, you and me must jine agin the common enemy. This town ain't big enough to hold us and this destroyer of our happiness, and we must find some way of smokin' him out."

The slumbers of both 'Zekiel and the Professor were broken when the jolly party returned home after midnight. 'Zekiel recalled Hiram's description of the arrangement of seats, and another deep sigh escaped him; but this time there were no leafless trees and winter wind to supply an echo.

The Professor's half-awakened mind travelled in very different channels. He imagined himself engaged in several verbal disputes with a number of fisticuff encounters in which he invariably proved to be too much for the city fellow. Just before he sank again into a deep sleep he imagined that the entire population of Mason's Corner escorted a certain young man forcibly to the railroad station at Eastborough Centre and put him in charge of the expressman, to be delivered in Boston. And that young man, in the Professor's dream, had a tag tied to the lapel of his coat upon which was written, "Quincy Adams Sawyer."

CHAPTER II.

IN 186— the town of Eastborough was located in the southeastern part of Massachusetts, in the county of Normouth. It was a large town, being fully five miles wide from east to west and from five to seven miles long, the northern and southern boundaries being very irregular.

The town contained three villages; the western one being known as West Eastborough, the middle one as Eastborough Centre, and the easterly one as Mason's Corner. West Eastborough was exclusively a farming section, having no store or post office. As the extreme western boundary was only a mile and a half from Eastborough Centre, the farmers of the western section of the town were well accommodated at the Centre. The middle section contained the railroad station, at which five trains a day, each way, to and from Boston, made regular stops. The Centre contained the Town Hall, two churches, a hotel, and express office, a bank, newspaper office, and several general stores. Not very far from the hotel, on a side road, was the Almshouse, or Poorhouse, as it was always called by the citizens of Eastborough.

Between the Centre and Mason's Corner was a long interval of three miles. The land bordering the lower and most direct route was, to a great extent, hilly and rocky, or full of sand and clay pits. The upper and longest road ran through a more fertile section. The village of Mason's Corner contained the best arable land in the town, and the village had increased in population and wealth much faster than the other sections of the town. To the east of the village of Mason's Corner lay the town of Montrose, and beyond that town was situated the thriving city of Cottonton, devoted largely, as its name indicated, to the textile manufacturing industries.

The best known and most popular resident of Mason's Corner was Deacon Abraham Mason. He was a retired farmer on the shady side of fifty. He had married young and worked very hard, his labors being rewarded with pecuniary success. When a little over fifty, he gave up active farm work and devoted his time to buying and selling real estate, and to church and town affairs, in both of which he was greatly interested. His house stood about halfway down a somewhat steep hill, the road over which, at the top, made a sharp turn. It was this turn which had received the appellation of Mason's Corner and from which the village eventually had taken its name.

Mrs. Sophia Mason, the Deacon's wife, was a little less than fifty years of age. She was a comely, bright-faced, bright-eyed, and energetic woman, who had been both a loving wife and a valued helpmeet to her husband. Their only living child was a daughter named Huldah Ann, about nineteen years of age, and considered by many to be the prettiest and smartest girl in Mason's Corner. The only other resident in Deacon Mason's house was Hiram Maxwell, a young man about thirty years of age. He had been a farm hand, but had enlisted in 1861, and served through the war. On his return home he was hired by Deacon Mason to do such chores as required a man's strength, for the Deacon's business took him away from home a great deal. Hiram was not exactly what would be called a pronounced stutterer or stammerer, but when he was excited or had a matter of more than ordinary importance to communicate, a sort of lingual paralysis seemed to overtake him and interfered materially with the vocal expression of his thoughts and ideas. Type would be inadequate to express the facial contortions and what might be termed the chromatic scales of vocal expression in which he often indulged, and they are, therefore, left for full comprehension to those of inventive and vivid imaginative powers. This fact should not be lost sight of in following the fortunes of this brave soldier, honest lover, good husband, and successful business man.

The Pettengill homestead was situated on the other side of the road, southwest from Deacon Mason's house. Ezekiel's grandfather had left three sons, Abraham, Isaac, and Jacob, the latter being Ezekiel's father. Abraham had died when he was a young man, and Jacob had been dead about five years. Uncle Ike was in his seventy-sixth year, and was Ezekiel's only living near relative, with the exception of his sister Alice, who had left home soon after her father's death and was now employed as bookkeeper in a large dry goods store in Boston.

Ezekiel was about twenty-eight years of age, being seven years older than his sister. He was a hardy, strong-willed, self-reliant young fellow. He loved farming and had resolved to make a better living out of it than his father had ever done. A strong incentive to win success proceeded from the fact that he had long been in love with "Huldy Ann," the Deacon's daughter, and he had every reason to believe that his affection was returned, although no formal engagement existed between them, and marriage had never been spoken of by them or the young lady's parents.

Uncle Ike Pettengill had been a successful business man in Boston, but at the age of sixty had wearied of city life, and decided to spend the rest of his days in the country. Despite the objections of his wife and two grown up daughters, he sold out his business, conveyed two-thirds of his property to his wife and children, and invested the remaining third in an annuity, which gave him sufficient income for a comfortable support. He did not live at the Pettengill

house, but in a little two-roomed cottage or cabin that he
had had built for him on the lower road, about halfway
between Mason's Corner and Eastborough Centre. A
short distance beyond his little house, a crossroad, not very
often used, connected the upper and lower roads. Uncle
Ike had a fair-sized library, read magazines and weekly
papers, but never looked at a daily newspaper. His only
companions were about two hundred hens and chickens and
a big St. Bernard dog which he had named "Swiss," after
his native land.

The other residents of the Pettengill homestead were
two young men named Jim and Bill Cobb, who aided
Ezekiel in his farm work, and Mandy Skinner, the "help,"
who was in reality the housekeeper of the establishment.
Jim and Bill Cobb were orphans, Jim being about twenty-
one and Bill three years older. When young they resembled each other very closely, for this reason they had
been nicknamed "Cobb's Twins," and the name had clung
to them, even after they had reached manhood.

Mandy Skinner was about twenty-three, and was the only
child of Malachi and Martha Skinner. Her father was dead,
but her mother had married again and was now Mrs. Jonas
Hawkins, the proprietor of Mrs. Hawkins's boarding house,
which was situated in the square opposite Hill's grocery,
and about a quarter of a mile from the top of Mason's Hill.
Mandy had a double burden upon her shoulders. One was
the care of such a large house and family, and the other
was the constant necessity of repelling the lover-like hints
and suggestions of Hiram Maxwell, who was always ready
and willing to overlook his work at Deacon Mason's so
that he could run down and see if Mandy wanted him to do
anything for her.

Hill's grocery was owned and carried on by Benoni Hill
and his son Samuel. Their residence was on the easterly
edge of the town, being next to the one occupied by old

Ben James, who was a widower with one daughter, Miss Matilda James.

About a quarter of a mile east of Hill's grocery was the village church, presided over by the Rev. Caleb Howe. He had one son, Emmanuel, who had graduated at Harvard and had intended to fit for the ministry, but his health had failed him and he had temporarily abandoned his studies. He was a great admirer of Miss Lindy Putnam, because, as he said, she was so pretty and accomplished. But after long debate one evening at the grocery store, it had been decided without a dissenting vote that "the minister's son was a lazy 'good-for-nothing', and that he wanted the money more than he did the gal." The village schoolhouse stood a short distance eastward from the church. The teacher, Miss Seraphina Cotton, a maiden lady of uncertain age, who boasted that the city of Cottonton was named after her grandfather, boarded at the Rev. Mr. Howe's, and was ardently attached to the minister's wife, who was an invalid and rarely seen outside of her home.

On the upper road, about half a mile to the west of Dea-con Mason's, lived Mr. and Mrs. Silas Putnam. They owned the largest house and best farm at Mason's Corner. They were reputed to be quite wealthy and it was known for a sure fact that their only daughter, Lindy, was worth one hundred thousand dollars in her own right, it having been left to her by her only brother, J. Jones Putnam, who had died in Boston about five years before.

Mrs. Hawkins had a large house, but it was always full of boarders, all of the masculine gender. Mrs. Hawkins had declared on several occasions that she'd "sooner have the itch than a girl boarder." She was a hard-working woman and had but one assistant, a young girl named Betsy Green, one of whose sisters was "working out" up at Mrs. Putnam's. Mrs. Hawkins's husband, his wife declared,

was "no account nohow," and for the present her estimate
of him must be accepted without question.

Among Mrs. Hawkins's twelve boarders were Robert
Wood and Benjamin Bates, two young men who were na-
tives of Montrose. Bates was a brick and stone mason,
and Wood was a carpenter, and they had been quite busily
employed during the two years they had lived at Mason's
Corner.

Mrs. Hawkins owned a buggy and carryall and a couple
of fairly good horses. They were cared for by Abner Stiles.
He was often called upon to carry passengers over to the
railway station at the Centre, and was the mail carrier between the Centre and Mason's Corner, for the latter village
had a post office, which was located in Hill's grocery, Mr.
Benoni Hill being the postmaster.

Since his return from the war Mr. Obadiah Strout had
been Mrs. Hawkins's star boarder. He sat at the head of
the table and acted as moderator during the wordy dis-
cussions which accompanied every meal. Abner Stiles be-
lieved implicitly in the manifest superiority of Obadiah
Strout over the other residents of Mason's Corner. He
was his firm ally and henchman, serving him as a dog does
his master, not for pay, but because he loves the service.

Mr. Strout was often called the "Professor" because he
was the singing-master of the village and gave lessons in
instrumental and vocal music. The love of music was another bond of union between Strout and Stiles, for the latter was a skilful, if not educated, performer on the violin.

The Professor was about forty years of age, stout in person, with smooth shaven face and florid complexion. In
Eastborough town matters he was a general factotum. He
had been an undertaker's assistant and had worked for the
superintendent of the Poorhouse. In due season and in
turn he had been appointed to and had filled the positions of
fence viewer, road inspector, hog reeve, pound keeper, and

the year previous he had been chosen tax collector. Abner
Stiles said that there "wasn't a better man in town for
selectman and he knew he'd get there one of these days."

To those residents of Mason's Corner whose names have
been given, whose homes have been described and some
whose personal peculiarities have been portrayed, must be
added a late arrival. The new-comer whose advent in town
during Christmas week had caused so much discussion at
the rehearsal in the old red schoolhouse, and whose liberality in providing a hot supper with all the fixings for the
sleighing party from Mason's Corner, when it arrived at
the Eagle Hotel at Eastborough Centre, had won, at a
bound, the hearts of the majority of the younger residents
of Mason's Corner. The village gossips wondered who he
was, what he was, what he came for, and how long he
intended to stay. If these questions had been asked of him
personally, he might have returned answers to the first
three questions, but it would have been beyond his power
to have answered the fourth inquiry at that time. But the
sayings and doings of certain individuals, and a chain of
circumstances not of his own creation and beyond his personal control, conspired to keep him there for a period of
nearly four months. During that time certain things were
said and done, certain people were met and certain events
took place which changed the entire current of this young
man's future life, which shows plainly that we are all crea-
tures of circumstance and that a man's success or failure
in life may often depend as much or even more upon his
environment than upon himself.

CHAPTER III.

IT was the evening of New Year's day, 186—. The leading people, in fact nearly all the people of the three villages forming the town of Eastborough, were assembled in the Town Hall at Eastborough Centre. The evening was pleasant and this fact had contributed to draw together the largest audience ever assembled in that hall. Not only was every seat taken, but the aisles were also crowded, while many of the younger citizens had been lifted up to eligible positions in the wide window seats of the dozen great windows on three sides of the large hall.

The large attendance was also due in part to the fact that a new and original musical composition by Mr. Strout, the singing-master, would be sung for the first time in public. Again, it had been whispered up at Hill's grocery at Mason's Corner that the young city fellow who was boarding at Deacon Mason's was going to be present, and this rumor led to a greatly increased attendance from that village.

The audience was a typical one of such communities at that period; horny-handed farmers with long shaggy beards and unkempt hair, dressed in ill-fitting black suits; matronly looking farmers' wives in their Sunday best; rosy-cheeked daughters full of fun and vivacity and chattering like magpies; tall, lank, awkward, bashful sons, and red-haired, black-haired, and tow-headed urchins of both sexes, the latter awaiting the events of the evening with the wild an-

ticipations that are usually called forth only by the advent
of a circus.

The members of the chorus were seated on the large platform, the girls being on the right and the fellows on the
left. A loud hum of conversation arose from the audience
and chorus, a constant turning over and rattling of programmes gave a cheerful and animated appearance to the
scene. The centre door at the rear of the platform was
opened and all eyes were turned in that direction, the chorus
twisting their necks or turning half 'round in their seats.

Professor Strout entered and was greeted with a loud
burst of applause. He wore a dress suit that he had hired
in Boston, and there was a large white rose in the lapel of
his coat. He was accompanied by Miss Tilly James, the
pianist, who wore a handsome wine-colored silk dress that
had been made for the occasion by the best dressmaker in
Cottonton. As she took her place at the piano and ran her
fingers over the keys, she, too, came in for a liberal round
of applause. Professor Strout bowed to the audience, then
turning his back upon them, he stood with baton uplifted
facing the chorus and waiting the advent of the town committee. Every eye in the audience was fixed upon the programme. It contained the information that the first number was an opening chorus entitled, "Welcome to the Town
Committee," written and composed by Professor Obadiah
Strout and sung for the first time with great success at the
last annual concert.

The door at the rear of the platform was opened again
and Deacon Abraham Mason, the Rev. Caleb Howe, and
Mr. Benoni Hill, the members of the town committee on
singing school, entered. Deacon Mason was accompanied
by Quincy Adams Sawyer, and all eyes were fastened on
the couple as they took their seats at the right of the platform, the Rev. Mr. Howe and Mr. Hill being seated on the
left.

Quincy Adams Sawyer in appearance and dress was a marked contrast to the stout, hardy, and rugged young farmers of Eastborough. He had dark hair, dark eyes, and a small black mustache curled at the ends. His face was pallid, but there was a look of determination in the firmly set jaw, resolute mouth, and sharp eye. He wore a dark suit with Prince Albert coat. Upon one arm hung an over-coat of light-colored cloth. He wore light-brown kid gloves and in one hand carried a light-colored Kossuth hat.

As soon as the committee and their guest had taken their seats, Professor Strout tapped upon his music stand with his baton and the members of the Eastborough Singing Society arose to their feet with that total disregard of uni-formity and unanimity of motion that always characterizes a body of undrilled performers. Each girl was obliged to look at her own dress and that of her neighbor to see if they were all right, while each fellow felt it absolutely nec-essary to shuffle his feet, pull down his cuffs, pull up his col-lar, and arrange his necktie. Despite the confusion and individual preparations the chorus took the opening note promptly and sang the "Welcome to the Town Committee" with a spirit and precision which well merited the applause it received. The words were not printed on the programme, but they conveyed the idea that the members of the sing-ing class were very much obliged to the town committee for hiring a singing-master and paying his salary. Also that the members of the chorus had studied hard to learn to sing and would do their best that evening as a return for the favors bestowed upon them by the town.

Professor Strout then advanced to the edge of the plat-form and called the attention of the audience to the second number upon the programme which read, "Address by Abraham Mason, Esq." Prof. Strout added that by special request Deacon Mason's remarks would relate to the sub-ject of "Education." The Deacon drew a large red bandanna handkerchief from his pocket, wiped the perspiration from his forehead, blew his nose vigorously, and then advanced to the centre of the platform near the music stand.

"I dote on eddikation," he began; "it makes the taxes high; I've lived in this town man and boy more'n fifty year and I never saw them anythin' but high." A general laugh greeted this remark. "But when I'm in town meetin' I allus votes an aye to make our schools as good as those found in neighborin' towns, and none of them are any too good. For my political actions I'm proud to give my grounds, for I never cast a vote that I was ashamed to give my reasons for." A burst of applause followed this declaration.

"Years back when I was young, we had no modern notions. We had to be satisfied with the three R's, Readin', 'Ritin', and 'Rithmetic, and larnin' was dealt out in rather meagre potions, 'bout three months in the winter after the wood was cut, sawed and split, and piled up in the wood-shed. We allus had to work in the summer, make hay and fill the barn in, and not till winter come could get a speck of larnin,' and then it took most of our time to pile wood into the stove and settle our personal accounts with the teacher." An audible titter ran through the audience at this sally. "And yet when I was young, though this community was rather behind in letters, no people in the land could say they were our betters. But now the world is changed, we live without such grubbin', learn Latin, French, and Greek, how to walk Spanish, talk Dutch, draw picters, keep books, fizziology, and lots of other 'ologies and much piano drubbin'. Now what brought this about? I think I have a notion; you know the immergrants from about every country under the sun have piled across the ocean. They've done the diggin' and other rough work and we've thruv on their labor. I have some ready cash. Mr. Strout comes 'round and gets some of't every year, and likewise

IT WAS A MARVELLOUS RIG THAT HE WORE WHEN HE REAPPEARED.

my neighbor has some put aside for a rainy day." Many
of the audience who probably had nothing laid aside
glanced at the well-to-do farmers who had the reputation of
being well fixed as regards this world's goods. "Perhaps
I'm doin' wrong, but I would like my darter to know as
much as those that's likely to come arter. But if the world
keeps on its progress so bewild'rin' and they put some more
'ologies into the schools together with cabinet organs and
fife and drum, I'm afraid it will cost my darter more than
it did me to eddikate her childrin."

A storm of applause filled the hall when the Deacon concluded his remarks. As he resumed his chair, Quincy
handed him a tumbler of water that he had poured from a
pitcher that stood upon a table near the piano. This act
of courtesy was seen and appreciated by the audience and a
loud clapping of hands followed. At the commencement
of the Deacon's speech, the Professor had left the platform,
for it gave him an opportunity for an intended change of
costume, for which time could be found at no other place
on the programme. It was a marvellous rig that he wore
when he reappeared. A pair of white duck pantaloons,
stiffly starched, were strapped under a pair of substantial,
well-greased, cowhide boots. The waistcoat was of bright-
red cloth with brass buttons. The long-tailed blue broad-
cloth coat was also supplied with big brass buttons. He
wore a high linen dickey and a necktie made of a small silk
American flag. On his head he had a cream-colored, woolly
plug hat and carried in his hand a baton resembling a small
barber's pole, having alternate stripes of red, white, and
blue with gilded ends.

The appearance of this apparition of Uncle Sam was
received with cries, cheers, and loud clapping of hands. The
Professor bowed repeatedly in response to this ovation, and
it was a long time before he could make himself heard by
the audience. At last he said in a loud voice:

"The audience will find the words of number three printed on the last page of the programme, and young and old are respectfully invited to jine in the chorus."

A fluttering of programmes followed and this is what the audience found on the last page, "Hark! and Hear the Eagle Scream, a new and original American national air written, composed, and sung for the first time in public by Professor Obadiah Strout, author of last season's great success, 'Welcome to the Town Committee.'"

I.

They say our wheat's by far the best;
Our Injun corn will bear the test;
Our butter, beef, and pork and cheese,
The furriner's appetite can please.
The beans and fishballs that we can
Will keep alive an Englishman;
While many things I can't relate
He must buy from us or emigrate.

CHORUS:

Raise your voices, swing the banners,
Pound the drums and bang pianners;
Blow the fife and shriek for freedom,
'Meriky is bound to lead 'em.
Emigrate! ye toiling millions!
Sile enuf for tens of billions!
Land of honey, buttermilk, cream;
Hark! and hear the eagle scream.

II.

In manufactures, too, we're some;
Take rubber shoes and chewing gum;

In cotton cloth, and woollen, too,
In time we shall outrival you;
Our ships with ev'ry wind and tide,
With England's own will sail beside,
In ev'ry port our flag unfurled,
When the Stars and Stripes will rule the world.

CHORUS:

III.

For gold and silver, man and woman,
For things that's raised, made, dug, or human,
'Meriky's the coming nation;
She's bound to conquer all creation!
Per'aps you call this brag and bluster;
No, 'taint nuther, for we muster
The best of brain, the mighty dollar;
We'll lead on, let others foller.

CHORUS:

Professor Strout sang the solo part of the song himself.
The singing society and many of the audience joined in the
chorus. Like many teachers of vocal music, the Professor
had very little voice himself, but he knew how to make
the best possible use of what he did possess. But the patri-
otic sentiment of the words, the eccentric make-up of the
singer, his comical contortions and odd grimaces, and what
was really a bright, tuneful melody won a marked success
for both song and singer. Encore followed encore. Like
many more cultured audiences in large cities the one assembled in Eastborough Town Hall seemed to think that
there was no limit to a free concert and that they were
entitled to all they could get. But the Professor himself
fixed the limit. When the song had been sung through
three times he ran up the centre aisle of the platform and
facing the audience, he directed the chorus, holding the

variegated baton in one hand and swinging his woolly plug
hat around his head with the other. At the close, amid
screams, cheers, and clapping of hands, he turned upon his
heel, dashed through the door and disappeared from sight.

The next number upon the programme was a piano solo
by Miss Tilly James. Nothing could have pleased her audience any better than the well-known strains of the ever
popular "Maiden's Prayer." In response to an encore
which Quincy originated, and dexterously led, Miss James
played the overture to Rossini's "William Tell" without
notes. A fact which was perceived by the few, but unnoticed by the many.

At the close of these instrumental selections, the Professor reappeared in evening costume and again assumed
the directorship of the concert. Robert Wood had a ponderous bass voice, which if not highly cultivated was highly
effective, and he sang "Simon the Cellarer" to great ac-
ceptation. Next followed a number of selections sung
without accompaniment by a male quartette composed of
Cobb's twins, who were both tenors, Benjamin Bates, and
Robert Wood. This feature was loudly applauded and one
old farmer remarked to his neighbor, who was evidently
deaf, in a loud voice that was heard all over the hall, "That's
the kind of music that fetches me," which declaration was a
signal for another encore.

The singing society then sang a barcarolle, the words of
the first line being, "Of the sea, our yacht is the pride." It
went over the heads of most of the audience, but was greatly
appreciated by the limited few who were acquainted with
the difficulties of accidentals, syncopations, and inverted
musical phrases.

According to the programme the next feature was to be
a duet entitled "Over the Bridge," composed by Jewell and
sung by Arthur Scates and Miss Lindy Putnam. The Pro-

fessor stepped forward and waved his hand to quiet the
somewhat noisy assemblage.

"The next number will have to be omitted," he said,
"because Mr. Scates is home sick abed. The doctor says
he's got a bad case of quinsy," with a marked emphasis on
the last word, which, however, failed to make a point. "In
response to requests, one verse of 'Hark! and Hear the
Eagle Scream' will be sung to take the place of the piece
that's left out." '

While the Professor was addressing the audience, Quincy
had whispered something in Deacon Mason's ear which
caused the latter to smile and nod his head approvingly.
Quincy arose and reached the Professor's side just as the
latter finished speaking and turned towards the chorus.
Quincy said something in a low tone to the Professor which
caused Mr. Strout to shake his head in the negative in a
most pronounced manner. Quincy spoke again and looked
towards Miss Putnam, who was seated in the front row,
and whose face wore a somewhat disappointed look.

Again the Professor shook his head by way of negation
and the words, "It can't be did," were distinctly audible to
the majority of both singing society and audience, at the
same time a look of contempt spread over the singing-
master's face. Quincy perceived it and was nettled by it.
He was not daunted, however, nor to be shaken from his
purpose, so he said in a loud voice, which was heard in all
parts of the hall: "I know the song, and will sing it if
Miss Putnam and the audience are willing."

With a smile upon her face, Miss Putnam nodded her
acquiescence. All the townspeople had heard of Quincy's
liberality in providing a hot supper for the sleighing party
the night before, and cries of "Go ahead! Give him a
chance! We want to hear him!" and "Don't disappoint
Miss Putnam," were heard from all parts of the hall. The
Professor was obliged to give in. He sat down with a

disgusted look upon his face, and from that moment war
to the knife was declared between these champions of city
and country civilization.

Mr. Sawyer went to the piano, opened Miss James's copy
of the music and placed it upon the music rack before her,
saying a few words to her which caused her to smile.
Quincy then approached Lindy, opened her music at the
proper place and passed it to her. Next he took her hand
and led her to the front of the platform. These little acts
of courtesy and politeness, performed in an easy, graceful,
and self-possessed manner, were seen by all and won a
round of applause.

The duet was beautifully sung. Quincy had a fine well-
trained tenor voice, while Miss Putnam's mezzo-soprano
was full and melodious and her rendition fully as artistic
as that of her companion. One, two, three, four, five, six
encores followed each other in quick succession, in spite of
Professor Strout's endeavors to quell the applause and
take up the next number. The ovation given earlier in the
evening to Professor Strout was weak in comparison with
that vouchsafed to Quincy and Lindy when they took their
seats. In vain did the Professor strive to make himself
heard. Audience and chorus seemed to be of one mind.
The Professor, his face as red as a beet, turned to Ezekiel
Pettengill and said:

"That was a mighty impudent piece of business, don't
you think so?"

"They're both mighty fine singers," Ezekiel responded
in a rather unsympathetic tone.

Quincy realized that something must be done to satisfy
the demands of the now thoroughly excited audience.
Going to Miss James, he asked her a question in a low
voice, in reply to which she nodded affirmatively. He next
sought Miss Putnam and evidently asked her the same
question, receiving a similar answer. Then he led her for-

ward, and she sang the opening part of "Listen to the Mocking Bird." After they had sung the chorus it was repeated on the piano and Quincy electrified the audience by whistling it, introducing all the trills, staccatos, and roulades that he had heard so many times come from under Billy Morris's big mustache at the little Opera House on Washington Street, opposite Milk, run by the Morris Brothers, Johnny Pell, and Mr. Trowbridge, and when he finished there flashed through his mind a pleasant memory of Dr. Ordway and his Æolians. An encore was responded to, but the tumult still continued. Turning to Ezekiel, Strout said:

"Ain't it a cussed shame to spoil a first-class concert this way?"

"He's a mighty fine whistler," replied Ezekiel in the same tone that he had used before.

Finally to quiet their exuberance Quincy was obliged to say a few words, which were evidently what the audience was waiting for.

"Ladies and gentlemen," he said, "the hour is getting late and there is another number on the programme. Miss Putnam is tired and I shall have to wet my whistle before I can use it again. I thank you for your kind indulgence and applause."

This little speech pleased the audience. It was down to their level, with "no sign of stuckupativeness about it," as one country girl remarked to her chum. Quincy bowed, the audience laughed, and quiet was restored.

The Professor had fidgeted, fumed, and fussed during Quincy's occupancy of the platform. He now arose with feelings impossible to express and took up his baton to lead the closing chorus. He brought it down with such a whack upon the music stand that it careened, tottered, and fell to the platform with a crash. Tilly James leaned over and whispered to Huldy Mason: "The Professor seems to

have a bad attack of Quincy, too." And the two girls
smothered their laughs in their handkerchiefs. If the singing society had not been so well acquainted with the closing
chorus the Professor certainly would have thrown them
out by his many mistakes in beating time. The piece was a
"sleighride" song. The Professor forgot to give the signal
for the ringing of the sleigh bells, but the members of the
singing society did not, and their introduction, which was
unexpected by the audience, to use a theatrical term,
"brought down the house." The number was well rendered, despite the manifest defects in leadership. The concert came to a close.

Deacon Mason and his wife, accompanied by their
daughter, Huldy, and Rev. Mr. Howe, occupied a double
sleigh, as did Hiram, Mandy, and Cobb's twins. Another
double-seated conveyance contained Mr. and Mrs. Benoni
Hill, their son, Samuel, and Miss Tilly James. Quincy also
had accommodations for four in his sleigh, but its only
occupants were Miss Putnam and himself. Abner Stiles
sat on the front seat of another double-seated sleigh, while
the Professor and Ezekiel were on the back one; the remainder of the Mason's Corner folks occupied the big
barge which had been used for the sleigh ride the night
before.

The barge led the procession to Mason's Corner,
followed by the vehicles previously mentioned and scores
of others containing residents of Mason's Corner, whose
names and faces are alike unknown. By a strange fatality,
the sleigh containing the Professor and Ezekiel was the
last in the line. Ezekiel was inwardly elated that Mr. Sawyer had gone home with Lindy instead of with Deacon
Mason's party. Strout's bosom held no feelings of elation.
He did not seem to care whether the concert was considered a success or not. He had but one thought in his mind,

"THE BARGE LED THE PROCESSION TO MASON'S CORNER."

and that was the "daring impudence of that city feller."
Turning to Ezekiel, he said:

"I'll get even with that city chap the next time I meet
him. As I said last night, Pettengill, this town ain't big
enough to hold both on us and one on us has got to git."

As he said this, he leaned back in the sleigh and puffed
his cigar savagely while Ezekiel was wondering if Huldy
was thinking half as much about him as he was about her.

CHAPTER IV.

ANCESTRY VERSUS PATRIOTISM.

FOUR days had passed since the concert in the Town Hall at Eastborough. The events of that evening had been freely discussed in barn and workshop, at table and at the various stores in Eastborough and surrounding towns, for quite a number had been present who were not residents of the town. All interest in it had not, however, passed away as subsequent occurrences proved.

It was the morning of the fifth of January. Benoni Hill, who ran the only grocery store at Mason's Corner, was behind his counter and with the aid of his only son, Samuel, was attending to the wants of several customers.

While thus engaged, Miss Tilly James entered, and young Samuel Hill forgot to ask the customer on whom he had been waiting the usual question, "Anything else, ma'am?" so anxious was he to speak to and wait upon the pretty Miss James, whose bright eyes, dark curly hair, and witty remarks had attracted to her side more suitors than had fallen to the lot of any other young girl in the village. As yet she had evinced no especial liking for any particular one of the young men who flocked about her, and this fact had only served to increase their admiration for her and to spur them on to renewed efforts to win her favor.

"Do you know, Miss James," said Samuel, "I can't get it out of my ears yet." As he said this, he leaned over the counter, and being a brave young man, looked straight into Miss James's smiling face.

"If all home remedies have failed," said Tilly, "why don't you go to Boston and have a doctor examine them?"

"What a joker you are!" remarked Samuel; "I believe you will crack a joke on the minister the day you are married."

"It may be my last chance," rejoined Tilly. "Mother says the inside of a boiled onion put into the ear is good for some troubles; give me a pound of tea, Oolong and green mixed, same as we always have."

As Samuel passed the neatly done up package to Miss James, he leaned across the counter again and said in a low voice, "You know what is in my ears, Miss James. How beautifully you played for Mr. Sawyer when he whistled 'Listen to the Mocking Bird.' I don't think I shall ever forget it."

"Well, I don't know about the playing, Mr. Hill. I came near losing my place several times, because I wanted so much to hear him whistle."

During this conversation Tilly and Samuel had been so preoccupied that they had not noticed the entrance of a new-comer and his approach towards them. Only one other customer, a little girl, was left in the store, and Mr. Hill, Sr., had gone down cellar to draw her a quart of molasses.

As Tilly uttered the words, "I wanted so much to hear him whistle," she heard behind her in clear, melodious, flute-like notes, the opening measures of "Listen to the Mocking Bird." Turning quickly, she saw Mr. Sawyer standing beside her.

"Why, how do you do, Mr. Sawyer? I am delighted to see you again," she said in that hearty, whole-souled way that was so captivating to her country admirers.

"The delight is mutual," replied Quincy, raising his hat and bowing.

Samuel Hill was evidently somewhat disturbed by the

great friendliness of the greetings that he had just witnessed. This fact did not escape Tilly's quick eye, and turning to Mr. Sawyer she said:

"Have you been introduced to my friend, Mr. Samuel
Hill?"

"I have not had that pleasure," replied Quincy. "This
is my first visit to the store."

"Then allow me," continued Tilly, "to present you to
Mr. Samuel Hill and to Mr. Benoni Hill, his father, both
valued friends of mine," and she added, as a roguish smile
came into her face, "as they keep the only grocery store in
the village, you will be obliged to buy what they have and
pay them what they ask, unless you prefer a three-mile
tramp to Eastborough Centre."

"I hope you're enjoyin' your stay at Mason's Corner,"
said Mr. Benoni Hill, "though I don't s'pose you city folks
find much to please yer in a country town, 'specially in the
winter."

"So far I have found two things that have pleased me
very much," replied Quincy.

"The milk and eggs, I suppose," remarked Tilly.

"No," said Quincy, "I refer to Miss Lindy Putnam's
fine singing and the beautiful playing of a young lady who
is called Miss James."

"I have heard," said Tilly, "that you city gentlemen are
great flatterers. That is not the reason why I am obliged
to leave you so suddenly, but the fact is the tea caddy ran
low this morning and grandma's nerves will remain un-
strung until she gets a cup of strong tea."

With a graceful bow and a parting wave of the hand to
the three gentlemen, the bright and popular young lady
left the store.

"Mr. Hill," said Quincy, addressing the elder gentleman, "I've smoked all the cigars that I brought from Boston, but Deacon Mason told me perhaps you had some

that would suit me. I like a good-sized, strong cigar and one that burns freely."

"Well," said Mr. Hill, "Professor Strout is the most par-tikler customer I have in cigars; he says he always smokes a pipe in the house, 'cause it don't hang round the room so long as cigar smoke does, but he likes a good cigar to smoke on the street or when he goes ridin.' I just had a new box come down for him last night. Perhaps some of them will satisfy yer till I can git jest the kind yer want."

Mr. Hill took his claw-hammer and opening the box passed it to Quincy, who took one of the cigars and lighted it. As he did so he glanced at the brand and the names of the makers, and remarked, "This is a good cigar, I've smoked this brand before. What do you ask for them?"

"I git ten cents straight, but as Mr. Strout always smokes up the whole box before he gits through, though he don't usually buy more than five at a time, I let him have 'em for nine cents apiece. There ain't much made on them, but yer see I have to obleege my customers."

"You don't ask enough for them," said Quincy, throw-ing down a twenty-dollar bill. "They sell for fifteen cents, two for a quarter, in Boston."

"How many will you have?" asked Mr. Hill, thinking that Boston must be a paradise for shopkeepers, when seven cents' profit could be made on a cigar that cost only eight cents.

"I'll take the whole box," said Quincy. "Call it ten dollars, that's cheap enough. No matter about the dis-count." As he said this he took half a dozen cigars from the box and placed them in a silver-mounted, silk-embroidered cigar case. "Please do them up for me, Mr. Hill, and the next time Hiram Maxwell comes in he will take them down to Deacon Mason's for me."

After much rummaging through till and pocketbook, Mr. Hill and his son found ten dollars in change, which

was passed to Quincy. He stuffed the large wad of small
bills and fractional currency into his overcoat pocket and
sitting down on a pile of soap boxes drummed on the lower
one with his boot heels and puffed his cigar with evident
pleasure.

While Quincy was thus pleasantly engaged, Professor
Strout entered the store and walked briskly up to the counter. He did not see, or if he did, he did not notice, Quincy
who kept his place upon the pile of soap boxes. Strout
was followed by Abner Stiles, Robert Wood, and several
other idlers, who had been standing on the store platform
when the Professor arrived.

"Did those cigars come down, Hill?" asked Strout in his
usual pompous way.   ·

"Yes!" replied Mr. Hill, "but I guess you'll have to wait
till I git another box down."

"What for?" asked Strout sharply. "Wa'n't it understood between us that them cigars was to be kept for me?"

"That's so," acknowledged Mr. Hill, "but you see, when
I told that gentleman on the soap box over yonder that you
smoked them, he bought the whole box, paid me a cent
more apiece than you do. A dollar's worth saving nowadays. He says they sell for fifteen cents, two for a quarter,
up in Boston."

"If he's so well posted on Boston prices," growled Strout,
"why didn't he pay them instead of cheatin' you out of two
dollars and a half? I consider it a very shabby trick, Mr.
Hill. I shall buy my cigars at Eastborough Centre in the
future. Perhaps you'll lose more than that dollar in the
long run."

"Perhaps the gentleman will let you have some of them,"
expostulated Mr. Hill, "till I can get another box."

"All I can say is," said Strout in snappish tones, "if the
man who bought them knew that you got them for me, he
was no gentleman to take the whole box. What do yer

say, Stiles?" he asked, turning to Abner, who had kept his eyes fixed on the placid Quincy since entering the store, though listening intently to what the Professor said.

"Well, I kinder reckon I agree to what you say, Professor," drawled Abner, "unless the other side has got some sort of an explanation to make. 'Tain't quite fair to judge a man without a hearin'."

"Allow me to offer you one of your favorite brand, Professor Strout," said Quincy, jumping down from the soap boxes and extending his cigar case.

"No! thank you!" said Strout, "I always buy a box at a time, the same as you do. Judging from the smell of the one you are smoking, I guess they made a mistake on that box and sent second quality. Give me a five-cent plug, Mr. Hill, if some gentleman hasn't bought out your whole stock. I fancy my pipe will have to do me till I get a chance to go over to Eastborough Centre."

During this conversation Hiram Maxwell had come in to do an errand for Mrs. Mason, and several more platform idlers, having heard the Professor's loud words, also entered.

Strout was angry. When in that condition he usually lost his head, which he did on this occasion. Turning to Quincy he said with a voice full of passion:

"What's yer name, anyway? You've got so many of them I don't know which comes fust and which last. Is it Quincy or Adams or Sawyer? How in thunder did you get 'em all, anyway? I s'pose they tucked 'em on to you when you was a baby and you was too weak to kick at being so abused."

At this sally a loud laugh arose from the crowd gathered in the store, and Abner Stiles, who was the Professor's henchman and man-of-all-work, cried out, "Fust blood for the Professor."

Quincy faced the Professor with a pale face and spoke in

clear, ringing tones, still holding his lighted cigar between
the fingers of his right hand. When he spoke all listened
intently.

"Your memory has served you well, Mr. Strout. You
have got my names correct and in the proper order, Quincy
Adams Sawyer. I do not consider that any child could be
abused by being obliged to wear such honored names as
those given me by my parents. My mother was a Quincy,
and that name is indissolubly connected with the history
and glory of our common country. My father's mother was
an Adams, a family that has given two Presidents to the
United States. If your knowledge of history is as great as
your memory for names you should be aware of these facts,
but your ignorance of them will not affect the opinion of
those knowing to them. My father, Nathaniel Adams Sawyer, has a world-wide reputation as a great constitutional
lawyer, and I am proud to bear his name, combined with
those of my illustrious ancestors. It is needless for me to
add that I, too, am connected with the legal profession."

Here Hiram Maxwell called out, "First round for Mr.
Sawyer."

"Shut up, you dough-head," cried Strout, his face pur-
ple with rage. Turning to Quincy he said in a choked
voice, "My name is Obadiah Strout, no frills or folderols
about it either. That was my father's name too, and he
lived and died an honest man, in spite of it. He raised
potatoes and one son, that was me. When the nation called
for volunteers I went to war to save the money bags of
such as you that stayed at home. It was such fellers as
you that made money out of mouldy biscuits and rotten
beef, shoddy clothin', and paper-soled boots. It was such
fellers as your father that lent their money to the government and got big interest for it. They kept the war going
as long as they could. What cared they for the blood of
the poor soldier, as long as they could keep the profits and

interest coming in? It wasn't the Quincys and the Adamses and the other fellers with big names that stayed at home and hollered who saved the country, but the rank and file that did the fightin', and I was one of them."

As he said this the irascible Professor shook his fist in Quincy's face, to which a red flush mounted, dyeing cheek and brow.

"That's the Lord's truth," said Abner Stiles. Then he called out in a loud voice, "Second round for the Professor. Now for the finish."

But the finish did not come then. The settlement between these two lingual disputants did not come for many days. The reason for a sudden cessation of the wordy conflict was a shrill, feminine voice, which cried out from the store platform:

"Hiram Maxwell, where are you? Mother's most out of patience waiting for you."

"Good Lord!" cried Hiram, breaking through the crowd and rushing to the counter to make the long-deferred purchase. "I'm coming in a minute."

"I think I had better see you home," remarked Huldy Mason, entering the store.

As she advanced the crowd separated and moved backward, leaving her a clear path.

"Why, how do you do, Mr. Sawyer?" said she in a pleasant voice and with a sweet smile, as she reached Quincy. "Won't you help me take Hiram home?"

"I should be happy to be of service to you," replied Quincy.

The professor turned his back toward Miss Mason and began talking in an animated manner to Abner Stiles, Bob Wood, and a few other ardent sympathizers who gathered about him.

The rest of the crowd were evidently more interested in watching the pretty Miss Mason and the genteel Mr. Sawyer. When Hiram left the store with his purchases under one arm and Quincy's box of cigars under the other, he was closely followed by Quincy and Huldy, who were talking and laughing together. The crowd of loungers streamed out on the platform again to watch their departure. As Quincy and Huldy turned from the square into the road that led to the Deacon's house they met Ezekiel Pettengill. Huldy nodded gayly and Quincy raised his hat, but Ezekiel was not acquainted with city customs and did not return the salutation. A few moments later the Professor and Abner Stiles were relating to him the exciting occurrences of the last half hour.

CHAPTER V.

QUINCY ADAMS SAWYER had not come down to Mason's Corner with any idea of becoming a hermit. His father was a great lawyer and a very wealthy man. He had made Quincy a large allowance during his college days, and had doubled it when his only son entered his law office to complete his studies.

Quincy had worked hard in two ways; first, to read law, so as to realize the great anticipations that his father had concerning him; second, he worked still harder between eight in the evening and one, two, and even four in the morning, to get rid of the too large allowance that his father made him.

Like all great men, his father was unsuspicious and easily hoodwinked about family matters; so when Quincy grew listless and on certain occasions fell asleep at his desk his renowned and indulgent father decided it was due to over-work and sent him down to Eastborough for a month's rest and change of scene.

His father had known Isaac Pettengill, and in fact had conducted many successful suits for him; besides this he had drawn up the papers when Uncle Ike divided his fortune. Quincy's father had written to Uncle Ike, asking him to find his son a boarding place, and Uncle Ike had selected Deacon Mason's as the best place for him.

Quincy's father had told him to be sure and get acquainted with Mr. Isaac Pettengill, saying he was a man of

fine education, and added, "I sometimes feel, Quincy, as
though I would like to go into the country and take care of
a chicken farm myself for a while."

His mother came of the best New England stock, and
although she had been named Sarah and her husband's
name was Nathaniel, we have seen that the son had been
endowed with the rather high-sounding name of Quincy
Adams, which his schoolmates had shortened to Quince,
and his college friends had still further abbreviated to
Quinn. Quincy had two sisters and they had been equally
honored with high-sounding appellations, the elder being
called Florence Estelle and the younger Maude Gertrude,
but to pa, ma, brother, and friends they were known as
Flossie and Gertie.

The next day after the affair at Hill's grocery, Quincy
put several of the best cigars in town in his pocket and
started towards Eastborough Centre for a walk, intending
to call upon Uncle Ike Pettengill.

The young man knew that late hours and their usual ac-
companiments were what had undermined his health, so
he determined to make his vacation of good service to him
and recover his accustomed health and strength, and when
he returned home cut his old acquaintances and settle down
earnestly and honestly to the battle of life.

He had been a favorite in city society; he was well educated, well read, had travelled considerably and was uniformly polite and affable to all classes, from young children to old men and women; he was very careful about his
dress, and always had that well-groomed appearance, which
in the city elicits commendation, but which leads the average countryman to say "dude" to himself and near friends
when talking about him.

Quincy was no dude; he had been prominent in all college
athletic games; he had been a member of the 'varsity eight
in one of its contests with Yale, and had won a game for

Harvard with Yale at base ball by making a home run in the
tenth inning on a tied score. He was a good musician and
fine singer. In addition he was a graceful dancer, and had
taken lessons in boxing, until his feather-weight teacher
suggested that he had better find a heavy-weight instructor
to practise on.

Quincy was in his twenty-third year. He had been in love
a dozen times, but, as he expressed it, had been saved from
matrimony by getting acquainted with a prettier girl just as
he was on the point of popping the question.

But we left him walking along on his way to Eastborough
Centre. Deacon Mason had told him Uncle Ike's house
was away from the road, some hundred feet back, and that
he could not mistake it, as he could see the chicken coop
from the road. He finally reached it after traversing about
a mile and a half, it being another mile and a half to Eastborough Centre.

He found the path that led to the house. As he neared
the steps a huge dog arose from a reclining posture and
faced him, not in an ugly mood, but with an expression that
seemed to say, "An introduction will be necessary before
you come any farther." The dog seemed to understand
that it was his duty to bring about the necessary introduction, so he gave a series of loud barks. The door was
quickly opened and Uncle Ike stood in the doorway.

"Do I address Mr. Isaac Pettengill?" asked Quincy.

Uncle Ike replied, "That's what they write on my letters."

Quincy continued, "My name is Quincy Adams Sawyer.
I am the only son of the Hon. Nathaniel Sawyer of Boston,
and I bear a letter of introduction from him to you."

Quincy took the letter from his pocket and held it in his
hand. The dog made a quick movement forward and before Quincy could divine his object, he took the letter in
his mouth and took it to Uncle Ike, and, returning, faced
Quincy again.

Uncle Ike read the letter slowly and carefully; then he turned to Quincy and said, "If you will talk about birds, fish, dogs, and chickens, you are welcome, and I shall be glad to see you now or any time. If you talk about law-suits or religion I shall be sorry that you came. I am sick of lawyers and ministers. If you insist upon talking on such subjects I'll tell Swiss, and the next time you come he won't even bark to let me know you're here."

Quincy took in the situation, and smiling said, "I am tired of lawyers and lawsuits myself; that is the reason I came down here for a change. The subjects you mention will satisfy me, if you will allow me to put in a few words about rowing, running, boxing, and football."

Uncle Ike replied, "The physically perfect man I admire, the intellectually perfect man is usually a big bore; I prefer the company of my chickens." Turning to Swiss he said with a marked change in his voice, "This is a friend of mine, Swiss." Turning to Quincy he said, "He will admit you until I give him directions to the contrary."

The dog walked quietly to one side and Quincy advanced with outstretched hand toward Uncle Ike.

Uncle Ike did not extend his. He said, "I never shake hands, young man. It is a hollow social custom. With Damon and Pythias it meant something. One was ready to die for the other, and that hand-clasp meant friendship until death. How many hand shakings mean that now-adays? Besides," with a queer smile, "I have just been cutting up a broiler that I intend to cook for my dinner. Come in, you are welcome on the conditions I have mentioned."

Quincy obeyed and stepped into the kitchen of Sleepy Hollow. He owned to himself in after years that that was the most important step he had taken in life—the turning-point in his career.

CHAPTER VI.

DID you ever kill a chicken?" asked Uncle Ike, as Quincy entered the room and took a seat in the willow rocker Uncle Ike pointed out to him.

"No," replied Quincy, "but out in Chicago I saw live hogs killed, bristles taken off, cut up, assorted according to kind and quality, and hung up to cool off, in three minutes."

Uncle Ike responded vehemently, "Yes, I know, and it is a shame to the American people that they allow such things."

"That may be true," said Quincy, "but even at that speed they cannot kill and pack as fast as it is wanted."

"Yes," said Uncle Ike, "in the old days man feared God, and he treated man and beast better for that reason. In these days man serves Mammon and he will do anything to win his favor."

"Do you think it is true that men were better in the old days?" asked Quincy.

"No," answered Uncle Ike, "I didn't say so. I said that in the old days man was afraid to do these things; now if he has money he is afraid of neither God, man, nor the devil. To speak frankly, that is why I am so independent myself. I am sure of enough to support me as long as I live; I owe no man anything, and I allow no man to owe me anything."

Quincy, changing the subject, inquired, "What is your method of killing chickens?"

Uncle Ike said, "Let me tell you why I devised a new plan. When I was about eight years old I went with my mother to visit an uncle in a neighboring town. I was born in Eastborough myself, in the old Pettengill house. But this happened some twenty miles from here. My uncle was chopping wood, and boy like, I went out to watch him. An old rooster kept running around the block, flapping its wings, making considerable noise. Uncle shooed him off three or four times. Finally uncle made a grab at him, caught him by the legs, whacked him down on the block and with his axe cut off his head close to his body, and then threw it out on the grass right in front of me. Was that rooster dead? I thought not. It got up on its legs, ran right towards where I was sitting, and before I could get away I was covered with the blood that came from its neck. I don't know how far the rooster ran, but I know I never stopped until I was safe in my mother's arms. The balance of the time I stayed there you could'nt get me within forty yards of my uncle, for every time I met him I could see myself running around without my head."

"That made a lasting impression on you," remarked Quincy.

"Yes," said Uncle Ike, "it has lasted me sixty-eight years, one month, and thirteen days," pointing to a calendar that hung on the wall.

As Quincy looked in the direction indicated he saw something hanging beside it that attracted his attention.

It was a sheet of white paper with a heavy black border. Within the border were written these words, "Sacred to the memory of Isaac Pettengill, who was killed at the battle of Gettysburg, July 4th, 1863, aged twenty-nine years. He died for his namesake and his native land."

Quincy said interrogatively, "Did you lose a son in the war?"

"No," was the reply. "I never had a son. That was my substitute."

"Strange that your substitute should have the same name as yourself."

"Yes, it would have been if he had, but he didn't. His right name was Lemuel Butters. But I didn't propose to put my money into such a name as that."

"Were you drafted?" asked Quincy.

"No," said Uncle Ike. "I might as well tell you the whole story, for you seem bound to have it. I came down here in 1850, when I was about sixty. Of course I knew what was going on, but I didn't take much interest in the war, till a lot of soldiers went by one day. They stopped here; we had a talk, and they told me a number of things that I hadn't seen in the papers. I haven't read the daily papers for thirteen years, but I take some weeklies and the magazines and buy some books. Well, the next day I went over to Eastborough Centre and asked the select-men how much it would cost to send a man to the war. They said substitutes were bringing $150 just then, but that I was over age and couldn't be drafted, and there was no need of my sending anybody. I remarked that in my opinion a man's patriotism ought not to die out as long as he lived. It seemed to me that if a man had $150 it was his duty to pay for a substitute, if he was a hundred. The selectmen said that they had a young fellow named Lem Butters who was willing to go if he got a hundred and fifty. So I planked down the money, but with the understanding that he should take my name. Well, to make a long story short, I got killed at Gettysburg and I wrote that out as a reminder."

"Don't you ever get lonesome alone here by yourself?" Quincy asked.

"Yes," said Uncle Ike. "I am lonesome every minute of the time. That's what I came down here for. I got tired

being lonesome with other people around me, so I thought
I would come down here and be lonesome all by myself,
and I have never been sorry I came."

Quincy opened his eyes and looked inquiringly at Uncle
Ike.

"I don't quite understand what you mean by being lonesome with other people around you," said he.

"No, of course you don't," replied Uncle Ike. "You are
too young. I was sixty. I was thirty-five when I got married and my wife was only twenty-two, so when I was
sixty she was only forty-seven. One girl was twenty-three
and the other twenty. I went to work at seven o'clock in
the morning and got home at seven at night. My wife
and daughters went to theatres, dinners, and parties, and of
course I stayed at home and kept house with the servant
girl. In my business I had taken in two young fellows as
partners, both good, honest men, but soon they got to fig-
uring that on business points they were two and I was one,
and pretty soon all I had to do was to put wood on the fire
and feed the office cat. So you can see I was pretty lonesome about eighteen hours out of the twenty-four."

Quincy said reflectively, "And your family——"

Uncle Ike broke in, "Are alive and well, I suppose.
They don't write me and I don't write them. I told my
partners they must buy me out, and I gave them sixty days
to do it in. I gave my wife and daughters two-thirds of
my fortune and put the other third into an annuity. I am
calculating now that if my health holds good I shall beat
the insurance company in the end."

Quincy, finding that his inquiries provoked such interesting replies, risked another, "Are your daughters married?"

Uncle Ike laughed quietly. "I don't read the daily
papers as I said, so I don't know, but they wouldn't send
me cards anyway. They know my ideas of marriage."

Quincy, smiling, asked, "Have you some new ideas on that old custom?"

"Yes, I have," replied Uncle Ike. "If two men go into business and each puts in money and they make money or don't make it, the law doesn't fix it so that they must keep together for their natural lives, but allows the firm to be dissolved by mutual consent."

"Why, sir, that would make marriage a limited partnership," said Quincy with a smile.

"What better is it now?" asked Uncle Ike. "The law doesn't compel couples to live together if they don't want to, and if they don't want to live together, why not let them, under proper restrictions, get up some new firms? Of course, there wouldn't be any objection to parties living together for their natural lives, if they wanted to, and the fact that they did would be pretty good proof that they wanted to."

Quincy started to speak, "But what—"

"I know what you were going to say," said Uncle Ike. "You are going to ask that tiresome old question, what will become of the children? Well, I should consider them part of the property on hand and divide them and the money according to law."

"But few mothers would consent to be parted from their children."

"Oh, that's nonsense," replied Uncle Ike. "I have a Massachusetts State Report here that says about five hundred children every year are abandoned by their mothers for some cause or other. They leave them on doorsteps and in railroad stations; they put them out to board and don't pay their board; and the report says that every one of these little waifs is adopted by good people, and they get a better education and a better bringing up than their own parents could or would give them. Have you ever read, Mr. Sawyer, of the Austrian baron who was crossed in love and decided he would never marry?"

Quincy shook his head.

"Well, he was wealthy and had a big castle, with no one to live in it, and during his life he adopted, educated, clothed, and sent out into the world, fitted to make their own living, more than a thousand children. To my mind, Mr. Sawyer, he was a bigger man than any emperor or king who has ever lived."

Quincy asked, "But how are you going to start such a reform, Mr. Pettengill? The first couple that got reunited on the partnership plan would be the laughing stock of the community."

"Just so," said Uncle Ike, "but I can get over that difficulty. The State of Massachusetts has led in a great many social reforms. Let it take the first step forward in this one; let it declare by law that all marriages on and after a certain day shall terminate five years from the date of marriage unless the couples wish to renew the bonds. Then let everybody laugh at everybody else if they want to."

"Well, how about those couples that were married before that day?"

"That's easy," was Uncle Ike's reply. "Give them all a chance five years after the law to dissolve by mutual consent, if they want to. Don't forget, Mr. Sawyer, that with such a law there would be no need of divorce courts, and if any man insulted a woman, imprisonment for life and even the gallows wouldn't be any too good for him. Will you stay to lunch, Mr. Sawyer? My chicken is about done."

Quincy arose and politely declined the invitation, saying he had been so much interested he had remained much longer than he had intended, but he would be pleased to call again some day if Mr. Pettengill were willing.

"Oh, yes, come any time," said Uncle Ike, "you're a good listener, and I always like a man that allows me to do most of the talking. By the way, we didn't get a chance to say much this time about shooting, fishing, or football."

Quincy went down the steps, and Uncle Ike stood at the door, as he did before he entered. Swiss looked at Quincy with an expression that seemed to say, "You have made a pretty long call." Quincy patted him on the head, called him "good dog," and walked briskly down the path towards the road. When he was about fifty feet from the house, Uncle Ike called out sharply, "Mr. Sawyer!" Quincy turned on his heel quickly and looked towards the speaker. Uncle Ike's voice, still sharp, spoke these farewell words:

"I forgot to tell you, Mr. Sawyer, that I always chloroform my chickens before I cut their heads off."

He stepped back into the house. Swiss, with a bound, was in the room beside him, and when Quincy again turned his steps towards the road the closed door had shut them both from view.

CHAPTER VII.

"THAT CITY FELLER."

A S usual, the next morning Hiram was down to the Pettengill house between nine and ten o'clock. He opened the kitchen door unobserved by Mandy and looked in at her. She was standing at the sink washing dishes and singing to herself. Suddenly Hiram gave a jump into the room and cried out in a loud voice, "How are you, Mandy?"

She dropped a tin pan that she was wiping, which fell with a clatter, breaking a plate that happened to be in the sink.

"I'm much worse, thank you," she retorted, "and none the better for seeing you. What do you mean by coming into the house and yelling like a wild Injin? I shall expect you to pay for that plate anyway."

"He who breaks pays," said Hiram with a laugh. "But why don't you shake hands with a fellow?"

"I will if I like and I won't if I like," replied Mandy, extending her hand, which was covered with soapsuds.

"Wipe your hand," said Hiram, "and I'll give you this ten cents to pay for the plate."

As he said this he extended the money towards her. Mandy did not attempt to take it, but giving her wet hand a flip threw the soapsuds full in Hiram's face. He rushed forward and caught her about the waist; as he did so he dropped the money, which rolled under the kitchen table.

Mandy turned around quickly and facing Hiram, caught

him by both ears, which she pulled vigorously. He released his hold upon her and jumped back to escape further punishment.

"Now, Mr. Hiram Maxwell," said she, facing him, "what do you mean by such actions? I've a good mind to put you outdoors and never set eyes on you again. What would Mr. Pettengill have thought if he'd a come in a minute ago?"

"I guess he'd a thought that I was gittin' on better'n I really am," replied Hiram, with a crestfallen look. "Now, Mandy, don't get mad, I didn't mean nothin', I was only foolin' and you began it fust, by throwin' that dirty water in my face, and no feller that had any spunk could stand that." As he said this, a broad smile covered his face. "Say, Mandy," he continued, "here comes Obadiah Strout, we'd better make up before he gits in or it'll be all over town that you and me have been fightin'. Got any chores this mornin', Mandy, that I can do for you?"

At this moment the kitchen door was again opened and Professor Strout entered.

"Where's Pettengill?" he asked of Mandy, not noticing Hiram.

"I guess he's out in the wood-shed, if he hasn't gone somewheres else," replied Mandy, resuming her work at the sink.

Strout turned towards Hiram and said, as if he had been unaware previously of his presence, "Oh! you there, Hiram? Just go find Pettengill for me like a good feller and tell him Professor Strout wishes to see him up to the house."

"At the same time, Hiram," said Mandy, "go find me that dozen eggs that I told you I wanted for that puddin'."

Hiram winked at Mandy, unseen by the Professor, and started for the chicken coop.

"Guess I'll have a chair," remarked the Professor.

"All right, if you don't take it with you when you go," replied Mandy, still busily washing dishes.

"Fine weather," said Strout.

"Sorter between," laconically replied Mandy.

"Did you enjoy the concert?" asked Strout.

"Some parts of it," said Mandy. "I thought Mr. Sawyer and Miss Putnam were just splendid. His whistling was just grand."

"He'll whistle another kind of a tune in a few days," remarked Strout.

"What? Are you going to give another concert?" asked Mandy, looking at him for the first time.

"If I do," replied the Professor, "you bet he won't be one of the performers."

"Oh, I see," said Mandy, "you're mad with him 'cause he hogged the whole show. Mr. Maxwell was just telling me as how Mr. Sawyer was going to hire the Town Hall on Washington's birthday and bring down a big brass band from Boston and give a concert that would put you in the shade, and somebody was telling me, I forget who, that Mr. Sawyer don't like to sit 'round doing nothin', and he's goin' to give music lessons."

These last two untruthful shots hit the mark, as she knew they would, and Strout, abandoning the subject, blurted out, "Where in thunder's that Hiram? I'll be blowed if I don't believe he went to look for the eggs first."

"I reckon he did," said Mandy, "if he means to keep on good terms with me. He ain't likely to tend to stray jobs till he's done up his regular chores."

"I s'pose Deacon Mason sends him down here to wait on you?" remarked Strout with a sneer.

"Did Deacon Mason tell you that you could have him to run your errands?" inquired Mandy, with a pout.

"Guess the best thing I can do," said Strout rising, "is to go hunt Pettengill up myself."

"I guess you've struck it right this time," assented
Mandy, as Strout left the room and started for the wood-
shed.

As he closed the door, Mandy resumed her singing as
though such conversations were of everyday occurrence.

She finished her work at the sink and was fixing the
kitchen fire when Hiram returned.

"All I could find," said he, holding an egg in each hand.
"The hens must have struck or think it's a holiday. S'pose
there's any out in the barn? Come, let's go look, Mandy.
Where's old Strout?"

"I guess he's gone to look for Mr. Pettengill," replied
Mandy, with a laugh.

"I kinder thought he would if I stayed long enough,"
said Hiram, with a grin; "but come along, Mandy, no hen
fruit, no puddin'."

"Mr. Maxwell," said Mandy, soberly, "I wish you'd be
more particular about your language. You know I abom-
inate slang. You know how careful I try to be."

"You're a dandy," said Hiram, taking her hand.

They ran as far as the wood-shed, when seeing the door
open, they hid behind it until Strout came out and walked
down towards the lane to meet Ezekiel, whom he had seen
coming up from the road. Then Hiram and Mandy sped
on their way to the barn, which they quickly reached and
were soon upon the haymow, apparently searching intently
for eggs.

When Strout reached Ezekiel he shook hands with him
and said, "Come up to the barn, Pettengill, I've got a little
somethin' I want to tell you and it's kinder private. It's
about that city feller that's swellin' round here puttin' on
airs and tryin' to make us think that his father is a bigger
man than George Washington. He about the same as
told me down to the grocery store that the blood of all the
Quincys flowed in one arm and the blood of all the Adams

in the other, but I kinder guess that the rest of his carcass is full of calf's blood and there's more fuss and feathers than fight to him."

By this time they had reached the barn and they sat down upon a pile of hay at the foot of the mow.

"Now my plan's this," said Strout. "You know Bob Wood; well, he's the biggest feller and the best fighter in town. I'm goin' to post Bob up as to how to pick a quarrel with that city feller. When he gets the lickin' that he deserves, I rayther think that Deacon Mason will lose a boarder."

"But s'posin' Mr. Sawyer licks Bob Wood?" queried Ezekiel.

"Oh! I don't count much on that," said Strout; "but if it should turn out that way we're goin' to turn in and get up a surprise party for Miss Mason and jist leave him out."

"I hope you ain't goin' to do any fightin' down to Deacon Mason's?" remarked Ezekiel.

"Oh, no!" protested Strout, "it'll be kind o' quiet, underminin' work, as it were. Remarks and sayin's and side whispers and odd looks, the cold shoulder business, you know, that soon tells a feller that his company ain't appreciated."

"Well, I don't think that's quite fair," said Ezekiel. "You don't like him, Mr. Strout, but I don't think the whole town will take it up."

The Professor said sternly, "He has insulted me and in doing that he has insulted the whole town of East-borough."

A smothered laugh was heard.

"By George! What was that?" cried Strout.

Ezekiel was at a loss what to say, and before he could reply, Mandy's laughing had caused the hay to move. As it began to slide she clutched at Hiram in a vain effort to save herself, and the next instant a large pile of hay, bearing Hiram and Mandy, came down, falling upon Ezekiel and Strout and covering them from sight.

When all had struggled to their feet, Ezekiel turned to Mandy and said sharply, "What were you doin' up there, Mandy?"

"Looking for eggs," said she, as she ran out of the barn and started for the house.

Hiram stood with his mouth distended with a huge smile. Strout turned towards him and said savagely, "Well, if you're the only egg she got, 'twas a mighty bad one."

Hiram retorted, "I would rather be called a bad egg than somethin' I heard about you."

Strout, in a passion, cried out, "Who said anything about me?"

Hiram made for the barn door and then said, "heard a gentleman say as how there was only one jackass in Eastborough and he taught the singin' school."

Strout caught up a rake to throw at him, but Hiram was out of sight before he could carry out his purpose. Turning to Ezekiel, Strout said, "I bet a dollar, Pettengill, it was that city feller that said that, and as I have twice remarked and this makes three times, this town ain't big enough to hold both on us."

CHAPTER VIII.

HIRAM MAXWELL was not called upon to perform very arduous duties at Deacon Mason's. The Deacon had given up farming several years before, and Hiram's duties consisted in doing the chores about the house. He had plenty of spare time, and he used it by going down to the Pettengill place and talking to Mandy Skinner.

The next morning after the adventure in the barn, Hiram went down as usual after his morning's work was done to see Mandy.

"How do you find things, Mandy?" said Hiram, opening the kitchen door and putting his head in.

"By looking for them," said Mandy, without looking up from her work.

"You are awful smart, ain't you?" retorted Hiram.

Mandy replied, "People's opinion that I think a good deal more of than yours have said that same thing, Mr. Maxwell."

Hiram saw that he was worsted, so he changed the conversation.

"Anybody to hum?"

Mandy answered sharply, "Everybody's out but me, of course I am nobody."

Hiram came in and closed the door.

"You needn't be so pesky smart with your tongue, Mandy. Of course I can't keep up with you and you know it. What's up?"

Mandy replied, "The thermometer. It isn't nearly as cold as it was yesterday."

Hiram, seeing a breakfast apparently laid out on a side table inquired, "Expectin' somebody to breakfast?"

"No," said Mandy, "I got that ready for Mr. Pettengill, but he didn't have time to eat it because he was afraid he would lose the train."

"Has he gone to the city?" asked Hiram.

"I 'spect he has," answered Mandy.

"Well," remarked Hiram, "s'posin' I eat that breakfast myself, so as to save you the trouble of throwin' it away."

"Well," said Mandy, "I was going to give it to the pigs; I suppose one hog might as well have it as another."

Hiram said, "Why, you don't call me a big eater, do you, Mandy?"

Mandy laughed and said, "I can't tell, I never saw you when you wasn't hungry. How do you know when you have got enough?"

Hiram said, "I haven't got but one way of tellin', I allus eats till it hurts me, then I stop while the pain lasts."

Then he asked Mandy, "What did 'Zekiel go to the city for?"

Mandy answered, "Mr. Pettengill does not confide his private business to me."

Hiram broke in, "I bet a dollar you know why he went, just the same."

Mandy said, "I bet a dollar I do."

Then she broke into a loud laugh. Hiram evidently thought it was very funny and laughed until the tears stood in his eyes.

"What are you laughing for?" asked Mandy.

Hiram's countenance fell.

"Come down to the fine point, Mandy, durned if I know."

"That's a great trick of yours, Hiram," said Mandy.

"You ought not to laugh at anything unless you understand it."

"I guess I wouldn't laugh much then," said Hiram. "I allus laugh when I don't understand anythin', so folks won't think that I don't know where the p'int comes in. But say, Mandy, what did Pettengill go to the city for?"

During this conversation Hiram had been eating the breakfast that had been prepared for Ezekiel. Mandy sat down near him and said, "I'll tell you, but it ain't nothing to laugh at. Mr. Pettengill had a telegraph message come last night."

"You don't say so!" said Hiram. "It must be pretty important for persons to spend money that way. Nobody dead, I s'pose?"

"Well," said Mandy, "Mr. Pettengill left the telegram in his room and I had to read it to see whether I had to throw it away or not, and I remember every word that was in it."

Hiram asked earnestly, "Well, what was it? Is his sister Alice goin' to get married?"

Mandy answered, "No, she is sick and she wanted him to come right up to Boston at once to see her."

Hiram said, "'Zekiel must think a powerful lot of that sister of his'n. Went right off to Boston without his breakfast."

"I guess it would have to be something nearer than a sister to make you do that," said Mandy. "I don't know but one thing, Hiram, that would make you go without your feed."

"What's that, Mandy?" said he. "You?"

"No," replied Mandy, "a famine."

"You ain't no sort of an idea as to what's the matter with her, have you?" he asked.

"No, I haven't," said Mandy, "and if I had I don't imagine I would tell you. Now you better run right home,

little boy, for I have to go upstairs and do the chamber
work."

She whisked out of the room, and Hiram, helping himself
to a couple of apples, left the house and walked slowly
along the road towards Eastborough Centre.

Suddenly he espied a man coming up the road and soon
saw it was Quincy Adams Sawyer.

"Just the feller I wanted to see," soliliquized Hiram.

As Quincy reached him he said, "Mr. Sawyer, I want
to speak to you a minute or two. Come into Pettengill's
barn, there's nobody to hum but Mandy and she's upstairs
makin' the beds."

They entered the barn and sat down on a couple of half
barrels that served for stools.

"Mr. Sawyer, you've treated me fust rate since you've
been here and I want to do you a good turn and put you
on your guard."

Quincy laughed.

Hiram continued, "Well, maybe you won't laugh if Bob
Wood tackles you. I won't tell you how I found it out
for I'm no eavesdropper, but keep your eye on Bob Wood
and look out he don't play no mean tricks on you."

Quincy remarked, "I suppose Mr. Strout is at the bottom
of this and he has hired this Bob Wood to do what he can't
do himself."

"I guess you have got it about right, Mr. Sawyer," said
Hiram. "Can you fight?" he asked of Quincy.

"I am a good shot with a rifle," Quincy replied. "I can
hit the ace of hearts at one hundred feet with a pistol."

"I don't mean that," said Hiram. "Can you fight with
yer fists?"

"I don't know much about it," said Quincy with a queer
smile.

"Then I am afraid you will find Bob Wood a pretty
tough customer. He can lick any two fellers in town. Why,

he polished off Cobb's twins one day in less than five min·
utes, both of 'em."

"Where does this Bob Wood spend most of his time?"
asked Quincy.

"He loafs around Hill's grocery. When he ain't wokin'
at his trade," said Hiram, "he does odd jobs for the Put·
nams in summer and cuts some wood for them in winter.
You know. Lindy Putnam, the gal you sang with at the
concert?"

"Come along," said Quincy, "I feel pretty good this
morning, we'll walk down to Hill's and see if that Mr.
Wood has anything to say to me."

"Don't you think the best plan, Mr. Sawyer, would be
to keep out of his way?" queried Hiram.

"Well, I can't tell that," said Quincy, "until I get better
acquainted with him. After that he may think .he'd better
keep out of my way."

"Why, he's twice as big as you," cried Hiram, with a
look of astonishment on his face.

"Come along, Hiram," said Quincy. "By the way, I
haven't seen Miss Putnam since the concert. I think I
will have to call on her."

Hiram laughed until his face was as red as a beet.

"By gum, that's good," he said, as he struck both legs
with his hands.

"What's good?" asked Quincy. "Calling on Miss Put·
nam?"

"Yes," said Hiram. "Wouldn't she be s'prised?"

"Why?" asked Quincy. "Such a call wouldn't be con·
sidered anything out of the way in the city."

"No, nor it wouldn't here," said Hiram, "but for the fact
that Miss Putnam don't encourage callers. She goes round
a visitin' herself ,and she treats the other girls fust rate,
'cause she has plenty of money and can afford it. But she
has got two good reasons for not wantin' visitors."

"What are they?" asked Quincy.

"Well, I'm country myself," said Hiram, "and there are others in Eastborough that are more country than I am. But if you want to see and hear the genooine old Rubes you want to see old Sy Putnam and his wife Heppy."

"But Miss Mason said Miss Putnam was quite wealthy."

"You bet she is," said Hiram. "She's worth hundreds of millions of dollars."

"I think you must mean thousands," remarked Quincy.

"Well, as far as I'm concerned," said Hiram, "when you talk about millions or thousands of money, one's just the same to me as t'other. I never seed so much money in my life as I seed since you've been here, but I don't want you to think I'm beggin' for more."

"No," said Quincy, "I should never impute such a motive to you."

Quincy took a dollar bill from his pocket and held it up before Hiram.

"What's that?" he asked.

"That's one hundred cents," said Hiram, "considerably more than I have got."

"Well," said Quincy, "if you tell me why Miss Putnam doesn't like callers I will give you that dollar."

"Stop a minute," replied Hiram. "Soon as we turn this next corner we'll be in full sight of the grocery store. You can go ahead and I'll slip 'cross lots and come up from behind the store. If Wood thought I'd told you he would lick me and I'm no fighter. Now about Miss Putnam," dropping his voice, "I heard it said, and I guess it's pretty near the truth, that she is so blamed stuck up and dresses so fine in city fashions that she is just 'shamed of her old pa and ma and don't want nobody to see 'em."

"But," asked Quincy, "where did she get her money?"

Hiram answered, "From her only brother. He went down to Boston, made a pile of money, then died and left it all to Lindy. If what I've told you ain't gospel truth it's mighty near it. Well, I'll see you later, Mr. Sawyer."

And Hiram ran down a path that led across the fields.

Quincy turned the corner and walked briskly towards Hill's grocery store. A dozen or more young men and as many older ones were lounging about the platform that ran the whole length of the store, for it was a very mild day in January, and the snow was rapidly leaving under the influence of what might be called a January thaw.

Quincy walked through the crowd, giving a friendly nod to several faces that looked familiar, but the names of whose owners were unknown to him. He entered the store, found a letter from his mother and another from his sister Gertie, and saying "Good morning" to Mr. Hill, who was the village postmaster, soon reached the platform again.

As he did so a heavily built young fellow, fully six feet tall and having a coarse red face, stepped up to him and said brusquely, "I believe your name's Sawyer."

"Your belief is well founded," replied Quincy. "I regret that I do not know your name."

"Well, you won't have to suffer long before you find out," said the fellow. "My name's Robert Wood, or Bob Wood for short."

"Ah! I see," said Quincy. "Robert for long wood and Bob for short wood."

Wood's face grew redder.

"I s'pose you think that's mighty smart makin' fun of folks' names. I guess there ain't much doubt but what you said what a friend of mine tells me you did."

Quincy remarked calmly, "Well, what did your friend say I said about you?"

By this time the loungers in and outside the store had gathered around the two talkers. Wood seemed encouraged and braced up by the presence of so many friends. He walked up close to Quincy and said, "Well, my friend told me that you said there was but one jackass in East-borough and he sang bass in the quartette."

Quincy paled a little, but replied firmly, "I never said it, and if your friend says I did he lies and he knows it."

At this juncture, as if prearranged, Obadiah Strout suddenly emerged from the grocery store.

"What's the matter, gentlemen?" asked Mr. Strout.

"Well," said Wood, "I told this young man what you said he said, and he says you're a liar."

"Well," said Strout pompously, "I know that he said it and I have witnesses to prove it. When you settle with him for calling you a jackass I'll settle with him for calling me a liar."

"Take your coat off, Mr. Sawyer, and get ready. I won't keep you waitin' but a few moments," said Bob.

A jeering laugh went up from the crowd. Quincy, turning, saw Hiram.

"Here, Hiram," said he, "hold my things."

He took off his overcoat and then his black Prince Albert coat and passed them to Hiram. Then he removed his hat, which he also handed to Hiram.

Turning to Wood he said, "Come right out here, Mr. Wood; here is a place where the sun has kindly removed the snow and we can get a good footing."

Wood followed him, and the crowd formed a ring about them.

"Now, Mr. Wood, or perhaps I should say Bob Wood for short, put up your hands."

Bob put them up in defiance of all rules governing boxing. This was enough for Quincy; he had sized up his man and determined to make the most of his opportunity.

"Mr. Wood," he said politely, "before I hit you I am going to tell you just exactly where I am going to strike, so you can't blame me for anything that may happen. I shall commence on your right eye."

Wood's face grew livid; he made a rush at Quincy as
though he would fall on him and crush him. Quincy easily
eluded him, and when Wood made his second rush at him
he parried a right-hander, and before Wood could recover,
he struck him a square blow full on his right eye. They
faced each other again.

"Now, Mr. Wood," said Quincy, "I see you have a watch
in your vest pocket. Is it an open-faced watch?"

"S'posin' you find out," said Wood, glaring at Quincy
with his left eye, his right one being closed up.

"Well, then," remarked Quincy, "you will be obliged to
have it repaired, for I am going to hit you just where
that watch is and it may injure it."

Wood was more wary this time and Quincy was more
scientific. He gave Wood a left-hander in the region of
the heart which staggered him.

They faced each other for the third time.

"I regret the necessity this time, but I will be obliged to
strike you full in the face and in my excitement may hit
your nose."

It required all of Quincy's dexterity to avoid the wild
rushes and savage thrusts made by Wood. But Quincy
understood every one of the boxer's secrets and was as
light and agile on his feet as a cat. It was three minutes
at least before Quincy got the desired opening, and then
he landed a blow on Wood's nose that sent him flat upon
his back.

"That's enough," cried the crowd, and several friends
led Wood to a seat on the platform.

Quincy turned to Strout. "Now, Mr. Strout, I am at
your service."

"No, sir," said Strout, "I am willing to fight a gentleman, but I don't fight with no professional prize fighter
like you." Turning to the crowd: "I know all about this
fellow. He is no lawyer at all, he is a regular prize fighter,

"AND THEN HE LANDED A BLOW ON WOOD'S NOSE."

and down in Boston he is known by the name of Billy Shanks."

Quincy smiled. Turning to the crowd he said, "The statement just made by Mr. Strout is like his statement to Mr. Wood. The first was a lie, the second is a lie, and the man who uttered them is a liar. Good morning, gentlemen."

Quincy went to Hiram, who helped him on with his coats. They walked along together. After they turned the corner and got out of sight of the grocery store, Hiram said:

"Geewhilikins! What a smasher you gave him. I thought you said you didn't know nothin' about fightin'."

"I don't know much," responded Quincy. "There are a dozen men in Boston who could do to me just exactly what I did to Bob Wood."

CHAPTER IX

QUINCY had a double purpose in calling on Lindy; he actually wished to see her, for they had not met since the concert, but his principal wish was to meet a real old-fashioned country couple. To be sure, Deacon Mason and his wife often dropped into the vernacular, but the Deacon was a very dignified old gentleman and his wife was not a great talker. What he desired was to find one of the old-fashioned style of country women, with a tongue hung in the middle and running at both ends. His wish was to be gratified.

When he clanged the old brass knocker on the door, Samanthy Green answered the call.

"Is Miss Putnam at home?" asked Quincy politely.

"No, she ain't," said Samanthy, "but Mr. and Mrs. Putnam is. They're allus to hum. They don't go nowheres from one year's end to t'other."

"I would like to see them," said Quincy.

"Yes, sir," said Samanthy, "walk right in."

She threw open the door of the sitting-room. "Here's a gentleman that wants to see you, Mis' Putnam. Leastwise he asked for Lindy fust."

Samanthy left the room, slamming the door after her.

"My name is Sawyer," said Quincy, addressing the old lady and gentleman who were seated in rocking chairs. "I met your daughter at the concert given at the Town Hall New-Year's night."

Mrs. Putnam said, "Glad to see ye, Mr. Sawyer; have a chair."

As Quincy laid his hand upon the chair, the old gentleman called out in a voice that would have startled a bull of
Bashan, "What's his name, Heppy?"

Mrs. Putnam answered in a shrill voice with an edge like
a knife, "Sawyer."

"Sawyer!" yelled the man. "Any relation to Jim Sawyer that got drunk, beat his wife, starved his children, and
finally ended up in the town Poorhouse?"

Quincy shook his head and replied, "I think not. I don't
live here; I live in Boston."

"Du tell," said Mrs. Putnam. "How long you been
here?"

Quincy replied that he arrived two days after Christmas.

"Where be you stoppin'?" asked Mrs. Putnam.

Quincy answered, "I am boarding at Deacon Mason's."

"He's a nice old gentleman," said Mrs. Putnam, "and
Mrs. Mason's good as they make 'em. Her daughter
Huldy's a pert young thing, she's pretty and she knows it."

Quincy remarked that he thought Miss Mason was a
very nice young lady.

"Oh, yes," said Mrs. Putnam, "you young fellers never
look more than skin deep. Now the way she trifles with
that young 'Zekiel Pettengill I think's shameful. They ust
to have a spat every week about somethin', but they allus
made it up. But I heard Lindy say that after you come
here, 'Zeke he got huffy and Huldy she got independent,
and they hain't spoke to each other nigh on two weeks."

This was a revelation to Quincy, but he was to hear more
about it very soon.

"How long be you goin' to stay, Mr. Sawyer?"

"I haven't decided," said Quincy.

"What's your business?" persisted Mrs. Putnam.

"I am a lawyer," replied Quincy.

Mrs. Putnam looked at him inquiringly and said, "Be n't
you rather young for a lawyer? How old be you, anyway?"

Quincy decided to take a good humored part in his cross examination and said without a smile, "I am twenty-three years, two months, sixteen days old."

"Be you?" exclaimed Mrs. Putnam. "I shouldn't have said you were a day over nineteen."

Quincy never felt his youth so keenly before. He determined to change the conversation.

"Did you attend the concert, Mrs. Putnam?"

"No," said she. "Pa and me don't go out much; he's deefer'n a stone post and I've had the rheumatiz so bad in my knees for the last five years that I can't walk without crutches;" and she pointed to a pair that lay on the floor beside her chair.

During this conversation old Mr. Putnam had been eying Quincy very keenly. He blurted out, "He's a chip of the old block, Heppy; he looks just as Jim did when he fust came to this town. Did yer say yer had an Uncle Jim?"

Quincy shook his head.

Mrs. Putnam turned to her husband and yelled, "Now you shet up, Silas, and don't bother the young man. Jim Sawyer ain't nothin' to be proud of, and I don't blame the young man for not ownin' up even if Jim is his uncle."

Quincy made another attempt to change the conversation. "Your daughter is a very fine singer, Mrs. Putnam."

"Well, I s'pose so," said she; "there's been enough money spent on her to make suthin' of her. As for me I don't like this folderol singin'. Why, when she ust to be practisin' I had to go up in the attic or else stuff cotton in my ears. But my son, Jehoiakim Jones Putnam, he sot everythin' by Lucinda, and there wasn't anythin' she wanted that she couldn't have. He's dead now, but he left more'n a hundred thousand dollars, that he made speculatin'."

"Then your daughter will be quite an heiress one of these days, Mrs. Putnam?"

She answered, "She won't get none of my money.
Jehoiakim left her all of his'n, but before she got it she had
to sign a paper, a wafer, I believe they call it, if you're a
lawyer you ought to know what it was, givin' up all claim
on my money. I made my will and the girl who'll get it
needs it and will make good use of it."

Quincy determined to get even with Mrs. Putnam for
the questioning she put him through, so he said, "Did you
make your money speculating, Mrs. Putnam?"

"No," said she, "pa made it by hard work on the farm;
but he gave it all to me more'n fifteen year ago, and he
hasn't got a cent to his name. He's just as bad off as Jim
Sawyer. I feed him and clothe him and shall have to bury
him. I guess it seems kinder odd to ye, so I reckon I'll
have to tell ye the hull story. I've told it a dozen times,
but I guess it'll bear tellin' once more. You see my husband here, Silas Putnam, was brought up religis and he's
allus been a churchgoin' man. We were both Methodists,
and everythin' went all right till one day a Second Advent
preacher came along, and then things went all wrong. He
canoodled my husband into believin' that the end of the
world was comin' and it was his duty to give all his property away, so he could stand clean handed afore the Lord,
My dander riz when I heerd them makin' their plans, but
afore my husband got deef he was great on argifyin' and
argumentin', and I didn't stand much show against two on
'em; but when Silas told me he was goin' to give his property away I sot up my Ebenezer, and I says, 'Silas Putnam,
if you gives your property to any one you gives it to me.'
So after a long tussle it was settled that way and the lawyers
drew up the papers. The night afore the world was goin'
to end he prayed all night. You can imagine with that air
voice of his'n I didn't sleep a wink. When mornin' came—
it was late in October and the air was pretty sharp—Silas
stopped prayin' and put on his white robe, which was a

shirt of hisn't I pieced out so it came down to his feet, and takin' a tin trumpet that he bought over to Eastborough Centre, he went out, climbed up on the barn, sot down on the ridgepole and waited for Kingdom Come. He sot there and tooted all mornin' and 'spected the angel Gabriel would answer back. He sot there and tooted all the arter-noon till the cows come home and the chickens went to roost. I had three good square meals that day, but Silas didn't get a bite. 'Bout six o'clock I did think of takin' him out some doughnuts, but then I decided if he was goin' up so soon it was no use a wastin' em, so I put 'em back in the pantry. He sot there and tooted all the evenin' till the moon come up and the stars were all out, and then he slid down off'n the barn, and barked both his shins doin' it, threw his trumpet into the pig pen, come into the house and huddled up close to the fire. He didn't say nothin' for a spell, but finally says he, 'I guess, Heppy, that feller made a mistake in figurin' out the date.' 'I guess, Silas,' says I, 'that you've made an all-fired fool of yerself. And if you don't go to bed quick and take a rum sweat, I shall be a widder in a very short time.' He was sick for more'n three weeks, but I pulled him through by good nussin', and the fust day he was able to set up, I says to him, 'Now, Silas Putnam, when I married ye forty-five year ago I promised to obey ye, ye was allus a good perwider and I don't per-pose to see yer want for nothin', but ye have got to hold up yer right hand and swear to obey me for the rest of yer nateral life,' and he did it. He got well, and he is tougher'n a biled owl, if he is eighty-six. But the cold sorter settled in his ears, and he's deef as an adder. Ef angel Gabriel blew his horn now I'm afeared Silas wouldn't hear him."

During this long story Quincy had listened without a smile on his face, but the manner in which the last remark was made was too much for him and he burst into a loud laugh. Silas, who had been eying him, also gave a loud laugh and said with his ponderous voice, "I guess Heppy's been tellin' ye about my goin' up."

Quincy laughed again and Mrs. Putnam took part. He arose, told Mr. and Mrs. Putnam he had enjoyed his visit very much, was very sorry Miss Putnam was not at home, and said he would call again, with their kind permission.

"Oh, drop in any time," said Mrs. Putnam; "we're allus to hum. You seem to be a nice young man, but you're too young to marry. Why, Lindy's twenty-eight, and I tell her she don't know enough to get married yet. Ef you'll take a bit of advice from an old woman, let me say, 'less you mean to marry the girl yourself, you'd better git away from Deacon Mason's."

And with this parting shot ringing in his ears, he left the house and made his way homeward.

In half an hour after Quincy's departure, Lindy Putnam entered the sitting-room and facing her mother said with a voice full of passion, "Samanthy says Mr. Sawyer called to see me."

Mrs. Putnam answered, "Well, ef ye wanted to see him so much why didn't ye stay to hum?"

Lindy continued, "Well, I have told you a dozen times that when people come to see me that you are not to invite them in."

"Wall, I didn't," said Mrs. Putnam. "When he found you wuz out he said he wanted to see pa and me, and he stayed here more'n an hour."

"Yes," said Lindy, "no doubt you told him all about pa's turning Second Advent and how much money I had, and you have killed all my chances."

"Well, I guess not," said Mrs. Putnam. "I told him about your brother leavin' yer all his money, and I guess that won't drive him away."

Lindy continued, "Money don't count with him; they say his father is worth more than a million dollars."

Mrs. Putnam answered, "Wall, I s'pose there's a dozen
or so to divide it among."

Lindy said, "Did you tell him who you were going to
leave your money to?"

"No, I didn't," replied Mrs. Putnam. "But I did tell
him that you wouldn't get a cent of it."

Lindy sobbed, "I think it is a shame, mother. I like him
better than any young man I have ever met, and now after
what you have told me I sha'n't see him again. I have a
good mind to leave you for good and all and go to Boston
to live."

"Wall, you're your own mistress," replied Mrs. Putnam,
"and I'm my own mistress and pa's. Come to think on't,
there was one thing I said to him that might sot him against
yer."

"What was that?" demanded Lindy fiercely.

"Wall," said Mrs. Putnam, "he said he was twenty-three,
and I sort a told him incidentally you was twenty-eight.
You know yer thirty, and p'raps he might object to ye on
account of yer age."

This was too much for Lindy. She rushed out of the
room and up to her chamber, where she threw herself on
her bed in a passion of tears.

"It's too bad," she cried. "I will see him again, I will
find some way, and I'll win him yet, even if I am twenty-
eight."

Two days afterwards Hiram told Mandy that he heard
down to Hill's grocery that that city chap had two strings
to his bow now. He was courting the Deacon's daughter,
but had been up to see Mr. and Mrs. Putnam to find out
how much money Lindy had in her own right, and to see
if there was any prospect of getting anything out of the
old folks.

CHAPTER X.

A FTER supper on the day he had been visiting Mr.
and Mrs. Putnam, Quincy went to his room and
wrote a long letter to his father, inquiring if he ever had an
uncle by the name of James Sawyer. Before retiring he sat
and thought over the experiences of the past fortnight since
his arrival in Eastborough, but the most of his thoughts
were given to the remark made by Mrs. Putnam about his
leaving Deacon Mason's. He had been uniformly polite
and to a slight degree attentive to Miss Mason. The Deacon's horse was a slow one, and so on several occasions he
had hired a presentable rig and a good stepper over to
Eastborough Centre, and had taken Miss Mason out to ride.
He reflected now, as he had never done before, that of
course the whole town knew this, and the thought came
home to him strongly that by so doing he might have in-
flicted a triple injury upon Miss Mason, Mr. Pettingill, and
himself. He was not in love with Miss Mason, nor Miss
Putnam; they were both pretty girls, and in the city it was
the custom to be attentive to pretty girls without regard to
consequences.

He had asked Miss Mason to go riding with him the next
day, but he inwardly resolved that it would be the last time
he would take her, and he was in doubt whether to go back
to the city at once or go to some other town and board at a
hotel, or look around and find some other place in Eastborough. One consideration kept him from leaving

Eastborough; he knew that if he did so the singing-master would claim that he had driven him out of town, and although he had a hearty contempt for the man, he was too high spirited to leave town and give the people any reason to think that Strout's antipathy to him had anything to do with it.

Finally a bright idea struck him. Why hadn't he thought of it before? He would go and see Uncle Ike, state the case frankly and ask him to let him live with him for a month. He could bunk in the kitchen, and he preferred Uncle Ike's conversation to that of any other of the male sex whom he had met in Eastborough. With this idea firmly fixed in his mind he retired and slept peacefully.

While Quincy was debating with himself and coming to the conclusion previously mentioned, another conversation, in which his name often occurred, took place in Deacon Mason's kitchen.

The old couple were seated by the old-fashioned fireplace, in which a wood fire was burning. The stove had super-seded the hanging crane and the tin oven for cooking purposes, but Deacon Mason clung to the old-fashioned fire-place for heat and light. The moon was high and its rays streamed in through the windows, the curtains of which had not been drawn.

For quite a while they sat in silence, then Deacon Mason said, "There is something I want to speak about, mother, and yet I don't want to. I know there is nothing to it and nothing likely to come of it, but the fact is, mother, Huldy's bein' talked about down to the Corner, 'cause Mr. Sawyer is boardin' here. You know she goes out ridin' with him, which ain't no harm, and she has a sort o' broken with 'Zekiel, for which I am sorry, for 'Zekiel is one of the likely young men of the town."

"So I do, father," said Mrs. Mason, "and if you don't meddle, things will come out all right. Mr. Sawyer don't

care nothing for Huldy, and I don't think she cares anything for him. He will be going back to the city in a little
while and then things will be all right again."

"Well," said the Deacon, "I think Huldy better stop
goin' out to ride with him anyway; she is high spirited,
and if I tell her not to go she'll want to know why."

"But," broke in Mrs. Mason, "ef you tell him won't he
want to know why?"

"Well, perhaps," said the Deacon, "but I will speak to
him anyway."

The next morning after breakfast Deacon Mason asked
Mr. Sawyer to step into the parlor, and remarking that
when he had anything to say he always said it right out, he
asked Quincy if he was on good terms with Mr. 'Zekiel
Pettengill.

"I don't know," said Quincy. "I don't know of anything
that I have done at which he could take offence, but he
keeps away from me, and when I do meet him and speak
to him, a 'yes' or 'no' is all I get in reply."

"Haven't you any idea what makes him treat you so?"
asked the Deacon.

Quincy flushed.

"Yes, Mr. Mason, I think I do know, but it never entered my mind until late yesterday afternoon, and then it
was called to my attention by a stranger. I am glad I have
this chance to speak to you, Mr. Mason, for while I have
had a very enjoyable time here, I have decided to find
another boarding place, and I shall leave just as soon as I
make the necessary arrangements."

The Deacon was a little crestfallen at having the business
taken out of his hands so quickly, and saying he was very
sorry to have the young man go, he sought his wife and told
her everything was fixed up and that Mr. Sawyer was going
away.

Quincy started to leave the house by the front door; in

the hallway he met Huldy, who had just come down stairs. He had asked her to go to ride with him that day, and as he looked at her pretty face he vowed to himself that he would not be deprived of that pleasure. It could do no harm, for it would be their last ride together and probably their last meeting.

He said, "Good morning, Miss Mason," and then added with that tone which the society belle considers a matter of course, but which is so pleasing to the village maiden, "You look charming this morning, Miss Mason. I don't think our ride to-day could make your cheeks any redder than they are now." Huldy blushed, making her cheeks a still deeper crimson. "I will be here at one o'clock with the team," said Quincy. "Will you be ready?"

"Yes," answered Huldy softly.

Quincy raised his hat, and a moment later he was on his way to Eastborough Centre.

He walked briskly and thought he would stop at Uncle Ike's and carry out the resolution he had made the night before, but as he turned up the path that led to the house he saw a man standing on the steps talking to Uncle Ike, who stood in the doorway. The young man was Ezekiel Pettengill. Shakespeare says,

" 'Tis conscience that makes cowards of us all,"

and although Quincy at heart was a gentleman, he also knew it was not quite right for him to take Miss Mason out riding again under the circumstances; but young men are often stubborn and Quincy felt a little stiff-necked and rebellious that morning.

He reached Eastborough Centre, mailed his father the letter relating to Jim Sawyer, and going to the stable, picked out the best rig it could supply. He always had the same horse. It was somewhat small in size, but a very plump, white mare; she was a good roadster and it was never necessary to touch her with the whip. Shake it in the stock and she would not forget it for the next two miles. The stable keeper told with much unction how two fellows hired her to go from Eastborough Centre to Montrose. On their way home they had drunk quite freely at the latter place, and thought they would touch the mare up with the whip; they were in an open team and the result was that she left them at different points along the road and reached home with no further impediment to her career than the shafts and the front wheels.

Instead of coming back by the main road which led by Uncle Ike's, Quincy went through by what was called The Willows, which increased the distance a couple of miles. Nevertheless, it lacked five minutes of one o'clock when he drove up to Deacon Mason's front door.

Huldy was all dressed for the occasion, and with a "Good-by, mother," to Mrs. Mason, who was in the kitchen, was out the front door, helped into the team, and they were off just as the startled matron reached the parlor window. Mrs. Mason returned to the kitchen and at that moment the Deacon came in from the barn.

"What's the matter, mother?" asked the Deacon, noticing her excited and somewhat troubled look.

"Huldy is gone out riding again with Mr. Sawyer," said she.

The Deacon was a good Christian man and didn't swear, but he was evidently thinking deeply. Finally he said, "Well, mother, we must make the best of it. I'll help him find a boarding place if he don't get one by to-morrow."

They had a splendid drive. The air was cool, but not biting, the sun was warm, the roads had dried up since the recent thaw, which had removed the snow, with the exception of some patches in the fields, and the high-topped buggy rolled smoothly over the ground.

They passed through the little square in front of Hill's grocery, and as luck would have it, Professor Strout was standing on the platform smoking a cigar. Huldy smiled and nodded to him, and Quincy, with true politeness, followed a city custom and raised his hat, but the Professor did not return the bow, nor the salute, but turning on his heel walked into the grocery store.

"Professor Strout is not very polite, is he, Mr. Sawyer?" asked Huldy, laughing.

Quincy replied, looking straight ahead, "He has never learned the first letter in the alphabet of the art."

Quincy had a disagreeable duty to perform. He enjoyed Miss Huldy's company, but she was not the sort of girl he could love enough to make his wife. Then the thought came to him, supposing she should fall in love with him; that was not impossible, and it must be prevented.

When they were about half a mile from Mason's Corner, on their way home, Quincy realized that he could not put the matter off any longer.

Just as he was going to speak to her she turned to him and said, "Let me drive the rest of the way home, Mr. Sawyer."

"Oh, no," replied Quincy, "I think I had better keep the reins. You know I am responsible for you until you are safe at home."

Huldy pouted. "You think I can't drive," said she, "I have driven horses all my life. Please let me, Mr. Sawyer," she added coaxingly. And she took the reins from his hands.

"Well," said Quincy, "you are now responsible for me and I shall expect you to be very careful."

They drove a short distance in silence; then Quincy turned to her and said abruptly, "This is our last ride together, Miss Mason."

"Why?" inquired she with an astonished look in her face.

"I am going to leave your very pleasant home to-morrow," said Quincy.

The girl's cheeks paled perceptibly.

"Are you going back to Boston?" she asked.

"No, not for some time," Quincy replied, "but I have had some advice given me and I think it best to follow it."

"You have been advised to leave my father's house," said she, holding the reins listlessly in her hand.

Quincy said, "You won't be offended if I tell you the whole truth?"

"No; why should I?" asked Huldy.

As she said this she gathered up the reins and gave them a sharp pull. The white mare understood this to be a signal to do some good travelling and she started off at a brisk trot.

Quincy said, "I was told yesterday by a friend that if I was not a marrying man they would advise me to leave Deacon Mason's house at once."

The blood shot into Huldy's face at once. He was not a marrying man and consequently he was going to leave. He did not care for her or he would stay. Then another thought struck her. Perhaps he was going away because he was afraid she would fall in love with him.

As the Deacon had said, she was high spirited, and for an instant she was filled with indignation. She shut her eyes, and her heart seemed to stop its beating. She heard Quincy's voice, "Look out for the curve, Miss Mason." She dropped the left rein and mechanically gave the right one a strong, sharp pull with both hands. Quincy grasped the reins, but it was too late.

Huldy's pull on the right rein had thrown the horse almost at right angles to the buggy. The steep hill and sharp curve in the road did the rest. The buggy stood for an instant on two wheels, then fell on its side with a crash, taking the horse off her feet at the same time.

Huldy pitched forward as the buggy was falling, striking her left arm upon the wheel, and then fell into the road.

Quincy gave a quick leap over the dasher, falling on the prostrate horse, and grasping her by the head, pressed it to the ground. The mare lay motionless. Quincy rushed to Miss Mason and lifted her to her feet, but found her a dead weight in his arms. He looked in her face. She had evidently fainted. Her left arm hung by her side in a help-less sort of way; he touched it lightly between the elbow and shoulder. It was broken. Grasping her in his arms he ran to the back door and burst into the kitchen where Mrs. Mason was at work.

Quincy said in quick, excited tones, "There has been an accident, Mrs. Mason, and your daughter's arm is broken; she has also fainted. I will take her right to her room and put her on her bed. You can bring her out of that." Suit-ing the action to the word, he took Huldy upstairs, saying, "I will go for the doctor at once."

Then he dashed down the stairs and out of the front door; as he reached the team he found Hiram standing beside it, his eyes wide open with astonishment.

"Had a smash-up, Mr. Sawyer?" he asked. "How did it happen?"

"All my carelessness," said Quincy. "Come, give me a lift on the buggy, quick."

How it was done Quincy could never tell afterwards, but in a very short time the buggy was righted, the mare on her feet and the harness adjusted. Hiram took off his cap and began dusting the mare, whose white coat showed the dust very plainly.

"Where does the nearest doctor live, Hiram?" asked Quincy.

"Second house up the road you just come down," said Hiram. "The folks say he don't know much, anyway."

"Well, you get him here as quick as possible," said Quincy. "I am going to Eastborough Centre to telegraph for a surgeon and a trained nurse. Can you remember that?"

Quincy passed him a dollar bill.

Hiram winked and said, "I guess I can," and darted off up the hill.

Quincy sprang into the team and the white mare dashed forward at full speed. As he reached the Pettengill house he saw Ezekiel standing at the front gate. With difficulty he pulled the mare up, for she was greatly excited.

"Mr. Pettengill," said he, "there has been a serious accident. Miss Mason has been thrown from her carriage and her left arm is broken. I sent Hiram for a doctor and I am on my way to Eastborough to telegraph to Boston for a surgeon and a nurse. I shall not return to-night. Go up to the Deacon's and stay with her."

As he said this the mare gave a bound forward and she never slackened pace until Eastborough Centre was reached.

Quincy sent his telegram and returned the injured buggy and the horse to the stable keeper, telling him to have it repaired and he would pay the bill. He arranged to have a driver and a four-seated team ready on the arrival of the train bearing the doctor and the nurse. In about an hour he received a telegram that they would leave on the 6.05 express and would reach Eastborough Centre at 7.15.

They arrived, and the hired driver, doctor, and nurse started for Mason's Corner.

The last train to Boston left at 9.20. Ten minutes before that hour the team returned with the doctor.

"She is all right," he said. "Everything has been done for her, and the other doctor will write me when my services are needed again. Good night."

The train dashed in and the doctor sped back to Boston.

Quincy had engaged a room at the hotel, and he at once

retired to it, but not to sleep. He passed the most uncomfortable night that had ever come to him.

The next afternoon Hiram told Mandy that he heard Professor Strout say to Robert Wood that he guessed that "accident would never have occurred if that city chap hadn't been trying to drive hoss with one hand."

Mandy said, "That Strout is a mean old thing, anyway, and if you tell me another thing that he says, I'll fill your mouth full o' soft soap, or my name isn't Mandy Skinner."

CHAPTER XI.

THE morning of the accident, when Quincy saw Ezekiel Pettengill standing on the steps of Uncle Ike's house, Ezekiel was the bearer of some sad tidings.

He recognized Quincy as the latter started to come up the path, and saw him retrace his steps, and naturally thought, as most men would, that the reason Quincy did not come in was because he did not wish to meet him.

"Who was you looking after?" asked Uncle Ike, as Ezekiel entered the room and closed the door.

"I think it was Mr. Sawyer," replied Ezekiel, "on his way to Eastborough Centre."

"That Mr. Sawyer," said Uncle Ike, "is a very level-headed young man. He called on me once and I like him very much. Do you know him, 'Zeke?"

"Yes, I know who he is," Ezekiel answered, "but I have never been introduced to him. He nods and I nod, or I say, 'good mornin',' and he says, 'good mornin'.'"

"Don't you go up to Deacon Mason's as much as you used to, 'Zeke?" asked Uncle Ike. "I thought Huldy and you were going to make a match of it."

Ezekiel replied, "Well, to be honest, Uncle Ike, Huldy and me had a little tiff, and I haven't seen her to speak to her for more than three weeks, but I guess it will all come out all right some day."

"Well, you're on the right track, 'Zeke," said Uncle Ike. "Do all your fighting before you get married. But what brings you down here so early in the morning?"

"I've got some bad news," replied Ezekiel. "Have you heard from Alice lately?"

"No," said Uncle Ike, "and I can't understand it. She has always written to me once a fortnight, and it's a month now since I heard from her, and she has sent me a book every Christmas until this last one."

"She has been very sick, Uncle Ike," said Ezekiel. "She was taken down about the middle of December and was under the doctor's care for three weeks."

"Is she better?" asked Uncle Ike eagerly.

"Yes, she is up again," said Ezekiel, "but she is very weak; but that ain't the worst of it," he added.

"Why, what's the matter?" asked Uncle Ike. "Why didn't her friends let us know?"

"She wouldn't let them," said Ezekiel. "If it hadn't been for what the eye doctor told her she wouldn't have telegraphed to me what she did."

"Well, what's the matter with her?" cried Uncle Ike almost fiercely.

"Well, Uncle Ike," said Ezekiel, and the tears stood in his eyes as he said it, "our Allie is almost blind, but the eye doctor says she will get better, but it will take a very long time. She has had to give up her job, and I am going to Boston again to-morrow to bring her home to the old house."

"What's the matter with her eyes?" asked Uncle Ike.

"He called them cataracts," said Ezekiel, "or something like that."

Uncle Ike sat down in his armchair and thought for a minute or two.

"Yes," he said, "I know what they are; I have read all about them, and I know people who have had them. One was a schoolmate of mine. He was a mighty smart fellow and I felt sorry for him and used to help him out in his studies. I heard he had his eyes operated on and recovered his sight."

"Well, the doctor she has," said Ezekiel, "is agin operations. He says they can be cured without them. She drops something in her eyes and blows something in them, and then the tears come, and then she sits quietly with her hands folded, thinking, I suppose, till the time comes to use the medicine again."

"What can I do to help you?" asked Uncle Ike. "You know I always loved Alice even better than I did my own children, because she is more lovable, I suppose. Now, 'Zeke, if you want any money for doctor's bills or anything else, I am ready to do everything in the world I can for Alice. Did she ask after me, 'Zeke?"

"Almost the first thing she said was, 'How is dear old Uncle Ike?' and then she said how glad she would be to get back to Eastborough, where she could have you to talk to. 'I am lonesome now,' she said, 'I cannot write nor read, and the time passes so slowly with no one to talk to.'"

"But the poor dear girl can't walk down here to see me," said Uncle Ike.

"That's just what I came to see you about," said Ezekiel. "The greatest favor you can do Alice and me is to come up to the old house and live with us for a while and be company for Alice. You can have the big front room that father and mother used to have, and Alice's room, you know, is just side of that. In a little while I shall have to be busy on the farm and poor Alice—"

"Don't talk any more about it, 'Zeke," said Uncle Ike. "Of course I'll come. She will do me as much good as I'll do her. Send down the boys with the team to-morrow noon and I'll be all settled by the time you get back."

"I'll do it," said Ezekiel. "It is very good of you, Uncle Ike, to give up your little home here that you like so much and come to live with us. I know you wouldn't do it for

anybody but Alice, and I'll leave her to thank you when
she gets down here."

Uncle Ike and Ezekiel shook hands warmly.

"Don't you need any money, 'Zeke?" asked Uncle Ike.

"No," replied Ezekiel. "Alice wouldn't let me pay out
a cent; she had some money saved up in the bank and she
insisted on paying for everything herself. She wouldn't
come home till I promised her I'd let her pay her board
when she got able to work again."

"She always was independent," said Uncle Ike, "and that
was one reason why I liked her. But more than that, she
is the fairest-minded and best-tempered woman I ever met
in my life, and I have seen a good many."

Ezekiel shook hands again with Uncle Ike, and then
started off briskly with a much lighter heart than he had
before the interview. Reaching home he astonished Mandy
Skinner by telling her that he was going to bring his sister
down from Boston and that Uncle Ike was coming to live
with them for a while.

"My Lord!" cried Mandy, "and do you expect me to do
all this extra work?"

"I don't expect nothing," said Ezekiel. "You can get
old Mrs. Crowley to come and do the heavy work, and I
guess you can get along. You allus said you liked her, she
was such a nice washer and ironer. She can have the little
room over the ell, and I'll give you a dollar a week extra for
your trouble. Do you think you can get along, Mandy?"

Mandy answered, "I know I can with your sister all
right, but if your Uncle Ike comes out here in the kitchen
and tells me how to roast meat and make pies, as he did
once, there will be trouble, and he may have to do all the
cooking."

Ezekiel smiled, but said nothing, and went off upstairs to
look at the two rooms that were to be occupied by Uncle
Ike and poor Allie.

CHAPTER XII.

WHEN Quincy awoke in his room at the hotel on the morning after the accident he found to his great surprise that it was nine o'clock. He arose and dressed quickly, and after a light breakfast started off towards Uncle Ike's. Reaching the house he was astonished at the sight that met his gaze. Everything was out of place. The bed was down and the bedding tied up in bundles; the books had been taken from the bookcase and had been piled up on the table. There was no fire in the stove, and the funnel was laid upon the top of it. Quincy had remembered that he had seen a pile of soot on the ground near the steps as he came up them. All of Uncle Ike's cooking utensils were packed in a soap box which stood near the stove.

"What's the matter, Mr. Pettengill, are you going to move?" asked Quincy.

"For a time at least," replied Uncle Ike. " 'Zeke Pettengill's sister has been struck blind and he is going to bring her down home this afternoon and I am going to live with them and be company for her. I always thought as much of Alice as if she was my own daughter, and now she is in trouble, her old uncle isn't going back on her. It isn't Ike Pettengill's way."

"Have you seen 'Zekiel Pettengill this morning?" asked Quincy.

"No, nor I didn't expect to," replied Uncle Ike. "I suppose he went to Boston on the nine o'clock train and will be back on the three o'clock express."

"Mr. Pettengill," said Quincy, "can you give me fifteen minutes' time for a talk?"

"Well," said Uncle Ike, looking at his watch, "it will be half an hour before Cobb's twins will be down here with the team, and I might as well listen to you as sit around and do nothing. They are coming down again by and by to get the chickens. I have a good mind to set the house on fire and burn it up. If I don't, I suppose some tramp will, and if I need another house like it, thank the Lord I've got money enough to build it."

"No, don't burn it up, Mr. Pettengill," said Quincy. "Let it to me. I am around looking for a boarding place myself."

"Why, what's the matter, what made you leave Deacon Mason's?"

"That's what I want to tell you," said Quincy. "Time is limited and I'll make my story short, but you are a friend of my father's, and I want you to understand the whole business."

"Why, what have you been up to?" asked Uncle Ike, opening his eyes.

"Nothing," said Quincy, "and that's the trouble. When I went to Deacon Mason's nobody told me that his daughter was engaged to Ezekiel Pettengill."

"And she isn't," interjected Uncle Ike.

"Well," said Quincy, "they have been keeping company together, but I didn't know it. Miss Mason is a pretty girl and a very pleasant one. Time hung heavily on my hands and I naturally paid her some attentions; gave her flowers and candy, and took her out to ride, but I never thought of falling in love with her, and I am not conceited enough to think she is in love with me."

"Well, I don't know," said Uncle Ike reflectively. "Perhaps she has heard your father was worth a million dollars."

"No, I don't believe that," said Quincy. "Miss Mason

is too true and honest a girl to marry a man simply for his money."

"Well, I think you are right there," remarked Uncle Ike.

"New Year's night," said Quincy, "at the concert in the Town Hall, Strout, the singing teacher, got down on me because Miss Putnam and I received so much applause for singing a duet together. Then I broke his heart by whistling a tune for the girls and boys, and then again he doesn't like me because I am from the city! he hired a fellow to whip me, but the fellow didn't know how to box and I knocked him out very quickly. Now that Strout can't hurt me any other way he has gone to work making up lies, and the village is full of gossip about Miss Mason and me. Deacon Mason was going to talk to me about it, but I told him yesterday morning that I was going to get another boarding place, and I should have done so yesterday but for a very unfortunate accident."

"Accident?" said Uncle Ike; "why, you seem to be all right."

"I wish I had been the victim," said Quincy, "instead of Miss Mason. I took her out riding yesterday and the buggy got tipped over right in front of Deacon Mason's house, and Miss Mason had her left arm broken above the elbow. I have done all I could to atone for my carelessness, but I am afraid 'Zeke Pettengill will never forgive me. I wish, Mr. Pettengill, you would make him understand my position in the matter. I would like to be good friends with him, for I have nothing against him. He is the most gentlemanly young man that I have seen in the town. I value his good opinion and I want him to understand that I haven't intentionally done anything to wrong or injure him."

Uncle Ike covered his eyes with his hands and mused for a few minutes; then he finally said, "Mr. Sawyer, I have got an idea. That fellow, Strout, thinks he runs this town,

and it would tickle him to death if he thought he made
things uncomfortable for you. Then, again, I happen to
know that he is sweet on Huldy Mason himself, and he
would do all he could to widen the breach between 'Zeke
and her. You see he isn't but forty himself, and he
wouldn't mind the difference in ages at all. Now, my plan
is this." Uncle Ike looked out the window and said, "Here
comes Cobb's twins with the team. Now we will take my
things up to the house, then you take the team and go up
to Deacon Mason's and get your trunk and bring it down
to Pettengill's house. You will be my guest for to-night,
anyway, and if I don't make things right with 'Zeke so you
can stay there, I'll fix it anyway so you can stay till you get
a place to suit you. Now don't say no, Mr.Sawyer. Your
father and I are old friends and he will sort o' hold me
responsible for your good treatment. I won't take no for
an answer. If you have no objections, Mr. Sawyer, I wish
you would keep your eye on those books when they are
put into the team, for those Cobb boys handle everything
as though it was a rock or a tree stump." And Uncle Ike,
taking his kerosene lamp in one hand and his looking
glass in the other, cried, "Come in," as one of the Cobb
boys knocked on the door.

CHAPTER XIII.

IT was not until Quincy had reached the Pettengill house and helped Uncle Ike get his things in order, that he finally decided to accept Uncle Ike's offer. If he went to Eastborough Centre to live at the hotel, he knew Strout would consider he had won a victory. He had thought of going to Mr. and Mrs. Putnam about a room and board, but then he remembered Lindy, and said to himself that Miss Putnam was a pretty girl and it would be the same old story over again. Then he thought, "There won't be any danger here with a blind girl and Mandy Skinner, and if Uncle Ike can arrange matters it will be the best thing I can do."

And so he drove up to Deacon Mason's with Cobb's twins, saw Mrs. Mason, went upstairs and packed his trunk quickly, and the Cobb boys drove away with it to his new, though perhaps only temporary, lodgings.

When Quincy went downstairs, Mrs. Mason was in the parlor, and she beckoned to him to come in. He entered and closed the door.

"I want to speak to you a few minutes," said she, "and I want to tell you first I don't blame you a bit. I know you told 'Zeke Pettengill that the tip-over was all your careless-ness, but Huldy says it ain't so. She said she was driving, though you didn't want her to, and the accident was all her fault. Now, I believe my daughter tells the truth, and the Deacon thinks so too."

"Well, Mrs. Mason," said Quincy, "what your daughter

says is partly true, but I am still to blame for allowing her
to drive a horse with which she was not acquainted."

"That warn't the trouble, Mr. Sawyer," said Mrs. Mason.
"Huldy told me the whole truth. You said something to
her about going away. She had heard what the village
gossips were saying. Huldy's got a high temper and she
was so mad that she got flustrated, and that's what caused
all the trouble. I like you, Mr. Sawyer, and Huldy likes
you. She says you have allus been a perfect gentleman,
and the Deacon now is awful sorry you are going, but I
hope you will come and see us often while you stay at
Mason's Corner."

"I certainly shall, Mrs. Mason," replied Quincy. "How
is Miss Mason?"

"Oh, she is fust rate," said the Deacon's wife. "That
doctor from the city fixed her arm all up in what he called
a jacket, and that nurse that you sent just seems to know
what Huldy wants before she can ask for it. I hear them
nurses are awful expensive, and I don't think she better
stay but a day or two longer."

"She can't leave till the surgeon comes from Boston and
says she can go," he remarked, thinking this was the easiest
way to get out of it. "May I see Miss Mason?" he added.

"Certainly," replied Mrs. Mason. "She is in the front
chamber. We moved her in there 'cause there is a fireplace
in the room and the nurse objected to the wood stove that
Huldy had in her room. She said it was either too hot or
too cold, and that Huldy must have an even temperature."

As Quincy entered the room Huldy looked up and a
faint smile lighted her face. Her usually rosy cheeks
showed only a faint touch of pink. The helpless left arm,
in its plaster of paris jacket, rested on the outside of the
white quilt, the fingers on her little hand projecting beyond
the covering.

Quincy advanced to the bedside and took a vacant chair.

The nurse was sitting by the window. She glanced up at him and at Mrs. Mason, who followed close behind him, but continued the reading of her book.

Quincy said lightly, as he reached over and took the right hand and gave it a little shake, "You're not shaking hands with the left, Miss Mason."

"No," said Huldy, "I wish I could shake it, but nurse says it will have to stay on for two or three weeks, and it is so heavy, Mr. Sawyer."

Mrs. Mason went to the nurse and whispered to her, "Don't let him stay too long." The nurse nodded and Mrs. Mason left the room.

Quincy said in a low tone, as he sat in the chair by the bedside, "Miss Mason, I can't express my sorrow for this unfortunate occurrence. Your mother says you have told her it was your fault. But I insisted it was my fault in allowing you to drive a strange horse."

Huldy smiled. "It wasn't the horse, Mr. Sawyer," she said, and quickly changing the subject asked, "Where are you going to board now?"

"Old Uncle Ike Pettengill has taken pity on me," replied Quincy, thinking he would not say anything about going to Ezekiel Pettengill's house.

"But," said Huldy, "Zekiel called here this morning before he went to Boston for his sister and told me that Uncle Ike was coming to live with him. Didn't I hear them take your trunk away a little while ago?"

Quincy saw it was useless to prevaricate, so he said, "My trunk was taken to Mr. Ezekiel Pettengill's house."

"I hope you and 'Zekiel will be good friends," said Huldy, with a grave look on her face.

"I trust we may become so," remarked Quincy. "I am afraid we are not now, and I am still more afraid it is my fault that we are not on the best of terms."

Huldy turned her face towards him, a red flush coloring

her cheeks and brow. "No," she said, with vehemence, "it was my fault, and you know it, Mr. Sawyer. How you must hate me for having caused you so much trouble." She gave a convulsive sob and burst into a flood of tears.

Quincy was on the point of assuring Huldy that he could never hate her and that they would always be good friends, but he had no opportunity to frame the words.

As Huldy sobbed and began to cry, the nurse jumped to her feet, dropped her book on the floor, and came quickly to the bedside. She said nothing, but the look upon her face convinced Quincy that he must wait for a more auspicious moment to declare his friendly sentiment. So with a "Good-by, Miss Mason, I'll call again soon," he quitted the apartment and left the victim to the ministrations of the nurse.

CHAPTER XIV.

A QUIET EVENING.

A FTER the somewhat exciting termination of his interview with Miss Mason, Quincy left the house quickly
and walked down to Ezekiel Pettengill's. Uncle Ike was
there and he told Mandy to show Mr. Sawyer to his room,
which proved to be the big front one upstairs.

When he was alone, Quincy sank into the capacious
rocking chair and fell to thinking. His mind went back to
his parting with Miss Mason. She had said that it wasn't
the horse, so it must have been what he said to her. Was
she angry because he had decided to go in order to stop
village gossip, or had she really cared for him? Well, it
was over now. He would never know what her real feelings were, and after all it was best for him not to know.
He would drop the whole matter where it was. Then he
began to think about his present position. Here he was
located in the house of the man who would naturally be
considered the last one to desire his company.

Uncle Ike had told him that he would make it all right.
If he failed in this and Ezekiel objected to his remaining
he could move again. He was determined not to leave
Mason's Corner till he got ready, and he felt sure he would
not be ready to go until he had squared accounts with
Strout.

Presently he heard the sound of wheels. The Pettengill
house faced the south and Eastborough Centre lay west of
Mason's Corner, so he could not see the team when it

arrived, as it drove up to the back door, but he knew that
Ezekiel had arrived with his sister. Uncle Ike and Cobb's
twins went down stairs quickly; there was a jumble of
voices, and then the party entered the house. A short time
after he heard persons moving in the room adjoining his,
and guessed that Ezekiel's sister was to occupy it.

Then he fell to imagining the conversation that was
doubtless going on between Uncle Ike and his nephew.
Quincy was not naturally nervous, but he did not like suspense; almost unconsciously he arose and walked back and
forth across the room several times. Then it occurred to
him that probably the uncle and nephew were having their
conversation in the parlor, which was right under him, and
he curbed his impatience and threw himself into the armchair, which stood near the open fireplace.

As he did so there came a sharp rap at the door. In
response to the quick uttered "Come in," the door opened
and Uncle Ike entered. He came forward, took a seat in
the rocking chair near Quincy and passed him two letters.

Quincy looked up inquiringly. He had had his mail
sent to Eastborough Centre, where he had hired a box.
At the Mason's Corner post office the letters were stuck
upon a rack, where every one could see them, and Quincy
did not care to have the loungers at Hill's grocery inspecting his correspondence.

Uncle Ike saw the look and understood it. Then he
said, " 'Zekiel brought these over from Eastborough Centre. He didn't want to, but the postmaster said one of
them was marked 'In haste,' and he had been over to the
hotel and found that you had gone to Mason's Corner, and
probably wouldn't be back to-day, and so he thought
'Zekiel better bring it over."

"It was very kind of Mr. Pettengill," said Quincy, "and
I wish you would thank him for me."

In the meantime he had glanced at his letters. One

bore, printed in the corner, the names, Sawyer, Crowninshield, & Lawrence, Counsellors at Law, Court Street, Boston, Mass. That was from his father. The other was
directed in a feminine hand and bore the postmark, Mason's
Corner, Mass. He could not imagine from whom it could
be.

"I have had a talk with 'Zekiel," said Uncle Ike, "and
the whole matter is satisfactorily arranged; he is a fair-
minded young fellow and he don't believe you have done
anything with the intention of injuring him. What did
you pay up to Deacon Mason's?"

"Five dollars a week," replied Quincy.

"Well, it will be the same here," said Uncle Ike. "You
can stay as long as you like. 'Zeke wouldn't charge you
anything, but I said no, you have got to look out for your
sister, and Mr. Sawyer can afford to pay."

Quincy broke in, "And I wouldn't stay unless I did pay.
I am able and willing to pay more, if he will take it."

"Not a cent more," said Uncle Ike. "He will give you
your money's worth, and then one won't owe the other
anything. When you come down to supper I'll introduce
you, just as if you had never seen each other, and you can
both take a fresh start."

Uncle Ike arose. "By the time you have read your letters supper will be ready, and I want to go in and have a
talk with Alice. She is my only niece, Mr. Sawyer, and I
think she is the finest girl in Massachusetts, and, as far
as I know, there ain't any better one in the whole world;"
and Uncle Ike went out, closing the door behind him.

Quincy resumed his seat by the window. The light had
faded considerably, but he could still see to read. Naturally enough he first opened the letter bearing the feminine handwriting. He looked at the signature first of all
and read "Lucinda Putnam." "What can she have to write
to me about?" he thought. He read the letter:

Mason's Corner, January 22, 186—

My dear Mr. Sawyer:—I regret very much that I was absent when you called, but am glad to learn from mother that you had a pleasant visit. Although you are from the city I am sure you would blush if you could hear the nice things mother said about you. I am conceited enough to think that you will find time to call on us again soon, for I wish to consult you regarding an important business matter. I am going to Boston next Monday in relation to this business and if you could make it convenient to call before then it would be greatly appreciated by

Yours very truly,

LUCINDA PUTNAM.

Quincy reflected. "What is she up to? Some legal business, I suppose. Well, I am not practising law now; I shall have to refer her to—"

He took up the other letter and read, "Sawyer, Crowninshield, & Lawrence."

His father's letter read as follows:

Boston, January 21, 186—

My dear Son:—Yours at hand, and inquiries carefully noted. I had a brother, James Edward Sawyer; he was five years older than I and must be about sixty. Father wished him to study law, but he wouldn't study anything. When father died he got his share of the money, about $50,000, but he squandered the most of it in high living. The next we heard of him he had married a country girl named Eunice Raymond, I think. He brought her to Boston and tried to introduce her into the society he had been brought up in. She was a nice, pretty woman, but uneducated, and naturally bashful, and James finally left the city and went to live somewhere in the country, I never

knew where! he never wrote me after leaving Boston. This
Jim Sawyer may be your uncle. I hope not, but if he is,
remember he is my brother, and if he needs any assistance
let me know at once. I hope your health is improving.
Your mother and sisters are well and send love, as does also

Your affectionate father,

NATHANIEL ADAMS SAWYER.

As Quincy finished his second letter there was another
rap at the door and Mandy's voice was heard outside
saying, "Supper's ready, Mr. Saw—yer."

Quincy jumped to his feet. He had not unlocked his
trunk, as he was not certain that it would be worth while
to do so. It was but the work of a few moments to make
the necessary changes in his toilet. He put on a black
Prince Albert coat in place of a sack coat that he usually
wore, but before he had completed this change there came
another tap on the door, and Mandy's voice was heard
saying, "The things will get cold if you don't come down
right away."

As Quincy entered the large room which was used for a
dining-room, he was met by Uncle Ike. Ezekiel was standing a short distance from his uncle. Uncle Ike said,
"'Zekiel, this is my friend, Mr. Sawyer. Mr. Sawyer, this
is my nephew, 'Zekiel Pettengill. I am good friends with
both of you, and I hope you will be good friends to each
other."

The two men shook hands. If each had any idea of what
the other was thinking about he did not betray it by look
or act.

Uncle Ike continued, "Mr. Sawyer, this is Jim Cobb and
this is Bill Cobb, and this," as Mandy entered bearing
something for the table, "is Miss Mandy Skinner. Now
that we are all acquainted, I think we had all better intro-

duce ourselves at once to the supper. I haven't done such
a hard day's work for sixteen years."

Ezekiel insisted upon Uncle Ike taking the head of the
table. He motioned Mr. Sawyer to take the second seat
from his uncle on the right, while he took the first seat on
the left, with Cobb's twins next to him.

Quincy immediately surmised that when the sister
appeared at the table she would probably sit between him
and Uncle Ike.

The meal was not a very lively one as far as conversation went. Quincy inquired politely concerning Miss Pettengill's health, and Uncle Ike said she was tired after her
trip, and Mandy was going to take her supper up to her.

The meal was plentiful and well cooked. Quincy thought
to himself, how much brighter it would have looked, and
how much better the food would have tasted if Miss Huldy
Mason had been present with her pretty face, joyous laugh,
and occasional bright sayings.

After supper the things were quickly taken out by
Mandy. The white tablecloth was removed, and one in
which the prevailing color was bright red took its place.

The three men drew up to the open fireplace. Uncle
Ike pulled out his pipe and said, "Do you allow smoking
here, 'Zeke?"

'Zekiel replied, "I wish you and Mr. Sawyer to make
yourselves perfectly at home and do just as you would if
you were in your own house."

"Well, if I did that," said Uncle Ike, "you wouldn't need
Mandy, for I should be chief cook and bottle washer
myself."

Uncle Ike lighted his pipe, and Ezekiel took a cigar from
his pocket, saying, "I guess I'll smoke, too." Then his face
reddened. He said, "Beg pardon, Mr. Sawyer, I have only
this one."

"That's all right," rejoined Quincy, "a cigar would be

too heavy for me to-night. I have a slight headache, and
if you will excuse me I will roll a cigarette."

He took his little case of rice paper from his pocket and
also a small pouch of tobacco, and deftly made and lighted
a cigarette. The three men sat smoking, and as Quincy
blew a ring into the air he wondered what Sir Walter
Raleigh would have said if he could have looked in upon
them.

Quincy broke the silence. "I am afraid, Uncle Ike, that
I have caused you much inconvenience by driving you out
of that pleasant front room where I found my trunk."

"Not a bit," replied Uncle Ike. "I hate carpets, and I
prefer to sleep in my own bed, and what's more, I wanted
to put up my stove, and there was no chance in that front
room. When real cold weather comes I always have a ton
of coal for my stove, so I am much better off where I am
than I would be downstairs. By the way, 'Zeke, just tell
me all about Alice again. You won't mind Mr. Sawyer; he
is one of the family now."

"Well," said Ezekiel, "Alice was taken sick about the
middle of December. The folks where she boarded sent
for a doctor. It was about eight o'clock in the morning
when she was taken, and it was noon before she got easy,
so they could get her to bed. She thought she was getting better; then she had another attack; then she thought
she was getting better again, and the third attack was the
worst of the three. The folks wanted to write to me, but she
wouldn't let them. When she really did begin to get better,
she found out there was something that was worse than
being sick. She found she couldn't see to read either print
or writing, but Alice is a spunky girl, and she wouldn't
give in, even then. A friend told her to go and see Dr.
Moses, who was an eye doctor, and put herself right under
his treatment. She thought she was going to get well right
off at first, but when she found it was likely to be a long

job, then she gave in and wrote to me. She has brought
her treatment down with her, and the doctor says she will
have to go to Boston once a month to see him, as he is too
busy to come down here."

At this point in the proceedings the door opened and
Mandy entered, bringing a large dish of big red apples and
another full of cracked shellbarks. She left the room and
returned almost immediately with a large dish full of pop-
corn.

"Have an apple?" said Ezekiel. "Help yourselves; we
don't pass anything round here. We put the things on the
table and each one helps himself."

Mandy came in again, bringing a large pitcher of cider
and some glasses, which she placed upon the table.

While the three men were discussing their country evening lunch in silence, an animated conversation was taking
place in the kitchen, the participants being Mandy, Mrs.
Bridget Crowley, and Hiram, who always dropped in during the evening to get his glass of cider, a luxury that was
not dispensed at Deacon Mason's.

"Well," said Mandy, "I think it's wasteful extravagance
for you Irish folks to spend so much money on carriages
when one of your friends happens to die. As you just said,
when you lived in Boston you own up you spent fourteen
dollars in one month going to funerals, and you paid a
dollar a seat each time."

"I did that," said Mrs. Crowley, "and I earned every bit
of it doing washing, for Pat, bless his sowl, was out of
work at the time."

"Just think of that!" said Mandy, turning to Hiram.

"Well, it can't be helped," said Mrs. Crowley, obstinately.
"Shure and if I don't go to folks' funerals they won't come
to mine."

This was too much for Mandy and Hiram, and they
began laughing, which so incensed Mrs. Crowley that she

"MANDY SKINNER," AS SHE APPEARS IN THE PLAY.

trudged off to her little room in the ell, which departure just suited Mandy and Hiram.

"Have you got any soft soap here in the kitchen?" asked Hiram.

"No," said Mandy, "I used the last this afternoon. I shall have to go out in the shed to-morrow morning and get some."

"You wouldn't be likely to go out to-night for any?" asked Hiram.

"I guess not," said Mandy. "Why, there is rats out in that shed as big as kittens. Did you want to use some?"

"No," said Hiram, "but I didn't want you to have any 'round handy, for I am bound to tell you I heard Strout telling the minister's son that Lindy Putnam writ a letter to Mr. Sawyer and mailed it at Mason's Corner post office this mornin', and it was directed to Eastborough Centre, and Strout said it looked as though they were keeping up correspondence. I tell you that made 'Manuel Howe mad, for he's gone on Lindy Putnam himself, and then Strout said that probably all the fellers in town would have to put off getting married until that city chap had decided which one of the girls he wanted himself. And now, hang it," said Hiram, "he has come to live in this house, and I sha'n't have any peace of mind."

Hiram dodged the first apple Mandy threw at his head, but the second one hit him squarely, and he gave a loud "Oh!"

"Stop your noise," said Mandy, "or Mr. Pettengill will be out here. I'll ask them if they want anything else," as she rapped on the door. There was no response and she opened it and looked in. "Why, they have all gone to bed," she said. At that moment the old clock in the kitchen struck nine. "It's nine o'clock and you had better be going home, Hiram Maxwell."

"I shall have to get some anarchy to put on my forehead," said Hiram. "See that big bump, Mandy, that you made."

Mandy approached him quite closely and looked at his forehead; as she did so she turned up her nose and puckered her mouth. Her arms were hanging by her side. Hiram grasped her around the waist, holding both of her arms tight, and before Mandy could break away he gave her a kiss full on the mouth.

He made a quick rush for the door, opened it and dashed out into the night. Luckily for him there was no moon and he was out of sight before Mandy could recover her self-possession and reach the door. She peered out into the darkness for a moment; then she closed the door and bolted it, took a lamp and went up to her own room. Standing in front of her looking glass, she turned up her nose and puckered up her mouth as she had done when facing Hiram.

"That's the first time Hiram Maxwell ever kissed me," she said to herself. "Mebbe it will be the last time and mebbe it won't." Then she said reflectively, "I didn't think the little fellow had so much spunk in him."

In a quarter of an hour she was dreaming of cupids, and hearts, and arrows, and St. Valentine's Day, which was not so very far away.

CHAPTER XV.

EZEKIEL PETTENGILL owned what Deacon Mason did not—a nice carryall and a good road horse. Ezekiel would fix no price, but Quincy would not drive him unless he paid for the use of the team. One dollar for half a day, two dollars for a whole day, were the prices finally fixed upon.

Quincy drove first to Mrs. Putnam's. As he was ascending the steps the front door was opened and Lindy stood there to welcome him, which she did by extending her hand and then showing him into the parlor. She was evidently on the point of going out, for she had on her outdoor garments. After a few commonplaces relating to health and the weather, Quincy abruptly approached the object of his visit by saying, "I received your letter, Miss Putnam, and I have come to see if I can be of any service to you."

"Oh! I know you can," said Lindy; "you are wealthy—"

"I beg your pardon," interposed Quincy, "I am not what they call a wealthy young man; the fact that my father is possessed of a large fortune has probably given rise to the incorrect impression just repeated by you."

"I understand," said Lindy, with a laugh. "What I meant to say was, that you are undoubtedly acquainted with wealthy gentlemen, who know the best ways of investing money. I find my money a great trouble to me," she continued. "I had $25,000 invested in a first mortgage, but the property has been sold and the money repaid to me, and I don't know what to do with it."

"The obvious thing to do," remarked Quincy, "is to invest it at once, so that it will begin paying you interest."

"That is just what I wished to see you about," responded Lindy. "How would you advise me to invest it?" she asked.

"I would not presume," replied Quincy, "to give positive advice in such a case. I would go either to Foss & Follansbee, or Braithwaite & Mellen, or perhaps Rothwell Brothers & Co., look over the securities they have for sale and make my own selection, if I were in your place.

Lindy was manifestly disappointed at Quincy's polite refusal to recommend any particular security, but she evidently realized that further argument or entreaty would be useless, so she quickly changed the subject by remarking that her mother had considerable money invested, but that she was a woman who never took any advice and never gave any.

"I wonder who my mother is going to leave her money to? Do you know, Mr. Sawyer?"

Quincy replied that he did not. "But she did tell me that by the terms of your brother's will you were not to inherit it."

"Well, if you ever find out," said Lindy, "you will tell me, won't you, Mr. Sawyer?"

"Yes," said Quincy, "unless I am requested to keep it a secret."

"But you wouldn't keep it from me, their own daughter," said Lindy.

"Well," he replied, "I don't think it at all likely that they will inform me; but I promise to tell you if I learn who it is and am not bound in any way to keep the information secret."

"And will you tell me just as soon as you know?" persisted Lindy.

"In less than twenty-four hours from the time I learn

the name you shall hear it from my own lips," he replied.

"Thank you," said Lindy. "Would you like to see father and mother? Father has been quite sick for a few days and they are in their own room. I will go up and tell them you are coming."

Quincy was left in the room. That gossip about Miss Putnam could not be true. Gossip said she was ashamed of her father and mother, and yet she had invited him to go up and see them. What a pretty girl she was, well educated and with a hundred thousand dollars; such a beautiful singer and their voices blended so nicely together. How pleased his mother and sisters would be if he should bring home a wife like her. On the wall hung an oil portrait of her, evidently painted within a short time. He sat looking at it as Lindy opened the door.

Before he could remove his eyes from the picture, Lindy had noticed his fixed gaze at it and smiled brightly.

"Mother would be delighted to see you."

Lindy rang a small bell that was on a table. In a moment Samanthy entered the room.

"Samantha, please show Mr. Sawyer to mother's room. Will you excuse me, Mr. Sawyer, if I am not here to say good-by to you after you have seen mother? I am going to the city this morning and there—" looking out of the window—"here comes Abner Stiles; he is going to drive me over to Eastborough. Did you ever meet Mr. Stiles, Mr. Sawyer?"

"I may have seen him," replied Quincy.

"Seeing him is nothing," said Lindy. "He must be heard to be appreciated. He is a most engaging talker; he has caught the biggest fish and killed the biggest bears—"

"And told the biggest lies," broke in Quincy,—

"Of any man in town," Lindy concluded.

"I think there is one man in town who can tell bigger

ones," Quincy said gravely; "he has been telling a good many lately."

Lindy looked up and smiled. "He will never forgive us for what we did at the concert," said she. "Well, I mustn't keep Mr. Stiles waiting any longer, if I do he may—"

"Try to compete with the other one," added Quincy.

She smiled again, and gave him her little gloved hand, which he took in his for an instant.

She ran out quickly and got into the team, which immediately drove off. Samanthy, who had been waiting impatiently in the hallway, ushered Quincy into an upper chamber, where sat Mrs. Putnam. Her husband was reclining on a lounge near the fire.

"Well, I am awful glad to see yer," said Mrs. Putnam. "Silas here hasn't been feelin' fust rate for more'n a week. He's most frozen to death all the time. So I got him up front of the fire, same as I used to roast turkeys. Set down, Mr. Sawyer, and tell me all the news. Have you heerd anybody going to git engaged or anybody going to git married? I heerd as how you had left Deacon Mason's. So you 'cided to take my advice. I'm kinder sorry you tipped the buggy over, for Huldy Mason's a nice girl. The fact is I was thinkin' more of her than I was of you, when I told yer you'd better git out. Where be yer boardin' now?"

"I am boarding at Mr. Ezekiel Pettengill's. His sister has got home and his Uncle Isaac has come back to live with him."

"Lord sakes, do tell!" said Mrs. Putnam. "I allus thought that old fool would die out there in the woods and they'd bury him in his chicken coop. But what on airth is Alice home for? Has she lost her job?"

"No," replied Quincy; "poor girl, she has almost lost

her sight. She has been very sick, and as a result she is almost blind, and had to give up work and come home."

Mrs. Putnam sank back in her chair.

"If I didn't think you were a truthful man, Mr. Sawyer, I wouldn't b'lieve a word you said. My poor Alice. Why, do you know, Mr. Sawyer, I never saw a human being in all my life that I liked so much as I have Alice Pettengill. Did you ever see her, Mr. Sawyer?"

"No," said Quincy, "she only arrived yesterday afternoon, and she did not appear at supper nor at breakfast this morning. She was tired and wished to rest, her brother told me."

"Well, I hope she won't die," said Mrs. Putnam. "I have left her every dollar I've got in the world, and if she should die I shouldn't know who on airth to give it to. Well, there, I've let the cat out of the bag, and my daughter Lindy, mean as she is about money, would give a thousand dollars to know who I am goin' to leave my money to. I wish I could see Alice. I can't walk, and that poor, dear girl can't see. Why, Mr. Sawyer, I think she's the prettiest, sweetest girl I ever sot eyes on in my life, and I've seed a good many on 'em. Now you tell me what you think of her the next time you come up, won't you, Mr. Sawyer?"

"I certainly will," said Quincy, "and if she will come with me I will bring her over to see you. If she came from Boston with her brother, she can surely ride as far as this," he added.

"Tell her I shall count every minute till she comes over here, but don't say a word to her about my money," said Mrs. Putnam.

"Certainly not," Quincy answered. "You did not intend to tell me."

"No, I didn't," acknowledged Mrs. Putnam, "it slipped out before I thought."

Quincy arose. "I must go now, Mrs. Putnam. I have business at Eastborough Centre, and I don't know how long it will take me, and besides, I am anxious to see Miss Pettengill after your glowing description of her beauty and her virtues."

"Well, I haven't put the paint on half as thick as it would stand," said Mrs. Putnam. "Well, good-by, Mr. Sawyer. It's very kind in you to come and see two old folks like us. No use saying good-by to Silas; he's stone deaf and besides he's sound asleep."

When Quincy took up the reins and started towards Eastborough Centre it was with conflicting emotions. If there had been no Alice Pettengill to see, his thoughts, no doubt, would have related chiefly to Lindy Putnam, who had never attracted his attention before as she had that morning. Could Alice Pettengill be as pretty and as good as Mrs. Putnam had portrayed? And she was to be an heiress. He was sorry that Mrs. Putnam had told him. When he was talking to Miss Pettengill what he knew would be continually in his mind. He was glad that she was to have the money, but very sorry that he knew she was to have it; he had promised not to tell her, but he had promised to tell Lindy. Mrs. Putnam had not told him not to tell Lindy, but she had said Lindy would give a thousand dollars to know. Now, was that the same as requesting him not to tell Lindy, and should he tell Lindy for nothing what her mother said she would give a thousand dollars to know? Anyhow, that question must be decided within the next twenty-four hours.

Then he began to think of his intended visit to Eastborough Poorhouse. Would the Jim Sawyer that he found there turn out to be his own uncle? What a sweet morsel that would be for Strout if it proved to be true. Anyhow, he would follow his father's instructions and do all he could for his uncle, come what might.

Since he had arrived at Mason's Corner everything that he had done seemed to give rise to gossip, and a little more of it could do no harm.

Quincy reached the Poorhouse and inquired for the keeper. A very stout, red-faced man answered the summons.

He informed Quincy that his name was Asa Waters, and that he had been keeper of the town Poorhouse for the last ten years.

Quincy thought from his size, as he evidently weighed between three and four hundred pounds, that he had probably eaten all the food supplied for the inmates. In reply to a direct question whether there was a man there by the name of Jim Sawyer, Mr. Waters said "yes," but that he was sick abed and had been for the last week.

"He coughs awful," said Waters; "in fact, I had to change his room because the rest of us couldn't sleep. When we tried to move him he became sort of crazy like, and it took three on us to get him out of the room and take him upstairs. He seems sot on getting back in that room. The other day he crawled down stairs and we found him trying to get into the room, but I had it locked and we had another fight to get him upstairs again."

"Well," said Quincy, "I would like to see him; it may be he is a distant relative of our family. My father wishes me to talk with him and make the inquiry anyway."

"What mought your name be?" asked Mr. Waters.

"My name is Quincy Adams Sawyer."

"Oh, yes, I remember you," said Waters. "Wasn't you the singer that Mr. Strout hired to come down from Boston to sing at his concert. Strout told me he paid you $50 for singing that night, and by gosh it was worth it."

Quincy was not a profane young man, but he had to smother an oath on hearing that. He replied, "Yes, I sang that night."

"And," said Waters, "didn't you whistle that piece, Listen to the Bobolink, fine?"

"Here, Sam," said he to a young fellow who appeared in sight, "show this gentleman up to Jim Sawyer's room; I'm getting kind of pussy, and I don't go upstairs much."

Sam performed his mission and Quincy was ushered into the room and found himself with the sick man.

"Is your name James Sawyer?" asked Quincy.

"Yes," said the man. "I used to be proud of it once."

"Did you have a brother?" asked Quincy.

"Well," said Jim, "I don't think he would be proud of me now, so I guess I won't claim any relationship."

Quincy stopped for a moment. Evidently the man's pride would keep him from telling anything about himself. He would try him on a new tack. The man had a long fit of coughing. When it had subsided, Quincy said, "It wearies you to talk. I will do the talking, and if what I say is true you can nod your head." Quincy continued, "Your name is James Edward Sawyer, your brother's name was Nathaniel." The man opened his eyes wide and looked steadfastly at him. "Your father, Edward Sawyer, left you fifty thousand dollars." The man clutched with both hands at the quilt on the bed. "You are about sixty years of age." The man nodded. "You married a young girl who lived in the country and took her to Boston with you; her maiden name was Eunice Raymond."

The man started up in bed, resting on his elbow. "How did you know all this?" asked he. "Who has told you this? Who are you?"

The exertion and the rapid speaking brought on another fit of coughing and he fell back on his pillow.

"If what I have said is true," remarked Quincy quietly, "your brother, Nathaniel, is my father, and I am your nephew, Quincy Adams Sawyer."

"Who sent you to see me?" asked the man.

"I heard," replied Quincy, "that a man named James Sawyer was in the Eastborough Poorhouse. I wrote to my father, and in his reply he told me what I have just said to you. If you are my uncle, father says to do everything I can to help you, and if he had not said so I would have done it anyway."

"It is all true," said the man faintly. "I squandered the money my father left me. I married a sweet, young girl and took her to the city. I tried to introduce her into the set to which I once belonged. It was a failure. I was angry, not with myself for expecting too much, but with her because she gave me too little, as I then thought. We had two children—a boy named Ray and a little girl named Mary, after my mother."

"My grandmother," said Quincy.

James Sawyer continued: "I took to drink. I abused the woman whose only fault had been that she had loved me. I neglected to provide for my family. My wife fell sick, my two little children died, and my wife soon followed them. I returned from a debauch which had lasted me for about a month to find that I was alone in the world. I fled from the town where we had lived, came here and tried to reform. I could not. I fell sick and they sent me here to the Poorhouse. I have had no ambition to leave. I knew if I did it would mean the same old life. I am glad you came. I cannot tell you how glad. I do not wish for any assistance; the town will care for me as long as I live, which will not be very long; but your coming enables me to perform an act of justice which otherwise I could not have done."

"Tell me in what way I can serve you," said Quincy, "and it shall be done."

"Look outside of the door," said the man, "and see if anybody is listening."

Quincy opened the door suddenly and the broad face of Mr. Asa Waters stood revealed.

"I thought I would come up and see if Mr. Sawyer wanted anything."

"If he does," said Quincy, "I will inform you;" and he closed the door in Mr. Waters's face.

Quincy waited till he heard his ponderous footsteps descending the stairs at the foot of the hallway.

"Was old Waters out there listening?" asked Jim Sawyer.

"I don't think he had time to hear anything," Quincy replied.

"Come closer," said Jim; "let me whisper. I am not penniless. I have got some money. I have five thousand dollars in government bonds. I sold some stock I owned just before I went off on that last debauch, but I didn't spend all the money. When I die I want you to pay back to the town of Eastborough every dollar I owe for board. Don't let anybody know you got the money from me. Pay it yourself and keep the balance of it yourself."

"Where is the money?" said Quincy.

"It is down in my old room, No. 24, one flight down from here, at the other end of the hallway. I have got a key that will open the door. I made it myself. I nearly got in there the other day, but they caught me before I had a chance to open the door. If you can get in there take up the fourth brick from the window, second row from the front of the fireplace, and you will find the bonds in an old leather wallet. What time is it?" he asked quickly.

"Half-past eleven," replied Quincy.

"Now is your time," said the man; "all the hands have their dinner from half-past eleven to twelve; at twelve they feed us; take this key, and if you get the money, for God's sake come around to-morrow and let me know. I sha'n't sleep a wink till I hear from you."

Quincy pressed the sick man's hand and left the room. He went downstairs on tiptoe and quickly reached room No. 24. He listened; all was quiet; it took but an instant to open the door, and, slipping quietly in, he locked it after him. With some difficulty he found the wallet, looked inside and saw five one thousand dollar United States bonds. He put the wallet in his pocket, replaced the brick, and listened at the door; all was quiet. He unlocked it, slipped out, locked it, and was retracing his steps, when he saw Sam coming upstairs at the other end of the hallway.

"I think I took the wrong turn," said Quincy. "I thought I came up that way."

"No," said Sam; "that's the back way."

"Thank you," said Quincy, as he ran lightly downstairs. At the foot he met Mr. Waters.

"Well, is he any relative of yours?" asked Waters.

"I don't know yet," replied Quincy; "he has given me some facts, and I am going to write to Boston, and when I hear from there I will be able to answer your question. I will come around in a few days, as soon as I hear from the city."

Quincy jumped into his team and drove to Eastborough Centre post office to see if there were any letters for him.

When he reached the post office he found a letter from his father, informing him his mother and sisters were going to New York for a two weeks' visit and would very much like to see him if he would run up the next day.

Quincy's mind was made up instantly. He drove to the hotel, left the team, with instructions to have it ready for him when he came down on the express that reached Eastborough Centre at 7.15 P. M., ran for the station and caught on to the back platform of the last car as it sped on its way to Boston.

Arriving there, he first took a hasty lunch, then hiring a coupe by the hour, drove to his bank on State Street.

Here he left the bonds with instructions to write to East-borough Centre the amount realized from them and passed to the credit of his account.

His next trip was to his father's house on Beacon Street, where he found his mother and sisters. They were over-joyed to see him, and his younger sister declared that he had grown better looking since he went away. She wanted to know if he had fallen in love with a country girl. Quincy replied that his heart was still free and if it wasn't for the law he would have her for his wife, and no one else. Maude laughed and slapped him.

He next rode to his father's office on Court Street. The Hon. Nathaniel had just lunched at Parker's and was en-joying a good cigar when his son came in.

Quincy told him that the Jim Sawyer at Eastborough Poorhouse was unquestionably their missing relative.

"Poor Jim," said Nathaniel; "I ought to go and see him."

"No; I wouldn't," said Quincy, "it will do no good, and his remorse is deep enough now without adding to it."

He then told his father about the money, and the latter agreed that Jim's idea was right and Quincy had best use the money as though it were his own.

"By the by," said his father, wheeling round in his office chair, "that Miss Putnam from Eastborough is a very pretty girl; don't you think so, Quincy?"

"Handsome is as handsome does," thought Quincy to himself, but he only said, "Where did you see her?"

"She was in here to-day," replied his father. "She said she had $25,000 to invest, and that you gave her the address of some broker, but that she had forgotten it."

"Her statement is partially true," said Quincy, "but not complete. I gave her three addresses, because I did not wish to recommend any particular one. I wished her to make her own choice."

"I was not so conservative," remarked his father. "I

advised her to go to Foss & Follansbee and even suggested
that Quinnebaug Copper Company was one of the most
promising investments before the public to-day."

"Did she confide in you any farther," said Quincy.

"Oh, yes," replied his father; "I gleaned she was worth
$100,000 and that her parents, who were very old people,
had nearly as much more. I remember her brother, J. Jones
Putnam. He was a 'plunger,' and a successful one. He
died suddenly of lung fever, I believe."

Quincy smiled.

"She seemed to be well educated," his father continued,
"and told me that you and she sang together at a concert."

"Did she tell you what her father's religion was?"
inquired Quincy.

"You don't seem to admire this young lady, Quincy. I
thought she would be likely to be a great friend of yours.
You might do worse than—"

"I know," said Quincy, "she is pretty, well educated,
musical, very tasteful in dress, and has money, but she can't
have me. But how did it end?" asked he; "how did you get
rid of her?"

"Well," replied his father, "as I said before, I thought
she must be a great friend of yours, and perhaps more, so I
went down to Foss & Follansbee's with her; then we went
to Parker's to lunch, then I sent her to the station in a
coupe."

"I am greatly obliged to you, father," said Quincy, "for
the kind attentions you paid her. I shall get the full credit
of them down in Eastborough; your name will not be mentioned; only," said Quincy with a laugh, "if she is coming
to the city very often I think perhaps I had better come
back to Boston and look after mother's interests."

The Hon. Nathaniel was nettled by this and said sternly,
"I do not like that sort of pleasantry, Quincy."

"Neither do I," said Quincy coolly, "and I hope there will be no further occasion for it."

"How long do you intend to remain in Eastborough?" asked his father.

"I don't know," replied Quincy. "I can't come home while Uncle Jim is sick, of course. I will ask him if he would like to see you, and if he says yes, I will telegraph you. Well, good-by. I was up to the house and saw mother and the girls. I am going up to the club to see if I can meet some of the boys and have some dinner, and I shall go down on the 6.05 express."

Quincy lighted a cigar, shook hands rather stiffly with his father and left the office.

When Quincy reached the Pettengill house it was a little after eight o'clock. Hiram came out to help him put up the horse. "Anybody up?" asked Quincy.

"Only Mandy and me," said Hiram. "Uncle Ike is up in his attic, and 'Zeke is up talkin' to his sister, and Mandy and me has been talkin' to each other; and, say, Mr. Sawyer, did you meet Lindy Putnam up in Boston to-day?"

"No," said Quincy between his shut teeth.

"Well, that's funny," said Hiram; "I heard Abner Stiles telling Strout as how Miss Putnam told him that Mr. Sawyer had been to the banker's with her to invest her money, and that Mr. Sawyer took her out to lunch and then rode down to the station in a carriage and put her aboard the train."

"There are a great many Mr. Sawyers in Boston, you must remember, Hiram," remarked Quincy. "Anything else, Hiram?"

"Well, not much more," replied Hiram; "but Strout said that if you got Lindy and her money and then cajoled the old couple into leavin' their money to you, that it would be the best game of bunco that had ever been played in Eastborough."

"Well, Strout ought to know what a good bunco game is," said Quincy. "Have the horse ready by nine o'clock in the morning if you can get over. Good night, Hiram," he said.

He passed through the kitchen, saying good night to Mandy, and went straight to his own room. He sat and thought for an hour, going over the events of the day.

"As soon as Uncle Jim is dead and buried," said he to himself, "I think I will leave this town. As the children say when they play 'hide and go seek,' I am getting warm."

CHAPTER XVI.

A PROMISE KEPT.

QUINCY was up next morning at eight o'clock and ate his breakfast with 'Zekiel. 'Zekiel said his sister did not sleep well nights, and so would not be down till later.

"Do you want the team this morning, Mr. Pettengill?" asked Quincy.

"No," said 'Zekiel, "but the Boston doctor wrote to Deacon Mason that he was comin' down this afternoon to take that stuff off Huldy's arm, and she wanted me to come up, so I shall be up there all the afternoon."

"That reminds me," said Quincy. "Will you tell Deacon Mason that I want the nurse to stay until to-morrow and I will be up to see her at nine o'clock?"

Quincy took up the reins and started for Eastborough Poorhouse.

He found his uncle weaker than on the day before. Quincy touched his hand, but did not lift it from the bed. Jim pointed towards the door.

"It's all right," said Quincy, "there is no one there."

"Did you get it?" asked Uncle Jim in a whisper.

"Yes," replied Quincy, "and it's safe in the bank in Boston."

"Thank God!" exclaimed Uncle Jim. "Now I don't care how soon I am called to judgment for my sins."

"Uncle Jim," said Quincy, "I saw my father yesterday afternoon. Would you like to have your brother come and see you?"

Uncle Jim shook his head. "It will do no good," said he. "You have done all I could wish for. Pay the town for my board. Give them what they ask. Do with the balance what you wish, Quincy. It is yours."

"Where do you wish to be buried, Uncle?" asked Quincy bravely.

"Right here," replied Uncle Jim. "One of the boys here died about a month ago; his name was Tom Buck. He was a good fellow and did many kind things for me. Bury me side of him."

"One more question, Uncle," said Quincy. "In what town did your wife and children reside when they died?"

"In Amesbury," said Uncle Jim. An idea seemed to strike him. "Well, Quincy, do you suppose you could find where they are buried?"

"Of course I can," Quincy answered.

"Well," continued Uncle Jim, "I don't deserve it, I am not worthy of it, but she always loved me, and so did the children. I never struck her, nor them, nor did I ever speak unkindly to them. I never went home when I was drunk. I deserted them and left them to suffer. I don't think she would object, do you?"

Quincy divined his thoughts and answered, "No, I do not, Uncle."

"If you will do it, Quincy," said Uncle Jim, "I shall die a happy man. Buy a little lot and put me beside Eunice and the children. Don't put my name on the stone, put her name and those of the children. That will please me best. She will know I am there, but others will not."

"It shall be done as you say, Uncle," said Quincy. "I will be here early to-morrow morning and I shall come every day to see you. Good-by."

He touched his uncle's hand again softly and left the room. Uncle Jim, with a smile upon his wasted face, fell asleep.

Quincy drove leisurely towards Mason's Corner. It was more than twenty-four hours since he had learned who was to be Mrs. Putnam's heiress. He had made a promise. Should he keep it? How could he avoid keeping it? He would see Miss Putnam and be governed by circumstances.

He reached the Putnam house and was shown into the same room as on the morning before. In a few minutes Lindy joined him. He had never seen her looking better. She had on a handsome gown that he had never seen before. Quincy opened the conversation.

"Did you enjoy your trip to Boston yesterday, Miss Putnam?"

"Oh, yes," replied Lindy, "I must tell you all about it."

"There is no need to, Miss Putnam, I am acquainted with the most important events of your trip already."

"Why, how?" asked Lindy. "Oh, I see," said she, "you had a letter from your father."

"No," said Quincy. "I had the pleasure of a conversation with my father yesterday afternoon in Boston."

"Is that so?" exclaimed Lindy.

"Yes," said Quincy, "but I might have learned all the principal facts without leaving Mason's Corner. In fact, I did learn them in a somewhat distorted shape late last evening."

Lindy colored until her forehead was as red as her cheeks.

"I do not understand you, Mr. Sawyer," she remarked.

"It is easily explained," said Quincy. "Mr. Stiles forgot to mention that it was my father who was your escort and not myself. Of course he would offer the similarity in names as his excuse."

"And so," said Lindy, recovering herself, "you have come here to scold me because Abner Stiles didn't tell the truth. I told you he was a wonderful story teller."

"No, Miss Putnam," said Quincy, "I did not come here for any such purpose. I made you a promise yesterday and I have come to keep it. I know who is to inherit your mother's money. She did not intend to tell me, but the name escaped her unintentionally."

"Did she ask you not to tell me?" asked Lindy.

"No," replied Quincy, "not in so many words."

"Then you must tell me," cried Lindy eagerly.

"Well, I don't know," said Quincy. "Your mother said you would give a thousand dollars to know the name of the person. This fixes the condition on which I shall divulge the name."

"And if I did give you a thousand dollars," inquired Lindy, "what would you do with the money?"

"I should give it to your mother," said Quincy. "She fixed the price of the secret, not I."

Lindy walked to the window and looked out. She wished to know the name. She had her suspicions, but she could not bear to give up a thousand dollars of her own money, for she knew that this, too, would go to the unknown heiress. She knew Alice Pettengill was in town and at her brother's house. She had been there for a whole day and parts of two others. She would save her money and at the same time learn the truth.

Turning to Quincy she said, "I cannot afford to pay you, or rather my mother, a thousand dollars for the secret. It is not worth it. I will not ask you again for her name, but if you will answer me one simple question I will absolve you from your promise."

Quincy reflected. He knew that Lindy was deep and that she was plotting something while she stood at the window. But he wished this matter over, he was tired of it, so he replied, "I will answer your simple question, Miss Putnam, on one condition. It is that you will not deem me guilty of any intentional discourtesy if, after replying to it, I at once take my leave."

They faced each other, she hardly able to conceal her impatience, he with a stern look upon his face.

"My simple question is this, Mr. Sawyer, have you ever eaten a meal at the same table with my mother's heiress?"

"I have never seen her," replied Quincy coldly. He took his hat, and with a low bow quitted the house and drove away.

Lindy threw herself in a passion on the sofa and burst into a flood of tears. She had played her last card and had lost.

CHAPTER XVII.

WHEN Quincy drove into the barn he found Jim Cobb there, and he turned the horse over to him. Entering by the back door he passed through the kitchen without seeing either Mandy or Mrs. Crowley, and went slowly upstairs. The house was very quiet. He remembered that Uncle Ike had gone to Eastborough Centre and 'Zekiel had gone to Deacon Mason's. It was necessary for him to pass the door of the room occupied by Alice Pettengill in order to reach his own room. The door of her room was open. He involuntarily glanced in and then stood still.

What vision was this that met his eye? The sun, now dropping to the westward, threw its rays in at the window and they fell upon the head of the young girl seated beside it.

The hair was golden in the sunlight, that real golden that is seldom seen excepting on the heads of young children. She seemed slight in figure, but above the average stature. She wore a loose-fitting dress of light blue material, faced down the front with white, and over her shoulders was thrown a small knitted shawl of a light pink color. Quincy could not see her face, except in profile, for it was turned towards the window, but the profile was a striking one. He turned to step forward and enter his own room. As he did so the board upon which he stood creaked. He stopped again suddenly, hoping that the noise would not attract her attention, but her quick ear had caught the sound, and, rising, she advanced towards the door, her hands extended before her.

"Is that you, Uncle Ike?" she asked in a clear, sweet voice. "I heard you drive in."

She had started in a straight line towards the door, but for some cause, perhaps the bright light coming from the wood fire in the open fireplace, she swerved in her course and would have walked directly towards the blazing wood had not Quincy rushed forward, caught her by the hand and stopped her further progress, saying as he did so, "Miss Pettengill, you will set your dress on fire."

"You are not Uncle Ike," said she, quickly. "He could not walk as fast as that. Who are you? You must know me, for you called me by name."

Quincy replied, "Under the circumstances, Miss Pettengill, I see no way but to introduce myself. I am your brother's boarder, and my name is Sawyer."

"I am pleased to meet you, Mr. Sawyer," said she, extending her hand, which Quincy took. "I feel acquainted with you already, for Uncle Ike speaks of you very often, and 'Zekiel said you used to board at Deacon Mason's. Don't you think Huldy is a lovely girl?"

Quincy avoided this direct question and replied, "Uncle Ike has been equally kind in speaking of his niece, Miss Pettengill, so that I feel acquainted with her even without this,—I was going to say formal introduction,—but I think that we must both confess it was rather informal."

Alice laughed merrily. "Won't you sit down, Mr. Sawyer? I have been alone nearly all day, and have really been very lonesome."

She turned and groped, as if feeling for a chair. Quincy sprang forward, placed a large rocking chair before the fire, then, taking her hand, saw her safely ensconced in it. He then took a seat in a large armchair at the end of the fireplace nearest the door.

"Thank you, Mr. Sawyer," said Alice. "Everybody has been so kind to me since I have had this trouble with my eyes. Of course 'Zekiel has told you about it."

"Yes," assented Quincy.

He really did not care to talk. He was satisfied to sit and look at her, and he could do this with impunity, for she could not see his earnest gaze fixed upon her.

"I have been used to an active life," said Alice. "I have had my business to attend to every day, and evenings I had my books, papers, pictures, and music. At first it seemed so hard to be shut out from them all, but years ago Uncle Ike taught me to be a philosopher and to take life as it came, without constantly fretting or finding fault. Uncle Ike says, 'It is not work but worry that wears men out.' That's why he came down here to live in the woods. He said they wouldn't let him work and so he worried all the time, but when he came here he had plenty to do, and in his work he found happiness."

"I am learning a good lesson," said Quincy with a laugh. "I have studied much, but I actually never did a day's work in all my life, Miss Pettengill."

"Then you are to be pitied," said Alice frankly; "but I see I should not blame you, you are studying now and getting ready to work."

"Perhaps so," Quincy remarked. "My father wishes me to be a lawyer, but I detest reading law, and have no inclination to follow in my father's footsteps."

"Perhaps you are too young," said Alice, "to settle upon your future career. I cannot see you, you know, and Uncle Ike did not say how old you were."

Quincy smiled. "I am in my twenty-fourth year," said he. "I graduated at Harvard two years ago."

"So old!" exclaimed Alice; "why, I am not twenty-one until next June, and I have been working for my living since I was sixteen."

Quincy said, "I wish I had as honorable a record."

"Now you are vexed with me for speaking so plainly,"
said Alice.

"Not at all," Quincy replied. "I thank you for it. I
have learned from Uncle Ike that frankness of speech and
honesty of heart are Pettengill characteristics."

"You might add," said Alice, "firmness in debate, for
none of us like to own up that we are beaten. I remember
years ago Uncle Ike and I had a long discussion as to
whether it were better to be stone blind or stone deaf. I
took the ground that it was better to be blind, for one could
hear music and listen to the voices of friends, and hear the
sound of approaching danger, and then, besides, everybody
is so kind to a person who is blind. But you see Uncle Ike
don't care for music, and had rather talk himself than listen,
so he decided that it was best to be stone deaf, for then
he could read and write to his friends. But of course
neither of us gave in, and the question, so far as we are
concerned, is still unsettled."

At that moment the sound of a team was heard, and a
few minutes later Uncle Ike came upstairs, followed by the
driver of the team bearing a big basket and a large bundle.
These contained Uncle Ike's purchases.

"Wait a minute and I will go upstairs with you," called
out Uncle Ike to the man. He entered the room, and
looking somewhat surprised at seeing Quincy, he said
somewhat sharply, "So you two have got acquainted, have
you? I have been waiting for two days to introduce you."

"I am greatly indebted to Mr. Sawyer," said Alice.
"When he passed my door, which was open, I thought it
was you and I started forward to meet you, but I missed
my way and was walking directly towards the fire, when
Mr. Sawyer interposed."

"I should have done the same thing had it been me,"

said Uncle Ike. "So I don't see as you were in any real danger."

Quincy thought that it was noticeably evident that the Pettengills were noted for plainness of speech.

"Here are three letters for you, Alice, and here is one for you, Mr. Sawyer. I thought I would bring it over to you as I met Asa Waters down to the post office and he said you'd started for home. I'll be down in a few minutes, Alice, and read your letters for you." And Uncle Ike showed the man the way up to his domicile.

Quincy arose, expressed his pleasure at having met Miss Pettengill, and presuming they would meet again at dinner, took his leave.

The letter was from Quincy's father. It was short, but was long enough to cause Quincy to smother an oath, crush the letter in his hands and throw it into the open fire. The flames touched it, and the strong draught took it still ablaze up the wide-mouthed chimney.

But Quincy's unpleasant thought did not go with it. The letter had said, "Quinnebaug stock has dropped off five points. Foss & Follansbee have written Miss Putnam that she must put up five thousand dollars to cover margin. Better see her at once and tell her the drop is only temporary, and the stock is sure to recover."

Quincy sat down in his easy-chair, facing the fire, upon which he put some more wood, which snapped and crackled.

"I won't go near that girl again," said he, with a determined look upon his face. The next moment he had banished Lindy Putnam from his mind, and was thinking of that other girl who was sitting not six feet from him. He could hear Uncle Ike's voice, and he knew that Alice's letters were being read to her. Then he fell into a reverie as the twilight shadows gathered round him. As the room grew darker the fire grew brighter, and in it he could seem to see a picture of a fair-haired girl sitting in a chair and listening with evident interest to a young man who was reading to her from a newspaper.

The young girl placed her hand upon his arm and asked a question. The young man dropped the paper and gazed into the girl's face with a look full of tenderness, and placing one of his hands upon that of the young girl clasped it fondly, and Quincy saw that the face of this young man was his own. He sat there until there came a loud rap upon the door and Mandy's voice called out, "Supper's ready."

CHAPTER XVIII.

WHILE Quincy was taking his first steps in Lover's Lane, which steps so often lead to the high road of Matrimony, 'Zekiel Pettengill had reached the end of his lane, which had been very long with many devious turns, and he found himself at that point where the next important question was to fix the day.

'Zekiel was a strong-minded, self-willed, self-reliant young man, but in the presence of Huldy Mason he was as big a coward as the world ever saw. She had sent a little note to him, saying that she wished to see him that afternoon, and he knew their fates would be decided that day. He was hopeful, but the most hopeful lover has spasms of uncertainty until his lady love has said yes and yes again.

Dressed in his best, 'Zekiel knocked at Deacon Mason's front door. For an instant he wished himself safe at home and debated whether he could get round the corner of the house before the door was opened. He turned his head to measure the distance, but at that moment the door was opened, and Mrs. Mason's smiling face was before him, and her pleasant, cheery voice said, "Come in, 'Zekiel."

He felt reassured by this, for he argued to himself that she would have called him Mr. Pettengill if there had been any change in her feelings towards him. They entered the parlor, and Mrs. Mason said, "Take off your things and leave them right here, and go right up and see Huldy. She is waitin' for you. The doctor's been and gone. He took that plaster thing off Huldy's arm, says she's all right now, only she must be keerful, not do any heavy liftin' with it till it gets good and strong. He said it would be some time before she could help me much with the housework, so I am going to get a girl for a month or two. I heerd your sister got home, 'Zeke. They do say she's blind. I am awful sorry, 'Zekiel. Hope she will get better of it. I am coming over to see her just as soon as I get me my girl. But you go right up, there's nobody there but Huldy. Mr. Sawyer is coming after the nurse to-morrow morning, and she is up in the spare room trying to catch up with her sleep. We told her there was no use in setting up with Huldy, but she said she had her orders from the doctor, and she wouldn't mind a single thing we said. But we will get rid on her to-morrow. Now you go right up, 'Zekiel;" and Mrs. Mason took him by the arm and saw him on his way up the front stairs before she returned to her work in the kitchen.

'Zekiel went upstairs deliberately, one step at a time. His footfalls, it seemed to him, must be heard all over the house. He paused before Huldy's door. He opened it a couple of inches, when the thought struck him that he ought to knock. He started to close the door and do so, when he heard a faint voice say, "Come in, 'Zekiel." So he was still 'Zekiel to Huldy. He opened the door and walked bravely into the room, but his bravery forsook him when he had taken a few steps. He had expected to find her in bed, as she had been every day before when he had called. But there she stood before him, the same Huldy as of old. Not exactly the same, however, for her cheeks had lost much of their rosy tint and there was a pensive look to the face that was new to it, which 'Zekiel saw, but could not understand.

There were two chairs close together before the fire. She sat down in the left-hand one and motioned 'Zekiel to the other, which he took.

"I thought I would find you abed," said 'Zekiel. "I didn't know you were up."

"Oh, yes," said Huldy. "I got up and dressed as soon as the doctor took the jacket, that's what he called it, off my arm. I felt so much better I couldn't stay in bed any longer."

"Well," said 'Zekiel, "when the schoolmaster used to tell me to take my jacket off I didn't feel near as well as I did before," and then they both laughed heartily.

They sat silent for a few moments, when Huldy, turning her face with that sad look towards him, said, "There is something on my mind, 'Zekiel, that I wish I could take off as easily as the doctor did that jacket."

"Oh, nonsense," cried 'Zekiel; "why should you have anything on your mind? You are a little bit low spirited because you have been cooped up in bed so long."

"No," said Huldy, "that isn't it. I have wronged a person and I am afraid that person will never fully forgive me. I am real sorry for what I have done, and I am going to tell the person and ask for pardon."

"Well," said 'Zekiel, "the person must be pretty mean spirited if he or she don't forgive you after you say you are sorry, 'specially if you promise not to do it again."

"Oh, I shall never do it again," said Huldy. "Once has nearly killed me. I suffered ten times more from that than from my broken arm."

"Well," said 'Zekiel, "if that person don't forgive you I don't want anything more to do with him."

"Let me tell you a little story," said Huldy. "A little boy and girl whose homes were not a quarter of a mile apart grew up together in a little country town. As children they loved each other, and as they grew older that love really grew stronger, though not so plainly shown or spoken. Everybody thought that one day they would be

married, though he had never asked her to be his wife.
Did you ever hear of anything like that, 'Zekiel?"

"Well," remarked 'Zekiel, "I have in my mind two persons whose relations were pretty similar up to a certain
point."

"Yes," said Huldy, eagerly, "and that point was reached
when a young man from the city, whose father was known
to be very wealthy, came to board in her father's house."
Huldy looked at 'Zekiel inquiringly.

"Yes, I've heard of something like that," said 'Zekiel.

"For a time," continued Huldy, "the young girl was
unfaithful to her old-time lover. She thought the young
man from the city was learning to love her because he was
polite and attentive to her. She thought it would be nice
to be rich and go to the city to live, but the young man
soon undeceived her. He took her to ride one day, and on
their way home he told her he was going to leave her
father's house. She wished to know the reason, but he
would not give it. She divined it, however, and in her agitation lost control of the horse she was driving. The
buggy was overturned and her arm was broken." She
looked up at 'Zekiel. His face was grave, but he nodded
for her to go on. "She stayed in bed for three weeks, and
during that time she lived over her short life a hundred,
yes, a thousand, times; she knew that her fancy had been
but a fleeting dream. A suspicion that perhaps the young
man had imagined her feelings towards him was what had
nearly broken her heart. Supposing you were the man,
'Zekiel, and I were the woman in this little story, could
you forgive me if I said I was sorry and would never do it
again?"

"I forgave you, Huldy, when I let him come to board in
my house. He told Uncle Ike why he left your father's
house. The folks were talking about you and him, but he
never imagined that you were in love with him, or thought

any more about him than you would have of any passing acquaintance."

"I am so glad," cried Huldy; "you have done me more good than the doctor, 'Zekiel;" and she dropped her head upon his shoulder.

'Zekiel was struck with an idea. "If I am a better doctor than the other one, Huldy, I ought to get a bigger price for my services than he does."

Huldy looked up. "What will your price be, Dr. Pettengill?"

"I think I shall charge," said 'Zekiel, "one hundred thousand dollars, and as I know you haven't got the money and can't raise it, I think I shall have to hold you for security."

He suited the action to the word, and they sat there so long, happy in their mutual love, that the Deacon and his wife came upstairs and entered the room quietly. When they saw the picture before them, thrown into prominence by the light of the fire, the Deacon said in a low tone to his wife, "I have thought so all along."

And as Mrs. Mason looked up into her husband's face she said, "I am glad on't."

CHAPTER XIX.

JIM SAWYER'S FUNERAL.

QUINCY obeyed the call to supper with alacrity. Possibly he thought he would be the first one at the table, but Cobb's twins were in their places when he entered the room. 'Zekiel came in next, and Quincy's quick eye discerned that there was a look of quiet contentment on his face which had not been there before.

Uncle Ike came down with Alice, and for the first time since her arrival she sat beside Quincy. For some reason or other the conversation lagged. Quincy surmised that 'Zekiel was too happy with his own thoughts to wish to talk, and Uncle Ike rarely conversed during meal time. He said he could not talk and eat at the same time, and as meal time was for eating he proposed to give his attention to that exclusively.

Quincy ventured a few commonplace remarks to Alice, to which she replied pleasantly. He was at a loss for a topic, when he remembered his last visit to Mrs. Putnam's and recalled his promise to bring Alice to see her some day.

He spoke of visiting Mrs. Putnam, and Alice's face immediately shone with pleasure. "Dear old Aunt Heppy! I must go and see her as soon as I can."

"If you can find no better escort than myself, I trust you will command my services, unless," said Quincy, "your brother thinks it unsafe to trust you with me."

"He won't be likely to let you drive, Alice," responded 'Zekiel dryly, "so I don't think there will be any danger."

Quincy knew by this remark that Huldy had told 'Zekiel

the facts of the case, but he maintained his composure and said, "Any time you wish to go, Miss Pettengill, I am at your service."

As they arose from the table 'Zekiel said to his uncle, "I am coming up in your room to-night, Uncle Ike, to see you."

Quincy knew by this that the pleasant chat in the dining-room beside the fireplace was to be omitted that evening, so he went up to his own room and read until it was time to retire.

Quincy was up early next morning. He knew his uncle could not live long, but he wished to take the trained nurse to Eastborough Centre, so he might have the best of care during the short time left to him on earth.

He found 'Zekiel at the breakfast table, and beyond a few commonplace remarks the meal was eaten in silence.

"Are you going to Eastborough Centre to-day, Mr. Sawyer?" asked 'Zekiel.

"Yes," said Quincy; "I intended to go just as soon as one of the boys could get the team ready."

"I'll speak to Jim about it," said 'Zekiel. "If you will step into the parlor, Mr. Sawyer, I would like to have a few minutes' talk with you."

'Zekiel went out into the barn and Quincy walked into the parlor, where he found a bright fire burning on the hearth. He threw himself into an easy-chair and awaited 'Zekiel's return. What was up? Could 'Zekiel and Huldy have parted, and was 'Zekiel glad of it? Quincy, as the saying is, passed a "bad quarter of an hour," for he did not like suspense. The truth, however bitter or unpalatable, was better than uncertainty.

'Zekiel entered the room and took a seat opposite to Quincy. He bent forward and placed his hands upon his knees.

"Mr. Sawyer," said he, "I am a man of few words, so I

will come right to the point. Huldy Mason and me are engaged to be married."

Quincy was equal to the occasion. He arose, stepped forward, and extended his hand. 'Zekiel rose also and grasped it unhesitatingly. Quincy said, "Accept my most sincere congratulations, Mr. Pettengill. I have known Miss Mason but a short time, but any man ought to be proud of her and happy in her love."

"Thank you, Mr. Sawyer," said 'Zekiel; "I agree with you in both the particulars you've mentioned, but both of us have what we consider good reasons for not having our engagement known in the village just at present, and to keep it a secret we need the assistance of a mutual friend."

"If I might aspire to that honor," said Quincy, "my time and services are at your disposal."

"That's what I told Huldy," said 'Zekiel, "but she was afraid that you would be vexed at what the gossips said about you and her; she's mad as a hornet herself, and she wants to teach them a lesson."

"Personally," said Quincy, "I don't care what the gossips say, but I was both sorry and indignant that they should have referred to Miss Mason in the way they did."

"Well," said 'Zekiel, "we have hatched up a sort of a plot, and if you will help us, all three of us will have some fun out of it."

"Well," inquired Quincy, "what's my share in the fun?"

"It's this," said 'Zekiel, "you know you used to take Huldy out to ride with you. To help out our plan, would you be willing to do it again?"

"Certainly," replied Quincy. "Miss Mason has been confined to her room so long I think she ought to have some fresh air."

"That's true," remarked 'Zekiel; "she's lost considerable flesh staying in so long; but if I took her out to ride they would jump at conclusions right off and say Huldy and

'Zekiel have made up, and they will guess we are going to make a match of it. Then, again," 'Zekiel continued, "Huldy says she's bound to have it out with the one that started the stories. There's no use mincing matters between us, because you know as well as I do who is at the bottom of all this tittle-tattle. Since I refused to join hands with him to try and drive you out of town, he has talked about me almost as bad as he has about you. 'So,' says Huldy to me, 'you know he is the only teacher of music in Eastborough. I want to take music lessons very much, and so I have got to have him for teacher.' Then she said, ''Zekiel, you leave the rest of it to me, and we will all have some fun before we get through.' I expect she is going to flirt with him, for it comes as nat'ral to her as it does to most women."

Quincy did not think it polite to assent to this last remark and changed the subject by remarking, "This is a beautiful day. I am going to drive the nurse over to East-borough; perhaps Miss Mason would like to accompany us. That is, if you can trust her with me."

"Oh, that's all right," said 'Zekiel; "Huldy had to pay pretty dearly for getting mad at the wrong time. Besides, I don't think she will want to drive horse again for a while."

Mandy rapped on the parlor door and called out that the team was ready.

Quincy assured 'Zekiel that he understood his part and would play it to the best of his ability.

When he arrived at Deacon Mason's house he found the latter just coming out of the front gate. As Quincy leaped from the team the Deacon came forward and shook hands with him. "You are just the man I want to see," he remarked. "I've paid our doctor, but I want to know what the bill is for the Boston doctor and the nurse."

"I don't know yet," said Quincy, "but there will be nothing for you to pay. It is my duty to settle that bill myself."

"No," said the Deacon firmly. "She is my daughter, and it is my place as her father to pay such bills, until she has a husband to pay them for her."

Quincy said, "Deacon Mason, when I took your daughter out to ride it was my duty to return her to her home without injury. I did not do so, and I trust that you will allow me to atone for my neglect. Remember, sir, you have lost her services for several weeks, and the board of the nurse has been an expense to you."

"I prefer," rejoined the Deacon, "that the bill should be sent to me."

"Well," said Quincy, to close the discussion, "I will ask him to send you one;" mentally resolving, when it was sent, it would be a receipted one.

Quincy received a hearty welcome from Mrs. Mason, who said the nurse had her things packed and was all ready to go. He then told Mrs. Mason that he had a message for Miss Mason from Mr. 'Zekiel Pettengill, and Mrs. Mason said she would send Huldy to the parlor at once. Huldy greeted Quincy with a happy face and without any show of confusion.

"I had a long talk with Mr. Pettengill," said Quincy, "and he has induced me to become a conspirator. The first act in our comedy is to ask you if you will ride over to Eastborough Centre this morning with the nurse and myself, and get a little fresh air?"

"I should be delighted," said Huldy, "if you can wait long enough for me to dress."

"That's what I came early for," remarked Quincy. "How long will it take you?"

"Fifteen minutes," said Huldy.

"It is now half-past seven," remarked Quincy, looking at his watch. "You mean you will be ready by quarter of nine?"

"No," said Huldy, with a flash of her eyes, "I am no city lady. I am a plain, country girl, and I mean just one-quarter of an hour. You can time me, Mr. Sawyer;" and she ran gayly out of the room.

Quincy looked out of the window and saw that Hiram had put the nurse's heavy valise on the front seat of the carryall. The nurse herself was standing by the side of the team, evidently uncertain which seat to take. Quincy was quickly at her side.

"You can sit in here, Miss Miller," said Quincy, pointing to one of the rear seats; and when she was seated Quincy told Hiram to put the valise on the seat beside her. He had no idea of having Huldy take a back seat.

True to her promise, Huldy made her toilet in the appointed time, and taking her seat beside Quincy, he took up the reins. Turning to Hiram he asked, "If I drive by Hill's grocery and take the road to the left, will it bring me round to the main road to Eastborough Centre again?"

"Yaas," said Hiram, "you take the road where Mis' Hawkins's boardin' house is on the corner. You remember that big yellow house. You know I told you Mandy's mother kept it."

"All right," said Quincy, and off they went.

Quincy gave a side glance at Huldy. He discovered she was throwing a side glance at him. They both smiled, but said nothing. He drove around the big tree that stood in the centre of the square in front of the grocery, which brought the team quite close to the store platform. No one was in sight, but just as he reached Mrs. Hawkins's boarding house the door opened and Obadiah Strout came out. Huldy placed her hand on Quincy's arm.

"Please hold up a minute, Mr. Sawyer."

Quincy brought the horse to a standstill with a jerk and looked straight ahead.

"Ah, good morning, Mr. Strout," said Huldy. "Did

you get the letter I sent up by Hiram last evening about my taking music lessons?"

"Yes," said Mr. Strout, "and I was coming down this morning to settle on the best time for you taking them."

"Could you come to-morrow afternoon from two to three?" asked Huldy.

Strout took a well-worn memorandum book from his pocket and consulted it. "Three to four would be the best I could do," said he, "for I have a lesson from half-past one to half-past two."

"That will do just as well," replied Huldy. "Three to four to-morrow afternoon. Isn't this a beautiful day, Mr. Strout? I am taking a little drive for my health;" and she nodded smilingly to Strout, who had recognized Quincy as her companion.

"That's all, Mr. Sawyer," said Huldy, and they drove on.

"By thunder," said Strout, "they say the hair of a dog is good for his bite. Just as soon as she got well, off she goes riding again with the same feller who tipped the team over and broke her arm. I guess 'Zeke Pettengill's chances ain't worth much now. It beats all how 'Zeke can let that feller board in his house, but I suppose he does it to let us folks see that he don't care. Well, Huldy Mason is a bright little girl, and I always liked her. That city chap don't mean to marry her, and if I don't make the best of my chances when I get to teaching her music, my name ain't Obadiah Strout, which I guess it is." And he walked across the square to Hill's grocery to smoke his morning cigar.

On the way to Eastborough Centre Quincy wondered what he would do with Huldy when he arrived there. He did not care to take her to the Poorhouse, and particularly he did not wish her to see his uncle. Quincy was proud, but he was also sensible, and he decided upon a course of action that would prevent any one from saying that his pride had made him do a foolish act.

As they neared the Poorhouse Quincy turned to Huldy and said, "The Jim Sawyer who has been at the Eastborough Poorhouse for the last five years is my father's brother and my uncle. His story is a very sad one. I will tell it to you some day. He is in the last stages of consumption, and I am taking Miss Miller over to care for him while he lives."

Huldy nodded, and nothing more was said until they reached the Poorhouse. Quincy jumped out and called to Sam, who was close at hand, to hold the horse. Sam looked at him with a peculiar expression that Quincy did not stop to fathom, but running up the short flight of steps entered the room that served as the office for the Poorhouse. Mr. Waters was there writing at his desk. He turned as Quincy entered.

"How is my uncle?" asked Quincy.

"He is better off than us poor mortals," replied Mr. Waters with a long-drawn countenance.

"What do you mean?" asked Quincy. "Is he dead?"

"Yes," said Mr. Waters, "he died about four o'clock this mornin'. Sam sat up with him till midnight, and I stayed with him the balance of the time."

"I am so sorry I was not here," said Quincy.

"It wouldn't have done any good," said Waters. "He didn't know what was going on after two o'clock, and you couldn't have been of any use if you'd been here. If 't had been daytime I should have sent over for you. He only spoke once after I went upstairs and that was to say that you would see to buryin' him."

"Yes," said Quincy, "I will take charge of the remains."

"Well," remarked Mr. Waters, "I called in the town undertaker and he has got him all ready."

"When does the next train leave for Boston?" asked Quincy, taking out his watch.

"In just twenty minutes," Waters replied, looking up at the clock.

"I will be back from Boston at the earliest possible moment," said Quincy; and before the astonished Waters could recover himself, the young man had left the room.

Quincy jumped into the team, grasped the reins, and started off at full speed for Eastborough Centre.

"My uncle died this morning," said he, turning to Huldy, "I must go to Boston at once to make the necessary arrangements for his funeral. He is to be buried at Amesbury with his wife and children, so please get word to Mr. Pettengill that I shall not be home for several days. I will get some one at the hotel to drive you home, Miss Mason. Only stern necessity compels me to leave you in this way."

"You will do nothing of the sort," said Huldy. "I am perfectly confident that I am able to drive this team home all by myself."

"I never can consent to it," said Quincy. "If anything happened to you, your father and—" Huldy glanced at him. "I mean," said Quincy, "I should never forgive myself, and your father would never forgive me. Your arm is still weak, I know."

"My arm is just as good as ever," said Huldy. "The doctor told me it wouldn't break in that place again. Besides, Mr. Sawyer," she said, as the hotel came in sight, "I shall drive back just the same way we came, and there are no hills or sharp corners, you know." She laughed heartily and added, "I shall enjoy it very much, it is part of the comedy."

"Well," said Quincy in an undertone, "rebellious young woman, do as you will, and bear the consequences. I will turn the team around so that you won't have any trouble, and Hiram can take it down to Mr. Pettengill's and deliver my message. Good-by," and he shook hands with her.

"We will get out here, Miss Miller," said he, and he helped the nurse to alight. Grasping the heavy valise, he started at a brisk pace for the station, and Miss Miller was obliged to run in order to keep up with him. They boarded the train and took their seats. The train was ahead of time and waited for a few minutes at the station.

Quincy did not know as he sped towards Boston on his sad errand that Miss Lindy Putnam was in the second car behind him, bound to the same place. Nor did he know for several days that Abner Stiles, who drove her to the station, had seen Huldy driving towards Mason's Corner. Nor did he know that Strout had told Abner of his seeing Huldy and Sawyer together. Nor did he know that Abner whipped up his horse in a vain attempt to overtake Huldy on her return to Mason's Corner. She, too, had whipped up her horse and had reached home, and was in the house, calling for Hiram, just as Abner turned into the square by Hill's grocery.

Quincy made the necessary purchases, and with the city undertaker returned to Eastborough Centre by the noon train. The body was placed in a leaden casket and Quincy and the undertaker with their sad burden returned to Boston by the five o'clock express.

His mother and sisters were still in New York, but he passed the evening with his father, who approved of all he had done and what he proposed doing.

Quincy went to Amesbury and purchased a small lot in the cemetery. After a day's search he discovered the place of burial of his uncle's wife and children. They were disinterred, and the four bodies were placed in the little lot.

On his return to Boston he made arrangements for two plain marble stones for his uncle and aunt, and two smaller ones for his little cousins, whom he had never seen.

The directions that he left with the monument maker and the undertaker at Amesbury were followed to the letter. If one should pass by that little lot he would see on one marble slab these words:

Eunice Raymond Sawyer,
Aged 29 yrs., 6 mos.

On the little slab at her feet the simple words:

Mary, Aged 4 yrs., 2 mos.

At its side another little stone bearing only these words:

Ray, Aged 6 yrs., 8 mos.

Adhering strictly to his uncle's request, the other large stone bore no name, but on it were engraved these words:

In Heaven we Know our Own.

CHAPTER XX.

A WET DAY.

WHEN Quincy alighted from the train at Eastborough Centre, after attending his uncle's funeral, he found the rain descending in torrents. He hired a closed carriage and was driven to Mason's Corner, arriving there about ten o'clock. He had taken his breakfast in Boston.

When he reached the Pettengill house he saw Hiram standing at the barn door. Bidding the driver stop, he got out and paid his score; he then took Hiram by the arm and led him into the barn. When he had primed the latter with a good cigar, he said, "Now, Hiram, I've been away several days and I want to know what has been going on. You know our agreement was that you should tell me the whole truth and nothing but the truth. I don't want you to spare my feelings nor anybody else's. Do you understand?" said he to Hiram. Hiram nodded. "Then go ahead," said Quincy.

"Well, first," said Hiram, puffing his cigar with evident satisfaction, "they got hold of the point that Miss Huldy drove back alone from Eastborough Centre. Abner Stiles took Lindy Putnam down to the station and she went to Boston on the same train that you did. Abner tried to catch up with Huldy, so he could quiz her, but she whipped up her horse and got away from him."

"Smart girl!" interjected Quincy.

"You can just bet," said Hiram, "there ain't a smarter one in this town, though, of course, I think Mandy is pretty smart, too."

"Mandy's all right," said Quincy; "go ahead."

"Well, secondly, as the ministers say," continued Hiram, "Lindy Putnam told Abner when he drove her home from the station that night that the copper company that Mr. Sawyer told her to put her money in had busted, and she'd lost lots of money. That's gone all over Mason's Corner, and if Abner told Asa Waters, it's all over Eastborough Centre by this time."

"The whole thing is a lie," said Quincy hotly; "the stock did go down, but my father told me yesterday it had rallied and would soon advance from five to ten points. What's the next confounded yarn?"

"Well, thirdly," continued Hiram, "of course everybody knows Jim Sawyer was your uncle, and somebody said— you can guess who—that it would look better if you would pay up his back board instead of spending so much money on a fancy funeral and cheating the town undertaker out of a job."

"I paid him for all that he did," said Quincy.

"Yes," said Hiram, "but this is how it is. You see the undertaker makes a contract with the town to bury all the paupers who die during the year for so much money. They averaged it up and found that about three died a year, so the town pays the undertaker on that calculation; but this year, you see, only two have died, and there ain't another one likely to die before town meeting day, which comes the first Monday in March, so, you see the undertaker gets paid for buryin' your uncle, though he didn't do it, and some one says—you can guess who—that he is going to bring the matter up in town meeting."

Quincy smothered an exclamation and bit savagely into his cigar.

"Anything else?" inquired he. "Have they abused the ladies as well as me?"

"No," said Hiram; "you see somebody—you know who —is giving Huldy music lessons and he will keep quiet

Quincy Adams Sawyer.

"AN OLD-FASHIONED HUSKING BEE."   (ACT III.)

—Penalty of red ear.

about her anyway; but he says he can't understand how
'Zeke Pettengill can let you board in his house and go out
riding with Huldy, unless things is up between 'Zeke and
Huldy."

"Well, I guess that's about the size of it," said Quincy.
"Now, for instance, Hiram, you and Mandy are good
friends, aren't you?"

"Yes," said Hiram, "after we get over our little difficulties we are."

"Well," said Quincy, "I happen to know that 'Zekiel and
Huldy have got over their little difficulties and they are
now good friends."

"Been't they going to get married?" asked Hiram.

"Are you and Mandy going to get married?" asked
Quincy.

"Well, we haven't got so far along as to set the day
exactly," said Hiram.

"And I don't believe 'Zekiel and Huldy will get married any sooner than you and Mandy will," remarked
Quincy. "But don't say a word about this, Hiram."

"Mum's the word," replied Hiram. "I am no speaker,
but I hear a thing or two."

"Now, Hiram," said Quincy, "run in and tell Mandy I'll
be in to lunch as usual, and then come back, for I have
something more to say to you."

Hiram did as directed, and Quincy sat and thought the
situation over. So far he had been patient and he had
borne the slings and arrows hurled at him without making
any return. The time had come to change all that, and
from now on he would take up arms in his own defence,
and even attack his opponents.

When he had reached this conclusion, Hiram reappeared
and resumed his seat on the chopping block.

Quincy asked, "In what regiment did the singing-master
go to war?"

"The same one as I did, —th Mass.," replied Hiram.

"Did you go to war?" inquired Quincy.

"Well, I rather guess," said Hiram. "I went out as a bugler; he was a corporal, but he got detailed for hospital duty, and we left him behind before we got where there was any fightin'."

"Was he ever wounded in battle?" asked Quincy

"One of the sick fellers in the hospital gave him a lickin' one day, but I don't suppose you'd call that a battle," remarked Hiram.

"Well, how about that rigmarole he got off down to the grocery store that morning?" Quincy interrogated.

"Oh, that was all poppycock," said Hiram. "He said that just to get even with you, when you were telling about your grandfathers and grandmothers."

Quincy laughed.

"Oh, I see," said he. "Were you ever wounded in battle, Hiram?"

"Well, I was shot onct, but not with a bullet."

"What was it," said Quincy, "a cannon ball?"

"No," said Hiram. "I never was so thunderin' mad in my life. When I go to regimental reunions the boys just joke the life out of me. You see I was blowin' my bugle for a charge, and the boys were goin' ahead in great style, when a shell struck a fence about twenty feet off. The shell didn't hit me, but a piece of that darned fence came whizzin' along and struck me where I eat, and I had a dozen stummick aches inside o' half a minute. I just dropped my bugle and clapped my hands on my stummick and yelled so loud that the boys told me afterwards that they were afraid I had busted my bugle."

Quincy laid back in his chair and laughed heartily.

"What do the boys say to you when you go to the reunions?" he asked.

"They tell me to take a little whiskey for my stummick's

sake," said Hiram, "and some of them advise me to put on a plaster, and, darn 'em, they always take me and toss me in a blanket every time I go, and onct they made me a present of a bottleful of milk with a piece of rubber hose on top of it. They said it would be good for me, but I chucked it at the feller's head, darn him."

Quincy had another good laugh. Then he resumed his usual grave expression and asked, "What town offices does the singing-master hold?"

"Well," said Hiram, "he is fence viewer and hog reeve and pound keeper, but the only thing he gets much money out of is tax collector. He gets two per cent on about thirty thousand dollars, which gives him about ten dollars a week on an average, 'cause he don't get no pay if he don't collect."

"Did he get a big vote for the place?" asked Quincy.

"No," said Hiram, "he just got in by the skin of his teeth; he had last town meetin' two more votes than Wallace Stackpole, and Wallace would have got it anyhow if it hadn't been for an unfortunate accident."

"How was that?" asked Quincy.

"Well, you see," said Hiram, "two or three days before town meetin' Wallace went up to Boston. He got an oyster stew for dinner, and it made him kinder sick, and some one gave him a drink of brandy, and I guess they gave him a pretty good dose, for when he got to Eastborough Centre they had to help him off the train, 'cause his legs were kinder weak. Well, 'Bias Smith, who lives over to West Eastborough, he is the best talker we've got in town meetin'. He took up the cudgels for Wallace, and he just lammed into those mean cusses who'd go back on a man 'cause he was sick and took a little too much medicine. But Abner Stiles,—you know Abner,—well, he's the next best talker to 'Bias Smith,—he stood up and said he didn'. think it was safe to trust the town's money to a man who couldn't go to Boston and come home sober, and that pulled over some of the fellers who'd agreed to vote for Wallace."

"Has the tax collector performed his duties satisfactorily?" asked Quincy.

"Well," said Hiram, "Wallace Stackpole told me the other day that he hadn't got in more than two-thirds of last year's taxes. He said the selectmen had to borrow money and there'd be a row at the next town meetin'."

"Well," said Quincy, rising, "I think I will go in and get ready for lunch. I had a very early breakfast in Boston."

"Did you have oyster stew?" asked Hiram.

"No," replied Quincy, "people who live in Boston never eat oyster stews at a restaurant. If they did there wouldn't be enough left for those gentlemen who come from the country."

He opened the door and Hiram grasped his arm.

"By Gosh! I forgot one thing," he cried. "You remember Tilly James, that played the pianner at the concert?"

"Yes," said Quincy, "and she was a fine player, too."

"Well," said Hiram, "she's engaged to Sam Hill, you know, down to the grocery store. That ain't all, old Ben James, her father, he's a paralytic, you know, and pretty well fixed for this world's goods, and he wants Benoni to sell out his grocery when Tilly gets married and come over and run the farm, which is the biggest one in the town, and I heerd Abner Stiles say to 'Manuel Howe, that he reckoned he—you know who I mean—would get some fellers to back him up and he'd buy out the grocery and get 'p'inted postmaster. I guess that's all;" and Hiram started off towards Deacon Mason's.

Quincy went to his room and prepared for the noonday meal. While doing so he mentally resolved that the singing-

master would not be the next tax collector if he could prevent it; he also resolved that the same party would not get
the grocery store, if he had money enough to outbid him;
and lastly he felt sure that he had influence enough to
prevent his being appointed postmaster.

Quincy met Ezekiel at lunch. He told Quincy that
everything was working smoothly; that the singing-master
evidently thought he had the field all to himself. He said
Huldy and Alice were old friends, and Huldy was coming
over twice a week to see Alice, and so he shouldn't go
up to Deacon Mason's very often.

"Where is Miss Pettengill?" said Quincy.

"Well," replied Ezekiel, "she isn't used to heavy dinners
at noon, so she had a lunch up in her room. I am going
over to West Eastborough this afternoon with the boys to
see some cows that 'Bias Smith has got to sell. The sun
is coming out and I guess it will be pleasant the rest of the
day."

"'Bias Smith?" asked Quincy.

"His name is Tobias," said Ezekiel, "but everybody calls
him 'Bias."

"I have heard of him," said Quincy. "You just mention
my name to him, Mr. Pettengill, and say I am coming over
some day with Mr. Stackpole to see him."

'Zekiel smiled. "Going to take a hand yourself?" asked
he.

"Yes," said Quincy, "the other fellow has been playing
tricks with the pack so long that I think I shall throw down
a card or two myself, and I may trump his next lead."

"By the way," said 'Zekiel, "while you were away Uncle
Ike had our piano tuned and fixed up. It hasn't been
played since Alice went to Boston five years ago. But the
tuner who came from Boston said it was just as good as
ever. So if you hear any noise underneath you this afternoon you will know what it means."

"Music never troubles me," said Quincy, "I play and sing myself."

"Well, I hope you and Alice will have a good time with the piano," remarked 'Zekiel as he left the room.

Quincy went back to his room and wrote a letter to a friend in Boston, asking him to get a certified copy of the war record of Obadiah Strout, Corporal —th Mass. Volunteers, and send it to him at Eastborough Centre as soon as possible. It was many days before that letter reached its destination.

He then sat down in his favorite armchair and began thinking out the details of his aggressive campaign against the singing-master. He had disposed of his enemy in half a dozen pitched battles, when the sound of the piano fell upon his ear.

She was playing. He hoped she was a good musician, for his taste in that art was critical. He had studied the best, and he knew it when he heard it sung or played. The piano was a good one, its tone was full and melodious, and it was in perfect tune.

He listened intently. He looked and saw that he had unintentionally left the door of his room ajar. The parlor door, too, must be open partly, or he could not have heard so plainly. What was that she was playing? Ah! Mendelssohn. Those "Songs Without Words" were as familiar to him as the alphabet. Now it is Beethoven, that beautiful work, "The Moonlight Sonata," she was evidently trying to recall her favorites to mind, for of course she could not be playing by note. Then she strayed into a "valse" by Chopin, and followed it with a dashing galop by some unknown composer. "She is a classical musician," said Quincy to himself, as the first bars of a Rhapsodie Hongroise by Liszt fell upon his ear. "I hope she knows some of the old English ballads and the best of the popular songs," thought Quincy.

As if in answer to his wish she played that sterling old song, " 'Tis but a Little Faded Flower," and Quincy listened with pleasure to the pure, sweet, soprano voice that rang out full and strong and seemed to reach and permeate every nook and corner in the old homestead.

Quincy could stand it no longer. He stepped quietly to his door, opened it wide, and listened with delight to the closing lines of the song.

Then she sang that song that thrilled the hearts of thousands of English soldiers in the Crimea on the eve of the battle of Inkermann, "Annie Laurie," and it was with difficulty that Quincy refrained from joining in the chorus. Surely Annie Laurie could have been no purer, no sweeter, no more beautiful, than Alice Pettengill; and Quincy felt that he could do and die for the girl who was singing in the parlor, as truly as would have the discarded suitor who wrote the immortal song.

But Quincy was destined to be still more astonished. Alice played a short prelude that seemed familiar to him, and then her voice rang out the words of that beautiful duet that Quincy had sung with Lindy Putnam at the singing-master's concert. Yes, it was Jewell's "Over the Bridge." This was too much for Quincy. He went quietly down the stairs and looked in at the parlor door, which was wide open. Alice was seated at the piano, and again the sun, in its westward downward course, shone in at the window, and lighted up her crown of golden hair. This time she had reversed the colors which she evidently knew became her so well, and wore a dress of light pink, while a light blue knitted shawl, similar to its pink companion, lay upon the chair beside her.

When she reached the duet Quincy did not attempt to control himself any further, but joined in with her, and they sang the piece together to the end.

Alice turned upon the piano stool, faced the door and clapped her hands.

"That was capital, Mr. Sawyer. I didn't know that you sang so well. In fact, I didn't know that you sang at all."

"How did you know it was I?" said Quincy, as he advanced towards her. "It is a little cool here, Miss Pettengill. Allow me to place your shawl about you;" and, suiting the action to the word, he put it gently over her shoulders.

"Yes," said Alice, "I put it on when I first came down. It interfered with my playing and I threw it into the chair."

"May I take the chair, now that it is unoccupied?" he asked.

"Yes," said Alice, "if you will give me your word of honor that you did not try to make me think it was cold here, so that you could get the chair."

Quincy replied with a laugh, "If I did my reward is a great return for my power of invention, but I assure you I was thinking of your health and not of the chair, when I tendered my services."

"You are an adept in sweet speeches, Mr. Sawyer. You city young men all are; but our country youth, who are just as true and honest, are at a great disadvantage, because they cannot say what they think in so pleasing a way."

"I hope you do not think I am insincere," remarked Quincy, gravely.

"Not at all," said Alice, "but I have not answered your question. How did I know that it was you? You must remember, Mr. Sawyer, that those who cannot see have their hearing accentuated, and the ear kindly sends those pictures to the brain which unfortunately the eye cannot supply."

"I have enjoyed your playing and singing immensely," said Quincy. "Let us try that duet again."

They sang it again, and then they went from piece to piece, each suggesting her or his favorite, and it was not till Mandy's shrill voice once more called out with more than usual force and sharpness, "Supper's ready," that the piano was closed and Quincy, for the first time taking Alice's hand in his, led her from the parlor, which was almost shrouded in darkness, into the bright light of the dining-room, where they took their accustomed seats. They ate but little, their hearts were full of the melody that each had enjoyed so much.

CHAPTER XXI.

WHEN Ezekiel and Cobb's twins returned from West Eastborough, they said the air felt like snow. Mandy had kept some supper for them. Ezekiel said they had supper over to Eastborough Centre, but the home cooking smelled so good that all three sat down in the kitchen and disposed of what Mandy had provided.

The other members of the Pettengill household were in their respective rooms. Uncle Ike was reading a magazine. Alice had not retired, for Mandy always came to her room before she did so to see that her fire was all right for the night. Alice was a great lover of music and she had enjoyed the afternoon almost as much as Quincy had. She could not help thinking what musical treats might be in store for them, and then the thought came to her how she would miss him when he went back to Boston.

In the next room, Quincy was pursuing a similar line of thought. He was thinking of the nice times that Alice and he could have singing together. To be sure he wished to do nothing to make his father angry, for Quincy appreciated the power of money. He knew that with his mother's third deducted, his father's estate would give him between two and three hundred thousand dollars. He had some money in his own right left him by a fond aunt, his father's sister, the income from which gave him a good living without calling upon his father.

He knew his father wished him to become a lawyer, and

keep up the old firm which was so well known in legal and business circles, but Quincy in his heart realized that he was not equal to it, and the future had little attraction for him, if it were to be passed in the law offices of Sawyer, Crowninshield, & Lawrence. At any rate his health was not fully restored and he determined to stay at Mason's Corner as long as he could do so without causing a break in the friendly relations existing between his father and himself. His present income was enough for his personal needs, but it was not sufficient to also support a Mrs. Quincy Adams Sawyer.

What Ezekiel had prophesied came true. No one knew just when the storm began, but the picture that greeted Mandy Skinner's eyes when she came down to get breakfast was a great contrast to that of the previous day.

The snow had fallen steadily in large, heavy flakes, the road and the fields showed an even, unbroken surface of white; the tops of the taller fences were yet above the snow line, each post wearing a white cap. As the morning advanced the storm increased, the wind blew, and great drifts were indications of its power. The thick clouds of white flakes were thrown in every direction, and only dire necessity, it seemed, would be a sufficient reason for leaving a comfortable fireside.

Mandy and Mrs. Crowley were busily engaged in preparing the morning meal, when a loud scratching at a door, which led into a large room that was used as an addition to the kitchen, attracted their attention. In bounded Swiss, the big St. Bernard dog belonging to Uncle Ike. At Uncle Ike's special request Swiss had not been banished to the barn or the wood-shed, but had been allowed to sleep on a pallet in the corner of the large room referred to.

Swiss was a great favorite with Mandy, and he was a great friend of hers, for Swiss was very particular about his food, and he had found Mandy to be a much better

cook than Uncle Ike had been; besides the fare was more
bounteous at the Pettengill homestead than down at the
chicken coop, and Swiss had gained in weight and strength
since his change of quarters.

After breakfast Uncle Ike came into the kitchen and
received a warm welcome from Swiss. Uncle Ike told
Mandy and Mrs. Crowley the well-known story of the
rescues of lost travellers made by the St. Bernard dogs on
the snow-clad mountains of Switzerland. When Mrs.
Crowley learned that Swiss had come from a country a
great many miles farther away from America than Ireland
was, he rose greatly in her estimation and she made no
objection to his occupying a warm corner of the kitchen.

About noon, when the storm was at its very worst,
Mandy, who was looking out of the kitchen window, espied
something black in the road about halfway between Deacon
Mason's and the Pettengill house. She called Mrs. Crowley to the window and asked her what she thought it was.

"That's aisy," said Mrs. Crowley. "It's a man coming
down the road."

"What can bring a man out in such a storm as this?"
asked Mandy.

"Perhaps he is going for the docther," remarked Mrs.
Crowley.

"Then he would be going the other way," asserted
Mandy.

"He's a plucky little divil anyway," said Mrs. Crowley.

"That's so," said Mandy. "He is all right as long as
he keeps on his feet, but if he should fall down—"

At that moment the man did fall down or disappear from
sight. Mandy pressed her face against the window pane
and looked with strained eyes. He was up again, she
could see the dark clothing above the top of the snow.

What was that! A cry? The sound was repeated.

"I do believe the man is calling for help," cried Mandy.

"MRS. PUTNAM'S ANGER, UPON DISCOVERY OF LINDY'S PARENTAGE." (ACT III.)

She rushed to the kitchen door and opened it. A gust of snow swept into the room, followed by a stream of cold, chilling air. Swiss awoke from his nap and lifted his head. Despite the storm, Mandy stood at the door and screamed "Hello!" with her sharp, strident voice. Could she believe her ears? Through the howling storm came a word uttered in a voice which her woman's heart at once recognized. The word was "Mandy," and the voice was Hiram's.

"What on earth is he out in this storm for?" said Mandy to herself. She called back in response, "Hello! Hello! Hello!" and once more her own name was borne to her through the beating, driving storm.

She shut the door and resumed her post at the window. Hiram was still struggling manfully against the storm and had made considerable progress.

Mandy turned to Mrs. Crowley and said, "Mr. Maxwell is coming, Mrs. Crowley."

"More fool he," remarked Mrs. Crowley, "to be out in a storm like this."

"Get some cider, Mrs. Crowley," said Mandy, "and put it on the stove. He will need a good warm drink when he gets here."

"If he was a son of mine he'd get a good warmin'," said Mrs. Crowley, as she went down cellar to get the cider.

Mandy still strained her eyes at the window. The dark form was still visible, moving slowly through the snow. At that moment a terrific storm of wind struck the house; it made every window and timber rattle; great clouds of snow were swept up from the ground to mingle with those coming from above, and the two were thrown into a whirling eddy that struck the poor traveller and took him from his feet, covering him from sight. Mandy rushed to the door and opened it. This time she did not scream "Hello." The word this time was "Hiram! He is lost! He is lost!" she cried. "His strength has given out; but

what shall I do? I could not reach him if I tried. Oh,
Hiram! Hiram!" and the poor girl burst into tears. She
would call Mr. Pettengill; she would call Cobb's twins;
she would call Mr. Sawyer; one of them would surely go
to his assistance.

She turned, and to her surprise found Swiss by her side,
looking up at her with his large, intelligent eyes. Quick
as lightning, Uncle Ike's story came back to her mind.
She patted Swiss on the head, and pointed out into the
storm.

Not another word was needed. With a bound Swiss
went into the snow and rapidly forward in the direction
of the road. Mandy was obliged to close the door again
and resume her place at the window. How her heart beat!
How she watched the dog as he ploughed his way through
the drifts? He must be near the place. Yes, he is scratching and digging down into the snow. Now the dark form
appears once more. Yes, Hiram is on his feet again and
man and dog resume their fight with the elements.

It seemed an age to Mandy, but it was in reality not
more than five minutes, before Hiram and Swiss reached
the kitchen door and came into the room.

"Come out into the back room," said Mandy to Hiram.
"I don't want this snow all over my kitchen floor." So
Hiram and Swiss were taken into the big room and in a
short time came back in presentable condition.

"Now, Mr. Maxwell, if you have recovered the use of
your tongue, will you kindly inform me what sent you
out in such a storm as this?"

"Well," replied Hiram, "I reckoned I'd git down kinder
early in the mornin' and git back afore dark."

"That's all right," said Mandy; "but that don't tell me
what you are out for, anyway."

"Well, you didn't suppose," said Hiram, "that I could go
all day long without seein' you, did yer, Mandy?"

Mrs. Crowley chuckled to herself and went into the side room. Even Swiss seemed to recognize that two were company and he followed Mrs. Crowley and resumed his old resting place in the corner on the pallet.

As Mrs. Crowley went about her work, she chuckled again, and said to herself, "It's a weddin' I'll be goin' to next time in place of a funeral."

Upstairs other important events were taking place. Quincy had gone to his room directly after breakfast, and looked out upon the wild scene of storm with a sense of loneliness that had not hitherto oppressed him. Why should he be lonely? Was he not in the same house with her, with only a thin wall of wood and plaster between them? Yes, but if that wall had been of granite one hundred feet thick, it could not have shut him off more effectually from seeing her lovely face and hearing her sweet voice.

There came a sharp rap at the door.

"Come in," called out Quincy.

"Ah!" said Uncle Ike as he entered, "I am glad to see you have a good fire. The snow has blown down into Alice's room and her fire is out. Will you let her step in here for a few moments, Mr. Sawyer, until 'Zeke and I get the room warm again?"

"Why, certainly," replied Quincy. "I am only too happy—"

But Uncle Ike was off, and returned in a few moments leading Alice. Quincy placed a chair for her before the fire. This cold wintry day she wore a morning dress of a shade of red which, despite its bright color, seemed to harmonize with the golden hair and to take the place of the sun, which was not there to light it up.

"If Miss Pettengill prefers," said Quincy, "I can make myself comfortable in the dining-room, and she can have my room to herself."

He had started this speech to Uncle Ike, who left the room abruptly in the middle of it, and Quincy's closing words fell on Alice's ears alone.

"Why, certainly not," said Alice; "sit down, Mr. Sawyer, and we will talk about something. Don't you think it is terrible?" As Quincy was contemplating his fair visitor, he could hardly be expected to say "yes" to her question. "Perhaps you enjoy it?" said she.

"I certainly do," answered Quincy, throwing his whole heart into his eyes.

"Well, I must differ with you," said Alice. "I never did like snow."

"Oh, you were talking about the weather!" remarked Quincy.

"Why, yes," said Alice. "What else did you think I was talking about?"

Quincy, cool and self-possessed as he invariably was, was a trifle embarrassed.

Turning to Alice he said, "I see, Miss Pettengill, that I must make you a frank statement in order that you may retain your respect for me. I know you will pardon me for not hearing what you said, and for what I am about to say; but the fact is, I was wondering whether you have had the best advice and assistance that the medical science of to-day can afford you as regards your eyes."

"It is very kind of you, Mr. Sawyer, to think of me, and my trouble, and I will answer you in the same friendly way in which you have spoken. I was taken sick one morning just as I was eating my breakfast. I never felt better in my life than I did that morning, but the pain in my side was so intense, so agonizing, that by the time I reached my room and threw myself on the bed, physically I was a complete wreck. A doctor was called at once and he remained with me from eight o'clock until noon before I became comfortable. I thought I was going to get better

right off, or I should have written to 'Zekiel. Two other
attacks, each more severe than the one preceding, followed
the first, and I was so sick that writing, or telling any one
else what to write, or where to write, was impossible. Then
I began slowly to recover, but I was very weak and what
made me feel worse than ever was the fact that the trouble
with my eyes, which before my illness I had attributed to
nearsightedness, was now so marked that I could not see
across the room. I could not even see to turn a spoonful
of medicine from a bottle on the table beside my bed. The
Pettengills, Mr. Sawyer, are a self-reliant race, and I concluded in my own mind that the trouble with my eyes was
due to my illness, and that when I recovered from that,
they would get well; but they did not. I was able, physically,
to resume my work, but I could not see to read or write. I
sent for my employer and told him my condition. He
advised me to consult an oculist at once. In fact, he got a
carriage and took me to one himself. The oculist said that
the treatment would require at least three months; so my
employer told me I had better come home, and that when
I recovered I could have my place back again. He is a
fine, generous-hearted man and I should be very miserable
if I thought I was going to lose my place."

"But what did the oculist say was the trouble with your
eyes?" Quincy asked.

"He didn't tell me," replied Alice. "He may have told
my employer. He gave me some drops to put in my eyes
three times a day; and a little metal tube with a cover to it
like the top of a pepper box; on the other end is a piece of
rubber tubing, with a glass mouthpiece attached to it."

"How do you use that?" asked Quincy.

Alice continued, "I hold the pepper box in front of my
wide-opened eye; then I put the glass mouthpiece in my
mouth and blow, for a certain length of time. I don't know
how long it is. It seems as though a thousand needles

were driven into my eyeball. The drops make me cry; but
the little tube brings the tears in torrents."

"Isn't that harsh treatment?" asked Quincy, as he looked
at the beautiful blue but sightless eyes that were turned
towards him.

"No," said Alice with a laugh, "the pain and the tears
are like an April shower, for both soon pass away."

At this moment Uncle Ike entered the room and Ezekiel's steps were heard descending the stairs. Uncle Ike
said, "We have got it started and 'Zeke's gone down to
bring up a good stock of wood. If you have no objection,
Mr. Sawyer, I will sit down here a few minutes. Don't let
me interrupt your conversation."

"I hope you will take a part in it," said Quincy. "You
put a lot of new ideas into my head the first time I came
to see you, and perhaps you may have some more new
ones for me to-day. Miss Pettengill was just saying she
would feel miserable if she lost her situation."

"I have no doubt of it," said Uncle Ike. "The Pettengills are not afraid to work. If a man is obliged to earn
his living by the sweat of his brow, I don't see why woman
shouldn't do the same thing."

"But the home is woman's sphere," said Quincy.

"Bosh!" cried Uncle Ike.

"Why, Uncle!" cried Alice.

"Oh, Mr. Sawyer understands me!" said Uncle Ike. "In
the Middle Ages, when women occupied the highest position that has fallen to her lot since the days of Adam, the
housework was done by menials and scullions. Has the
world progressed when woman is pulled down from her
high estate and this life of drudgery is called her sphere?
Beg your pardon, Mr. Sawyer, but there should be no
more limit fixed to the usefulness of woman than there is to
the usefulness of man."

"But," persisted Alice, "I don't think Mr. Sawyer means

that exactly. He means a woman should stay at home and look after her family."

"Well," said Uncle Ike, "so should the man. I am inclined to think if the father spent more time at home, it would be for the advantage of both sons and daughters."

"But," said Quincy, "do you think it is for the best interests of the community that woman should force her way into all branches of industry and compete with man for a livelihood?"

"Why not?" said Uncle Ike. "In the old days when they didn't work, for they didn't know how and didn't want to, because they thought it was beneath them, if a man died, his wife and children became dependent upon some brother or sister or uncle or aunt, and they were obliged to provide for them out of their own small income or savings. In those days it was respectable to be genteelly poor, and starve rather than work and live on the fat of the land. Nothing has ever done so much to increase the self-respect of woman, and add to her feeling of independence, as the knowledge of the fact that she can support herself." Alice bowed her head and covered her eyes with her hand. "There's nothing personal in what I say," said Uncle Ike. "I am only talking on general principles."

Quincy yearned to say something against Uncle Ike's argument, but how could he advance anything against woman's work when the one who sat before him was a workingwoman and was weeping because she could not work? There was one thing he could do, he could change the subject to one where there was an opportunity for debate. So he said, "Well, Mr. Pettengill, I presume if you are such an ardent advocate of woman's right or even duty to work, that you are also a supporter of her right to vote."

"That does not follow," replied Uncle Ike. "To be self-reliant, independent, and self-supporting is a pleasure and a duty, and adds to one's self-respect. As voting is done at the present day, I do not see how woman can take part in it and maintain her self-respect. Improvements no doubt will be made in the manner of voting. The ballot will become secret, and the count will not be disclosed until after the voting is finished. The rum stores will be closed on voting day and an air of respectability will be given to it that it does not now possess. It ought to be made a legal holiday."

"Granted," said Quincy, "but what has that to do with the question of woman's right to vote?"

"Woman has no inherent right to vote," said Uncle Ike. "The ballot is a privilege, not a right. Why, I remember reading during the war that young soldiers, between eighteen and twenty-one years of age, claimed the ballot as a right, because they were fighting for their country. If voting is a right, what argument could be used against their claim?"

"I remember," added Quincy, "that they argued that 'bullets should win ballots.' Do you think any one should vote who cannot fight?" asked Quincy.

"If he does not shirk his duty between eighteen and forty-five," said Uncle Ike, "he should not be deprived of his ballot when he is older; but the question of woman's voting does not depend upon her ability to fight. The mother at home thinking of her son, the sister thinking of her brother, the wife thinking of her husband, are as loyally fighting for their native land as the soldiers in the field, and no soldier is braver than the hospital nurse, who, day after day and night after night, watches by the bedsides of the wounded, the sick, and the dying. No, Mr. Sawyer, it is not a question of fighting or bravery."

During the discussion Alice had dried her eyes and was listening to her uncle's words. She now asked a question, "When will women vote, Uncle?"

"When it is deemed expedient for them to do so," replied
Uncle Ike. "The full privilege will not be given all at once.
They will probably be allowed to vote on some one matter
in which they are deeply interested. Education and the
rum question are the ones most likely to be acted upon
first. But the full ballot will not come, and now I know
Alice will shake her head and say, 'No!' I repeat it—the
full ballot will not come for woman until our social super-
structure is changed. Woman will not become the political
equal of man until she is his social and industrial equal; and
until any contract of whatever nature made by a man and a
woman may be dissolved by them by mutual consent, without their becoming criminals in the eye of the law, or out-
casts in the eyes of society."

At this moment Ezekiel looked in the door and said,
"Alice's room is nice and warm now." Advancing, he
took her hand and led her from the room. Uncle Ike
thanked Quincy for his kindness and followed them.
Quincy sat and thought. The picture that his mind drew
placed the woman who had just left his room in a large
house, with servants at her command. She was the head
of the household, but no menial nor scullion. She did not
work, because he was able and willing to support her. She
did not vote, because she felt with him that at home was
her sphere of usefulness; and then Quincy thought that
what would make this possible was money, money that not
he but others had earned, and he knew that without this
money the question could not be solved as his mind had
pictured it; and he reflected that all women could not have
great houses and servants and loving husbands to care for
them, and he acknowledged to himself that his solution
was a personal, selfish one and not one that would **answer**
for the toiling millions of the working world.

CHAPTER XXII.

MANDY was, of course, greatly pleased inwardly because Hiram had come through such a great storm
to see her, but, woman-like, she would not show it.

So she said to Hiram, "Your reason is a very good one,
and of course I am greatly flattered, but there must be
something else besides that. Now, what have you got to
tell me?"

"Well, the fact is, Mandy, I've got two things on my
mind. One of 'em is a secret and t'other isn't. I meant
to have told you yesterday; but Mr. Sawyer kept me busy
till noon, and the Deacon kept me busy all the afternoon,
and I was too tired to come over last night."

"Well," said Mandy, "tell me the secret first. If the
other one has kept so long it won't spoil if it's kept a little
longer."

Hiram had kept his eyes on the stove since taking his
seat, and he then remarked, "I am afraid that cider will
spoil unless I get a drink of it pretty soon."

"Well, I declare," cried Mandy, "if I didn't forget to
give it to you, after sending Mrs. Crowley down stairs for
it, when you was out there in the road."

"That's all right," said Hiram, as he finished the mugful
she passed him, and handed it back to be refilled. "That
sort o' limbers a feller's tongue a bit. Well, the secret is,"
said Hiram, lowering his voice, "that when Huldy saw me
gettin' ready to go out, sez she, 'Where are you goin'?'

'Over to Mr. Pettengill's,' sez I. Then sez she, 'Will you
wait a minute till I write a note?' 'Certainly,' sez I. And
when she brought me the note, sez she, 'Please give that
to Mr. Pettengill and don't let anybody else see it.' Then
sez I to her, 'No, ma'am;' but I sez to myself, 'Nobody
but Mandy.'" And Hiram took from an inside pocket
an envelope, addressed to Mr. Ezekiel Pettengill, and
showed it to Mandy. Then he put it back quickly in his
pocket.

"Well, what of that?" asked Mandy. "That's no great
secret."

"Well, not in itself," said Hiram; "but I am willing to
bet a year's salary agin a big red apple that those two
people have made up and are engaged reg'lar fashion."

"You don't say so," cried Mandy, "what makes you
think so?"

"Well, a number of things," said Hiram. "I overheard
the Deacon say to Huldy, 'It will be pretty lonesome for
us one of these days,' and then you see Mrs. Mason, she is
just as good as pie to me all the time, and that shows something has pleased her more than common; and then you
see Huldy has that sort of look about her that girls have
when their market's made, and they feel so happy that they
can't help showing it. You see, Mandy, I'm no chicken.
I've had lots of experience."

What Mandy might have said in reply to this remark
will never be known, for at this juncture Ezekiel entered
the room and passed through on his way to the wood-shed.

"Now's my time," said Hiram, and he arose and followed
him out.

Ezekiel was piling up some wood which he was to take
to Alice's room, when Hiram came up beside him and
slyly passed him the note. Then Hiram looked out of the
wood-shed window at the storm, which had lost none of its
fury, while Ezekiel read the note.

"Are you going home soon?" asked Ezekiel.

"Well, I guess I'll try it again," said Hiram, "as soon as
I get warm and kinder limbered up."

"I guess I'll go back with you," said Ezekiel. "We will
take Swiss with us; two men and a dog ought to be enough
for a little snowstorm like this."

"You won't find it a little one," said Hiram, "when you
get out in the road, but I guess the three on us can pull
through."

Ezekiel went upstairs with the wood and Hiram resumed
his seat before the kitchen fire.

"What did I tell you?" said Hiram to Mandy. " 'Zeke's
going back with me. She has writ him to come over and
see her. Now you see if you don't lose your apple."

"I didn't bet," said Mandy; "but what was that other
thing you were going to tell me that was no secret?"

"Oh, that's about another couple," said Hiram. "Tilly
James is engaged."

"Well, it's about time," said Mandy. "Which one of
them?"

"Samuel Hill," replied Hiram, "and she managed it fust
rate. You know the boys have been flocking round her
for more than a year. Old Ben James, her pa, told me
he'd got to put in a new hitchin' post. You see, there has
been Robert Wood and 'Manuel Howe and Arthur Scates
and Cobb's twins and Ben Bates and Sam Hill, but Samuel
was the cutest one of the lot."

"Why, what did he do that was bright?" asked Mandy.

"Well," replied Hiram, "you see, Tilly sot down and
writ invites to all the boys that had been sparkin' 'round
her to come to see her the same night. She gave these
invites to her brother Bill to deliver. Well, Sam Hill
met him, found out what he was about, and kinder surmised what it all meant. Wall, the night came 'round and
Sam Hill was the only one that turned up at the time

app'inted. After talkin' about the weather, last year's crops, and spring plantin', Sam just braced up and proposed, and Tilly accepted him on the spot."

"Where were the other fellers?" asked Mandy. "I always surmised that she thought more of Ben Bates than she did of Sam Hill."

"Well, it didn't come out till a couple of days afterwards," said Hiram. "You see, the shortest way to old James's place is to go over the mill race, and all of the fellers but Sam Hill went that way, and the joke of it was that they all fell over into the river and got a duckin'."

"Well," said Mandy, "they must have been drinking. Tilly is well rid of the whole lot of them. Why, I've walked over that log time and time again."

"Well, they hadn't been drinkin'," said Hiram. "You see it was pretty dark and they didn't get on to the fact that the log was greased till it was kinder too late to rectify matters."

"And did Sam Hill do that?" asked Mandy.

"He did," said Hiram; and he burst into a loud laugh, in which Mandy joined.

The laughing was quickly hushed as the kitchen door opened and Ezekiel entered, warmly dressed for his fight with the snow and carrying a heavy cane in his hand.

"Call the dog, Hiram," said Ezekiel, "and we'll start. Mandy, tell Jim and Bill to come over to Deacon Mason's for me about four o'clock, unless it looks too bad; if it does they needn't try it till to-morrow morning."

"All ready," said he to Hiram, who was patting Swiss's head, and off they started.

Again Mandy went to the window and watched the progress of the travellers. Mrs. Crowley came into the kitchen and seeing Mandy at the window quietly turned out a mug of the hot cider and drank it. She then ap-

proached Mandy and said, "What was all the laughin'
about? I like a good joke myself."

Mandy said, "Oh, he was telling me about a girl that
invited all her fellers to come and see her the same evening, and only one of them got there because he greased the
log over the mill race, and all the rest of them fell into the
water."

"It was a mane trick," said Mrs. Crowley. "Now, when
all the boys were after me, for I was a good-lookin' girl
once, Pat Crowley, he was me husband, had a fight on
hand every night for a fortnight and all on account of me;
and they do say there were never so many heads broken
in the County of Tipperary on account of one girl since the
days of St. Patrick."

Mandy had paid but little attention to Mrs. Crowley's
speech. She was too busy watching the travellers. Mrs.
Crowley filled and emptied the mug once more.

The last potation was too much for her equilibrium, and
forgetting the step that led from the kitchen to the side
room, she lost her balance and fell prone upon the floor.
Her loud cries obliged Mandy to turn from the window,
but not until she had seen that the travellers had reached
the fence before Deacon Mason's house, and she knew they
were safe for the present. Mrs. Crowley was lifted to her
feet by Mandy. The old woman declared that she was
"kilt intirely," but Mandy soon learned the cause of the
accident, and returning to the kitchen closed the door and
continued her morning duties.

Before Ezekiel left the house he had interrupted
Quincy's meditations by knocking on his door, and when
admitted told him that he had had a letter from Huldy.

"She is kind of lonesome," he said, "and wants me to
come over to see her."

"But it is a terrible storm," said Quincy, looking out of
the window.

"Oh," said Ezekiel, "we'll be all right! Hiram is going with me, and we are going to take Swiss along with us. Now, Mr. Sawyer, I am going to ask you to do me and Alice a favor. Uncle Ike is upstairs busy reading, and if you will kinder look out for Alice till I get back I shall be greatly obliged."

Quincy promised and Ezekiel departed.

Quincy thought the fates had favored him in imposing upon him such a pleasant task. But where was she, and what could he do to amuse her? Then he thought, "We can sing together as we did yesterday."

He went down stairs to the parlor, thinking she might be there, but the room was empty. The fire was low, but the supply of wood was ample, and in a short time the great room was warm and comfortable. Quincy seated himself at the piano, played a couple of pieces and then sang a couple; he did not think while singing the second song that he had possibly transcended propriety, but when he sang the closing lines of "Alice, Where Art Thou?" it suddenly dawned upon him, and, full of vexation, he arose and walked to the window and looked out upon the howling storm.

Suddenly he heard a sweet voice say, "I am here." And then a low laugh reached his ear.

Turning, he saw Alice standing in the middle of the room, while Mandy's retreating figure showed who had been her escort. Her brother Ezekiel had rigged a bell wire from her room to the kitchen, so that she could call Mandy when she needed her assistance.

"I beg your pardon, Miss Pettengill," said Quincy, advancing towards her. "The song has always been a favorite of mine, but I never thought of its personal application until I reached the closing words. I trust you do not think I was so presuming as to—"

Alice smiled and said, "The song is also a favorite one of

mine, Mr. Sawyer, and you sang it beautifully. No apologies are needed, for the fact is I was just saying to myself, 'Mr. Sawyer, where are you?' for 'Zekiel told me that he was going to speak to you and ask you to help me drive away those lonesome feelings that always come to me on a day like this. I cannot see the storm, but I can hear it and feel it."

As Quincy advanced towards her he saw she held several sheets of paper in her hand.

"I am at your service," said he. "I am only afraid that your requirements will exceed my ability."

"Very prettily spoken," said Alice, as Quincy led her to a seat by the fire, and took one himself. "I am going to confess to you," said she, "one of my criminal acts. I am going to ask you to sit as judge and mete out what you consider a suitable punishment for my offence."

"What crime have you committed?" asked Quincy gravely.

Alice laughed, shook the papers she held in her hand, and said, "I have written poetry."

"The crime is a great one," said Quincy. "But if the poetry be good it may serve to mitigate your sentence. Are those the evidences of your crime you hold in your hand, Miss Pettingill?"

"Yes," she answered, as she passed a written sheet to him; "I wrote them before my eyes failed me. Perhaps you will find it hard to read them. Which one is that?" she asked.

"It is headed, 'On the Banks of the Tallahassee,'" replied Quincy.

"Oh!" cried Alice, "I didn't write that song myself. A gentleman friend, who is now dead, was the author of it. But he couldn't write a chorus and he asked me to do it for him. The idea of the chorus is moonlight on the river."

"Shall I read it?" asked Quincy.

"Only the chorus part, if you please," replied Alice, "and be as lenient as you can, good Mr. Judge, for that was my first offence."

Quincy, in a smooth, even voice, read the following words:

> The moon's bright rays,
> In a silver maze,
>> Fall on the rushing river;
> Each ray of light
> Like an arrow white
>> Drawn from a crystal quiver.
> They romp and play,
> In a wond'rous way,
>> On tree and shrub and flower;
> And fill the night
> With a radiant light,
>> That falls like a silver shower.

"You do not say anything," said Alice, as Quincy finished reading and remained silent.

He replied, "You have conferred judicial functions upon me and a judge does not give his opinion until the evidence is all in."

"Ah! I see," said Alice. "My knowledge of metrical composition," she continued, "is very limited. What I know of it I learned from an old copy of Fowler's Grammar that I bought at Burnham's on School Street soon after I went to Boston. I have always called what you just read a poem. Is it one?" she asked, looking up with a smile.

"I think it is," replied Quincy, "and," he added inadvertently, "a very pretty one, too."

"Oh! Mr. Judge," laughing outright. "you have given aid and comfort to the prisoner before the evidence was all in."

And Quincy was forced to laugh heartily at the acuteness she had shown in forcing his opinion from him prematurely."

"Now, this one," said Alice, "I call a song. I know which one it is by the size and thickness of the paper." And she handed him a foolscap sheet.

Quincy took it and glanced over it a moment or two before he spoke, Alice leaning forward and listening intently for the first sound of his voice. Then Quincy uttered those ever pleasing words, "Sweet, Sweet Home," and delivered, with great expression, the words of the song.

"You read it splendidly," cried Alice, with evident delight. "Would it be presuming on your kindness if I asked you to read the refrain and chorus once more, Mr. Sawyer?"

"I shall enjoy reading it again myself," remarked Quincy, as he proceeded to comply with Alice's pleasantly worded request.

REFRAIN:

There is no place like home, they say,
No matter where it be;
The lordly mansion of the rich,
The hut of poverty.
The little cot, the tenement,
The white-winged ship at sea;
The heart will always seek its home,
Wherever it may be.

CHORUS:

Sweet, sweet home!
To that sweet piace where youth was passed our
    thoughts will turn;
Sweet, sweet home!
Will send the blood to flaming face, and hearts will burn.

Sweet, sweet home!
It binds us to our native land where'er we roam,
No land so fair, no sky so blue,
As those we find when back we come to sweet, sweet home!

"Of course you know that lovely song, 'Juanita'?" said Alice.

"Certainly," said Quincy, and he sang the first line of the chorus.

Alice's voice joined in with his, and they finished the chorus together. A thrill went through Quincy as he sang the last line, and he was conscious that his voice quivered when he came to the words, "Be my own fair bride."

"You sing with great expression," said Alice. "If you like these new words that I have written to that old melody we can sing them together. I have called it Loved Days. I think this is the one," she said, as she passed him several small sheets pinned together.

"It is," said Quincy, as he took the paper and read it slowly.

As before, he said nothing when he had finished.

"Mr. Judge," said Alice, "would it be improper, from a judicial point of view, for me to ask you which lines in the song you have just read please you the most? But perhaps," said she, looking up at him, "none of them are worthy of repetition."

"If you will consider for a moment," replied Quincy, "that I am off the bench and am just sitting here quietly with you, I will say, confidentially, that I am particularly well pleased with this;" and he read a portion of the first stanza:

On Great Heaven's beauties,
    Gaze the eyes I loved to see,
Done earth's weary duties,
    Now, eternity.

"And," continued Quincy, "I think these lines from the second stanza are fully equal to those I have just read."

But my soul, still living,
Speaks its words of comfort sweet,
Grandest promise giving
That again we'll meet.

"I should think," continued Quincy, "that those words were particularly well suited to be sung at a funeral. I shall have to ask my friend Bradley to have his quartette learn them, so as to be ready when I need them."

"Oh! Mr. Sawyer," cried Alice, with a strong tone of reproof in her voice, "how can you speak so lightly of death?"

"Pardon me," replied Quincy, "if I have unintentionally wounded your feelings, but after all life is only precious to those who have something to live for."

"But you certainly," said Alice, "can see something in life worth living for."

"Yes," assented Quincy, "I can see it, but I am not satisfied in my own mind that I shall ever be able to possess it."

"Oh, you must work and wait and hope!" cried Alice.

"I shall be happy to," he said, "if you will be kind and say an encouraging word to me, so that I may not grow weary of the battle of life."

"I should be pleased to help you all I can," she said sweetly.

"I shall need your help," Quincy remarked gravely, and then with a quick change in tone he said playfully, "I think it is about time for the judge to get back upon the bench."

"This," said Alice, as she passed him a manuscript enclosed in a cover, "is my capital offence. If I escape punishment for my other misdemeanors, I know I shall not when you have read this." And she handed him the paper.

Quincy opened it and read, The Lord of the Sea, a Cantata.

CHARACTERS.

Canute, the Great, King of England and Denmark.
A Courtier.
An Irish Harper.
Queen Emma, the "Flower of Normandy."
Courtiers, Monks, and Gleemen.

PLACE.

Part I.—The palace of the king.
Part II.—The seashore at Southampton.
Time- -About A. D. 1030.

As he proceeded with the reading he became greatly interested in it. He had a fine voice and had taken a prize for oratory at Harvard.

When he finished he turned to Alice and said, "And you wrote that?"

"Certainly," said she. "Can you forgive me?"

Quincy said seriously, "Miss Pettengill, that is a fine poem; it is grand when read, but it would be grander still if set to music. I can imagine," Quincy continued, "how those choruses would sound if sung by the Handel and Haydn Society, backed up by a full orchestra and the big organ." And he sang, to an extemporized melody of his own, the words:

> God bless the king of the English,
> The Lord of the land,
> The Lord of the sea!

"I can imagine," said he, as he rose and stood before Alice, "King Canute as a heavy-voiced basso. How he would bring out these words!

> Great sea! the land on which I stand, is mine;
> Its rocky shores before thy blows quail not.
> Thou, too, O! sea, are part of my domain,
> And, like the land, must bow to my command.
> I'll sit me here! rise not, nor dare to touch,
> With thy wet lips, the ermine of my robe!

"And," cried he, for the moment overcome by his enthusiasm, "how would this sound sung in unison by five hundred well-trained voices?

> For God alone is mighty,
> The Lord of the sea,
> The Lord of the land!
> For He holds the waves of the ocean
> In the hollow of His hand,
> And the strength of the mightiest king
> Is no more than a grain of sand.
> For God alone is mighty,
> The Lord of the sea,
> The Lord of the land!"

As Quincy resumed his seat, Alice clapped her hands to show her approbation of his oratorical effort. Then they both sat in silence for a few minutes, each evidently absorbed in thought.

Suddenly Alice spoke:

"And now, Mr. Sawyer, will you let me ask you a serious question? If I continue writing pieces like these, can I hope to earn enough from it to support myself?"

Quincy thought for a moment, and then said, "I am afraid not. If you would allow me to take them to Boston the next time I go I will try and find out their market value, but editors usually say that poetry is a drug, and they have ten times as much offered them as they can find room for. On the other hand, stories, especially short ones, are eagerly sought and good prices paid for them. Did you ever think of writing a story, Miss Pettengill?"

"Oh, yes!" said Alice, "I have several blocked out, I call it, in my own mind, but it is such a task for me to write that I dare not undertake them. If I could afford to pay an amanuensis it would be different."

Quincy comprehended the situation in a moment. "I like to write, Miss Pettengill," said he, "and time hangs heavily upon my hands. We are likely to have a long spell of winter weather, during which I shall be confined to the house as well as yourself. Take pity on me and give my idle hands something to do."

"Oh, it would be too much to ask," said Alice.

"But you have not asked," answered Quincy. "I have offered you my services without your asking."

"But when could we begin?" asked Alice, hesitatingly.

"At once," replied Quincy. "I brought with me from Boston a half ream of legal paper and a dozen good pencils. I can write faster and much better with a pencil than I can with a pen, and as all legal papers have to be copied, I have got into the habit of using pencils for everything."

It took Quincy but a few minutes to go to his room and secure his paper and pencils. He drew a table close to Alice's chair and sat down beside her.

"What is the name of the story?" asked he.

Alice replied, "I have called it in my mind, 'How He Lost Both Name and Fortune.'"

CHAPTER XXIII.

IT must not be supposed that Alice's story was written out by Quincy in one or even two days. The oldest inhabitants will tell you that the great snowstorm lasted three days and three nights, and it was not till the fourth day thereafter that the roads were broken out, so that safe travel between Eastborough Centre and Mason's Corner became possible.

The day after the storm the sad intelligence came to Quincy and Alice that old Mr. Putnam had passed quietly away on the last day of the storm. Quincy attended the funeral, and he could not help acknowledging to himself that Lindy Putnam never looked more beautiful than in her dress of plain black. The only ornament upon her was a pair of beautiful diamond earrings, but she always wore them, and consequently they were not obtrusive.

Quincy bore an urgent request from Mrs. Putnam that Alice should come to see her. As the story was finished and copied on the seventh day after the storm, Quincy had the old-fashioned sleigh brought out and lined with robes. Taking the horse Old Bill, that sleigh bells or snow slides could not startle from his equanimity, Alice was driven to Mrs. Putnam's, and in a few minutes was clasped to Mrs. Putnam's bosom, the old lady crying and laughing by turns.

Quincy thought it best to leave them alone, and descending the stairs he entered the parlor, the door being halfway open. He started back as he saw a form dressed in black, seated by the window.

"Come in, Mr. Sawyer," said Lindy. "I knew you were

here. I saw you when you drove up with Miss Pettengill.
What a beautiful girl she is, and what a pity that she is
blind. I hope with all my heart that she will recover her
sight."

"She would be pleased to hear you say that," remarked
Quincy.

"We were never intimate," said Lindy. "You can tell
her from me, you are quite the gallant chevalier, Mr. Sawyer, and what you say to her will sound sweeter than if it
came from other lips. Are you going to marry her, Mr.
Sawyer?"

"I do not think that our acquaintance is of such long
standing that you are warranted in asking me so personal
a question," replied Quincy.

"Perhaps not," said Lindy, "but as I happened to know,
though not from your telling, that she is to be my mother's
heiress, I had a little curiosity to learn whether you had
already proposed or were going—"

"Miss Putnam," said Quincy sternly, "do not complete
your sentence. Do not make me think worse of you than
I already do. I beg your pardon for intruding upon you.
I certainly should not have done so had I anticipated such
an interview."

Lindy burst into a flood of tears. Her grief seemed un-
controllable. Quincy closed the parlor door, thinking that
if her cries and sobs were heard upstairs it would require
a double explanation, which it might be hard for him to
give.

He stood and looked at the weeping girl. She had evidently known all along who her mother's heiress was. She
had been fooling him, but for what reason? Was she in
love with him? No, he did not think so; if she had been
she would have confided in him rather than have sought
to force him to confide in her. What could be the motive
for her action? Quincy was nonplussed. He had had

considerable experience with society girls, but they either
relied upon languid grace or light repartee. They never
used tears either for offence or defence.

A surprise was in store for Quincy. Lindy rose from
her chair and came towards him, her eyes red with weeping.

"Why do you hate me so, Mr. Sawyer?" she asked.
"Why will you not be a friend to me, when I need one so
much? What first turned you against me?"

Quincy replied, "I will tell you, Miss Putnam. They told
me you were ashamed of your father and mother because
they were old-fashioned country people and did not dress
as well or talk as good English as you did."

"Who told you so?" asked Lindy.

"It was common talk in the village," he replied.

"I should think you had suffered enough from village
gossip, Mr. Sawyer, not to believe that all that is said is
true."

Quincy winced and colored. It was a keen thrust and
went home.

"Where there is so much smoke there must be some
fire," he answered, rather lamely, as he thought, even to
himself.

"Mr. Sawyer, when I asked you to tell me a little secret
you had in your possession, you refused. I wanted a
friend, but I also wanted a proven friend. No doubt I
took the wrong way to win your friendship, but I am going
to tell you something, Mr. Sawyer, if you will listen to
me, that will at least secure your pity for one who is rich
in wealth but poor in that she has no friends to whom she
can confide her troubles."

Quincy saw that he was in for it, and like a gentleman,
determined to make the best of it, so he said, "Miss Putnam, I will listen to your story, and if, after hearing it, I
can honorably aid you I will do so with pleasure."

Lindy took his hand, which he had half extended, and said, "Come, sit down, Mr. Sawyer. It is a long story, and I am nervous and tired," and she looked down at her black dress.

They sat upon the sofa, he at one end, she at the other.

"Mr. Sawyer," she began abruptly, "I am not a natural-born child of Mr. and Mrs. Putnam. I was adopted by them when but two years of age. I do not know who my father and mother were. I am sure Mrs. Putnam knows, but she will not tell me."

"It could do no harm now that you are a woman grown," said Quincy.

"At first they both loved me," Lindy continued, "but a year after I came here to live their son was born, and from that time on all was changed. Mr. Putnam was never unkind to me but once, but Mrs. Putnam seemed to take delight in blaming me, and tormenting me, and nagging me, until it is a wonder that my disposition is as good as it is, and you know it is not very good," said she to Quincy with a little smile. She resumed her story: "I loved the little boy, Jones I always called him, and as we grew up together he learned to love me and took my part, although he was three years younger than myself. This fact made Mrs. Putnam hate me more than ever. He stayed at home until he was twenty-two, then he went to his father and mother and told them that he loved me and wished to marry me. Both Mr. and Mrs. Putnam flew into a great rage at this. The idea of a brother marrying his sister! They said it was a crime and a sacrilege, and the vengeance of God would surely fall upon us both. Jones told them he had written to a lawyer in Boston, and he had replied that there was no law prohibiting such a marriage. 'But the law of God shines before you like a flaming sword,' said Mrs. Putnam; and Mr. Putnam agreed with her, for she had all his property in her possession." Quincy smiled. "They

packed Jones off to the city at once," said Lindy, "and his
mother gave him five thousand dollars to go into business
with. Jones began speculating, and he was successful from
first to last. In three months he paid back the five thousand dollars his mother had given him, and he never took
a dollar from them after that day. At twenty-six he was
worth one hundred thousand dollars. When I went to Boston I always saw him, and he at last told me he could stand
it no longer. He wanted me to marry him and go to
Europe with him. I told him I must have a week to think
it over. If I decided to go I would be in Boston on a certain day. I would bring my trunk and would stop at a
certain hotel and send word for him to come to me. I used
all possible secrecy in getting my clothes ready, and packed
them away, as I thought, unnoticed, in my trunk, which was
in the attic. Mrs. Putnam must have suspected that I
intended to leave home, and she knew that I would not go
unless to meet her son. The day before I planned going to
Boston, or rather the night before, she entered my room
while I was asleep, took every particle of my clothing, with
the exception of one house dress and a pair of slippers,
and locked me in. They kept me there for a week, and I
wished that I had died there, for when they came to me it
was to tell me that Jones was dead, and I was the cause
of it. I who loved him so!" And the girl's eyes filled with
tears.

"What was the cause of his death?" asked Quincy.

"He was young, healthy, and careless," answered Lindy.
"He took a bad cold and it developed into lung fever.
Even then he claimed it was nothing and would not see a
doctor. One morning he did not come to the office, his
clerk went to his room, but when the doctor was called it
was too late. It was very sad that he should die so, believ-
ing that I had refused to go with him, when I would have
given my life for him. He loved me till death. He left

me all his money, but in his will he expressed the wish that
I would never accept a dollar from his parents. So now
you see why Mrs. Putnam does not make me her heiress.
You think I hate Miss Pettengill because she is going to
give it to her, but truly I do not, Mr. Sawyer. What I
said when you came in I really meant, and I hope you will
be happy, Mr. Sawyer, even as I hoped to be years ago."

Quincy had been greatly interested in Lindy's story, and
that feeling of sympathy for the unhappy and suffering
that always shows itself in a true gentleman rose strongly
in his breast.

"Miss Putnam," said he, "I have wronged you both in
thought and action, but I never suspected what you have
told me. Will you forgive me and allow me to be your
friend? I will try to atone in the future for my misdoings
in the past."

He extended his hand, and Lindy laid hers in his.

"I care not for the past," said she. "I will forget that. I
have also to ask for forgiveness. I, too, have said and done
many things which I would not have said or done, but for
womanly spite and vanity. You see my excuse is not so
good as yours," said she, as she smiled through her tears.

"In what way can I serve you?" asked Quincy. "Why
do you not go to Boston and live? I could introduce you
to many pleasant families."

"What!" cried Lindy. "Me, a waif and a stray! You
are too kind-hearted, Mr. Sawyer. I shall not leave the
woman every one but you thinks to be my mother. When
she is dead I shall leave Eastborough never to return. My
sole object in life from that day will be to find some trace
of my parents or relatives. Now it may happen that
through Mrs. Putnam or Miss Pettengill you may get
some clew that will help me in my search. It is for this
that I wish a friend, and I have a presentiment that some
day you will be able to help me."

Quincy assured her that if it lay in his power any time to be of assistance to her, she could count upon him.

"By the way, Miss Putnam," said he, "how did your investment with Foss & Follansbee turn out? I heard a rumor that the stock fell, and you lost considerable money."

Lindy flushed painfully. "It did drop, Mr. Sawyer, but it rallied again, as you call it, and when they sold out for me I made nearly five thousand dollars; but," and she looked pleadingly up into Quincy's face, "you have forgiven me for that as well as for my other wrong doings."

"For everything up to date," said Quincy, laughing.

At that instant a loud pounding was heard on the floor above.

"Mrs. Putnam is knocking for you," said Lindy. "Miss Pettengill must be ready to go home. Good-by, Mr. Sawyer, and do not forget your unhappy friend."

"I promise to remember her and her quest," said Quincy.

He gave the little hand extended to him a slight pressure and ran up the stairs. As he did so he heard the parlor door close behind him.

As they were driving home, Alice several times took what appeared to be a letter from her muff and held it up as though trying to read it. Quincy glanced towards her.

"Mr. Sawyer, can you keep a secret?" asked Alice.

"I have a big one on my mind now," replied Quincy, "that I would like to confide to some one."

"Why don't you?" asked Alice.

"As soon as I can find a person whom I think can fully sympathize with me I shall do so, but for the present I must bear my burden in silence," said he.

"I hope you will not have to wait long before finding that sympathetic friend," remarked Alice.

"I hope so, too," he replied. "But I have not answered

your question, Miss Pettengill. If I can serve you by sharing a secret with you, it shall be safe with me."

"Will you promise not to speak of it, not even to me?" she asked.

"If you wish it I will promise," he answered.

"Then please read to me what is written on that envelope."

Quincy looked at the envelope. "It is written in an old-fashioned, cramped hand," he said, "and the writing is 'confided to Miss Alice Pettengill, and to be destroyed without being read by her within twenty-four hours after my death. Hepsibeth Putnam.'"

"Thank you," said Alice simply, and she replaced the envelope in her muff.

Like a flash of lightning the thought came to Quincy that the letter to be destroyed had some connection with the strange story so recently told him by Lindy. He must take some action in the matter before it was too late. Turning to Alice he said, "Miss Pettengill, if I make a strange request of you, which you can easily grant, will you do it, and not ask me for any explanation until after you have complied?"

"You have worded your inquiry so carefully, Mr. Sawyer, that I am a little afraid of you, you being a lawyer, but as you have so graciously consented to keep a secret with me, I will trust you and will promise to comply with your request."

"All I ask is," said Quincy, "that before you destroy that letter, you will let me read to you once more what is written upon the envelope."

"Why, certainly," said Alice, "how could I refuse so harmless a request as that?"

"I am greatly obliged for your kindness," said Quincy to her; but he thought to himself, "I will find out what is in that envelope, if there is any honorable way of doing so."

Hiram came over to see Mandy that evening, and Mrs. Crowley, who was in the best of spirits, sang several old-time Irish songs to them, Hiram and Mandy joining in the choruses. They were roasting big red apples on the top of the stove and chestnuts in the oven. Quincy, attracted by the singing, came downstairs to the kitchen, and was invited to join in the simple feast. He then asked Mrs. Crowley to sing for him, which she did, and he repaid her by singing, "The Harp That Once Thro' Tara's Halls" so sweetly that tears coursed down the old woman's cheeks, and she said, "My poor boy Tom, that was killed in the charge at Bala-klava, used to sing just like that."

Then the poor woman began weeping so violently that Mandy coaxed her off to bed and left the room with her.

When Hiram and Quincy were alone together, the latter said: "Any news, Hiram?"

"Not much," replied Hiram. "The snow is too deep, and it's too darned cold for the boys to travel 'round and do much gossipin' this weather. A notice is pasted up on Hill's grocery that it'll be sold by auction next Tuesday at three o'clock in the afternoon. And I got on to one bit of news. Strout and his friends are goin' to give Huldy Mason a surprise party. They have invited me and Mandy simply because they want you to hear all about it. But they don't propose to invite you, nor 'Zeke, nor his sister."

"Has Strout got anybody to back him up on buying the grocery store?" asked Quincy.

"Yes," said Hiram, "he has got two thousand dollars pledged, and I hear he wants five hundred dollars more. He don't think the whole thing will run over twenty-five hundred dollars."

"How much is to be paid in cash?" Quincy inquired.

"Five hundred dollars," said Hiram; "and that's what troubles Strout. His friends will endorse his notes and take a mortgage on the store, for they know it's a good

"QUINCY READING ALICE'S LETTER TO HER." (ACT III.)

payin' business. They expect to get their money back with good interest, but it comes kinder hard on them to plunk down five hundred dollars in cold cash."

At that moment Mandy returned, and after asking her for a spoon and a plate upon which to take a roast apple and some chestnuts upstairs, Quincy left the young couple together. As he sat before the fire enjoying his lunch, he resolved that he would buy that grocery store, cost what it might, and that 'Zeke Pettengill, Alice, and himself would go to that surprise party.

CHAPTER XXIV.

THE NEW DOCTOR.

QUINCY improved the first opportunity offered for safe travelling to make a visit to the city. He had several matters to attend to. First, he had not sent his letter to his friend, requesting him to make inquiries as to Obadiah Strout's war record, for the great snowstorm had come the day after he had written it. Second, he was going to take Alice's story to show to a literary friend, and see if he could secure its publication. And this was not all; Alice had told him, after he had finished copying the story she had dictated to him, that she had written several other short stories during the past two years.

In response to his urgent request, she allowed him to read her treasured manuscripts. The first was a passionate love story in which a young Spanish officer, stationed on the island of Cuba, and a beautiful young Cuban girl were the principals. It was entitled "Her Native Land," and was replete with startling situations and effective tableaus. Quincy was delighted with it, and told Alice if dramatized it would make a fine acting play. This was, of course, very pleasing to the young author. Quincy was her amanuensis, her audience, and her critic, and she knew that in his eyes she was already a success.

She also gave him to read a series of eight stories, in a line usually esteemed quite foreign to feminine instincts. Alice had conceived the idea of a young man, physically weak and suffering from nervous debility, being left an immense fortune at the age of twenty-one. His money was well invested, and in company with a faithful attendant he travelled for fifteen years, covering every nook and corner of the habitable globe. At thirty-six he returned home much improved in health, but still having a marked aversion to engaging in any business pursuit. A mysterious case and its solution having been related to him, he resolved to devote his income, now amounting to a million dollars yearly, to amateur detective work. His great desire was to ferret out and solve mysteries, murders, suicides, rob- beries, and disappearances that baffled the police and eluded their vigilant inquiry.

The titles that Alice had chosen for her stories were as mysterious, in their way, as the stories themselves. Ar- ranged in the order of their writing, they were: Was it Signed? The Man Without a Tongue; He Thought He Was Dead; The Eight of Spades; The Exit of Mrs. Del- monnay; How I Caught the Fire-Bugs; The Hot Hand; and The Mystery of Unreachable Island.

When Quincy reached the city, his first visit was to his father's office, but he found him absent. He was told that he was conducting a case in the Equity Session of the Supreme Court, and would not return to the office that day.

Instead of leaving his letter at his friend's office, he went directly to the Adjutant-General's office at the State House. Here he found that an acquaintance of his was employed as a clerk. He was of foreign birth, but had served gal- lantly through the war and had left an arm upon the battle- field. He made his request for a copy of the war record of Obadiah Strout, of the —th Mass. Volunteers. Then a thought came suddenly to him and he requested one also of the record of Hiram Maxwell of the same regiment.

Leaving the State House on the Hancock Avenue side, he walked down that narrow but convenient thoroughfare, and was standing at its entrance to the sidewalk on Beacon Street, debating which publisher he would call on first, when a cheery voice said, "Hello, Sawyer." When he

looked up he saw an old Latin School and college chum,
named Leopold Ernst. Ernst was a Jew, but he had been
one of the smartest and most popular of the boys in school
and of the men at Harvard.

"What are you up to?" asked Ernst.

"Living on my small fortune and my father's bounty,"
said Quincy. "Not a very creditable record, I know, but
my health has not been very good, and I have been resting
for a couple of months in the country."

"Not much going on in the country at this time of the
year I fancy," remarked Ernst.

"That's where you are wrong," said Quincy. "There
has been the devil to pay ever since I landed in the town,
and I've got mixed up in so many complications that I don't
expect to get back to town before next Christmas. But
what are you doing, Ernst?"

"Oh, I am in for literature; not the kind that consists in
going round with a notebook and prying into people's business, with a hope one day of becoming an editor, and working twenty hours out of the twenty-four each day. Not a
bit of it, I am reader for ——;" and he mentioned the name
of a large publishing house. "I have my own hours and a
comfortable salary. I sit like Solomon upon the efforts
of callow authors and the productions of ripened genius.
Sometimes I discover a diamond in the rough, and introduce
a new star to the literary firmament; and at other times I
cut up some egotistical old writer, who thinks anything he
turns out will be sure to please the public."

"How fortunate that I have met you?" said Quincy.
"I have in this little carpet bag the first effusions of one of
those callow authors of whom you spoke. She is poor,
beautiful, and blind."

"Don't try to trade on my sympathies, old boy," said
Ernst. "No person who is poor has any right to become
an author. It takes too long in these days to make a hit,

and the poor author is bound to die before the hit comes. The 'beautiful' gag don't work with me at all. The best authors are homelier than sin and it's a pity that their pictures are ever published. As regards the 'blind' part, that may be an advantage, for dictating relieves one of the drudgery of writing one's self, and gives one a chance for a fuller play of one's fancies than if tied to a piece of wood, a scratchy pen, and a bottle of thick ink."

"Then you won't look at them," said Quincy.

"I didn't say so," replied Ernst. "Of course, I can't look at them in a business way, unless they are duly submitted to my house, but I have been reading a very badly written, but mightily interesting manuscript, for the past two days and a half, and I want a change of work or diversion, to brush up my wits. Now, old fellow," said he, taking Quincy by the arm, "if you will come up to the club with me, and have a good dinner with some Chianti, and a glass or two of champagne, and a pousse cafe to finish up with, then we will go up to my rooms on Chestnut Street—I have a whole top floor to myself—we will light up our cigars, and you may read to me till to-morrow morning and I won't murmur. But, mind you, if the stories are mighty poor I may go to sleep, and if I do that, you might as well go to bed too, for when I once go to sleep I never wake up till I get good and ready."

Quincy had intended after seeing a publisher to leave the manuscripts for examination, then to take tea with his mother and sisters, and go back to Eastborough on the five minutes past six express. But he was prone to yield to fate, which is simply circumstances, and he accepted his old college chum's invitation with alacrity. He could get the opinion of an expert speedily, and that fact carried the day with him.

When they were comfortably ensconced in their easy-chairs on the top floor, and the cigars lighted, Quincy commenced reading. Leopold had previously shown him his suite, which consisted of a parlor, or rather a sitting-room, a library, which included principally the works of standard authors and reference books, his sleeping apartment, and a bathroom.

There was a large bed lounge in the sitting-room, and Quincy determined to read every story in his carpet bag, if it took him all night. He commenced with the series of detective or mystery stories. He had read them over before and was able to bring out their strong points oratorically, for, as it has been said before, he was a fine speaker.

Quincy eyed Ernst over the corner of the manuscript he was reading, but the latter understood his business. Occasionally he was betrayed into a nod of approval and several times shook his head in a negative way, but he uttered no word of commendation or disapproval.

After several of the stories had been read, Ernst called a halt, and going to a cupboard brought out some crackers, cake, and a decanter of wine, with glasses, which he put upon a table, and placed within comfortable reach of both reader and listener. Then he said, "Go ahead," munched a cracker, sipped his wine, and then lighted a fresh cigar.

When the series was finished, Leopold said, "Now we will have some tea. I do a good deal of my reading at home, and I don't like to go out again after I have crawled up four flights of stairs, so my landlady sends me up a light supper at just about this hour. There is the maid now," as a light knock was heard on the door.

Leopold opened it, and the domestic brought in a tray with a pot of tea and the ingredients of a light repast, which she placed upon another table near a window.

"There is always enough for two," said Leopold. "Reading is mighty tiresome work, and listening is too, and a cup of good strong tea will brighten us both up immensely.

You can come back for the tray in fifteen minutes, Jennie," said Ernst.

The supper was finished, the tray removed, and the critic sat in judgment once more upon the words that fell from the reader's lips. Leopold's face lighted up during the reading of "Her Native Land." He started to speak, and the word "That's—" escaped him, but he recovered himself and said no more, though he listened intently.

Quincy took a glass of wine and a cracker before starting upon the story which had been dictated to him. Leopold gave no sign of falling asleep, but patted his hands lightly together at certain points in the story, whether contemplatively or approvingly Quincy could not determine. As he read the closing lines of the last manuscript the cuckoo clock struck twelve, midnight.

"You are a mighty good reader, Quincy," said Leopold, "and barring fifteen minutes for refreshments, you have been at it ten hours. Now you want my opinion of those stories, and what's more, you want my advice as to the best place to put them to secure their approval and early publication. Now I am going to smoke a cigar quietly and think the whole thing over, and at half past twelve I will give you my opinion in writing. I am going into my library for half an hour to write down what I have to say. You take a nap on the lounge there, and you will be refreshed when I come back after having made mince meat of your poor, beautiful, blind *protégé*."

Leopold disappeared into the library, and Quincy stretching himself on the lounge, rested, but did not sleep. Before he had realized that ten minutes had passed, Leopold stood beside him with a letter sheet in his hand, and said, "Now, Quincy, read this to me, and I will see if I have got it down straight."

Quincy's hand trembled nervously as he seated himself

in his old position and turning the sheet so that the light would fall upon it, he read the following:

Opinion of Leopold Ernst, Literary Critic, of certain manuscripts submitted for examination by Quincy A. Sawyer, with some advice gratis.

1.   Series of eight stories.   Mighty clever general idea; good stories well written.   Same style maintained throughout; good plots.   Our house could not handle them—not of our line.   Send to ——.   (Here followed the name of a New York publisher.)   I will write Cooper, one of their readers.   He is a friend of mine, and will secure quick decision, which, I prophesy, will be favorable.

2.   "Her Native Land" is a fine story.   I can get it into a weekly literary paper that our house publishes.   I know Jameson, the reader, will take it, especially if you would give him the right to dramatize it.   He is hand and glove with all the theatre managers and has had several successes.

3.   That story about the Duke, I want for our magazine. It is capital, and has enough meat in it to make a full-blown novel.   All it wants is oysters, soup, fish, entrees, and a dessert prefixed to and joined on to the solid roast and game which the story as now written itself supplies.

In Witness Whereof, I have hereunto set my hand, this 24th day of February, 186—.

LEOPOLD ERNST, Literary Critic.

Quincy remained all night with Leopold, sleeping on the bed lounge in the sitting-room.   He was up at six o'clock the next morning, but found that his friend was also an early riser, for on entering the library he saw the latter seated at his desk regarding the pile of manuscript which Quincy had read to him.

Leopold looked up with a peculiar expression on his face.

"What's the matter," asked Quincy, "changing your mind?"

"No," said Leopold, "I never do that, it would spoil my value as a reader if I did. My decisions are as fixed as the laws of the Medes and Persians, and are regarded by literary aspirants as being quite as severe as the statutes of Draco; but the fact is, Quincy, you and your *protégé*—you see I consider you equally culpable—have neglected to put any real name or pseudonym to these interesting stories. Of course I can affix the name of the most popular author that the world has ever known,—Mr. Anonymous,—but you two probably have some pet name that you wish immortalized."

"By George!" cried Quincy, "we did forget that. I will talk it over with her, and send you the *nom de plume* by mail.

"Very well," said Leopold, rising. "And now let us go and have some breakfast."

"My dear fellow, you must excuse me. I have not seen my parents this trip, and I ought to go up to the house and take breakfast with the family."

"All right," said Leopold, "rush that pseudonym right along, so I can send the manuscripts to Cooper. And don't forget to drop in and see me next time you come to the city."

On his way to Beacon Street Quincy suddenly stopped and regarded a sign that read, Paul Culver, M. D., physician and surgeon. He knew Culver, but hadn't seen him for eight years. They were in the Latin School together under *pater* Gardner. He rang the bell and was shown into Dr. Culver's office, and in a few minutes his old schoolmate entered. Paul Culver was a tall, broad-chested, heavily-built young man, with frank blue eyes, and hair of the color that is sometimes irreverently called, or rather the wearers of it are called, towheads.

They had a pleasant talk over old school days and college experiences, which were not identical, for Paul had grad-

uated from Yale College at his father's desire, instead of
from Harvard. Then Quincy broached what was upper-
most in his mind and which had been the real reason for
his call. He stated briefly the facts concerning Alice's case,
and asked Paul's advice.

Dr. Culver sat for a few moments apparently in deep
study.

"My advice," said he, "is to see Tillotson. He has an
office in the Hotel Pelham, up by the Public Library, you
know."

"Is he a 'regular'?" asked Quincy.

"Well," said Culver, "I don't think he is. For a fact I
know he is not an M. D., but I fancy that the diploma that
he holds from the Almighty is worth more to suffering
humanity than a good many issued by the colleges."

"You are a pretty broad-minded allopath," said Quincy,
"to give such a sweeping recommendation to a quack."

"I didn't say he was a quack," replied Culver. "He is a
natural-born healer, and he uses only nature's remedies in
his practice. Go and see him, Quincy, and judge for yourself."

"But," said Quincy, "I had hoped that you—"

"But I couldn't," broke in Paul. "I am an emergency
doctor. If baby has the croup, or Jimmy has the measles, or
father has the lung fever, they call me in, and I get them
well as soon as possible. But if mother-in-law has some
obscure complaint I am too busy to give the time to study
it up, and they wouldn't pay me for it if I did. Medicine,
like a great many other things, is going into the hands of
the specialists eventually, and Tillotson is one of the first of
the new school."

At that moment a maid announced that some one wished
to see Dr. Culver, and Quincy took a hurried leave.

He found his father, mother, and sisters at home, and
breakfast was quickly served after his arrival. They all

said he was looking much better, and all asked him when
he was coming home. He gave an evasive answer, saying
that there were lots of good times coming down in Eastborough and he didn't wish to miss them. He told his
father he was improving his time reading and writing, and
would give a good account of himself when he did return.

He had to wait an hour before he could secure an interview with Dr. Tillotson. The latter had a spare day in each
week, that day being Thursday, which he devoted to cases
that he was obliged to visit personally. Quincy arranged
with him to visit Eastborough on the following Thursday,
and by calling a carriage managed to catch the half-past
eleven train for that town, and reached his boarding place
a little before two o'clock. He had arranged with the driver
to wait for a letter that he wished to have mailed to Boston
that same afternoon.

He went in by the back door, and as he passed through
the kitchen, Mandy made a sign, and he went to her.

"Hiram waited till one o'clock," said she, "but he had to
go home, and he wanted me to tell you that the surprise
party is coming off next Monday night, and they are going
to get there at seven o'clock, so as to have plenty of time
for lots of fun, and Hiram suspects," and her voice fell to a
whisper, "that Strout is going to try and work the Deacon
for that five hundred in cash to put up for the grocery store
next Tuesday. That's all," said she.

"Where is Miss Pettengill?" Quincy inquired.

"She's in the parlor," said Mandy. "She has been playing the piano and singing beautifully, but I guess she has
got tired."

Quincy went directly to the parlor and found Alice seated
before the open fire, her right hand covering her eyes.

She looked up as Quincy entered the room and said, "I
am so glad you've got back, Mr. Sawyer. I have been very
lonesome since you have been away."

Alice did not see the happy smile that spread over
Quincy's face, and he covered up his pleasure by saying,
"How did you know it was I?"

"Oh," said Alice, "my hearing is very acute. I know
the step of every person in the house. Swiss has been with
me all the morning, but he asked a few minutes ago to be
excused, so he could get his dinner."

Quincy laughed, and then said, "Miss Pettengill, we forgot a very important matter in connection with your stories;
we omitted to put on the name of the author." He told her
of his meeting with Ernst, and what had taken place, and
Alice was delighted. Quincy did not refer to the coming
visit of Dr. Tillotson, for he did not mean to speak of it
until the day appointed arrived. "Now, Miss Pettengill,
I have some letters to write to send back by the hotel carriage, so that they can be mailed this afternoon. While I
am doing this you can decide upon your pseudonym, and I
will put it in the letter that I am going to write to Ernst."

Quincy went up to his room and sat down at his writing
table. The first letter was to his bankers, and enclosed a
check for five hundred dollars, with a request to send the
amount in bills by Adams Express to Eastborough Centre,
to reach there not later than noon of the next Tuesday,
and to be held until called for. The second letter was to a
prominent confectioner and caterer in Boston, ordering
enough ice cream, sherbet, frozen pudding, and assorted
cake for a party of fifty persons, and fifty grab-bag presents;
all to reach Eastborough Centre in good order on Monday
night on the five minutes past six express from Boston.
The third letter was to Ernst. It was short and to the point.
"The pseudonym is—" And he left a blank space for the
name. Then he signed his own. He glanced over his writing table and saw the three poems that Alice had given him
to read. He added a postscript to his letter to Ernst. It
read as follows:

"I enclose three poems written by the same person who wrote the stories. Tell me what you think of them, and if you can place them anywhere do so, and this shall be your warrant therefor. Q. A. S."

When his mail was in readiness he went downstairs to the parlor, taking a pen and bottle of ink with him, and saying to himself, "That pseudonym shall not be written in pencil."

"I am in a state of hopeless indecision," remarked Alice. "I can think of Christian names that please me, and surnames that please me, but when I put them together they don't please me at all."

"Then we will leave it to fate," said Quincy. He tore a sheet of paper into six pieces and passed three, with a book and pencil, to Alice. "Now you write," said he, "three Christian names that please you, and I will write three surnames that please me; then we will put the pieces in my hat, and you will select two and what you select shall be the name."

"That's a capital idea," said Alice, "it is harder to select a name than it was to write the story."

The slips were written, placed in the hat, shaken up, and Alice selected two, which she held up for Quincy to read.

"This is not fair," said Quincy. "I never thought. Both of the slips are mine. We must try again."

"No," said Alice, "it is 'Kismet.' What are the names?" she asked.

"Bruce Douglas, or Douglas Bruce, as you prefer," said Quincy.

"I like Bruce Douglas best," replied Alice.

"I am so glad," said Quincy, "that's the name I should have selected myself."

"Then I will bear your name in future," said Alice, and Quincy thought to himself that he wished she had said those words in response to a question that was in his mind, but which he had decided it was not yet time to ask her. He was too much of a gentleman to refer in a joking manner to the words which Alice had spoken and which had been uttered with no thought or idea that they bore a double meaning.

Quincy wrote the selected name in the blank space in Leopold's letter, sealed it and took his mail out to the carriage driver, who was seated in the kitchen enjoying a piece of mince pie and a mug of cider which Mandy had given him.

As Quincy entered the kitchen he heard Mandy say, "How is 'Bias nowadays?"

"Oh, dad's all right," said the young man; "he is going to run Wallace Stackpole again for tax collector against Obadiah Strout."

"Is your name Smith?" asked Quincy, advancing with the letters in his hand.

"Yes," replied the young man, "my name is Abbott Smith. My dad's name is 'Bias; he is pretty well known 'round these parts."

"I have heard of him," said Quincy, "and I wish to see him and Mr. Stackpole together. Can you come over for me next Wednesday morning and bring Mr. Stackpole with you? I can talk to him going back, and I want you to drive us over to your father's place. Don't say anything about it except to Mr. Stackpole and your father, but I am going to take a hand in town politics this year."

The young man laughed and said, "I will be over here by eight o'clock next Wednesday."

"I wish you would have these letters weighed at the post office, and if any more stamps are needed please put them on. Take what is left for your trouble," and Quincy passed Abbott a half dollar.

He heard the retreating carriage wheels as he went upstairs to his room. He made an entry in his pocket diary, and then ran his eye over several others that preceded and followed it.

"Let me see," soliloquized he, as he read aloud, "this is Friday; Saturday, expect war records from Adjutant-General; Monday, hear from Ernst, surprise party in the evening; Tuesday, get money at express office; Tuesday afternoon, buy Hill's grocery and give Strout his first knock-out; Wednesday, see Stackpole and Smith and arrange to knock Strout out again; Thursday, Dr. Tillotson." He laughed and closed the book. Then he said, "And the city fellows think it must be dull down here because there is nothing going on in a country town in the winter."

CHAPTER XXV.

THE next day was Saturday; the sun did not show itself from behind the clouds till noon, and Quincy put off his trip to the Eastborough Centre post office with the hope that the afternoon would be pleasant. His wish was gratified, and at dinner he said he was going to drive over to Eastborough Centre, and asked Miss Pettengill if she would not like to accompany him. Alice hesitated, but Uncle Ike advised her to go, telling her that she stayed indoors too much and needed outdoor exercise. Ezekiel agreed with his uncle, and Alice finally gave what seemed to Quincy to be a somewhat reluctant consent.

He saw that the sleigh was amply supplied with robes, and Mandy, at his suggestion, heated a large piece of soapstone, which was wrapped up and placed in the bottom of the sleigh.

Alice appeared at the door equipped for her journey. Always lovely in Quincy's eyes, she appeared still more so in her suit of dark blue cloth. Over her shoulders she wore a fur cape lined with quilted red satin, and on her head a fur cap, which made a strong contrast with her light hair which crept out in little curls from underneath.

They started off at a smart speed, for Old Bill was not in the shafts this time. Alice had been familiar with the road to Eastborough before leaving home, and as Quincy described the various points they passed, Alice entered into the spirit of the drive with all the interest and enthusiasm of a child. The sharp winter air brought a rosy bloom to her cheeks, and as Quincy looked at those wonderful large blue eyes, he could hardly make himself believe that they could not see him. He was sure he had never seen a handsomer girl.

As they passed Uncle Ike's little house, Quincy called her attention to it. Alice said:

"Poor Uncle Ike, I wish I could do more for him, he has done so much for me. He paid for my lessons in book-keeping and music, and also for my board until I had finished my studies and obtained a position. He has been a father to me since my own dear father died."

Quincy felt some inclination to find out the real reason why Uncle Ike had left his family, but he repressed it and called attention to some trees, heavily coated with snow and ice, which looked beautiful in the sunshine, and he described them so graphically, bringing in allusions to pearls and diamonds and strings of glistening jewels, that Alice clapped her hands in delight and said she would take him as her literary partner, to write in the descriptive passages. Quincy for an instant felt impelled to take advantage of the situation, but saying to himself, "The time is not yet," he touched the horse with his whip and for half a minute was obliged to give it his undivided attention.

"Did you think the horse was running away?" said he to Alice, when he had brought him down to a trot. "Were you afraid?"

"I am afraid of nothing nowadays," she replied. "I trust my companions implicitly, knowing that they will tell me if I am in danger and advise me what to do. I had a debate a long time ago with Uncle Ike about blind people and deaf people. He said he would rather be stone deaf than blind. As he argued it, the deaf person could read and write and get along very comfortably by himself. I argued on the other side. I wish to hear the voices of my friends when they talk and sing and read, and then, you know, everybody lends a helping hand to a person who is blind, but the deaf person must look out for himself."

"Either state is to be regretted, if there is no hope of re-lief," remarked Quincy. He thought he would refer to Dr. Tillotson, but they were approaching the centre of the town, and he knew he would not have time to explain his action before he reached the post office, so he determined to postpone it until they were on the way home.

There were three letters for himself, two for Alice and a lot of papers and magazines for Uncle Ike. He resumed his seat in the sleigh and they started on their journey homeward.

"Would you like to go back the same way that we came?" asked Quincy, "or shall we go by the upper road and come by Deacon Mason's?"

"I should like to stop and see Huldy," said Alice, and Quincy took the upper road.

Conversation lagged on the homeward trip. Alice held her two letters in her hand and looked at them several times, apparently trying to recognize the handwriting. As Quincy glanced at her sidewise, he felt sure that he saw tears in her eyes, and he decided that it would be an in-appropriate time to announce the subject of the new doctor. In fact, he was beginning to think, the more his mind dwelt upon the subject, that he had taken an inexcusable liberty in arranging for Dr. Tillotson to come down without first speaking to her, or at least to her brother or uncle. But the deed was done, and he must find some way to have her see the doctor, and get his opinion about her eyes.

Quincy spent so much time revolving this matter in his mind, that he was quite astonished when he looked around and found himself at the exact place where he spoke those words to Huldy Mason that had ended in the accident. This time he gave careful attention to horse and hill and curve, and a moment later he drew up the sleigh at Deacon Mason's front gate.

Mrs. Mason welcomed them at the door and they were

shown into the parlor, where Huldy sat at the piano. The young girls greeted each other warmly, and Mrs. Mason and Huldy both wished Quincy and Alice to stay to tea. They declined, saying they had many letters to read before supper and 'Zekiel would think something had happened to them if they did not come home.

"I will send Hiram down to let them know," said Mrs. Mason.

"You must really excuse us this time," protested Quincy. "Some other time perhaps Miss Pettengill will accept your hospitality."

"But when?" asked Mrs. Mason. "We might as well fix a time right now."

"Yes," said Huldy, "and we won't let them go till they promise."

"Well, my plan," said Mrs. Mason, "is this. Have 'Zekiel and Alice and Mr. Sawyer come over next Monday afternoon about five o'clock, and we will have tea at six, and we will have some music in the evening. I have so missed your singing, Mr. Sawyer, since you went away."

"Yes," said Huldy, "I think it is real mean of you, Alice, not to let him come and see us oftener."

Alice flushed and stammered, "I—I—I do not keep him from coming to see you. Why, yes, I have too," said she, as a thought flashed through her mind. "I will tell you the truth, Mrs. Mason. Mr. Sawyer offered to do some writing for me, and I have kept him very busy."

She stopped and Quincy continued:

"I did do a little writing for her, Mrs. Mason, during the great snowstorm, and it was as great a pleasure to me, as I hope it was a help to her, for I had nothing else to do."

"Well," said Mrs. Mason, "you can settle that matter between yer. All that Huldy and me wants to know is, will all three of you come and take tea with us next Monday night?"

"I shall be greatly pleased to do so," said Quincy.

"If 'Zekiel will come, I will," said Alice, and Quincy for an instant felt a slight touch of wounded feeling because Alice had ignored him entirely in accepting the invitation.

As they drove home, Alice said: "Mrs. Mason managed that nicely, didn't she? I didn't wish to appear too eager to come, for Huldy might have suspected."

"What mystery is this?" asked Quincy. "I really don't know what you are talking about."

"What!" said Alice. "Didn't 'Zekiel tell you about the surprise party that Mr. Strout was getting up, and that you, 'Zekiel, and I were not to be invited?"

"Oh! I see," said Quincy. "How stupid I have been! I knew all about it and that it was to be next Monday, but Mrs. Mason asked us so honestly to come to tea, and Huldy joined in so heartily, that for the time being I got things mixed, and besides, to speak frankly, Miss Pettengill, I was thinking of something else."

"And what was it?" asked Alice.

"Well," said Quincy, determined to break the ice, "I will tell you. I was wondering why you said you would come to tea if 'Zekiel would come."

"Oh!" said Alice, laughing. "You thought I was very ungenerous to leave you out of the question entirely."

"Honestly I did think so," remarked Quincy.

"Well, now," said Alice, "I did it from the most generous of motives. I thought you knew about the surprise party as well as I did. I knew 'Zekiel would go with me and I thought that perhaps you had some other young lady in view for your companion."

"What?" asked Quincy. "Whom could I have had in view?"

"Shall I tell you whom I think?" asked Alice.

"I wish you would," Quincy replied.

"Well," said Alice, "I thought it might be Lindy Putnam."

Quincy bit his lip and gave the reins a savage jerk, as
he turned up the short road that led to the Pettengill
house. "What could make you think that, Miss Pettengill?"

"Well, I have only one reason to give," Alice replied,
"for that opinion, but the fact is, when we made our call
on Mrs. Putnam she pounded on the floor three times with
her crutch before you came upstairs. Am I justified, Mr.
Sawyer?"

"I'm afraid you are," said Quincy. "I should have
thought so myself if I had been in your place."

But when he reached his room he threw his letters on
the table, his coat and hat on the bed, and thrusting his
hands into his pockets, he walked rapidly up and down the
room, saying to himself in a savage whisper, "Confound
that Putnam girl; she is a hoodoo."

Quincy was philosophical, and his excited feelings soon
quieted down. It would come out all right in the end.
Alice would find that he had not intended to take Miss
Putnam to the surprise party. He could not betray Lindy's
confidence just at that time, even to justify himself. He
must wait until Mrs. Putnam died. It might be years from
now before the time came to destroy that letter, and he
could not, until then, disclose to Alice the secret that Lindy
had confided to him. Yes, it would come out all right in
the end, for it might be if Alice thought he was in love with
Lindy that she would give more thought to him. He had
read somewhere that oftentimes the best way to awaken a
dormant love was to appear to fall in love with some one
else.

Somewhat reconciled to the situation by his thoughts,
he sat down to read his letters. The first one that he took
up was from the confectioner. It informed him that his

order would receive prompt attention, and the writer
thanked him for past favors and solicited a continuance of
the same. The second was from Ernst. It was short and
to the point, and written in his characteristic style. It said:

"Dear Quincy:—Pseudonym received. Bruce Douglas is
a name to conjure with. It smacks of 'Auld Lang Syne.'
The Scotch are the only people on the face of the earth who
were never conquered. You will remember, if you haven't
forgotten your ancient history, that the Roman general sent
back word to his emperor that the d—d country wasn't
worth conquering. Enclosures also at hand. The shorter
ones are more songs than poems. I will turn them over to a
music publisher, who is a friend of mine. Will report his
decision later.

"I gave the long poem to Francis Lippitt, the well-known
composer, and he is delighted with it and wishes to set it to
music. He is great on grand choruses, Bach fugues, and
such like. If he sets it to music he will have it sung by the
Handel and Haydn Society, for he is a great gun among
them just now. The eight stories have reached New York
by this time, and Jameson is reading 'Her Native Land.'

"With best regards to Mr. Bruce Douglas and yourself.

LEOPOLD ERNST.

The third letter was from the Adjutant-General's office,
and Quincy smiled as he finished the first sheet, folded it
up and replaced it in the envelope. As he read the second
the smile left his face. "Who would have thought it?" he
said to himself. "Well, after all, heroes are made out of
strange material. He is the man for my money and I'll
back him up, and beat that braggart."

On the following Sunday, after dinner, Quincy had a
chat with Uncle Ike. He took the opportunity of asking
the old gentleman if he was fully satisfied with the progress
towards recovery that his niece was making.

"I don't see that she is making any progress," said Uncle Ike frankly. "I don't think she can see a bit better than she could when she came home. In fact, I don't think she can see as well. She had a pair of glasses made of black rubber, with a pinhole in the centre of them, that she could read a little with, but I notice now that she never puts them on."

"Well," remarked Quincy, "perhaps I have taken an unwarrantable liberty, Uncle Ike; but when I was last in Boston I heard of a new doctor who has made some wonderful cures, and I have engaged him to come down here next week and see your niece. Of course, if you object I will write to him not to come, and no harm will be done."

Quincy did not think it necessary to state that he had paid the doctor his fee of one hundred dollars in advance.

"Well," said Uncle Ike, "I certainly sha'n't object, if the doctor can do her any good. But I should like to know something about the course of treatment, the nature of it, I mean, before she gives up her present doctor."

"That's just what I mean," said Quincy. "I want you to be so kind as to take this whole matter off my hands, just as though I had made the arrangement at your suggestion. I am going down for the doctor next Thursday noon. Won't you ride down with me and meet Dr. Tillotson? You can talk to him on the way home, and then you can manage the whole matter yourself, and do as you think best about changing doctors."

"You have been very kind to my niece, Mr. Sawyer, since you have been here," said Uncle Ike, "and very helpful to her. I attribute your interest in her case to your kindness of heart and a generosity which is seldom found in the sons of millionaires. But take my advice, Mr. Sawyer, and let your feelings stop there."

"I do not quite understand you," replied Quincy, though from a sudden sinking of his heart he felt that he did.

"Then I will speak plainer," said Uncle Ike. "Don't fall in love with my niece, Mr. Sawyer. She is a good girl, a sweet girl, and some might call her a beautiful one, but she has her limitations. She is not fitted to sit in a Beacon Street parlor; and your parents and sisters would not be pleased to have you place her there. Excuse an old man, Mr. Sawyer, but you know wisdom cometh with age, although its full value is not usually appreciated by the young."

Quincy, for the first time in his life, was entirely at a loss for a reply. He burned to declare his love then and there; but how could he do so in the face of such a plain statement of facts? He did the best thing possible under the circumstances; he quietly ignored Uncle Ike's advice, and thanking him for his kindness in consenting to meet the new doctor he bade him good afternoon and went to his room.

After Quincy had gone Uncle Ike rubbed his hands together gleefully and shook with laughter.

"The sly rogue!" he said to himself. "Wanted Uncle Ike to help him out." Then he laughed again. "If he don't love her he will take my advice, but if he does, what I told him will drive him on like spurs in the side of a horse. He is a good fellow, a great deal better than his father and the rest of his family, for he isn't stuck up. I like him, but my Alice is good enough for him even if he were a good deal better than he is. How it would tickle me to hear my niece calling the Hon. Nathaniel Sawyer papa!" And Uncle Ike laughed until his sides shook.

Monday promised to be a dull day. 'Zekiel told Quincy at breakfast, after the others had left the table, that Alice had spoken to him about Mrs. Mason's invitation to tea, and, of course, he was going. Quincy said that he had accepted the invitation and would be pleased to accompany him and his sister.

After breakfast he heard Alice singing in the parlor, and joining her there told her that he had received a letter from Mr. Ernst, which he would like to read to her. Alice was delighted with the letter, and they both laughed heartily over it, Quincy humorously apologizing for the swear word by saying that being historical it could not be profane.

Alice had in her hand the two letters that she had received on Saturday.

"Have you answered your letters?" he asked.

"No, I have not even heard them read," she replied. "Uncle Ike has grown tired all at once and won't read to me nor write for me. I don't understand him at all. I sent for him yesterday afternoon, after you came down, and told him what I wanted him to do. He sent back word that he was too busy and I must get somebody else, but who can I get? Mandy and 'Zekiel are both too much occupied with their own duties to help me."

"If I can be of any service to you, Miss Pettengill, you know—"

"Oh, I don't think I should dare to let you read these letters," interrupted Alice, laughing. "No doubt they are from two of my lady friends, and I have always heard that men consider letters that women write to each other very silly and childish."

"Perhaps I have not told you," said Quincy, "that I have two sisters and am used to that sort of thing. When I was in college hardly a day passed that I did not get a letter from one or the other of them, and they brightened up my life immensely."

"What are their names and how old are they?" asked Alice.

"The elder," replied Quincy, "is nineteen and her name is Florence Estelle."

"What a sweet name!" said Alice.

"The younger is between fifteen and sixteen, and is named Maude Gertrude."

"Is she as dignified as her name?" asked Alice.

"Far from it," remarked Quincy. "She would be a tomboy if she had an opportunity. Mother and father call them Florence and Maude, for they both abhor nicknames, but among ourselves they are known as Flossie, or Stell, and Gertie."

"What was your nickname?" asked Alice.

"Well," said Quincy, "they used to call me Quinn, but that had a Hibernian sound to it, and Maude nicknamed me Ad, which she said was short for adder. She told me she called me that because I was so deaf that I never heard her when she asked me to take her anywhere."

"Well, Mr. Sawyer, if you will promise not to laugh out loud, I will be pleased to have you read these letters to me. You can smile all you wish to, for of course I can't see you."

"I agree," said Quincy; and he advanced towards her, took the two letters and drew a chair up beside her.

"My dear May," read Quincy. He stopped suddenly, and turning to Alice said, "Is this letter for you?"

"Before we go any further," said Alice, "I must explain my various names and nicknames. I was named Mary Alice, the Mary being my mother's name, while the Alice was a favorite of my father's. Mother always called me Mary and father always called me Alice! and brother 'Zekiel and Uncle Ike seem to like the name Alice best. When I went to Commercial College to study they asked me my name and I said naturally Mary A. Pettengill. Then the girls began to call me May, and the boys, or young men I suppose you call them, nicknamed me Miss Atlas, on account of my initials. Now that I have given you a chart of my names to go by, the reading will no doubt be plain sailing in future."

Quincy laughed and said, "I should call it a M. A. P. instead of a chart."

"Fie! Mr. Sawyer, to make such a joke upon my poor name. No doubt you have thought of one that would please you better than any I have mentioned."

Quincy thought he had, but he wisely refrained from saying so. He could not help thinking, however, that Miss Atlas was a very appropriate name for a girl who was all the world to him. It is evident that Uncle Ike's words of advice the previous afternoon had not taken very deep root in Quincy's heart.

He resumed his reading:

"My dear May:—How are you getting along in that dismal country town, and how are your poor eyes? I know you can't write to me, but I want you to know that I have not forgotten you. Every time I see my sister, Stella, she waves your photograph before my eyes. You know you promised me one before you were sick. Just send it to me, and it will be just as nice as a good, long letter. As somebody else will probably read this to you, in order to keep them from committing a robbery I send you only one kiss.

From your loving,

EMMA FARNUM."

"Are you smiling, Mr. Sawyer?" asked Alice.

"Not at all," he answered. "I am looking grieved because Miss Farnum has such a poor opinion of me."

Alice laughed merrily. "Emma is a very bright, pretty girl," said Alice. "She boarded at the same house that I did. Her sister Stella is married to a Mr. Dwight. I will answer her letter as she suggests by sending her the promised photograph. On the bureau in my room, Mr. Sawyer, you will find an envelope containing six photographs. I had them taken about a month before I was sick. Underneath you will find some heavy envelopes that the photographer gave me to mail them in."

Quincy went upstairs three steps at a time. He found the package, and impelled by an inexplicable curiosity he counted the pictures and found there were seven. "She said six," he thought to himself. "I am positive she said there were only six." He took one of the pictures and put it in one of the mailing envelopes. He took another picture, and after giving it a long, loving look he placed it in the inside pocket of his coat, and with a guilty flush upon his face he fled from the room.

Just as he reached the open parlor door a second thought, which is said to be the best, came to him, and he was about turning to go upstairs and replace the picture when Alice's acute ear heard him and she asked, "Did you find them?"

Quincy, seeing that retreat was now impossible, said, "Yes," and resumed his seat beside her.

"Did you find six?" said Alice.

"There are five upstairs in the envelope and one here ready to address," replied Quincy.

"Her address," continued Alice, "is Miss Emma Farnum, care Cotton & Co., Real Estate Brokers, Tremont Row."

Quincy went to the table, wrote the address as directed, and tied the envelope with the string attached.

"I am afraid the other letter cannot be so easily answered," said Alice. "Look at the signature, please, and see if it is not from Bessie White."

"It is signed Bessie," said Quincy.

"I thought so," exclaimed Alice. "She works for the same firm that I did."

Quincy read the following:

"My dear May:—I know that you will be glad to learn what is going on at the great dry goods house of Borden,

Waitt, & Fisher. Business is good, and we girls are all tired out when night comes and have to go to a party or the theatre to get rested. Mr. Ringgold, the head book-keeper, is disconsolate over your absence, and asks one or more of us every morning if we have heard from Miss Pettengill. Then, every afternoon, he says, 'Did I ask you this morning how Miss Pettengill was getting along?' Of course it is his devotion to the interest of the firm that leads him to ask these questions."

Alice flushed slightly, and turning to Quincy said, "Are you smiling, Mr. Sawyer? There is nothing in it, I assure you; Bessie is a great joker and torments the other girls unmercifully."

"I am glad there is nothing in it," said Quincy. "If I were a woman I would be afraid to marry a bookkeeper. My household cash would have to balance to a cent, and at the end of the year he would insist on housekeeping showing a profit."

Alice regained her composure and Quincy continued his reading:

"What do you think! Rita Sanguily has left, and they say she is going to marry a Dr. Culver, who lives up on Beacon Hill somewhere."

Quincy started a little as he read this, but made no com-ment.

"I was out to see Stella Dwight the other day, and she showed me a picture of you. Can you spare one to your old friend,

BESSIE WHITE.

"P. S.—I don't expect an answer, but I shall expect the picture. I shall write you whenever I get any news, and send you a dozen kisses and two big hugs.   B. W."

"She is more liberal than Miss Farnum," remarked Quincy. "She is not afraid that I will commit robbery."

"No," rejoined Alice, "but I cannot share with you. Bessie White is the dearest friend I have in the world."

"Miss White is fortunate," said Quincy, "but who is Rita Sanguily, if I am not presuming in asking the question?"

"She is a Portuguese girl," answered Alice, "with black eyes and beautiful black hair. She is very handsome and can talk Portuguese, French, and Spanish. She held a certain line of custom on this account. Do you know her?"

"No," replied Quincy, "but I think I know Dr. Culver."

"What kind of a looking man is he?" asked Alice.

"Oh! he is tall and heavily built, with large bright blue eyes and tawny hair," said Quincy.

"I like such marked contrasts in husband and wife," remarked Alice.

"So do I," said Quincy, looking at himself in a looking glass which hung opposite, and then at Alice; "but how about Miss White's picture?"

"Can I trouble you to get one?" said Alice.

"No trouble at all," replied Quincy; but he went up the stairs this time one step at a time. He was deliberating whether he should return that picture that was in his coat pocket or keep it until the original should be his own. He entered the room, took another picture and another envelope and came slowly downstairs. His crime at first had been unpremeditated, but his persistence was deliberate felony.

"Now there are four left," said Alice, as Quincy entered the room.

"Just four," he replied. "I counted them to make sure." He sat at the table and wrote. "Will this do?" he asked: "Miss Bessie White, care of Borden, Waitt, & Fisher, Boston, Mass.?"

"Oh, thank you so much," said Alice.

At this moment Mandy appeared at the door and an-nounced dinner, and Quincy had the pleasure of leading Alice to her accustomed seat at the table.

"I took the liberty while upstairs," said Quincy, "to glance at a book that was on your bureau entitled, 'The Love of a Lifetime.' Have you read it?"

"No," replied Alice. "I commenced it the night before I was taken sick."

"I shall be pleased to read it aloud to you," said Quincy.

"I should enjoy listening to it very much," she replied.

So after dinner they returned to the parlor and Quincy read aloud until the descending sun again sent its rays through the parlor windows to fall upon Alice's face and hair, and Quincy thought to himself how happy he should be if the fair girl who sat beside him ever became the love of his lifetime.

Alice finally said she was tired and must have a rest. Quincy called Mandy and she went to her room. A few moments later Quincy was in his own room and after lock-ing his door sat down to inspect his plunder.

Alice did not rest, however; something was on her mind. She found her way to the bureau and took up the pictures.

"Only four," she said to herself, after counting them. "Let me see," she continued, "the photographer gave me thirteen,—a baker's dozen he called it. Now to whom have I given them? 'Zekiel, one; Uncle Ike, two; Mrs. Putnam, three; Stella Dwight, four; Bessie White, five; Emma Farnum, six; Mr. Ringgold, seven; Mr. Fisher, eight. That would leave five and I have only four. Now to whom did I give that other picture?"

And the guilty thief sat on the other side of the parti-tion and exulted in his crime. There came a loud rap at his door, and Quincy started up so suddenly that he dropped the picture and it fell to the floor. He caught it up quickly and placed it in his pocket. As he unlocked the door and opened it he heard loud rapping on the door of Miss Pettengill's room.

Looking into the entry he saw 'Zekiel, who cried out, "Say, you folks, have you forgotten that you have been invited out to tea this evening, and that we are going to give a surprise party to Mr. Strout and his friends? I am all dressed and the sleigh is ready."

Without waiting for a reply he dashed downstairs.

While Quincy was donning his sober suit of black, with a Prince Albert coat and white tie, Alice had put on an equally sober costume of fawn colored silk, with collar and cuffs of dainty lace, with little dashes of pink ribbon, by way of contrast in color.

CHAPTER XXVI.

AFTER Alice had taken her place on the back seat in the double sleigh, Quincy started to take his place on the front seat, beside 'Zekiel, but the latter motioned him to sit beside Alice, and Quincy did so without needing any urging.

As 'Zekiel took up the reins, Quincy leaned forward and touched him on the shoulder.

"I've just thought," said he, "that I've made a big blunder and I can't see how I can repair it."

"What's the matter?" asked 'Zekiel; and Alice turned an inquiring face towards Quincy.

"The fact is," Quincy continued, "I ordered some ice cream and cake sent down from the city for the show to-night, but I forgot, I am ashamed to say, to make arrangements to have it sent up to Deacon Mason's. It will be directed to him, but the station agent won't be likely to send it up before to-morrow."

"What time is it?" asked 'Zekiel.

Quincy looked at his watch and replied, "It is just half-past four."

"Why do we go so early?" inquired Alice, "they will not have tea till six."

"Oh," said 'Zekiel, "I intended to give you a sleigh ride first anyway. Now with this pair of trotters I am going to take you over to Eastborough Centre and have you back at Deacon Mason's barn door in just one hour and with appetites that it will take two suppers to satisfy."

With this 'Zekiel whipped up his horses and they dashed

off towards the town. A short distance beyond Uncle Ike's chicken coop they met Abner Stiles driving home from the Centre. He nodded to 'Zekiel, but Quincy did not notice him, being engaged in conversation with Alice at the time. They reached the station, and Quincy gave orders to have the material sent up, so that it would arrive at about half-past nine. 'Zekiel more than kept his promise, for they reached Deacon Mason's barn at exactly twenty-nine minutes past five. Hiram was on hand to put up the horses, and told Quincy in a whisper that some of the boys thought it was mighty mean not to invite the Pettengill folks and their boarder.

The sharp air had whetted the appetites of the travellers during their six-mile ride, and they did full justice to the nicely-cooked food that the Deacon's wife placed before them. Supper was over at quarter before seven, and in half an hour the dishes were washed and put away and the quartette of young folks adjourned to the parlor.

Quincy took his seat at the piano and began playing a popular air.

"Oh, let us sing something," cried Huldy. "You know I have been taking lessons from Professor Strout, and he says I have improved greatly. If he says it you know it must be so; and, did you know Alice, that 'Zekiel has a fine baritone voice?"

"We used to sing a good deal together," said Alice, "but I was no judge of voices then."

"Well, 'Zeke don't know a note of music," continued Huldy, "but he has a quick ear and he seems to know naturally just how to use his voice."

"Oh, nonsense," said 'Zekiel, "I don't know how to sing, I only hum a little. Sing us something, Mr. Sawyer," said he.

Quincy sang a song very popular at the time, entitled "The Jockey Hat and Feather." All four joined in the chorus, and at the close the room rang with laughter. Quincy then struck up another popular air, "Pop Goes the Weasel," and this was sung by the four with great gusto. Then he looked over the music on the top of the piano, which was a Bourne & Leavitt square, and found a copy of the cantata entitled, "The Haymakers," and for half an hour the solos and choruses rang through the house and out upon the evening air.

Mrs. Mason looked in the door and said, "I wouldn't sing any more now, it is nearly eight o'clock."

And thus admonished they began talking of Tilly James's engagement to Sam Hill and the sale of the grocery store, which was to come off the next day.

"I wonder who will buy it?" asked Huldy.

"Well, I hear Strout has got some backers," said 'Zekiel, "but I don't see what good it will be to him unless he is appointed postmaster. They say he has written to Washington and applied for the position."

Quincy pricked up his ears at this. He had almost forgotten this chance to put another spoke in Mr. Strout's wheel. He made a mental memorandum to send telegrams to two Massachusetts congressmen with whom he was well acquainted to hold up Strout's appointment at all hazards until they heard from him again.

A little after seven o'clock the advance guard of the surprise party arrived at Hill's grocery, which was the appointed rendezvous. Abner Stiles drew Strout to one side and said, "I saw the Pettengill folks and that city feller in 'Zeke's double sleigh going over to the Centre at about five o'clock."

"So much the better," said Strout.

"Do you know where they've gone?" inquired Stiles.

"No, but I guess I can find out," Strout replied.

He had spied Mandy Skinner among a crowd of girls on the platform. He called her and she came to him.

"Did Mr. Pettengill and his sister take tea at home to-
night?"

"No," said Mandy. "I told them I was going away to-
night, and Mr. Pettengill said they were going away too.
And Cobb's twins told me at dinner time that they wouldn't
be home to supper; and as I didn't wish to eat too much,
considering what was coming later, I didn't get no supper
at all. I left Crowley to look out for Uncle Ike, who
is always satisfied if he gets toast and tea."

"Don't you know where they've gone?" inquired Strout.

"Over to the hotel, I guess," said Mandy. "I heard Mr.
Sawyer tell Miss Alice that they had good oysters over
there, and she said as how she was dying to get some raw
oysters."

"Things couldn't have worked better," remarked Strout,
as he rejoined Abner, who was smoking a cheap cigar.
"The Pettengill crowd has gone over to the hotel to supper. You ought not to smoke, Abner, if you are going to
kiss the girls to-night," said Strout.

"I guess I sha'n't do much kissin'," replied Abner, "except what I give my fiddle with the bow, and that fiddle of
mine is used to smoke."

Strout looked around and saw that the whole party had
assembled. There were about fifty in all, very nearly
equally divided as regarded numbers into fellows and girls.

"Now I am going ahead," said Strout, "to interview the
old lady, before we jump in on them. The rest of you just
follow Abner and wait at the top of the hill, just round the
corner, so that they can't see you from the house. I have
arranged with Hiram to blow his bugle when everything is
ready, and when you hear it you just rush down hill laughing and screaming and yelling like wild Injuns. Come in
the back door, right into the big kitchen, and when Miss
Huldy comes into the room you just wait till I deliver my
speech."

Strout started off, and the party followed Abner to the appointed waiting place.

Strout knocked lightly at the kitchen door, and it was opened by Mrs. Mason.

"Is the Deacon at home?" inquired he, endeavoring to disguise his voice.

"No," said Mrs. Mason, "he has gone to Eastborough Centre on some business, but told me he would be back about half past nine."

"Is Hiram here?" asked Strout.

"He's out in the kitchen polishing up his bugle," said Mrs. Mason. "But come in a minute, Mr. Strout, I have got something to tell you."

Strout stepped in and quietly closed the door.

"What's the matter, Mrs. Mason? I hope Huldy isn't sick."

"No," said she, "it's unfortunate it has happened as it has, but it couldn't be avoided. You see she invited some company to tea, and I supposed that they would have gone home long 'fore this. You see, Huldy don't suspect nothing, and she has asked them to spend the evening, and I don't see how in the world I am going to get rid of them."

"Don't do it," said Strout. "Extend to them an invitation in my name to remain and enjoy the evening's festivities with us. No doubt Miss Huldy will be pleased to have them stay."

"I know she will," said Mrs. Mason, "and I'll give them your invite as soon as you're ready."

"Well, Mrs. Mason," said Strout, "just tell Hiram I am ready to have him blow that bugle, and when you hear it you can just tell your daughter and her friends what's up."

Hiram soon joined Strout outside the kitchen door. The latter went out in the road and looked up the hill to see if his party was all ready. Abner waved his hand, and

Strout rushed back to Hiram and cried, "Give it to 'em now, Hiram, and do your darnedest!"

Huldy and her friends were engaged in earnest conversation, when a loud blast burst upon the air, followed by a succession of piercing notes from Hiram's old cracked bugle.

Huldy jumped to her feet and exclaimed, "What does Hiram want to blow that horrid old bugle at this time of night for? I will tell ma to stop him."

She started towards the parlor door, when the whole party heard shouts of laughter, screams from female voices, and yells from male ones that would have done credit to a band of wild Comanches.

All stood still and listened. Again the laughter, screams, and yells were heard. This time they seemed right under the parlor window,

A look of surprise and almost terror passed over Alice's face, and turning to Quincy unthinkingly she said in a low whisper, "What was that, Quincy? What does it mean?"

Quincy's heart jumped as his Christian name fell from the girl's lips. He put his left hand over his heart (her picture was in the pocket just beneath it) and said as naturally as he could, although with a little tremor in his voice, "It's all right, Alice, that's Mr. Strout's idea of a surprise party."

"A surprise party!" cried Huldy, "who for? Me?"

At this moment Mrs. Mason opened the door and entered the room.

"Huldy," said she, "Professor Strout wishes me to tell you that he and his friends have come to give you a surprise party, and he wished me to invite you," turning to the others, "as Huldy's friends to remain and enjoy the festivities of the evening."

Then the poor old lady, who had been under a nervous strain for the past ten days, and who had come nearer tell-

"SAMANTHY GREEN," AS SHE APPEARS IN THE PLAY.

ing untruths than she ever had before in her life, began to laugh, and then to cry, and finally sank into a chair, overcome for the moment.

"I wish Abraham was here," said she, "I guess I'm getting a little bit nervous."

Let us return to the great kitchen, which the members of the surprise party now had in their possession. A dozen of the men produced lanterns, which they lighted, and which were soon hung upon the walls of the kitchen, one of the number having brought a hammer and some nails."

It was a pound party, and two young men fetched in a basket containing the goodies which had been brought for the supper. Strout had made arrangements to have the hot coffee made at the grocery store, and it was to be brought down at half-past nine.

He arranged his party so that all could get a good view of the door through which Huldy must come. He stepped forward within ten feet of the door and stood expectantly. Why this delay? Strout looked around at the party. There were Tilly James and Sam Hill; Cobb's twins, and each brought a pretty girl; Robert Wood, Benjamin Bates, and Arthur Scates were equally well supplied; Lindy Putnam, after much solicitation, had consented to come with Emmanuel Howe, the clergyman's son, and he was in the seventh heaven of delight; Mandy stood beside Hiram and his bugle, and Samantha Green had Farmer Tompkins's son George for escort. It was a real old-fashioned, democratic party. Clergymen's sons, farmers' sons, girls that worked out, chore boys, farm hands, and an heiress to a hundred thousand dollars, met on a plane of perfect equality without a thought of caste, and to these were soon to be added more farmers' sons and daughters and the only son of a millionaire.

"Just give them a call," said Strout, turning to Hiram, and the latter gave a blast on his bugle, which sent fingers to the ears of his listeners. The handle of the door turned and opened and Huldy entered, her mother leaning upon her arm.

They were greeted by hand clapping and cries of "Good evening" from the party, and all eyes were fixed upon Strout, who stood as if petrified and gazed at the three fig- ures that came through the open door and stood behind Huldy and her mother. Hamlet following the fleeting apparition on the battlements of the castle at Elsinore, Macbeth viewing Banquo at his feast, or Richard the Third gazing on the ghostly panorama of the murdered kings and princes, could not have felt weaker at heart than did Pro- fessor Strout when he saw the new-comers and realized that they were there by his express invitation.

The members of the surprise party thought Strout had forgotten his speech, and cries of "Speech!" "Speech!" "Give us the speech!" fell upon his ear, but no words fell from his lips. It was a cruel blow, but no crueler than the unfounded stories that he had started and circulated about the town for the past three months. Those who had thought it was mean not to invite the Pettengills and Mr. Sawyer enjoyed his discomfiture and were the loudest in calling for a speech.

The situation became somewhat strained, and Huldy looked up to Quincy with an expression that seemed to say, How are we going to get out of this?

Quite a number of the party saw this look and imme- diately began calling out, "Mr. Sawyer, give us a speech!" "A speech from Mr. Sawyer!"

Huldy smiled and nodded to Quincy, and then there were loud cries of "Speech! "Speech!" and clapping of hands.

Abner Stiles got up and gave his chair to Professor Strout, who sank into it, saying as he did so, "I guess it was the heat."

Quincy stepped forward and bowing to Huldy and then to Mrs. Mason, addressed the party in a low but clearly distinct voice.

"Authorized by these ladies to speak for them, I desire to return sincere thanks for this manifestation of your regard for them. Your visit was entirely unexpected by Miss Mason and a great surprise to her. But it is a most pleasant surprise, and she desires me to thank you again and again for your kind thoughts and your good company this evening. She and her mother join in giving you a most hearty welcome. They wish you to make yourselves at home and will do all in their power to make the evening a happy one and one long to be remembered by the inhabitants of Mason's Corner. The inception of this happy event, I learn, is due to Professor Strout, who for some time, I understand, has been Miss Mason's music teacher, and the ladies, whose ideas I am expressing, desire me to call upon him to take charge of the festivities and bring them to a successful close, as he is no doubt competent and willing to do."

Quincy bowed low and retired behind the other members of the party.

Quincy's speech was greeted with cheers and more clapping of hands. Even Strout's friends were pleased by the graceful compliment paid to the Professor, and joined in the applause.

Strout had by this time fully recovered his equanimity. A chair was placed upon the kitchen table and Abner Stiles was boosted up and took his seat thereon. While he was tuning up his fiddle the Professor opened a package that one of the girls handed to him and passed a pair of knitted woollen wristers to each lady in the company. He gave three pairs to Huldy, who in turn gave one pair to her mother and one to Alice. There were several pairs over, as several girls who had been expected to join the party had not come.

"Now, Mrs. Mason," said the Professor, "could you kindly supply me with a couple of small baskets, or if not, with a couple of milk pans?"

The Professor took one of the pans and Robert Wood the other.

"The ladies will please form in line," cried the Professor; which was done. "Now will each lady," said the Professor, "as she marches between us, throw one wrister in one pan and t'other wrister in the other pan? Give us a good, lively march, Abner," he added, and the music began.

The procession passed between the upheld pans, one wrister of each pair thrown right and the other left, as it moved on.

The music stopped. "Now, will the ladies please form in line again," said the Professor, "and as they pass through each one take a wrister from the pan held by Mr. Wood."

The music started up again and the procession moved forward and the work of selection was completed.

Again the music stopped. "Now will the gentlemen form in line, and as they march forward each one take a wrister from the pan that I hold," said the Professor.

Once more the music started up. The line was formed, the procession advanced, 'Zekiel and Quincy bringing up the rear. As Quincy took the last wrister from the pan that the Professor held, the latter turned quickly away and beat a tattoo on the bottom of the pan with his knuckles and cried out, "Gentlemen will please find their partners. The wristers become the property of the gentlemen."

Then a wild rush took place. Screams of laughter were heard on every side, and it was fully five minutes before the excitement subsided, and in response to another tattoo upon the milk pan by the Professor, the couples, as arranged by the hand of Fate, formed in line and marched

around the great kitchen to the music of a sprightly march
written by the Professor and called "The Wrister March,"
and respectfully dedicated to Miss Hulda Mason. This an-
nouncement was made by Mr. Stiles from his elevated position upon the kitchen table.

The hand of Fate had acted somewhat strangely. The
Professor and Mandy Skinner stood side by side, as did
'Zekiel Pettengill and Mrs. Mason. Lindy Putnam and
Huldy by a queer twist of fortune were mated with Cobb's
twins.

But Fate did one good act. By chance Quincy and
Alice stood side by side. She looked up at him and said to
her partner, "What is your name, I cannot see your face?"

"My name is Quincy," said Sawyer in a low voice.

"I am so glad!" said Alice, leaning a little more heavily
on his arm.

"So am I," responded Quincy ardently.

After the procession had made several circuits of the
great kitchen, Professor Strout gave a signal, and it broke
up, each gentleman being then at liberty to seek the lady
of his own choice.

"What games shall we play fust?" asked Strout, taking
the centre of the room, and looking round upon the company with a countenance full of smiles and good nature.

"Who is it?" "Who is it?" came from a dozen voices.

"All right," cried Strout; "that's a very easy game to
play. Now all you ladies git in a line and I'll put this
one chair right front of yer. Now all the gentlemen must
leave the room except one. I suppose we can use the parlor,
Mrs. Mason?"

Mrs. Mason nodded her head in the affirmative.

"I'll 'tend door," said Hiram; and he took his position
accordingly. After the rest of the gentlemen had left the
room, Hiram closed the door, and turning to Huldy said,
"Shall I call them, or will you?"

"You call them," said Huldy.

"Got the handkerchief ready?" asked Hiram.

Huldy swung a big red bandanna in the air. Opening a door, Hiram called out in a loud voice, "Obadiah Strout."

As Strout walked towards the line of young girls they called out together, "Mister, please take a chair."

Strout sat down in a chair. One of the girls who had the bandanna handkerchief in her hand passed it quickly over his eyes and tied it firmly behind his head. Two of the girls then stepped forward and each one taking one of his hands and extending it at right angles with his body held it firmly in their grasps. At the same instant his head was pulled back by one of the girls and a kiss was imprinted on his upturned mouth.

"Who is it?" screamed the girls in unison. The holds on the Professor's head and hands were released and he sat upright in the chair.

"I kinder guess it was Miss Huldy Mason," said he.

A loud laugh burst from the girls, mixed with cries of "You're wrong!" "You ain't right!" "You didn't get it!" "You're out!" and similar ejaculations.

The handkerchief was taken from his eyes and he was marched to the left of the line of girls, which ran lengthwise of the kitchen.

Abner Stiles was the next one called in, and he was subjected to the same treatment as had befallen his predecessor, but to the intense disgust of Professor Strout he saw Hiram Maxwell come on tiptoe from the parlor door, lean over and kiss Abner Stiles. The thought of course ran through his mind that he had been subjected to the same treatment. He was on the point of protesting at this way of conducting the game when the idea occurred to him that it would be a huge satisfaction to have that city chap subjected to the same treatment, and he decided to hold his peace.

The next one called was 'Zekiel Pettengill, and he was treated in the same manner as the Professor and Abner had been; but as Hiram leaned over to kiss him, 'Zekiel's foot slipped upon the floor and struck against Hiram's, Hiram being in front of him. 'Zekiel then put up both of his feet and kicked with them in such a way that Hiram was unable to approach him.

'Zekiel called out, "It's Hiram Maxwell," and the room rang with the laughs and cries of the girls.

'Zekiel, having guessed who it was, was marched off to the right of the line of girls.

Strout called out, "Let's play something else," but the sentiment of the company seemed to be that it wasn't fair to the others not to give them a chance, so the game continued. Quincy was the next one called, and to still further increase the disgust of Strout and Abner, instead of Hiram leaving the door, as before, one of the girls stepped out from the line, at a signal from Huldy, and kissed Quincy. He guessed that it was Miss Huldy Mason, and was greeted with the same cries that Strout had heard. He took his place at the left with the latter.

Strout leaned over and whispered in Abner's ear, "That was a put-up job. I'll get even with Hiram Maxwell before I get through."

The game continued until all the men had been called in. With the exception of Emmanuel Howe, none of them were able to guess who it was. When Emmanuel took his place by the side of 'Zekiel he confided the fact to him that he guessed it was Miss Putnam on account of the perfumery which he had noticed before he left the house with her.

After this game others followed in quick succession. There were "Pillow," "Roll the Cover," "Button, Button, Who's Got the Button?" "Copenhagen," and finally "Post Office." From all of these games Alice begged to be excused. She told the Professor that she was not bashful nor diffident, but that her eyesight was so poor that she knew she would detract from the pleasure of the others if she engaged in the games. The Professor demurred at first, but said finally that her excuse was a good one. Then he turned to Abner and remarked that he supposed Mr. Sawyer would ask to be excused next 'cause his girl wasn't going to play.

But Quincy had no such intention. After leading Alice to a seat beside Mrs. Mason, he returned to the company and took part in every game, entering with spirit and vivacity into each of them. He invented some forfeits that one girl objected to the forfeit exacted of her as being all out of proportion to her offence, the matter was referred to Quincy. He said that he would remit the original forfeit and she could kiss him instead. But she objected, saying that forfeit was worse than the other one. This pleased Strout greatly, and he remarked to Abner, who kept as close to him as the tail to a kite, that there was one girl in town who wasn't afraid to speak her mind.

The game of Post Office was the most trying one to Quincy. Of his own free will he would not have called either Huldy or Lindy, but Strout and Abner and all the rest of them had letters for both of these young ladies. He was afraid that his failure to call them out might lead to remark, as he knew that Strout and Abner and Robert Wood were watching his actions closely. So, near the middle of the game, when he had been called out, he had a letter from England for Miss Lindy Putnam.

As she raised her face to his for the kiss on the cheek that he gave her, she said, "I was afraid you had not forgiven me, after all."

"Oh, yes, I have," said Quincy, and carried away by the excitement of the occasion, he caught her again in his arms and gave her another kiss, this time upon the lips.

At this instant Abner Stiles, who was tending door, opened it and called out, "Takes a long time to pay the postage on one letter!"

A little later Quincy was again called out, and this time

he had a letter from Boston for Miss Mason. He kissed
her on the cheek, as he had done with Lindy. Huldy looked
up with a laugh and said, "Were you as bashful as that
with Miss Putnam?"

"Yes," said Quincy, "at first, but there was double postage on her letter, the same as on yours." And though
Huldy tried to break away from him he caught her and
kissed her upon the lips, as he had done to Lindy.

Again Abner opened the door and cried out that the
mails would close in one minute, and he'd better get the
stamps on that letter quick.

All such good times come to an end, and the signal for
the close was the return of Deacon Mason from his visit to
town. He was popular with all parties, and Stroutites,
Anti-Stroutites, and neutrals all gathered 'round him and
said they were having a beautiful time, and could they have
a little dance after supper?

The Deacon said he didn't know that dancing in itself
was so bad, for the Bible referred to a great many dances.
"But," said he, "I have always been agin permiscuous dancing."

"But we ain't permiscuous," said Tilly James. "We are
all friends and neighbors."

"Most all," said Strout; but his remark was unnoticed
by all excepting Quincy.

"Well, under the circumstances," concluded the Deacon,
"I don't object to your finishing up with an old-fashioned
reel, and mother and me will jine in with you, so as to countenance the perceedings."

The call was now made for supper. A procession was
again formed, each gentleman taking the lady who had
accompanied him to the party. They all filed into the
dining-room and took their places around the long table.
The most of them looked at its contents with surprise and
delight. Instead of seeing only home-made cakes, and pies,
and dishes of nuts, and raisins, and apples, that they had

expected, occupying the centre of the table, they gazed
upon a large frosted cake, in the centre of which arose what
resembled the spire of a church, made of sugar and adorned
with small American flags and streamers made of various
colored silk ribbons. Flanking the centrepiece at each corner were large dishes containing mounds of jelly cake,
pound cake, sponge cake, and angel cake. On either side of
the centrepiece, shaped in fancy moulds, were two large
dishes of ice cream, a third full of sherbet, and the
fourth one filled with frozen pudding. In the vacant spaces
about the larger dishes were smaller plates containing the
home-made pies and cake, and the apples, oranges, dates,
figs, raisins, nuts, and candy taken from the pound packages
brought by the members of the surprise party. Piled upon
the table in heaps were the fifty boxes containing the souvenir gifts that Quincy had ordered.

As they took their places about the table, Quincy felt it
incumbent upon him to say something. Turning to the
Professor he addressed him:

"Professor Strout, I think it is my duty to inform you
that I have made this little addition to the bountiful supper
supplied by you and the members of this party, on behalf
of my friends, Mr. and Miss Pettengill, and myself. I
trust that you will take as much pleasure in disposing of it
as I have in sending it. In the language of the poet I
would now say, 'Fall to and may good digestion wait on
appetite!'"

Quincy's speech was received with applause. The hot
coffee had arrived and was soon circulating in cups, mugs,
and tumblers. Everybody was talking to everybody else at
the same time, and all petty fueds, prejudices, and animosities were, apparently, forgotten.

The young fellows took the cue from Quincy, who, as
soon as he had finished his little speech, began filling the
plates with the good things provided, and passing them to
the ladies, and in a short time all had been waited upon.

When both hunger and appetite had been satisfied, Quincy again addressed the company.

"In those small paper boxes," said he, "you will find some little souvenirs, which you can keep to remind you of this very pleasant evening, or you can eat them and remember how sweet they were." A general laugh followed this remark. "In making your selection," continued Quincy, "bear in mind that the boxes tied up with red ribbon are for the ladies, while those having blue ribbons are for the gentlemen."

A rush was made for the table, and almost instantly each member of the company became possessed of a souvenir and was busily engaged in untying the ribbons.

Again Quincy's voice was heard above the tumult.

"In each package," cried he, "will be found printed on a slip of paper a poetical selection. The poetry, like that found on valentines, is often very poor, but the sentiment is there just the same. In the city the plan that we follow is to pass our own slip to our left-hand neighbor and he or she reads it."

This was too much for the Professor.

"I don't think," said he, "that we ought to foller that style of doin' things jest because they do it that way in the city. We are pretty independent in the country, like to do things our own way."

"Oh! it don't make any difference to me," said Quincy; "in the city when we get a good thing we are willing to share it with our partners or friends; you know I said if you didn't wish to keep your souvenir, you could eat it, and of course the poetical selection is part of the souvenir."

A peal of laughter greeted this sally, which rose to a shout when Strout took his souvenir out of the box. It proved to be a large sugar bee, very lifelike in appearance and having a little wad of paper rolled up and tucked under one of the wings.

As Strout spread out the slip of paper with his fingers, loud cries of "Eat it!" "Read it!" and "Pass it along!" came from the company. The Professor stood apparently undecided what course to pursue, when Tilly James, who was standing at his left, grabbed it from his fingers, and running to the end of the table, stood beside young Hill with an expression that seemed to say, "This is my young man, and I know he will protect me."

Loud cries of "Read it, Tilly!" came from all parts of the table.

"Not unless Professor Strout is willing," said Tilly with mock humility.

All eyes were turned upon Strout, who, seeing that he had nothing to gain by objecting, cried out, "Oh, go ahead; what do I care about such nonsense!"

Tilly then read with much dramatic expression the following poetical effusion:

"How does the wicked bumblebee
    Employ the shining hours,
In stinging folks that he dislikes,
    Instead of sipping flowers."

Another loud laugh greeted this; largely due to the comical expression on Tilly James's face, which so far upset Quincy's habitual gravity that he was obliged to smile in spite of himself.

If Strout felt the shot he did not betray it, but turned to Huldy, who stood at his right, and said, "Now, Miss Mason, let me read your poetry for you, as they do it in the city."

Huldy hesitated, holding the slip of paper between her fingers, "Oh! that ain't fair," said Strout. "I've set you a good example, now you mustn't squeal. Come, walk right up to the trough."

"I'm no pig," protested Huldy.

As Strout leaned over to take the paper he said in an

undertone, "No, you are a little dear;" whereat Huldy's
face flushed a bright crimson.

Strout cleared his voice and then read:

> "Come wreathe your face with smiles, my dear,
> A husband you'll find within the year."

This was greeted with laughter, clapping of hands, and
cries of "Who is it, Huldy?"

The Professor looked at Huldy inquiringly, but she
averted her eyes. He leaned over and said in an undertone,
"May I keep this?"

Huldy looked up and said in a tone that was heard by
every one at the table, "I don't care; if you like it better than
that one about the bumblebee you can have it."

The Professor then turned to Quincy and said, "Perhaps
Mr. Sawyer will oblige the company by passing his poetry
along, as they do it in the city."

Quincy answered quickly, "Why, certainly, and handed
the slip to his left-hand neighbor, who chanced to be Miss
Seraphina Cotton, who was the teacher in the public school
located at Mason's Corner.

She prided herself on her elocutionary ability, and read
the following with great expression:

> "Though wealth and fame fall to my lot,
> I'd much prefer a little cot,
> In which, apart from care and strife,
> I'd love my children and my wife."

Strout laughed outright.

"By the way, Mr. Sawyer," said he, "have you seen any
little cot round here that you'd swap your Beacon Street
house for?"

"I've got my eye on some real estate in this town," said
Quincy, "and if you own it perhaps we can make a trade."

'Zekiel Pettengill passed his slip to Lindy Putnam; it ran
thus:

"'An honest man's the noblest work of God,'
 No nobler lives than he who tills the sod."

This was greeted with shouts and cries of "Good for
'Zeke!" while one of Cobb's twins, who possessed a thin,
high voice, cried out, "He's all wool and a yard wide."
This provoked more shouts and hand-clapping, and
'Zekiel blushed like a peony.

Lindy Putnam handed her slip to Quincy; he took in its
meaning at a glance and looked at her inquiringly.

Strout saw the glance and cried out, "Oh, come, now;
don't leave out nothin'; read it jist as it's writ."

Lindy nodded to Quincy and he read:

"There is no heart but hath some wish unfilled,
 There is no soul without some longing killed,
 With heart and soul work for thy heart's desire,
 And turn not back for storm, nor flood, nor fire."

"This is gittin' quite tragic," said Strout. "I guess we've
had all we want to eat and drink, and have listened to all the
bad poetry we want ter, and I move—"

"Second the motion," cried Abner Stiles.

"And I move," continued Strout, "that we git back inter
the kitchen, and have a little dance jist to shake our suppers down."

After the company returned to the kitchen, Abner was
again lifted to his elevated position on the kitchen table,
and the fun began again. There was no doubt that in telling stories Abner Stiles often drew the long bow, but it was
equally true that he had no superior in Eastborough and
vicinity on the violin, or the fiddle, as he preferred to call it.
He was now in his glory. His fiddle was tucked under his

chin, a red silk handkerchief with large yellow polka dots protecting the violin from injury from his stubbly beard rather than his chin from being injured by the instrument.

After a few preliminary chords, Abner struck up the peculiar dance movement very popular in those days, called "The Cure." As if prearranged, Hiram Maxwell and Mandy Skinner ran to the centre of the room and began singing the words belonging to the dance. Abner gradually increased the speed of the melody, and the singers conformed thereto. Faster and faster the music went, and higher and higher the dancers jumped until the ceiling prevented any further progress upward. They leaned forward and backward, they leaned from side to side, but still kept up their monotonous leaps into the air. Finally, when almost exhausted, they sank into chairs hastily brought for them, amid the applause of the party.

Quincy had seen the dance at the city theatres, but acknowledged to himself that the country version was far ahead of the city one. At the same time it seemed to him that the dance savored of barbarism, and he recalled pictures and stories of Indian dances where the participants fell to the ground too weak to rise.

"I put my right hand in," called out one of the fellows. Cries of "Oh, yes, that's it!" came from the company, and they arranged themselves in two rows, facing each other and running the length of the long room. They were in couples, as they came to the party. Abner played the melody on his violin, and the fellows and girls sang these words:

"I put my right hand in,
I put my right hand out,
I give my right hand a shake, shake, shake,
And I turn myself about."

As they sang the last line they did turn themselves about

so many times that it seemed a wonder to Quincy, who was
an amused spectator, how they kept upon their feet.

Seeing that one of the young ladies in the line was without a partner, Quincy took his place beside her and joined
in the merriment as heartily as the rest. Then followed all
the changes of "I put my left hand in," "I put my right
foot in," "I put my left foot in," and so on until the whole
party was nearly as much exhausted as Hiram and Mandy
had been.

At this moment the door leading to the parlor opened
and Deacon Mason entered, accompanied by his wife.
They were greeted with shouts of laughter. Quincy looked
at them with astonishment, and had it not been for their
familiar faces, which they had not tried to disguise, he
would not have recognized them.

Out of compliment to their guests, the Deacon and his
wife had gone back to the days of their youth. Probably
from some old chest in the garret each had resurrected a
costume of fifty years before. They advanced into the
room, smiling and bowing to the delighted spectators on
either side. They went directly to Abner, and the latter
bent over to hear what the Deacon whispered in his ear.
The Deacon then went to Strout and whispered something
to him.

Strout nodded, and turning to the company said, "As
it's now half past 'leven and most time for honest folks to
be abed and rogues a runnin', out of compliment to Miss
Huldy's grandpa and grandma, who have honored us with
their presence this evenin', we will close these festivities
with a good old-fashioned heel and toe Virginia reel.
Let 'er go, Abner, and keep her up till all the fiddle strings
are busted."

Like trained soldiers, they sprang to their places. Quincy
and his partner took places near the end of the line. He
explained to her that he had never danced a reel, but

"THE DEACON AND HIS WIFE LED OFF."

thought he could easily learn from seeing the others, and he told her that when their turn came she need not fear but that he would do his part.

The Deacon and his wife led off, and their performance caused great enthusiasm. Sam Hill was not a good dancer, so he resigned Miss Tilly James to Professor Strout. Miss James was a superb dancer, and as Quincy looked at her his face showed his appreciation.

His partner saw the glance, and looking up to him said, "Don't you wish you could dance as well as that?"

"I wish I could," said Quincy. "I have no doubt you can," he added, looking at his partner's rosy face.

"Well," said she, "you do the best you can, and I'll do the same."

Professor Strout and Tilly did finely, and their performance gained them an encore, which they granted. One by one the couples went under the arch of extended arms, and one by one they showed their Terpsichorean agility on the kitchen floor, over which Mandy Skinner had thoughtfully sprinkled a handful of house sand.

At last came the turn of Quincy and his little partner, whose name was unknown to him. He observed the grace with which she went through the march, and when the dance came he wished he could have stood still and watched her. Instead, he entered with his whole soul into the dance, and at its conclusion he was astonished to hear the burst of applause and cheers that fell upon his ears.

"Come along!" said his partner, and taking him by the hand she drew him back through the arch, and the dance was repeated.

Three times in succession was this done in response to enthusiastic applause, and Quincy was beginning to think that he would soon fall in his tracks. He had no idea that any such fate would befall his partner, for she seemed equal to an indefinite number of repetitions.

But, as has been said before, to all good things an end
must come at last, and when the old-fashioned Connecticut
clock on the mantelpiece clanged out the midnight hour, as
if by magic a hush came over the company and the jollities
came to an end. Then followed a rush for capes, and coats,
and jackets, and shawls, and hats. Then came good-byes
and good-nights, and then the girls all kissed Huldy and
her mother, wished them long life and happiness, while
their escorts stood quietly by thinking of the pleasant
homeward trips, and knowing in their hearts that they
should treasure more the pressure of the hand or the single
good-night kiss yet to come than they did the surprise
party kisses that had been theirs during the evening.

Mrs. Mason and 'Zekiel had prepared Alice for her
homeward trip. Quincy took occasion to seek out his partner in the reel to say good night, and as he shook hands
with her he said, "Would you consider me rude if I asked
your name and who taught you to dance?"

"Oh! no," she replied; "my name is Bessie Chisholm. I
teach the dancing school at Eastborough Centre, and Mr.
Stiles always plays for me."

"Is he going to see you home to-night?" asked Quincy.

"Oh! no," said she; "I came with my brother. Here,
Sylvester," cried she, and a smart-looking, country fellow,
apparently about twenty-one years of age, came towards
them. "I'm ready," said Bessie to him, and then, turning
to Quincy, "Mr. Sawyer, make you acquainted with my
brother, Sylvester Chisholm."

"Ah, you know my name," said Quincy.

"I guess everybody in Eastborough knows who you are,"
retorted she with a toss of her head, as she took her brother's arm and walked away.

Hiram had brought 'round the Pettengill sleigh from the
barn. 'Zekiel, Alice, Quincy, and Mandy were the last of

the party to leave. Quincy took his old place beside Alice, while Mandy sat on the front seat with 'Zekiel.

It was a beautiful moonlight night and the ride home was a most enjoyable one.

"I am sorry," said Quincy to Alice, "that you could not take part in more of the games. I enjoyed them very much."

"Oh, Mrs. Mason kept me informed of your actions," said Alice with a laugh.

Halfway to Hill's grocery they passed the Professor and Abner walking home to Mrs. Hawkins's boarding house. They called out, "Good night and pleasant dreams," and drove rapidly on. In the Square a number of the party had stopped to say good night again before taking the various roads that diverged from it, and another interchange of "Good nights" followed.

When Strout and Abner reached the Square it was deserted. There was no light shining in the boarding house. The kerosene lamps and matches were on a table in the front entry. Strout lighted his lamp and went upstairs. Strout's room was one flight up, while Abner's was up two. As they reached Strout's room he said, "Come in, Abner, and warm up. Comin' out of that hot room into this cold air has given me a chill." He went to a closet and brought out a bottle, a small pitcher, and a couple of spoons. "Have some rum and molasses, nothin' better for a cold."

They mixed their drinks in a couple of tumblers, which Strout found in the closet. Then he took a couple of cigars from his pocket and gave one to Abner. They drank and smoked for some time in silence.

At last Abner said, "How are you satisfied with this evenin's perceedin's?"

"Wall, all things considered," said Strout, "I think it was the most successful party ever given in this 'ere town, if I did do it."

"That's so," responded Abner sententiously. "Warn't you a bit struck up when that city feller come in?"

"Not a bit," said Strout. "You know when I come back, you see it was so cussed hot, yer know I said it was the heat, but I knew they wuz there. Mrs. Mason told me."

"Did she?" asked Abner, with wide-opened eyes. "I thought it was one on you."

"When I went down to the road before the bugle was blown," said Strout, "Mrs. Mason told me they was there. You see, Huldy didn't suspect nothin' about the party and so she asked them over to tea. She sorter expected they would go right after tea, but they got singin' songs and tellin' stories, and Huldy saw they had come to stay."

"But," said Abner, "that city feller must have known all about it aforehand or how could he git that cake and frozen stuff down from Bosting so quick?"

"Didn't you say," said Strout, "that you seen them going over to Eastborough Centre about five o'clock?"

"Yes," replied Abner, "but how did he know when it was? Some one must have told him, I guess."

"There are times, Abner Stiles," exclaimed Strout, "when you are too almighty inquisitive."

"Wall, I only wanted to know, so I could tell the truth when folks asked me," said Abner.

"That's all right," said Strout. "Cuddent you guess who told him? 'Twas that Hiram Maxwell. I've been pumping him about the city chap, and of course, I've had to tell him somethin' for swaps. But to-morrow when I meet him I'll tell him I don't want anythin' more to do with a tittle-tattle tell-tale like him."

"What d'ye think of that pome 'bout the bumblebee?" drawled Abner.

"Oh, that was a put-up job," said Strout.

"How could that be?" asked Abner, "when you took it out of your own box?"

"Well," rejoined Strout, "he'll find I'm the wustest kind of a bumblebee if he stirs me up much more. When my dander's up a hornet's nest ain't a patch to me."

"I kinder fancied," continued Abner, "that the reason he had them fancy boxes sent down was because he sorter thought our pound packages would be rather ornary."

"I guess you've hit it 'bout right," remarked Strout; "them city swells would cheat their tailor so as to make a splurge and show how much money they've got. I guess he thought as how I'd never seen ice cream, but I showed him I knew all about it. I eat three sassersful myself."

"I beat you on that," said Abner; "I eat a sasserful of each kind."

As Abner finished speaking he emptied his glass and then reached forward for the bottle in order to replenish it. Strout's glass was also empty, and being much nearer to the bottle than Abner was, he had it in his possession before Abner could reach it. When he put it down again it was beyond his companion's reach. Abner turned some molasses into his tumbler, and then said, "Don't you think 'twas purty plucky of that city feller to come to our party to-night?"

"No, I don't," said Strout, "he jest sneaked in with 'Zeke Pettengill and his sister. He'll find out that I'm no slouch here in Eastborough. When I marry the Deacon's daughter and git the Deacon's money, and am elected tax collector agin, and buy the grocery store, and I'm app'inted post-master at Mason's Corner, he'll diskiver that it's harder fightin' facts like them than it is Bob Wood's fists. I kinder reckon there won't be anybody that won't take off their hats to me, and there won't be any doubts as to who runs this 'ere town. That city feller's health will improve right off, and he'll go up to Boston a wiser man than when he come down."

"That's so," remarked Abner; and as he spoke he stood

up as if to emphasize his words. Before he sat down, however, he reached across the table for the bottle, but again
Strout was too quick for him.

"I was only goin' to drink yer health an' success to yer,"
said Abner.

"All right," said Strout, "make it half a glass and I'll
jine yer."

The two men clinked their glasses, drank, and smacked
their lips.

"If you don't go to bed now you won't git up till to-
morrer," said the Professor.

"Yer mean ter-day," chuckled Abner, as he got up and
walked 'round to the other side of the table, where he had
left his lamp.

"I guess," remarked Strout, "I'll have some more fire.
I ain't goin' to bed jest yet. I've got some heavy thinkin'
to do."

While he was upon his knees arranging the wood, starting up the embers with the bellows, Abner reached across
the table and got possession of his tumbler, from which he
had fortunately removed the spoon. Grasping the bottle
he filled it to the brim and tossed it down in three big
swallows. As he replaced the tumbler on the table, Strout
turned round.

"There was 'bout a spoonful left in the bottom of my
tumbler," said Abner, apologetically. "Them that drinks
last drinks best," said he, as he took up his lamp. "I guess
that nightcap won't hurt me," he muttered to himself as he
stumbled up the flight of stairs that led to his room.

The fire burned brightly and Strout resumed his seat
and drew the bottle towards him. He lifted it up and
looked at it.

"The skunk!" said he half aloud; "a man that'll steal
rum will hook money next. Wall, it won't be many days
before that city chap will buy his return ticket to Boston.

Then I sha'n't have any further use for Abner. Let me see," he soliloquized, "what I've got to do to-morrer? Git the Deacon's money at ten, propose to Huldy 'bout half past, git home to dinner at twelve, buy the grocery store 'bout quarter-past three; that'll be a pretty good day's work!"

Then the Professor mixed up a nightcap for himself and was soon sleeping soundly, regardless of the broad smile upon the face of the Man in the Moon, who looked down upon the town with an expression that seemed to indicate that he considered himself the biggest man in it.

CHAPTER XXVII.

A T the table next morning the conversation was all about the surprise party. The Cobb twins declared that without exception it was the best party that had ever been given at Mason's Corner, to their knowledge.

After breakfast Quincy told Ezekiel that he was going over to Eastborough Centre that morning; in fact, he should like the single horse and team for the the next three days, as he had considerable business to attend to.

He drove first to the office of the express company; but to his great disappointment he was informed that no package had arrived for him on the morning train. Thinking that possibly some explanation of the failure of the bank to comply with his wishes might have been sent by mail, he went to the post office; there he found a letter from the cashier of his bank, informing him that he had taken the liberty to send him enclosed, instead of the five hundred dollars in bills, his own check certified for that amount, and stated that the local bank would undoubtedly cash the same for him.

As he turned to leave the post office he met Sylvester Chisholm. Quincy greeted the young man pleasantly, and asked him if he were in business at the Centre. Sylvester replied that he was the compositor and local newsman on the "Eastborough Express," a weekly newspaper issued every Friday. The bank being located in the same building, Quincy drove him over. Sylvester asked Quincy if he would not step in and look at their office. Quincy did so. A man about thirty years of age arose from a chair and stepped forward as they entered, saying, "Hello, Chisholm, I have been waiting nearly half an hour for you."

"Mr. Appleby, Mr. Sawyer," said Sylvester, introducing the two men.

"Mr. Appleby occupies a similar position on the 'Montrose Messenger' to the one that I hold on the 'Eastborough Express,'" said Sylvester, by way of explanation to Quincy. "We exchange items; that is, he supplies me with items relating to Montrose that are supposed to be interesting to the inhabitants of Eastborough, and I return the compliment. Here are your items," said Sylvester, passing an envelope to Mr. Appleby.

Mr. Appleby seemed to be in great haste, and with a short "Good morning" left the office.

"He is a great friend of Professor Strout's," remarked Sylvester.

"You speak as though you were not," said Quincy.

"Well," replied Sylvester, "I used to think a good deal more of him at one time than I do now, not on account of anything that he has done to me, but I do not think he has treated one of my dearest friends just right. Did you hear anything, Mr. Sawyer, about his being engaged or likely to be engaged to Deacon Mason's daughter, Huldy?"

Quincy looked at Sylvester and then laughed outright.

"No, I haven't heard of any such thing," he replied, "and considering certain information that I have in my mind and which I know to be correct, I do not think I ever shall."

"Will you tell me what that information is?" asked Sylvester.

"Well, perhaps I will," said Quincy, "if you will inform me why you wish to know."

"Well, the fact is," remarked Sylvester, "that for quite a while Professor Strout and my sister Bessie, whom you saw last night at the party and with whom you danced, kept company together, and everybody over here to the Centre

thought that they would be engaged and get married one
of these days; but since that concert at the Town Hall,
where you sang, a change of mind seems to have come over
the Professor, and he has not seen my sister except when
they met by accident. She thinks a good deal of him still,
and although the man has done me no harm personally, of
course I do not feel very good toward the fellow who makes
my sister feel unhappy."

"Now," said Quincy, "what I am going to say I am
going to tell you for your personal benefit and not for publication. I happen to know that Miss Huldy Mason is engaged definitely to Mr. Ezekiel Pettengill, and has been
for some time. Now, promise me not to put that in your
paper."

"I promise," said Sylvester, "unless I obtain the same information from some other source."

"All right," rejoined Quincy, and shaking hands with
the young man he crossed the passageway and went into
the bank.

He presented his certified check, and the five hundred
dollars in bills were passed to him, and he placed them in
his inside coat pocket. He was turning to leave the bank
when he met Deacon Mason just entering.

"Ah, Deacon," said he, "have you come to draw some
money? I think I have just taken all the bank bills they
have on hand."

"I hope not," said the Deacon, "I kinder promised some
one that I'd be on hand about noon to-day with five hundred
dollars that he wants to use on a business matter this afternoon."

Quincy took the Deacon by the arm and pulled him one
side, out of hearing of any other person in the room.

"Say, Deacon Mason, I am going to ask you a question,
which, of course, you can answer or not, as you see fit; but
if this business matter turns out to be what I think it is, I
may be able to save you considerable trouble."

"I don't think you would ask me any question that I ought not to answer," replied the Deacon, glancing up at Quincy with a sly look in his eye and a slight smile on his face.

"Well," continued Quincy, "are you going to let Strout have that money to pay down on account of the grocery store?"

"Why, yes," said the Deacon, "I guess you have hit it about right. Strout seemed to think that there warn't any doubt but what he could get the store, but as he said the town clerk was willing to endorse his note, I came over here last night just on purpose to find that out. I kinder thought I was perfectly safe in letting him have the money."

"Oh, you would be all right, Deacon, financially, if the town clerk or any other good man endorsed his note; but you see Strout won't need the money. I happen to know of another man that is going to bid on that grocery store. How much money do you think Strout can command; how high will he bid?"

"Well, he told me," the Deacon answered, "that he had parties that would back him up to the extent of two thousand dollars, and this five hundred dollars that I was goin' to lend him would make twenty-five hundred, and he had sort o' figured that the whole place, including the land and buildings and stock, warn't wuth any more than that, and that Benoni Hill would be mighty glad to get such a good offer."

"That's all right," said Quincy, "but I happen to know a man that's going to bid on that grocery store and he will have it if he has to bid as high as five thousand dollars, and he is ready to put down the solid cash for it without any notes."

The Deacon glanced up at Quincy, and the sly look in his eye was more pronounced than ever, while the smile on his face very much resembled a grin.

"I guess it must be some outside feller that is a-going to

buy it then," said the Deacon, "for I don't believe there is a man in Eastborough that would put up five thousand dollars in cold cash for that grocery store, unless he considered that he was paying for something besides groceries when he bought it."

"Well, I don't think, Deacon," continued Quincy, "that we need go further into particulars; I think we understand each other; all is, you come up to the auction this afternoon, and if the place is knocked down to Strout I will let you have the five hundred dollars that I have here in my pocket; besides, it would have been poor business policy for you to let him have the money on that note before the sale; for if the store was not sold to him you could not get back your money until the note became due."

"That's so," assented the Deacon. "Well, I've got to get home, cuz I promised to meet him by twelve o'clock."

"So have I," said Quincy, "for I have got to see the man who is going to buy the grocery store and fix up a few business matters with him."

Both men left the bank and got into their respective teams, which were standing in front of the building.

"Which road are you going, Deacon?" asked Quincy.

"Waal, I guess, for appearance's sake, Mr. Sawyer, you better go on the straight road, while I'll take the curved one. Yer know the curved one leads right up to my barn door."

"Yes, I know," said Quincy, "I found that out last night;" and the two men parted.

Quincy made quick time on his homeward trip. As he neared the Pettengill house he saw Cobb's twins and Hiram standing in front of the barn. He drove up and threw the reins to Bill Cobb, saying, "I shall want the team again right after dinner;" and turning to Hiram, he said, "Come down to Jacob's Parlor, I want to have a little talk with you."

They entered the large wood-shed that Ezekiel's father

had called by the quaint name just referred to, and took
their old seats, Quincy in the armchair and Hiram on the
chopping block facing him. Hiram looked towards the
stove and Quincy said, "It is not very cold this morning, I
don't think we shall need a fire; besides, what I have got to
say will take but a short time. Now, young man," continued he, "how old did you say you were?"

"I am about thirty," replied Hiram.

"You are about thirty?" repeated Quincy, "and yet you
are satisfied to stay with Deacon Mason and do his odd jobs
for about ten dollars a month and your board, I suppose."

"Well, he isn't a mean man," said Hiram, "he gives me
ten dollars a month and my board, and two suits of clothes
a year, including shoes and hats."

"Have you no ambition to do any better?" asked Quincy.

"Ambition?" cried Hiram, "why I'm full of it. I've
thought of more than a dozen different kinds of business
that I would like to go into and work day and night to
make my fortune, but what can a feller do if he hasn't any
capital and hasn't got any backer?"

"Well, the best thing that you can do, Hiram, is to find a
partner; that's what people do when they have no money;
they look around and find somebody who has."

"You mean," said Hiram, "that I've got to look 'round
and find some one who has got some money, who's willin' to
let me have part of it. There's lots of fellers in Eastborough that have got money, but they hang to it tighter'n the
bark to a tree."

"And yet," said Quincy, "a man like Obadiah Strout
can go around this town and get parties to back him up to
the extent of twenty-five hundred dollars."

"Yes, I know," answered Hiram, "but he couldn't do
that if the parties didn't have a mortgage on the place, and
o' course if Strout can't keep up his payments they'll grab
the store and get the hull business. I happen to know that
one of the parties that's goin' to put his name on one of

Strout's notes said quietly to another party that told a
feller that I heerd it from that it wouldn't be more'n a year
afore he'd be runnin' that grocery store himself."

"Well, Hiram Maxwell, I've got some money that I am
not using just now. You know that I've got quite a large
account to settle with that Professor Strout, and I can afford to pay pretty handsomely to get even with him. Now
do you think if you had that grocery store that you could
make a success of it?"

"Could I?" cried Hiram, "waal, I know I could. I know
every man, woman, and child in this town, and there isn't
one of them that's got anythin' agin me that I knows of."

"I'd back you up," said Quincy, "but I've got something
against you, and I will not agree to put my money into that
store until you explain to me something that you told me
several weeks ago. I don't say but that you told me the
truth as far as it went, but you didn't tell me the whole
truth, and that's what I find fault with you for."

Hiram's eyes had dilated, and he looked at Quincy with a
wild glance of astonishment. Could he believe his ears?
Here was this young man, a millionaire's son, saying that
he would have backed him up in business but for the fact
that he had told him a wrong story. Hiram scratched his
head and looked perplexed.

"True as I live, Mr. Sawyer, I don't remember ever
tellin' you a lie since I've known yer. I may have added
a little somethin' to some of my stories that I have brought
inter yer, jest to make them a little more interestin', and
p'r'aps ter satisfy a little pussonal spite that I might have
agin some o' the parties that I was tellin' yer about, but I
know as well's I'm standin' here that I never told yer
nothin' in the way of a lie to work yer any injury. You've
alwus treated me white, and if there's one thing that Mandy
Skinner says she can't abear, it's a man that tells lies."

"Then," remarked Quincy with a smile, "you think a
good deal of Miss Mandy Skinner's opinion?"

"I ain't never seen any girl whose opinion I think more of," answered Hiram.

"Did you ever see any girl that you thought more of?" continued Quincy.

"Waal, I guess it's an open secret 'round town," said Hiram, "that I'd marry her quicker'n lightnin', if she'd have me."

"Well, why won't she have you?" persisted Quincy.

"That's easy to answer," said Hiram. "You stated the situation purty plainly yourself when you counted up my income, ten dollars a month and my food and two suits of clothes. How could I pervide for Mandy out o' that?"

"Well," asked Quincy, "supposing I bought that grocery store for you and you got along well and made money. Do you think Mandy would consent to become Mrs. Maxwell?"

"I can't say for sure, Mr. Sawyer, but I think Miss Mandy Skinner would be at a loss for any good reason for refusin' me, in case what you jest talked about come to pass," said Hiram.

"Now," proceeded Quincy, "we will settle that little matter that I referred to a short time ago. You remember you were telling me your war experiences. You said you were never shot, but that you were hit with a fence rail at the battle of Cedar Mountain."

"Waal, I guess if you git my war record you will find I didn't tell yer any lie about that."

"Well, no," said Quincy, "that's all right; but why didn't you tell me that on one occasion, when the captain of your company was shot down, together with half the attacking force, that you took his body on your back and bore him off the field, at the same time sounding the retreat with your bugle? Why didn't you tell me that on two separate occasions, when the color sergeants of your company were

shot and the flag fell from their grasp, that you took the
flag and bore it forward, sounding the charge, until you
were relieved of your double duty? In other words, when
there were so many good things that you could say for
yourself, why didn't you say them?"

Hiram thought for a moment and then he said, "Waal,
I didn't think that I had any right to interduce outside matters not connected with what we were talkin' about. You
asked me if I'd ever been shot, and I told yer how I got
hit; but I didn't consider the luggin' the cap'n off the field
or h'istin' Old Glory, when there wasn't anybody else to
attend to it jest that minute, come under the head of bein'
shot."

Quincy laughed outright and extended his hand, which
Hiram took. Quincy gave it a hearty shake and said,
"Hiram, I think you're all right. I've decided to buy that
grocery store for you for two reasons. The first is that
you have served me well; Mandy has been very kind and
attentive to me, and I want to see you both prosper and be
happy. My second reason relates to the Professor, and,
of course, does not need any explanation, so far as you're
concerned. Now, you go up to the house, put on your best
suit of clothes, tell the Deacon that I want your company
this afternoon; I will drive up your way about two o'clock,
and we will go to the auction."

While these events were taking place, others, perhaps
equally interersting, were transpiring in another part of
Mason's Corner. The Professor had not arisen until late,
but ten o'clock found him dressed in his best and survey-
ing his personal appearance with a pleased expression. He
felt that this was a day big with the fate of Professor Strout
and Mason's Corner!

When he left Mrs. Hawkins's boarding house he went
straight to Deacon Mason's.

"Is the Deacon in?" he asked, as pleasant-faced Mrs.
Mason opened the door.

"No, he has gone over to the Centre. He said he'd got to go to the bank to get some money for somebody, but that he'd be back 'tween 'leven and twelve."

"Oh, that's all right," said Strout, stepping inside the door; "is Miss Huldy in?"

"Yes, she's in the parlor; she went in to practise on her music lesson, but I guess she's reading a book instead, for I haven't heard the piano since she went in half an hour ago."

"Waal, I'll step in and have a little chat with her whilst I'm waiting for the Deacon," said the Professor; "but you just let me know as soon as the Deacon comes, won't you, Mrs. Mason?"

Mrs. Mason replied that she would, and the Professor opened the parlor door and stepped in.

"Oh, good morning, Miss Mason," said the Professor; "I hope I see you enjoying your usual good health after last evening's excitement."

Huldy arose and shook hands with the Professor.

"Oh, yes," said she, "I got up a little late this morning, but I never felt better in my life. It was very kind of you, Mr. Strout, and of my other friends, to show your appreciation in such a pleasant manner, and I shall never forget your kindness."

"Waal, you know, I've always taken a great interest in you, Miss Mason."

"I know you have in my singing," answered Huldy, "and I know that I have improved a great deal since you have been giving me lessons."

"But I don't refer wholly to your singin'," said the Professor.

"Oh, you mean my playing," remarked Huldy. "Well, I don't know that I shall ever be a brilliant performer on the piano, but I must acknowledge that you have been the cause of my improving in that respect also."

"Waal, I don't mean," continued the Professor, "jest

your singin' and your playin'. I've been interested in you
as a whole."

"I don't exactly see what you mean by that, Mr. Strout,
unless you mean my ability as a housekeeper. I am afraid
if you ask my mother, she will not give me a very flattering
recommendation."

"Oh, you know enough about housekeepin' to satisfy
me," said the Professor.

Huldy by this time divined what was on the Professor's
mind; in fact, she had known it for some time, but had assured herself that he would never have the courage to put
his hints, and suggestions, and allusions, into an actual declaration. So she replied with some asperity, "What made
you think I was looking for a situation as housekeeper?"

"Oh, nothin'," said he, "I wasn't thinkin' anythin' about
what I thought you thought, but I was a-thinkin' about
somethin' that I thought myself."

Huldy looked up inquiringly.

"What would you say," asked the Professor, "if I told
you that I thought of gettin' married?"

"Well," replied Huldy, "I think my first question would
be, 'have you asked her?'"

"No, I haven't yet," said the Professor.

"Well, then, my advice to you," continued Huldy, "is
don't delay; if you do perhaps some other fellow may ask
her first, and she may consent, not knowing that you think
so much of her."

"Well, I've thought of that," said the Professor. "I
guess you're right. What would you say," continued he,
"if I told you that I had asked her?"

"Well, I should say," answered Huldy, "that you told
me only a minute or two ago that you hadn't."

"Well, I hadn't then," said the Professor.

"I don't really see how you have had any chance to ask
her, as you say you have," remarked Huldy, "in the short

time that has passed since you said you hadn't. I am not very quick at seeing a joke, Professor, but p'r'aps I can understand what you mean, if you will tell me when you asked her, and where you asked her to marry you."

"Just now! Right here!" cried the Professor; and before Huldy could interpose he had arisen from his chair and had fallen on his knees before her.

Huldy looked at him with a startled expression, then as the whole matter dawned upon her she burst into a loud laugh. The Professor looked up with a grieved expression on his face. Huldy became grave instantly.

"I wasn't laughing at you, Professor. I'm sure I'm grateful for your esteem and friendship, but it never entered my head till this moment that you had any idea of asking me to be your wife. What made you think such a thing possible?"

The Professor was quite portly, and it was with some little difficulty that he regained his feet, and his face was rather red with the exertion when he had succeeded.

"Well, you see," said he, "I never thought much about it till that city feller came down here to board; then the whole town knew that you and 'Zeke Pettengill had had a fallin' out, and then by and by that city feller who was boardin' with your folks went away, and I kinder thought that as you didn't have any steady feller—"

Huldy broke in,—"You thought I was in the market again and that your chances were as good as those of any one else?"

"Yes, that's jest it," said the Professor. "You put it jest as I would have said it, if you hadn't said it fust."

"Well, really, Professor, I can't understand what gave you and the whole town the idea that there was any falling out between Mr. Pettengill and myself. We have grown up together, we have always loved each other very much, and we have been engaged to be married—"

"Since when?" broke in the Professor, excitedly.

"'Since the day before I last engaged you to give me music lessons," replied Huldy.

What the Professor would have said in reply to this will never be known; for at that moment Mrs. Mason opened the door, and looking in, said, "The Deacon's come."

Strout grasped his hat, and with a hurried bow and "Good morning" to Huldy, left the room, closing the door behind him. It must be said for the Professor that he bore defeat with great equanimity, and when he reached the great kitchen and shook hands with Deacon Mason, who had just come in from the barn, the casual observer would have noticed nothing peculiar in his expression.

"Waal, Deacon," said he in a low tone, "did you git the money?"

"Oh, I've 'ranged 'bout the money," said the Deacon; "but I had a talk with my lawyer, and he said it wasn't good bizness for me to pay over the five hundred dollars till the store was actually knocked down to you. Here's that note of yourn that the town clerk endorsed las' night. Neow, when the auctioneer says the store is yourn I'll give yer the five hundred dollars and take the note. I'll be up to the auction by half-past two, so you needn't worry, it'll be jest the same as though yer had the money in yer hand."

Strout looked a little disturbed; but thinking the matter over quickly, he decided that he had nothing to gain by arguing the question with the Deacon; so saying, "Be sure and be on hand, Deacon, for it's a sure thing my gettin' that store, if I have the cash to pay down," he left the house.

He went up the hill and turned the corner on the way back to his boarding house. When he got out of sight of the Deacon's house he stopped, clenched his hands, shut his teeth firmly together and stamped his foot on the ground; then he ejaculated in a savage whisper, "Women are wussern catamounts; you know which way a catamount's goin' to jump. I wonder whether she was honest about that, or whether she's been foolin' me all this time; she'll be a sorry girl when I git that store and 'lected tax collector, and git app'inted postmaster. I've got three tricks left, ef I have lost two. I wonder who it was put that idea into the Deacon's head not ter let me have thet money till the sale was over. I bet a dollar it wuz thet city feller. Abner says thet he met Appleby on his way back to Montrose, and he told him thet he saw thet city feller and the Deacon drive off tergether from front o' the bank. Oh! nonsense, what would the son of a millionaire want of a grocery store in a little country town like this?" and he went into his boarding house to dinner.

A few moments after two o'clock Strout could restrain his impatience no longer, and leaving his boarding house he walked over to the grocery store. Quite a number of the Mason's Corner people were gathered in the Square, for to them an auction sale was as good as a show. Quincy had not arrived, and the Professor tried to quiet his nerves by walking up and down the platform and smoking a cigar. The crowd gradually increased, quite a number coming in teams from Montrose and from Eastborough Centre. One of the teams from Montrose brought the auctioneer, Mr. Beers, with whom Strout was acquainted. He gave the auctioneer a cigar, and they walked up and down the platform smoking and talking about everything else but the auction sale. It was a matter of professional dignity with Mr. Barnabas Beers, auctioneer, not to be on too friendly terms with bidders before an auction. He had found that it had detracted from his importance and had lowered bids, if he allowed would-be purchasers to converse with him concerning the articles to be sold. It was their business, he maintained in a heated argument one evening in the hotel at Montrose, to find out by personal inspection the condition and value of what was to be sold, and it was his

business, he said, to know as little about it as possible, for
the less he knew the less it would interfere with his descrip·
tive powers when, hammer in hand, he took his position on
the bench. Having established a professional standing,
Barnabas Beers was not a man to step down, and though
the Professor, after a while, endeavored to extract some
information from the auctioneer as to whether there was
likely to be many bidders, he finally gave it up in despair,
for he found Mr. Beers as uncommunicative as a hitching
post, as he afterwards told Abner Stiles.

About half-past two Deacon Mason drove into the
Square, and the Professor went to meet him, and shook
hands with him. In a short time his other backers, who had
agreed to endorse his notes to the amount of two thousand
dollars, arrived upon the scene, and he took occasion to
welcome them in a manner that could not escape the atten·
tion of the crowd. It was now ten minutes of three, and the
auctioneer stepped upon the temporary platform that had
been erected for him, and bringing his hammer down upon
the head of a barrel that had been placed in front of him,
he read, in a loud voice, which reached every portion of
the Square, the printed notice that for several weeks had
hung upon the fences, sheds, and trees of Mason's Corner,
Eastborough Centre, West Eastborough, and Montrose.

It was now three o'clock, for that hour was rung out by
the bell on the Rev. Caleb Howe's church. The auctioneer
prefaced his inquiry for bids by the usual grandiloquence
in use by members of that fraternity, closing his oration
with that often-heard remark, "How much am I offered?"

The Professor, who was standing by the side of Deacon
Mason's team, called out in a loud voice, "Fifteen hundred!"

"Well, I'll take that just for a starter," said the auction·
eer, "but of course no sane man not fitted to be the inmate
of an idiotic asylum thinks that this fine piece of ground,
this long-built and long-established grocery store, filled to
overflowing with all the necessities and delicacies of the

season, a store which has been in successful operation for nearly forty years, and of which the good will is worth a good deal more than the sum just bid, will be sold for any such preposterous figure! Gentlemen, I am listening."

Suddenly a voice from the rear of the crowd called out, "T-o-o-t-o to to-oo-two thousand!"

As if by magic, every head was turned, for the majority of those in the crowd recognized the voice at once. There was but one man in Mason's Corner who stammered, and that man was Hiram Maxwell.

They turned, and all saw seated in the Pettengill team Hiram Maxwell, and beside him sat Mr. Sawyer from Boston.

"Oh, that's more like it," said the auctioneer. "Competition is the life of trade, and is particularly pleasing to an auctioneer. The first gentleman who bid now sees that there is another gentleman who has a better knowledge of the value of this fine property than he has evinced up to the present moment. There is still an opportunity for him to see the error of his ways, and put himself on record as being an observing and intelligent person."

All eyes were turned upon Strout at these words from the auctioneer; his face reddened, and he called out, "Twenty-five hundred!"

"Still better," cried the auctioneer; "the gentleman, as I supposed, has shown that he is a person of discernment; he did not imagine that I was engaged simply to make a present of this fine establishment to any one who would offer any sum that suited his convenience for it. He knew as well as I did that there would be a sharp contest to secure this fine property. Now, gentlemen, I am offered twenty-five hundred, twenty-five hundred I am offered, twenty-five hundred—"

Again a voice was heard from the team on the outer limits of the crowd, "Twenty-five fifty!"

The crowd again turned their gaze upon Strout; the

Professor was not an extravagant man, and he had saved a little money. He had in his pocket at the time a little over a hundred dollars; he would not put it in the bank, for, he argued, if he did everybody in town would know how much money he had; so he called out, "Twenty-six hundred!"

"Ah, gentlemen," continued the auctioneer, "let me thank you for the keen appreciation that you show of a good thing. When I looked this property over I said to myself, 'the bidders will tumble over themselves to secure this fine property'; and I have not been disappointed."

Again the faces of the crowd were turned towards the team in which sat Quincy and Hiram. Hiram stood up in the team, and making a horn with his hands, shouted at the top of his voice, for the time overcoming his propensity to stammer, "Twenty-seven hundred!"

"Better! still better!" cried the auctioneer; "we are now approaching the figure that I had placed on this property, and my judgment is usually correct. I am offered twenty-seven hundred, twenty-seven hundred; who will go one hundred better?"

At this moment Abner Stiles, who had been watching the proceedings with eyes distended and mouth wide open, went up to Strout and whispered something in his ear. Strout's face brightened, he grasped Abner's hand and shook it warmly, then turning towards the auctioneer cried out, "Twenty-eight hundred!"

By this time the crowd was getting excited. To them it was a battle royal; nothing of the kind had ever been seen at Mason's Corner before. A great many in the crowd were friends of Strout's, and admired his pluck in standing out so well. They had seen at a glance that Abner Stiles had offered to help Strout.

Again the auctioneer called out in his parrot-like tone, "Twenty-eight hundred! I am offered twenty-eight hundred!"

And again Hiram put his hands to his mouth, and his voice was heard over the Square as he said, "Three thousand!"

"Now, gentlemen," continued the auctioneer, "I am proud to be with you. When it is my misfortune to stand up before a company, the members of which have no appreciation of the value of the property to be sold, I often wish myself at home; but, as I said before, on this occasion I am proud to be with you, for a sum approximating to the true value of the property offered for sale has been bidden. I am offered three thousand—three thousand—three thousand—going at three thousand! Did I hear a bid? No, it must have been the wind whistling through the trees." At this sally a laugh came up from the crowd. "Going at three thousand—going—going—going—gone at three thousand to—"

"Mr. Hiram Maxwell!" came from the score of voices.

"Gone at three thousand to Mr. Hiram Maxwell!" said the auctioneer, as he brought down his hammer heavily upon the barrel head with such force that it fell in, and, losing his hold upon the hammer, that dropped in also. This slight accident caused a great laugh among the crowd.

The auctioneer continued, "According to the terms of the sale, five hundred dollars in cash must be paid down to bind the bargain, and the balance must be paid within three days in endorsed notes satisfactory to the present owner."

Quincy and Hiram alighted from the Pettengill team and advanced towards the auctioneer. Reaching the platform, Quincy took from his pocket a large wallet and passed a pile of bills to the auctioneer.

"Make out a receipt, please," he said to Mr. Beers, "in the name of Mr. Hiram Maxwell; the notes will be made out by him and endorsed by me. If you will give a discount of six per cent, Mr. Maxwell will pay the entire sum

in cash within ten days; whichever proposition is accepted
by Mr. Hill will be satisfactory to Mr. Maxwell.''

The show was over and the company began to disperse.
Deacon Mason nodded to Strout and turned his horse's
head homeward. While Quincy and Hiram were settling
their business matters with the auctioneer, everybody had
left the Square with the exception of a few loungers about
the platform of the grocery store, and Strout and Abner,
who stood near the big tree in the centre of the Square,
talking earnestly to each other.

The auctioneer, together with Quincy and Hiram, entered the store to talk over business matters with Mr. Hill
and his son. Mr. Hill argued that Mr. Sawyer was good
for any sum, and he would just as soon have the notes; in
fact, he would prefer to have them, rather than make any
discount.

This matter being adjusted, Mr. Hill treated the party
to some of his best cigars, which he kept under the counter
in a private box, and when Quincy and Hiram came out and
took their seats in the team, they looked about the Square
and found that the Professor and his best friend were not
in sight.

The next morning at about nine o'clock, Abbott Smith
arrived at Pettengill's, having with him Mr. Wallace Stackpole. Quincy was ready for the trip, and they started immediately for Eastborough Centre. On the way Quincy had
plenty of time for conversation with Mr. Stackpole. The
latter gave a true account of the cause that had led to his
losing his election as tax collector at the town meeting a
year before. He had been taken sick on the train while
coming from Boston, and a kind passenger had given him
a drink of brandy. He acknowledged that he took too
much, and that he really was unable to walk when he
reached the station at Eastborough Centre; but he said
that he was not a drinking man, and would not have taken
the brandy if he had not been sick. They reached East-

borough Centre in due season, but made no stop, continuing on to West Eastborough to the home of Abbott Smith's father.

Here Quincy was introduced to 'Bias Smith, and found that what had been said about him was not overstated. He was a tall, heavily-built man, with a hard, rugged face, but with a pleasant and powerful countenance, and, in the course of conversation, ran the whole gamut of oratorical expression. He was what New England country towns have so often produced—a natural-born orator. In addition he was an up-to-date man. He was well read in history, and kept a close eye on current political events, including not only local matters, but State and National affairs as well.

Quincy gave him Strout's war record that he had obtained from the Adjutant-General's office, and it was read over and compared with that of Wallace Stackpole, which was also in 'Bias Smith's possession. Mr. Stackpole had obtained from the town clerk a statement of taxes due and collected for the past twenty years, and this was also delivered to Mr. Smith. Quincy confided to Mr. Smith several matters that he wished attended to in town meeting, and the latter agreed to present them, as requested.

It was finally settled that 'Bias Smith and Mr. Stackpole should come over to Mason's Corner the following Saturday and see if Deacon Mason would agree to act as moderator at the annual town meeting on the following Monday, the warrants for same having already been posted.

When Quincy reached home he found Hiram waiting for him. They went into Jacob's Parlor and took their accustomed seats.

"Any news?" asked Quincy.

"Not a word," said Hiram, "neither Strout or Abner have been seen on the street sence the sale wuz over, but Strout has got hold of it in some way that Huldy's engaged to 'Zeke Pettengill, and it's all over town."

At that moment Ezekiel opened the door and stepped into the shed. There was a roguish twinkle in his eye and a smile about his lips as he advanced towards Quincy.

"Waal, the cat's out o' the bag," said he to Quincy.

"Yes, Hiram was just telling me that Strout got hold of it in some way."

"Yaas," said Ezekiel, "he got hold of it in the most direct way that he possibly could."

"How's that," asked Quincy, "did Miss Mason tell him?"

"Yaas," said Ezekiel, "he seemed to want a satisfactory reason why she couldn't marry him, and it sorter seemed to her that the best reason that she could give him was that she was engaged to marry me."

Hiram nearly lost his seat on the chopping block while expressing his delight, and on Quincy's face there was a look of quiet satisfaction that indicated that he was quite well satisfied with the present condition of affairs.

"By the way, Hiram," said Quincy, "I believe you told me once that Mrs. Hawkins, who keeps the house where the Professor boards, is Mandy Skinner's mother."

"Yaas," said Hiram, "Mandy's father died and her mother married Jonas Hawkins. He wasn't much account afore he was married, but I understand that he has turned out to be a rale handy man 'round the boardin' house. Mrs. Hawkins's a mighty smart woman, and she knew just what kind of a man she wanted."

"Well," said Quincy, "I want you to tell Mandy to see her mother as soon as she can, and engage the best room that she has left in the house for a gentleman that I expect down here from Boston next Monday night. Here's ten dollars, and have Mandy tell her that this is her week's pay in advance for room and board, counting from to-day."

"Waal, I don't believe she'll take it," said Hiram; "she's a mighty smart woman and mighty clus in money matters, but she's no skin, and I don't believe she'll take ten dollars for one week's board and room."

"Well, if she won't take it," remarked Quincy, "Mandy may have the balance of it for her trouble. The man wants the room, and he is able to pay for it."

Then Quincy and Ezekiel went into the house for supper.

The next morning Quincy found that Uncle Ike had not forgotten his promise, for he was on hand promptly, dressed for a trip to Eastborough Centre. This time they took the carryall and two horses, and Uncle Ike sat on the front seat with Quincy.

They reached Eastborough Centre and found Dr. Tillotson awaiting them. The return home was quickly made and Uncle Ike took the doctor to the parlor. Then he went to Alice's room, and Quincy heard them descend the stairs. The conversation lasted for a full hour, and Quincy sat in his room thinking and hoping for the best. Suddenly he was startled from his reveries by a rap upon the door, and Uncle Ike said the doctor was ready. Quincy drove him back to Eastborough Centre, and on the way the doctor gave him his diagnosis of the case and his proposed treatment. He said it would not be necessary for him to see her again for three weeks, or until the medicine that he had left for her was gone. He would come down again at a day's notice from Quincy.

On his return Mandy told him that Miss Alice was in the parlor and would like to see him. As he entered the room she recognized his footstep, and starting to her feet turned towards him. He advanced to meet her and took both her hands in his.

"How can I thank you, my good friend," said she, "for the interest that you have taken in me, and how can I repay you for the money that you have spent?"

Quincy was at first disposed to deny his connection with the matter, but thinking that Uncle Ike must have told of it, he said, "I don't think it was quite fair for Uncle Ike, after promising to keep silent!"

"It was not Uncle Ike's fault," broke in Alice; "it was

nobody's fault. Nobody had told the doctor that there was any secret about it, and so he spoke freely of your visit to the city, and of what you had said, and of the arrangements that you had made to have the treatment continued as long as it produced satisfactory results. But," continued Alice, "how can I ever pay you this great sum of money that it will cost for my treatment?"

"Do not worry about that, Alice," said he, using her Christian name for the second time, "the money is nothing. I have more than I know what to do with, and it is a pleasure for me to use it in this way, if it will be of any benefit to you. You can repay me at any time. You will get money from your poems and your stories in due time, and I shall not have to suffer if I have to wait a long time for it. God knows, Alice," and her name fell from his lips as though he had always called her by that name, "that if half, or even the whole of my fortune would give you back your sight, I would give it to you willingly. Do you believe me?" And he took her hands again in his.

"I believe you," she said simply.

At that moment Mandy appeared at the door with the familiar cry, "Supper's ready," and Quincy led Alice to her old place at the table and took his seat at her side.

"QUINCY MAKES A SPEECH." (ACT III.)

CHAPTER XXVIII.

THE TOWN MEETING.

THE next day was Friday. After breakfast Quincy went to his room and looked over the memorandum pad upon which he had taken pleasure in jotting down the various items of his campaign against the singing-master. As he looked at the pad he checked off the items that he had attended to, but suddenly started back with an expression of disgust.

"Confound it," said he, "I neglected to telegraph to those congressmen when I was at Eastborough Centre last Tuesday. I hope I'm not too late." He reflected for a moment, then said to himself, "No, it's all right; this is the long session, and my friends will be in Washington."

He immediately wrote two letters to his Congressional friends, stating that he had good reasons for having the appointment of Obadiah Strout as postmaster at Mason's Corner, Mass., held up for a week.

"At the end of that time," he wrote, "I will either withdraw my objections or present them in detail, accompanied by affidavits in opposition to the appointment."

Having finished the letters, he went downstairs to the kitchen, and, as usual, found Hiram engaged in conversation with Mandy.

"You are just the man I want," said he to Hiram; "I would like to have you take these letters to the Mason's Corner post office and mail them at once. You can tell Mr. Hill that the papers relating to the store are nearly ready, and if he and his son will come here this afternoon we will

execute them. I would like to have you and Mr. Pettengill
on hand as witnesses."

Hiram started off on his mission, and Quincy returned to
his room and busied himself with the preparation of the
documents for the transfer of the grocery store, and the
making out of the necessary notes to cover the twenty-five
hundred dollars due for the same.

He had not seen Alice at breakfast, nor did she appear
at the dinner table. He had followed the rule since she
came to the house not to make any open inquiries about her
health, but from words dropped by Ezekiel and Uncle Ike,
he had kept fairly well informed as to the result of her
treatment. At dinner Ezekiel remarked that his sister
had commenced to take her new medicine, and that he
reckoned it must be purty powerful, for she had said that
she didn't wish anything to eat, and didn't want anything
sent to her room.

Quincy politely expressed his regrets at her indisposition
and trusted that she would soon be able to join them again
at meal time.

About three o'clock in the afternoon, Samuel Hill and
his father arrived, and Hiram, remembering Quincy's instructions, had found Ezekiel Pettengill, and all came to the
room together. It took a comparatively short time to
sign, seal, and deliver the documents and papers. It was
arranged that Samuel Hill and his father should take
charge of the grocery store and carry on the business until
a week from the following Monday; as Quincy told young
Hill that he had some business to attend to the early part
of the following week that would prevent his giving any
attention to the store until the latter part of the week.

Quincy treated his principals and witnesses to cigars, and
an interchange of ideas was made in relation to the result
of the auction sale.

"How does Strout take it?" inquired Quincy.

"I don't know," spoke up Hiram. "He acts as though

he thought I was pizen. Every time he sees me he crosses over on t'other side of the street, if we happen to be comin' towards each other."

"Well, I imagine," said Quincy, "that your usefulness to him has departed in some respects, but it's just as well."

"Well," said young Hill, "I can tell you what he said the other night in the grocery store. There was a crowd of his friends there, and he remarked that you," turning to Quincy, "might own Hill's grocery store, but that wasn't the whole earth. He said that he had no doubt that he would be elected unanimously as tax collector, and he was sure of his appointment as postmaster, and if he got it he should start another grocery store on his own hook and make it lively for you."

"Well," said Quincy with a laugh, "competition is the life of trade, and I sha'n't object if he does go into the business; but if he does, I will guarantee to undersell him on every article, and I will put on a couple of teams and hire a couple of men, and we'll scour Eastborough and Mason's Corner and Montrose for orders in the morning, and then we'll deliver all the goods by team in the afternoon in regular Boston style. I never knew just exactly what I was cut out for. I know I don't like studying law, and it may be, after all, that it's my destiny to become a grocery-man."

Quincy took Ezekiel by the arm, led him to the window, and whispered something to him.

Ezekiel laughed, then turned red in the face, then finally said in an undertone, "Waal, I dunno, seems kinder early, but I dunno but it jest as well might be then as any other time. I hain't got nuthin' ter do this afternoon, so I think I'll take a walk up there to see how the land lays."

He said, "Good afternoon" to the others and left the room.

Quincy then took Samuel Hill by the arm in the same manner as he had done to Ezekiel, led him to the window, and said something to him which wrought a similar effect to that produced upon Ezekiel.

Samuel thought for a moment and then said, "That ain't a bad idea; I'm satisfied if the other party is. I'm going to drive over this afternoon and tell the old gentleman that matters are all fixed up, and I'll find out if there's any objection to the plan. Guess I'll go now, as I've got to git back to-night."

So he said "Good afternoon," and, accompanied by his father, took his departure.

"Sit down, Hiram," said Quincy, "I want to have a talk with you. Have you settled up that little matter with Mandy?"

"No," said Hiram, "not yet; I've ben tryin' to muster up courage, but I haven't ben able to up to the present moment."

"I should think," remarked Quincy, "that a man who had carried his captain off the field with a shower of bullets raining about him, or who had pushed forward with his country's flag in the face of a similar storm of bullets, ought not to be afraid to ask a young girl to marry him."

"Waal, do yer know," said Hiram, "I'm more afraid o' Mandy than I would be of the whole army."

"Well," said Quincy, "I don't see ony other way for you except to walk up like a man and meet your fate. Of course if I could do it for you I'd be willing to oblige you."

"No, thank yer," said Hiram, "I kinder reckon thet little matter had better be settled between the two principals in the case without callin' in a lawyer."

Quincy leaned over and whispered something to him.

"By crickey!" said Hiram, "what put thet idea inter yer head?"

"Oh," said Quincy, "since I've had to spend so much time plotting against my enemies, I've got into the habit of thinking out little surprises for my friends."

"Waal, I swan!" cried Hiram, "that would be the biggest

thing ever happened in Mason's Corner. Well, I rather
think I shall be able to tend to that matter now, at once.
One, two, three," said Hiram, "just think of it; well, that's
the biggest lark that I've ever ben connected with; beats
buying the grocery store all holler."

"Well," continued Quincy, "you three gentlemen understand it now, and if matters can be arranged I will do
my part, and I promise you all a grand send-off; but not a
word of it must be breathed to outside parties, remember.
It won't amount to anything unless its' a big surprise."

"All right," said Hiram, "I kinder reckon Sawyer's surprise party will be a bigger one than Strout's was."

"Oh," continued Hiram, "I 'most forgot. Mandy was
up ter see her mother abeout thet room for thet man that's
comin' down from Boston Monday night, and Mis' Hawkins says the price of the room is three dollars per week
and the board fifty cents a day. Mandy paid for the room
for a week, and Mis' Hawkins says after she takes out what
the board comes to she'll give the balance back ter Mandy."

"That's all right," said Quincy, "I've heard from the
man in Boston, and he'll surely occupy the room next
Monday night. Mandy can tell her mother to have it all
ready."

Next morning about ten o'clock, Abbott Smith drove
over from Eastborough Centre, accompanied by his father
and Wallace Stackpole. Quincy took his place beside Mr.
Stackpole on the rear seat of the carryall, and Abbott drove
off as though he intended to return to Eastborough Centre,
but when he reached the crossroad he went through, then
turning back towards Mason's Corner, drove on until he
reached Deacon Mason's barn, following the same plan that
Ezekiel had on the night of the surprise party.

They found the Deacon at home, and all adjourned to
the parlor, where 'Bias Smith stated his business, which
was to ask the Deacon to act as Moderator at the town
meeting on the following Monday. The Deacon objected

at first, but finally consented, after Mr. Smith had explained several matters to him.

"Yer know," said the Deacon, "my fellow citizens have tried on several occasions to have me run for selectman, but I reckoned thet I wuz too old to be out so late nights and have to drive home from Eastborough at ten or 'leven o'clock at night. Besides I've worked hard in my day, and there's no place I like so well as my own home. I'm alwus sorry to go away in the mornin' and alwus glad ter git home at night, and although I consider that every citizen ought ter do everything he can for the public good, I reckon thet there's a good many more anxious than I am to serve the town, and I'm not so consated but thet I think they know how ter do it better'n I could. But as that Moderator work comes in the daytime, as I stand ready to do all I can for my young friend here," turning towards Quincy, "I'll be on hand Monday mornin' and do the best I can to serve public and private interests at the same time."

Wallace Stackpole, while the others were talking, had taken a couple of newspapers from his pocket, and as Deacon Mason finished, he looked up and said, "There's an item here in the 'Eastborough Express,' Deacon, that I imagine you'll be interested in. I'll read it to you: 'We are informed on the best authority that Miss Huldy Mason, only daughter of Deacon Abraham Mason of Mason's Corner, is engaged to Mr. Ezekiel Pettengill. The day of the marriage has not been fixed, but our readers will be informed in due season.'"

"I'm afraid, Deacon," said Quincy, "that's all my fault. I met young Chisholm last Tuesday when I was over to the Centre, and he told me something that actually obliged me to confide in him the fact that I knew that your daughter was not likely to become Mrs. Obadiah Strout, but he promised me on his word of honor that he would not put it in the paper unless he got the same information from some other source."

The Deacon haw-hawed in good old-fashioned country style.

"Waal," said he, "young Chisholm tackled me, and said he heard a rumor abeout Huldy and Strout, and, as you say, Mr. Sawyer, he kinder 'bliged me to set him right. But he made me a promise, as he did you, thet he wouldn't say anythin' abeout it unless some other feller told him the same thing."

"That young man is sure to get ahead in the world; he buncoed us both, Deacon," said Quincy.

"Waal, I dunno as I know just what you mean by buncoed," said the Deacon, "but I kinder think he got the best of both on us on thet point."

As they took their places again in the carryall, Quincy said to Mr. Smith, "If you can drive to Mr. Pettengill's house and wait a few minutes, I think I'll go over to Eastborough Centre with you. I'm going to Boston this afternoon, and shall not be back again until Monday night."

This they consented to do, and after Quincy had obtained certain papers and had packed his travelling bag, he left word with Mandy that he would not be back to the house until Tuesday of the following week, and it might be Wednesday, as he was going to Boston to see his parents.

When they reached Eastborough Centre, Quincy went at once to the post office; there he found a short letter from Leopold Ernst. It read as follows:

"Dear Q:—

"Come up and see me as soon as you can; I shall be at home all day Sunday. Am ready to report on the stories, but have more to say than I have time to write.

Invariably thine,
LEOPOLD ERNST."

Quincy then crossed the Square and entered the office of
the "Eastborough Express." Sylvester flushed a little as
Quincy came in, but the latter reassured him by extending
his hand and shaking it heartily.

"Is the editor in?" asked Quincy.

"No," replied Sylvester, "he never shows up on Satur-
days."

"Who is going to report the town meeting?" continued
Quincy.

"I am," answered Sylvester. "The editor will be on
hand, but he told me yesterday that he should depend on
me to write the meeting up, because he had a little political
work to attend to that would take all his time. He told
me he was going over to see 'Bias Smith on Sunday, so I
imagine that Mr. Smith and he are interested on the same
side."

"Well, Mr. Chisholm," said Quincy, "you managed that
little matter about Miss Mason's engagement so neatly that
I have something for you to do for me. I'm going to Boston this afternoon, and shall not be back until half-past
seven Monday night. I'm going over to see Mr. Parsons
when I leave here, and shall arrange with him to supply all
our boys with all they want to eat and drink next Monday."

"Well, the boys, as you call them, will be pretty apt to
be hungry and thirsty next Monday," laughed Sylvester.

"That's all right," said Quincy, "I'll stand the bills."

"How's Parsons going to know which are our boys?"
continued Chisholm. "They ought to have some kind of
badge or some kind of a password, or your enemies, as well
as your friends, will be eating up your provisions."

"That's what I want you to attend to," added Quincy.
"I'll arrange with Parsons that if anybody gives him the
letters B D on the quiet, he is to consider that they are on
our side, and mustn't take any money from them, but chalk
it up on my score. Now, I depend upon you, Mr. Chis-

holm, to give the password to the faithful, and to pay you for your time and trouble just take this."

And he passed a twenty-dollar bill to Sylvester. The latter drew back.

"No, Mr. Sawyer," said he, "I cannot take any money for that service. This work is to be done, for I understand the whole business, to defeat the man who, I think, has treated my sister in a very mean manner, and I'm willing to work all day and all night without any pay to knock that fellow out. Let's put it that way,—I'm working against him, and not for you; and, looking at it that way, of course, there's no reason why you should pay me anything."

"All right," rejoined Quincy, "I should have no feeling if you took the money, but I can appreciate your sentiments, and will have no feeling because you do not take it. One of these days I may be able to do as great a service for you, as you are willing to do for me between now and next Monday."

They shook hands and parted, and Quincy made his way to the Eagle Hotel, of which Mr. Seth Parsons was the proprietor. Mr. Parsons greeted him heartily and invited him into his private room. Here Quincy told the arrangement that he had made with young Chisholm, and gave him the password.

"Don't stint them," said Quincy, "let them have a good time; but don't let anybody know who pays for it. I shall be down on the half-past seven express, Monday night, and I would like to have a nice little dinner for eight or nine people ready in your private dining-room at eight o'clock. Mr. Tobias Smith knows who my guests are to be, and if I am delayed from any cause, he will tell you who are entitled to go in and eat the dinner."

The next train to Boston was due in ten minutes, and shaking hands with the hotel proprietor, he made his way quickly to the station. As he reached the platform he noticed that Abner Stiles was just driving away; the thought flashed through his mind that somebody from Mason's Corner was going to the city; but that was no uncommon event, and the thought passed from him.

He entered the car, and, to his surprise, found that it was filled; every seat in sight was taken. He walked forward and espied a seat near the farther end of the car. He noticed that a lady sat near the window; when he reached it he raised his hat, and leaning forward, said politely, "Is this seat taken?"

"No, sir," replied a pleasant, but somewhat sad voice, and he sank into the seat without further thought as to its other occupant.

When they reached the first station beyond Eastborough Centre he glanced out of the window, and as he did so, noticed that his companion was Miss Lindy Putnam.

"Why, Miss Putnam," cried he, turning towards her, "how could I be so ungallant as not to recognize you?"

"Well," replied Lindy, "perhaps it's just as well that you didn't; my thoughts were not very pleasant, and I should not have been a very entertaining companion."

"More trouble at home?" he inquired in a low voice.

"Yes," answered Lindy, in a choked voice, "since Mr. Putnam died it has been worse than ever. While he lived she had him to talk to; but now she insists on talking to me, and sends for me several times a day, ostensibly to do something for her, but really simply to get me in the room so she can talk over the old, old story, and say spiteful and hateful things to me. May Heaven pardon me for saying so, Mr. Sawyer, but I am thankful that it's nearly at an end."

"Why, what do you mean," asked Quincy, "is she worse?"

"Yes," said Lindy, "she is failing very rapidly physically, but her voice and mental powers are as strong as ever; in fact, I think she is more acute in her mind and sharper in her words than she has ever been before. Dr. Budd ordered some medicine that I could not get at the Centre, and so

there was no way for me except to go to the city for it.
Let me tell you now, Mr. Sawyer, something that I should
have been obliged to write to you, if I had not seen you.
I shall stay with Mrs. Putnam until she dies, for I promised Jones that I would, and I could never break any promise that I made to him; but the very moment that she's dead
I shall leave the house and the town forever!"

"Shall you not stay to the funeral?" said Quincy; "what
will the townspeople say?"

"I don't care what they say," rejoined Lindy, in a sharp
tone; "she is not my mother, and I will not stay to the
funeral and hypocritically mourn over her, when in my
secret heart I shall be glad she is dead."

"Those are harsh words," said Quincy.

"Not one-tenth nor one-hundredth as harsh and unfeeling
as those she has used to me," said Lindy. "No, my mind
is made up; my trunks are all packed, and she will not be
able to lock me in my room this time. I shall leave town
by the first train after her death, and Eastborough will
never see me nor hear from me again."

"But how about your friends," asked Quincy, "supposing that I should find out something that would be of interest to you; supposing that I should get some information
that might lead to the discovery of your real parents, how
could I find you?"

"Well," replied Lindy, "if you will give me your promise
that you will not disclose to any one what I am going to
say, I will tell you how to find me."

"You have my word," replied Quincy.

"Well," answered Lindy, "I'm going to New York! I
would tell you where, but I don't know. But if you wish
to find me at any time advertise in the Personal Column of
the 'New York Herald'; address it to Linda, and sign it
Eastborough," said she, after a moment's thought. "I shall
drop the name of Putnam when I arrive in New York, but
what name I shall take I have not yet decided upon; it will

depend upon circumstances. But I shall have the 'New
York Herald' every day, and if you advertise for me I
shall be sure to see it."

She then relapsed into silence, and Quincy forbore to
speak any more, as he saw she was busy with her own
thoughts. They soon reached the city and parted at the
door of the station. She gave him her hand, and as he held
it in his for a moment, he said, "Good-by, Miss Linda."
She thanked him for not saying "Miss Putnam" with a
glance of her eyes. "I may not see you again, but you may
depend upon me. If I hear of anything that will help you
in your search for your parents, my time shall be given to
the matter, and I will communicate with you at the earliest
moment. Good-by."

He raised his hat and they parted.

Town Meeting Day proved to be a bright and pleasant
one. At nine o'clock the Town Hall was filled with the
citizens of Eastborough. They had come from the Centre,
they had come from West Eastborough and from Mason's
Corner. There were very nearly four hundred gathered
upon the floor, the majority of them being horny-handed
sons of toil, or, more properly speaking, independent New
England farmers.

When Jeremiah Spinney, the oldest man in town, who
had reached the age of ninety-two, and who declared that
he hadn't "missed a town meetin' for seventy year," called
the meeting to order, a hush fell upon the assemblage. In
a cracked, but still distinct voice, he called for a nomination
for Moderator of the meeting. Abraham Mason's name,
of Mason's Corner, was the only one presented. The choice
was by acclamation; for it was acknowledged on all sides
that Deacon Mason was as square a man as there was in
town.

The newly-elected Moderator took the chair and called
upon the clerk to read the warrant for the meeting. This
was soon done, and the transaction of the town's business

begun in earnest. It will be, of course, impossible and unnecessary to give a complete and connected account of all
that took place in town meeting on that day. For such an
account the reader is referred to the columns of the "Eastborough Express," for it was afterwards acknowledged on
all sides that the account of the meeting written by Mr.
Sylvester Chisholm was the most graphic and comprehen-
sive that had ever appeared in that paper. We have to do
only with those items in the warrant that related directly
or indirectly to those residents of the town with whom we
are interested.

When the question of appropriating a certain sum for
the support of the town Almshouse was reached, Obadiah
Strout sprang to his feet and called out, "Mister Moderator," in a loud voice. He was recognized, and addressed
the chair as follows:

"Mister Moderator, before a vote is taken on the questions of appropriatin' for the support of the town poor, I
wish to call the attention of my fellow-citizens to a matter
that has come to my knowledge durin' the past year. A
short time ago a man who had been a town charge for more
than three years, and whose funeral expenses were paid by
the town, was discovered by me to be the only brother of
a man livin' in Boston, who is said to be worth a million
dollars. A very strange circumstance was that the son of
this wealthy man, and a nephew of this town pauper, has
been livin' in this town for several months, and spendin'
his money in every way that he could think of to attract
attention, but it never occurred to him that he could have
used his money to better advantage if he had taken some of
it and paid it to the town for takin' care of his uncle.
These facts are well known to many of us here, and I move
that a ballot—"

Tobias Smith had been fidgeting uneasily in his seat
while Strout was speaking, and when he mentioned the
word "ballot," he could restrain himself no longer, but

jumped to his feet and called out in his stentorian voice, "Mister Moderator, I rise to a question of privilege."

"I have the floor," shouted Strout, "and I wish to finish my remarks. This is only an attempt of the opposition to shut me off. I demand to be heard!"

"Mister Moderator," screamed Abner Stiles, "I move that Mr. Strout be allowed to continue without further interruption."

The Moderator brought his gavel down on the table and called out, "Order, order." Then turning to Tobias, he said, "Mr. Smith, state your question of privilege."

Strout sank into his seat, his face livid with passion; turning to Stiles, he said, "This is all cooked up between 'em. You know you told me you saw Smith and Stackpole and that city chap drivin' away from the Deacon's house last Saturday mornin'."

Stiles nodded his head and said, "I guess you're right.

Mr. Smith continued, "My question of privilege, Mister Moderator, is this: I desire to present it now, because when I've stated it, my fellow citizen," turning to Strout, "will find that it's unnecessary to make any motion in relation to the matter to which he has referred. I hold in my hand a letter from Mr. Quincy Adams Sawyer, whose father is the Hon. Nathaniel Sawyer of Boston, and whose uncle was Mr. James Sawyer, who died in the Eastborough Poorhouse several weeks ago. By conference with Mr. Waters, who is in charge of the Poorhouse, and with the Town Treasurer, he ascertained that the total expense to which the town of Eastborough has been put for the care of his uncle was four hundred and sixty-eight dollars and seventy-two cents. I hold his check for that sum, drawn to the order of the Town Treasurer, and certified to be good by the cashier of the Eastborough National Bank. He has requested me to offer this check to the town, and that a receipt for the same be given by the Town Treasurer."

Strout jumped to his feet.

"Mister Moderator, I am glad to learn," cried he, "that this son of a millionaire has had his heart touched and his conscience pricked by the kindness shown by the town of Eastborough to his uncle, and I move the check be accepted and a receipt given by the Town Treasurer, as requested."

"Second the motion!" called out Abner Stiles.

"Before puttin' the question," said the Moderator slowly, "I want to say a few words on this matter, and as it may be thought not just proper for me to speak from the chair, I will call upon the Rev. Caleb Howe to take the same durin' my remarks."

The well-known clergyman at Mason's Corner came forward, ascended the platform, took the chair, and recognized Deacon Mason's claim to be heard.

"I have heerd the motion to accept this check, an' I desire ter say thet I am teetotally opposed to the town's takin' this money. If the Hon'rable Nathaniel Sawyer, who's the dead man's brother, or Mr. Quincy Adams Sawyer, who's his nephew, had known that he wuz a pauper, they would 'er relieved the town of any further charge. We hev no legal claim agin either of these two gentlemen. Our claim is agin ther town of Amesbury, in which Mr. James Sawyer was a citizen and a taxpayer. If Mr. Quincy Adams Sawyer wishes to pay ther town of Amesbury after ther town of Amesbury has paid us, thet's his affair and none o' our business, but we've no legal right to accept a dollar from him, when our legal claim is agin the town in which he hed a settlement, and I hope this motion will not prevail."

As Deacon Mason regained the platform loud cries of "Vote! Vote! Vote!" came from all parts of the hall.

Tellers were appointed, and in a few moments the result of the vote was announced. In favor of Mr. Strout's motion to accept the check, eighty-five. Opposed, two hundred and eighty. And it was not a vote.

"We will now proceed," said the Moderator, as he resumed the chair, "to consider the question of appropriating money for the support of the Poor-farm."

The next matter on the warrant of general interest was the appropriation of a small sum of money to purchase some reference books for the town library, which consisted of but a few hundred volumes stowed away in a badly-lighted and poorly-ventilated room on the upper floor of the Town Hall.

This question brought to his feet Zachariah Butterfield, who was looked upon as the watchdog of the town treasury. He had not supported Strout on the question of accepting the check, because he knew the position taken by the Moderator was legally correct, and he was very careful in opposing appropriations to attack only those where, as it seemed to him, he had a good show of carrying his point. He had been successful so often, that with him success was a duty, for he had a reputation to maintain.

"Mister Moderator," he said, "I'm agin appropriatin' any more money for this 'ere town lib'ry. We hev got plenty of schoolbooks in our schools; we hev got plenty of books and newspapers in our houses, and it's my opinion thet those people who spend their time crawlin' up three flights er stairs and readin' those books had better be tillin' ther soil, poundin' on ther anvil, or catchin fish. Neow, I wuz talkin' with Miss Burpee, the librari'n, and she sez they want a new Wooster's Dictshuneery, 'cause ther old one iz all worn eout. Neow, I looked through the old one, and I couldn't see but what it's jest as good as ever; there may be a few pages missin', but what's thet amount ter when there's more'n a couple of thousan' on 'em left?"

Mr. Tobias Smith was again fidgeting in his seat. He evidently had something to say and was anxious to say it.

Mr. Butterfield continued: "Neow, to settle this question onct fer all, I make ther motion that this 'ere lib'ry be closed up and the librari'n discharged; she gits a dollar a week, and ther town ken use that fifty-two dollars a year, in my opinion, to better advantege."

"Mister Moderator," came again from Mr. Tobias Smith, "I rise to a question of privilege—"

Mr. Butterfield kept on talking: "Mister Moderator, this is not a question of privilege; this is a question of expenditure of money for a needless purpose. Yes, Mister Moderator, for a needless purpose."

Mr. Butterfield had evidently lost the thread of his discourse, and Mr. Smith, taking advantage of his temporary indecision, said, "I agree with the gentleman who has just spoken; I am in favor of closing up this musty, dusty old room, and saving the further expenditure of money upon it."

Mr. Butterfield, hearing these words, and not having sufficiently collected his thoughts to say anything himself, nodded approvingly and sank into his seat.

Mr. Smith continued, "I have a proposition to submit in relation to the town library. I hold in my hand a letter from Mr. Quincy Adams Sawyer, whose name has been previously mentioned—"

Mr. Strout jumped to his feet.

"Mister Moderator, I rise to a question of privilege."

"I second the motion!" cried Abner Stiles.

"State your question of privilege, Mr. Strout," said the Moderator.

"I wish to inquire," answered Strout, "if the time of this town meetin' is to be devoted to the legitimate business of the town, or is it to be fooled away in hearin' letters read from a person who is not a citizen of the town, and who is not entitled to be heard in this town meetin'?"

"Mister Moderator," said Mr. Smith, "I am a citizen of this town, and I'm entitled to be heard in this meeting, and the matter that I'm about to bring to the attention of this meeting is a most important one and affects the interests of the town materially. I consider that I have a right to read this letter or any other letter that relates to the question before the meeting, which is, 'Shall money be appropriated to buy books for what is called the town library?' I say NO; and my reason for this is contained in this letter, which I propose to read."

"Go on, Mr. Smith," said the Moderator.

"Well," continued Mr. Smith, "Mr. Quincy Adams Sawyer, in this letter, offers to the town of Eastborough the sum of five thousand dollars, to be used either for purchasing books and paying the expenses of a library to be located in the Town Hall; or a portion of the money may be used to build a suitable building, and the balance for the equipment and support of the library."

Mr. Butterfield was on his feet again.

"Mister Moderator, I'm agin acceptin' this donation. If we take it, we shall only jump out er the fryin-pan inter the fire; instead of buyin' a few books and payin' the librari'n a dollar a week, we shall hev to hev a jan'ter for the new buildin', and pay fer insurance, and we shell hev ter hev a librari'n ev'ry day in ther week, and by'm by the ungodly will want ter hev it open on a Sunday, so thet they kin hev a place to loaf in; and I'm agin the whole bizness teetotally. I've sed my say; neow, you kin go ahead, and do jest as you please."

This was Mr. Butterfield's usual wind-up to his arguments; but on this occasion it seemed to fail of its effect.

The Moderator said, "Was Mr. Butterfield's motion seconded?" There was no response. "Then the matter before the meeting is the question of appropriating money for the support of the town library."

"Mister Moderator," said Mr. Smith, "I move that the donation from Mr. Quincy Adams Sawyer be accepted, and that the library be named 'The Sawyer Free Public Library of the Town of Eastborough.'"

"Second the motion!" came from a hundred voices.

Strout was on his feet again.

"Mister Moderator," said he, "I move to amend the motion by havin' it read that we decline, that the town declines the donation without thanks."

A loud laugh arose from the assemblage.

Abner Stiles had evidently misinterpreted Mr. Strout's motion, for he called out, "Mister Moderator," and when he got the floor, "I move to amend so that the motion would read, this library shall be called the Strout Free Library of the Town of Eastborough."

This was greeted with shouts of laughter, and Strout grasped Abner by his coat collar and pulled him violently back upon the settee.

"Shut up, you fool," cried he between his teeth to Abner; "do you want to make a laughin' stock of me?"

"I kinder thought I wuz a-helpin' yer," said Abner, as he ran his fingers down under his chin and pulled away his shirt collar, which had been drawn back so forcibly that it interfered with his breathing.

"The question now," said the Moderator, "is on the adoption of Mr. Smith's motion. Those in favor will please stand up and be counted."

When the tellers had attended to their duty the Moderator said, "Those opposed will now rise and be counted."

The vote was soon announced. In favor of accepting the donation, three hundred and one; opposed, fifty-eight.

"It's a vote," declared the Moderator.

A dozen matters of minor importance were quickly disposed of, and but one remained upon the warrant, with the exception of the election of town officers. Little squads of the members were now gathered together talking over the most important question of the meeting, which was the election of town officers for the ensuing year. The last item on the warrant read: "Will the town appropriate money to buy a new hearse?"

Mr. Butterfield had evidently been holding himself in

reserve, for he was on his feet in an instant, and he secured the eye of the Moderator and the floor.

"Mister Moderator," began Mr. Butterfield, "I desire to raise my voice agin this biznez of unnecessary and unexampled extravagance. What do we want of a new hearse? Those who are dead and in the cemetery don't find any fault with the one we've got, and those who are livin' have no present use for it, and why should they complain? I know what this means. This is only an enterin' wedge. If this 'ere bill passes and we git a new hearse, then it'll be said thet ther horses don't look as well as the hearse, and then if ther hearse gits out in ther storm, we shell hev ter pay money to git it polished up agin, and we who are livin' will hev to work harder and harder for the benefit of those who are jest as well satisfied with the old hearse as they would be with a new one. I move, Mister Moderator, that instid of buyin' a new hearse, thet ther old one be lengthened six inches, which ken be done at a slight expense."

Mr. Tobias Smith now took the floor.

"I am glad that my friend has not opposed this measure entirely, but has provided for my proper exit from this world when my time comes. I must confess that it has troubled me a great deal when I have thought about that hearse. I was born down in the State of Maine, where the boys and the trees grow up together. I stand six feet two in my stockings and six feet three with my boots on, and I haven't looked forward with any pleasure to being carried to my last resting place in a hearse that was only six feet long. I second Mr. Butterfield's motion, but move to amend it by extending the length to seven feet."

The vote was taken, and Mr. Butterfield's motion was carried by a vote of three hundred and forty to twenty-two. Mr. Butterfield sank back in his seat with an expression on his face that seemed to say, "I've done the town some service to-day."

The Moderator then rose and said, "Fellow-citizens, all

the business matters upon the warrant have now been disposed of. We will now proceed to the election of town officers for the ensuing year."

Mr. Stackpole rose and called out, "Mister Moderator, it is now nearly twelve o'clock, and some of us had to leave home quite early this morning in order to be in time at the meeting. I move that we adjourn till one o'clock, at which time balloting for town officers usually commences."

Forty voices cried out, "Second the motion," and although Strout, Stiles, and several others jumped to their feet and endeavored to secure the Moderator's eye, the motion was adopted by an overwhelming vote, and the greater portion of the members made their way out of the hall and directed their steps towards the Eagle Hotel, as if the whole matter had been prearranged. Here, Mr. Parsons, the proprietor, had set out a most tempting lunch in the large dining-room, and those who were able to give the password were admitted to the room, and feasted to their heart's content.

Abner Stiles, impelled by curiosity, had followed the party, and had noticed that each one said something to the proprietor before he was admitted to the dining-room. Going up to Parsons, he said, "What's goin' on in there?"

"Oh, I guess they're having a caucus," replied Mr. Parsons.

"When thet last feller went in," said Abner, "I saw that the table was all set, and I kinder 'magined they must be havin' a dinner. I'd kinder like some myself."

"Well, I'm sorry," said Mr. Parsons, "but I cannot accommodate any more than have already applied. You can get a lunch over to the railroad station, you know, if you want one."

"I know," answered Abner, "but I kinder 'magine they're talkin' over 'lection matters in there, and I'd rather like ter know what's goin' on."

"Well, I guess you'll find out when they get back to the Town Hall," remarked Mr. Parsons; and he stepped forward to greet three or four other citizens, who leaned over and whispered in his ear.

Mr. Parsons smiled and nodded, and opening the door admitted them to the dining-room.

"Well, that beats all," said Abner, as he went out on the platform in front of the hotel. "They jest whispered somethin' to him and he let 'em right in. I kinder think somethin's goin' on and thet Strout ain't up to it. Guess I'll go back and tell him," which he proceeded to do.

He found Strout and some sixty or seventy of the citizens still remaining in the Town Hall, the majority of whom were eating the luncheons that they had brought with them from home. Taking Strout aside, Abner confided to him the intelligence of which he had become possessed..

" 'D'yer know what it means?" asked Abner.

"No, I don't," said Strout, "but I bet a dollar that it's some of that city chap's doin's. Is he 'round about town this mornin'?"

"No," said Abner, "he went to Bosting on the same train with Miss Lindy Putnam, for I fetched her down, and I saw him git inter the same car with her as I wuz drivin' off."

One o'clock soon arrived, and the large party that had regaled themselves with the appetizing viands and non-alcoholic beverages supplied by mine host of the Eagle Hotel came back to the Town Hall in the best of spirits. The majority of them were smoking good cigars, which had been handed to them by the proprietor, as they passed from the dining-room.

When asked if there was anything to pay, Mr. Parsons shook his head and remarked sententiously, "This is not the only present that the town has received to-day," which was a delicate way of insinuating the name of the donor of the feast without actually mentioning it.

The election of a dozen minor officers calls for no special attention, except to record the fact that Abner Stiles, who had cautiously taken a position several settees removed from Strout, arose as the nominations were made for each office, and in every case nominated Mr. Obadiah Strout for the position, and it is needless to add that Mr. Obadiah Strout had at least one vote for each office in the gift of the town.

The nomination of a collector of taxes for the town was finally reached. Abner Stiles was first on his feet, and being recognized by the Moderator, nominated "Mr. Obadiah Strout, who had performed the duties of the office so efficiently during the past year."

Now the battle royal began. Mr. Tobias Smith next obtained the floor and nominated Mr. Wallace Stackpole.

"In presenting this nomination, Mister Moderator, I do it out of justice to an old soldier who served the country faithfully, and who lost the election a year ago on account of an untrue statement that was widely circulated and which could not be refuted in time to affect the question of his election. I hold in my hand three documents. The first one is a certified copy of the war record of Wallace Stackpole, who entered one of our regiments of Volunteers as a private, served throughout the war, and was honorably discharged with the rank of captain. This record shows that during his four years of service he was three times wounded; in one instance so badly that for weeks his life hung by a thread, and it was only by the most careful treatment that amputation of his right arm was avoided. I hold here also the war record of the present incumbent of the office. From it I learn that he entered the army as a private and was discharged at the end of two years still holding the rank of private, and sent home as an invalid. He is not to blame for this, but inspecting his record I find that within a month after he joined the army he was detailed for service in the hospital, and during the two years of his connection with the army (he was never engaged in a single battle, not even in a skirmish."

Cries rose from certain parts of the hall in opposition to the speaker, and Deacon Mason remarked that while it was perfectly proper to compare the war records of the two candidates for the position, it must be borne in mind that because a man was a soldier, or, rather, because he did a little more fighting than the other one, was no reason that he would make a better tax collector.

The Moderator's remarks were greeted with applause, and Strout's face brightened.

"I am glad to see the Deacon's bound to have fair play," said he to an old farmer who sat next to him.

"Waal, I guess you're more liable to git it than you are disposed to give it," drawled the old farmer, who evidently was not an adherent of the present incumbent of the office.

Mr. Tobias Smith continued his remarks:

"I acknowledge the correctness of the remarks just made by our honored Moderator, and desire to say that I hold in my hand a third document, which is a statement of the taxes due and collected during the past twenty years by the different persons who have held the office of tax collector. I find during nineteen years of that time that the lowest percentage of taxes left unpaid at the end of the year was five per cent; the highest percentage during these nineteen years, and that occurred during the war, was fourteen per cent; but I find that during the past year only seventy-eight per cent of the taxes due have been collected, leaving twenty-two per cent still due the town, and the non-receipt of this money will seriously hamper the selectmen during the coming year, unless we choose a man who can give his entire time to the business and collect the money that is due. This statement is certified to by the town treasurer, and I do not suppose that the present incumbent will presume to question its accuracy."

Strout evidently thought that a further discussion of the

matter might work to his still greater disadvantage, for he leaned over and spoke to one of his adherents, who rose and said:

"Mister Moderator, this discussion has taken a personal nature, in which I am not disposed to indulge. I don't think that anything will be gained by such accusations and comparisons. It strikes me that the last speaker is trying to give tit for tat because his candidate lost at the last election; but I am one of those who believe that criminations and recriminations avail nothing, and I move that we proceed to vote at once."

"Second the motion!" screamed Abner Stiles from the settee on which he had assumed a standing posture.

The vote was taken. Those in favor of Obadiah Strout being called upon to stand up first, they numbered exactly one hundred and one. Then those in favor of Wallace Stackpole were called upon to rise, and they numbered two hundred and eighty-four; several citizens having put in an appearance at one o'clock who had not attended the morning session.

The next matter was the election of the Board of Selectmen; and the old board was elected by acclamation without a division. The meeting then adjourned without day.

The five minutes past six train, express from Boston, arrived on time, and at twenty minutes of eight, Mr. Quincy Adams Sawyer entered the private dining-room in the Eagle Hotel. There he found gathered Mr. Tobias Smith, Mr. Wallace Stackpole, Mr. Ezekiel Pettengill, Mr. Sylvester Chisholm, and the Board of Selectmen, making the party of eight which Quincy had mentioned. It was eleven o'clock before the dinner party broke up, and during that time Quincy had heard from one or another of the party a full account of the doings at the town meeting.

It is needless to say that he was satisfied with the results, but he said nothing to indicate that fact in the presence of the Board of Selectmen. They were the first to leave, and

then there was an opportunity for mutual congratulations
by the remaining members of the party. To these four
should be added Mr. Parsons, the proprietor, upon whose
face rested a broad smile when he presented his bill for the
day's expenses, and the sum was paid by Quincy.

"We had a very pleasant time," remarked Mr. Parsons to
Mr. Sawyer as he bade him good evening.

"I am delighted to hear it," said Quincy, "and I regret
very much that my business in the city prevented my being
here to enjoy it."

On the way home with Ezekiel they went over the events
of the day again together, and Ezekiel told him many little
points, that for obvious reasons had been omitted at the
dinner party.

Quincy was driven directly to Mrs. Hawkins's boarding
huose, for he had explained his programme to Ezekiel. He
turned up his coat collar and pulled his hat down over his
eyes, as he was admitted; and, although Mrs. Hawkins's
eyes were naturally sharp, she did not recognize the late
comer, who proceeded upstairs to his room, which Mrs.
Hawkins intormed him was right opposite the head of the
stairs, and there was a light burning in the room and a good
warm fire, and if he needed anything, if he would just call
to her inside of the next ten minutes, she would get it for
him.

Quincy said nothing, but went into his room and shut the
door, and there we will leave him.

As Strout and Abner drove back to Mason's Corner, after
the adjournment of the town meeting, nothing was said for
the first mile of the trip.

Then Abner turned to him and remarked, "You ought
ter be well satisfied with to-day's perceedin's."

"How do you make that out?" growled Strout.

"Waal, I think the events proved," said Abner, "that
you wuz the most pop'lar man in ther town."

"How do you make that out?" again growled Strout.

"Why," said Abner, "you wuz nominated for every office in the gift o' ther town, and that's more'n any other feller could say."

"If you don't shut up," said Strout, "I'll nominate you for town idyut, and there won't be any use of any one runnin' agin yer!"

Abner took his reproof meekly. He always did when Strout spoke to him. No more was said until they reached home. Strout entered the boarding house and went upstairs to his room, forgetting that there was a man from Boston, to arrive late that evening, who was to have the next room to his.

Abner put up the horse and went home. As he went by Strout's door, thoughts of the rum and molasses, and the good cigar that he had enjoyed the night of the surprise party one week ago went through his mind, and he stopped before Strout's door and listened attentively, but there was no sound, and he went upstairs disconsolately, and went to bed feeling that his confidence in the Professor had been somewhat diminished by the events of the day.

CHAPTER XXIX.

MRS. HAWKINS' BOARDING HOUSE.

MRS. HAWKINS waited patiently until eight o'clock for the gentleman from Boston to come down to breakfast. She then waited impatiently from eight o'clock till nine. During that time she put the breakfast on the stove to keep it warm, and also made several trips to the front entry, where she listened to see if she could hear any signs of movement on the part of her new boarder.

When nine o'clock arrived she could restrain her impatience no longer, and, going upstairs, she gave a sharp knock on the door of Quincy's room.

"What is it?" answered a voice, somewhat sharply.

"It's nine o'clock, and your breakfast's most dried up," replied Mrs. Hawkins.

"I don't wish for any breakfast," said the voice within the room, but in a much pleasanter tone. "What time do you have dinner?"

"Twelve o'clock," said Mrs. Hawkins.

"All right," answered the voice, cheerfully. "I'll take my breakfast and dinner together."

"That beats all," said Mrs. Hawkins, as she entered the kitchen.

"What beats all?" asked Betsy Green, who worked for Mrs. Hawkins.

"It beats all," repeated Mrs. Hawkins, "how these city folks can sit up till twelve o'clock at night, and then go without their breakfast till noontime. I've fixed up somethin' pretty nice for him, and I don't propose to see it wasted."

"What are you goin' to do with it?" asked Betsy. "'Twon't keep till to-morrer mornin'.'"

"I'm goin' to eat it myself," said Mrs. Hawkins. And suiting the action to the word, she transferred the appetizing breakfast to the kitchen table, and, taking a seat, began to devour it.

"Have you seen your sister, Samanthy, lately?" she asked.

"I was up there Sunday evening," replied Betsy, "and she said Mis' Putnam was failin' very fast. She keeps her bed all the time now, and Samanthy has to run up and down stairs 'bout forty times a day. She won't let Miss Lindy do a thing for her."

"Well, if I was Lindy," said Mrs. Hawkins, "I wouldn't do anything for her if she wanted me to. She used to abuse that child shamefully. Is Miss Lindy goin' to keep house arter her mother dies?"

"No," said Betsy, "she's got her things all packed up, and she told Samanthy she should leave town for well and good as soon as her mother was buried."

"I don't blame her," exclaimed Mrs. Hawkins. "Where's Samanthy goin'?"

"Oh, she says she wants to rest awhile afore she goes anywheres else to live. She's all run down."

"P'r'aps she'll go and stay with yer mother for a while."

"No," said Betsy, "she won't go there."

"Ain't yer mother 'n' her on good terms?"

"Oh, yes," replied Betsy, "but the four boys send mother five dollars a month apiece, and us girls give her two dollars a month apiece, and it's understood that none of us is to go and loaf 'round at home, 'less we pay our board."

"That's all right," said Mrs. Hawkins. "You can tell Samanthy for me that she can come here and stay a couple o' weeks with you. Your bed's big enough for two, and I won't charge her no board if she's willin' to wait on table

at dinner time.   You'll get the benefit of it, ye know,
Betsy, for you kin get the dinner dishes done so much earlier."

"That's very kind of you, Mrs. Hawkins," said Betsy,
and the conversation lapsed for a moment till she inquired, "Will your daughter Mandy stay with Mr. Pettengill arter he marries Huldy Mason?"

"I don't know," replied Mrs. Hawkins.   "Mandy says
that Hiram Maxwell is the biggest fool of a man she ever
saw."

"Then she must think a good deal of him," laughed
Betsy.

"Wall, I fancy she does," replied Mrs. Hawkins; "and
I've no objections to him, seein' as that Mr. Sawyer is goin'
to put him inter the grocery store and back him up.   But
Mandy says that he won't come to the pi'nt.   He hints and
hints and wobbles all 'round the question, but he don't ask
her to marry him right out and out.   Mandy says she won't
gin in until he does, for if she does, she says he'll be
chuckin' it at her one of these days that he didn't ask her
to marry him and be sayin' as how she threw herself at
him, but there's too much of the old Job Skinner spirit in
Mandy for her to do anythin' like that."

At this moment Mrs. Hawkins looked up and saw Hiram
Maxwell standing in the half-open doorway that led into
the wood-shed.

"List'ners never hear any good of themselves," remarked
Mrs. Hawkins, as Hiram advanced into the room.

"I didn't hear nothin'," said Hiram.   "I've got too
many things in my head to tell yer to mind any women's
talk," he continued.

"What is it?" cried Mrs. Hawkins and Betsy simul-
taneously.

"Well, fust," said Hiram, "early this mornin' your sister
Samanthy," here he looked at Betsy, "came tearin' down

to Deacon Mason's house and said as how Mis' Hepsey
Putnam was powerful bad, and she wanted me to run
down to 'Zeke Pettengill's and have him bring his sister
right up to the house, 'cause Mis' Putnam wanted to see
her afore she died, and the Deacon's wife said as how I
could go up with him and her, and so we druv up, and a
little while ago your sister Samanthy," here he looked at
Betsy again, "asked me if I'd drive over and ask Mis'
Hawkins if you," here he looked at Betsy for the third
time, "could come up and stay with her this arternoon, for
she thinks Mis' Putnam is goin' to die, and she don't want
to be left alone up in that big house."

Betsy looked at Mrs. Hawkins inquiringly.

Mrs. Hawkins saw the glance and said, "I can't spare
yer till arter dinner, Betsy; say 'bout one o'clock. You
kin go and stay till the fust thing to-morrer mornin'. I
guess I kin manage supper alone."

"Samanthy will be much obleeged, Mis' Hawkins," said
Hiram. "I'll drive right back and tell her, and I'll drive
down agin about one o'clock arter Betsy."

"List'ners get a good p'int now and then," remarked
Hiram to himself. "Now I see what made Mandy so
durned offish. Wall, she won't have any excuse in the
future. I guess I kin ask her a straight question when I
git good and ready, Mother Hawkins."   And he struck
the horse such a violent blow with the whip that it required
all his attention for the next few minutes to bring him
down to a trot. When he had done so he had reached his
destination and his resentful feelings had subsided.

After Hiram had gone, Mrs. Hawkins and Betsy busied
themselves getting dinner. Happening to glance out of
the window, the former exclaimed, "Why, there's Jonas,
and what on airth has he got in his hands?"

Betsy ran to the window and looked out.

"I guess it's a head of lettuce," said she.

At that moment the door opened and Jonas Hawkins entered, bearing a huge head of lettuce in his hand.

"Wall, Marthy," said Mr. Hawkins, "how did the man from Bosting like his breakfast? I kalkilated them fresh-laid eggs would suit him to a T."

"He ain't got up yet," replied Mrs. Hawkins.

"Must have been putty tired," continued Mr. Hawkins. "I kinder envy him. Do yer know, Marthy, if I wuz rich I wouldn't git up any day till it wuz time to go to bed agin." And he laughed loudly at his own remark.

"What do yer expect me to do with that head of lettuce?" asked Mrs. Hawkins with some asperity in her tone.

"Wall," said Jonas, "I was over to Hill's grocery and he'd ordered some from Bosting for Mis' Putnam, but she's too sick to eat 'em, so Sam gave me this one, 'cause we're putty good customers, you know, and I kalkilated that if you made up one of them nice chicken salads o' yourn it might please the new boarder and the old ones too;" and chuckling to himself he laid the lettuce on the kitchen table and walked out into the wood-shed. In a few moments he was vigorously at work chopping wood, whistling to himself as he worked.

"Mr. Hawkins is an awful good-natured man, isn't he?" asked Betsy.

"Yes," replied Mrs. Hawkins, "he's too all-fired good-natured for his own good. If I'd known him twenty-five years ago he'd have money in the bank now. His fust wife wuz slacker'n dish water. But I guess we've talked enough for one mornin', Betsy. You jest git that chicken I boiled and bone it and chop it up, and I'll make the dressin'."

When twelve o'clock sounded from the bell in the church tower, dinner was on the table at Mrs. Hawkins's boarding house. By five minutes past twelve there were fourteen seated at the table, with one vacant chair. Professor Strout sat at the head of the table. At his left was Abner Stiles, while Robert Wood sat next to Stiles. The vacant seat was at the Professor's right hand, and all eyes were turned toward it, for all had heard of the Boston man who had arrived the night before, but who, much to their disappointment, had not appeared at breakfast.

At ten minutes past twelve the door leading into the dining-room from the front entry was opened quietly, and the young man who entered, seeing the vacant chair near the head of the table, took possession of it.

For a moment nobody looked up, each apparently waiting for some one else to take the initiative.

Quincy, for it was he, broke the silence, and immediately every face at the table was turned towards him.

"How do you do, Professor?" said he. "Good afternoon, Mr. Stiles and Mr. Wood. Ah, glad to see you, Mr. Hill," he added, as he espied Samuel Hill at the farther end of the table.

The Professor's face grew crimson, then bright red, and finally assumed a bluish tinge. Abner sat transfixed. The others at the table had a charming diversity of expressions on their faces, ranging from "grave to gay, from lively to severe." No one at the table enjoyed the situation any more than Samuel Hill, who was very fond of a joke and who knew of Quincy's intention to meet his enemy at close quarters.

For several minutes no one spoke. Betsy flew from one to the other waiting upon table, but a solemn hush seemed to have fallen upon the dinner party. Again Quincy broke the silence.

"I trust, gentlemen," said he, "that you will not let my presence interfere with your usual conversation. I have no doubt Mr. Stiles can tell us a good story, and I am

equally sure that Professor Strout has some entertaining
bit of village gossip that he would like to circulate."

Here Samuel Hill purposely dropped his fork upon the
floor and was obliged to get under the table to recover it,
Betsy assisting him in the search.   When they emerged
from under the table their faces were red with their exertions.

As we have seen on other occasions, the Professor was
very quick in rescuing himself from any dilemma into
which he might be thrown.   He saw an opportunity to
divert attention from himself and speedily improved it.

"I think I'll have to walk over and see Miss Tilly James
this afternoon," said the Professor.

At this shot at Samuel Hill and Betsy everybody
laughed, including Quincy, and thus the ice was broken.

"I've heard some pretty big lies told in my life," said
Robert Wood, "but I think Abel Coffin, yer know him,
Professor, old Jonathan Coffin's son, the one that goes car-
penterin', he lives over in Montrose, yer know, can beat
anybody we've got in this town, not exceptin' you, Stiles;"
and he gave the latter a nudge with his elbow that nearly
knocked him out of his chair.

"Tell us the story, Robert," said the Professor, who had
recovered his self-complacency; "we're dyin' to hear it."

"Well," continued Robert Wood, "Abel had been shin-
glin' a house, and I told him there wuz a place where he'd
left off a shingle.   Abel laughed and, sez he, 'If I hadn't
better eyesight than you've got I'd carry a telescope 'round
with me.'   'Well,' sez I, thinkin' I'd fool him, 'let's see
which one of us has got the best eyesight.'   I pointed up
to the ridgepole of the house, which was 'bout a hundred
feet off from where we stood, and sez I to Abel, 'Can you
see that fly walkin' along on the ridgepole near the chimney? I ken.'   Abel put his hand up back of his ear, and

sez he, 'No, I can't see him, but I can hear him walkin' 'round.'"

As Robert concluded, a loud shout of laughter went up from the table. Quincy had no desire to be considered "stuck up," so he joined in the laugh, although he had heard the story in a different form before.

So had the Professor, and he never allowed an old story to be told in his presence without working in two lines of doggerel which he had composed, and of which he was very proud. So, turning to Robert Wood he said patron-izingly, "That was very well told, Robert. The story is an old one, but you worked it up very nicely; but," con-tinued the Professor, "as I have often remarked on similar occasions:

It makes no difference whether a story's new or old,
Everything depends on the way it's told."

Turning quickly to Quincy he said, "No doubt Mr. Saw-yer can favor us with a story that we've never heard be-fore."

Quincy was a little taken aback, for the appeal was un-expected, but he quickly recovered his self-possession and said in a low but pleasant voice, "I am afraid that my story will have to depend on the way it is told rather than upon its novelty." He wondered if his hearers were acquainted with the travels of Baron Munchausen, but decided to try the experiment. "About a year ago," resumed Quincy, "I went down to Maine on some law business. I transacted it, but had to travel some ten miles to the county town to record my papers. I had a four-wheeled buggy, and a strong, heavily-built horse. It began to snow very fast after I started, but I knew the road and drove steadily on. As I approached the county town I noticed that the snow was deeper than the highest building in the town, in fact, none of the town was visible, excepting about three feet of the spire of the tallest church in the place."

Quincy stopped and glanced about the table. Every eye was fastened upon him, and all, including the Professor and Stiles particularly, were listening intently. Quincy continued his story:

"I was well supplied with buffalo robes, so after tying my horse firmly to the weather vane on the spire, I made up a bed on the snow with my buffalo robes, and slept soundly and comfortably all night. When I woke in the morning I was still enveloped in the robes, but found to my surprise that I was lying upon the ground. I looked around, but there was no sign of snow anywhere. I arose and looked about for my horse and buggy, but they were not in sight. Then I remembered that I had tied my horse to the weather vane. Casting my eyes upward I saw my horse and buggy hanging by the strap, the horse having secured a footing on the side of the spire. Happily I had a revolver with me, and with one shot I severed the broad leathern strap. Naturally the horse and buggy fell to the ground. I put my buffalo robes back into the buggy, rode to the court house, had my papers recorded, and then drove back ten miles to town, none the worse for my adventure, but the stableman charged me fifty cents for the strap that I was obliged to leave on the church spire."

A number of low whistles, intermixed with several "whews!" were heard, as Quincy finished his story.

"Wall, by thunder!" ejaculated Stiles, "how do yer account for—"

"I think it must have been a sudden thaw," remarked Quincy, with a grave face.

"One thing puzzles me," said the Professor.

"What is that?" asked Quincy politely, "perhaps I can explain."

"Before you left the church," asked the Professor, "why didn't you reach up and ontie that strap?"

Another loud shout of laughter broke from the company, and Quincy, realizing that the Professor had beaten him fairly by putting a point on his own story, joined heartily in the laugh at his own expense.

"That reminds me," said Abner Stiles, "of an adventure that I had several years ago, down in Maine, when I wuz younger and spryer'n I am now."

"How old be you?" said the Professor.

"Wall," replied Abner, "the family Bible makes me out to be fifty-eight, but jedgin' from the fun I've had I'm as old as Methooserlar."

This remark gave Stiles the preliminary laugh, which he always counted upon when he told a story.

"Did yer ever meet a b'ar?" asked he, directing his remark to Quincy.

"Yes," said Quincy, "I've stood up before one many a time."

"Well, really," exclaimed Abner, "how'd yer come off?"

"Usually with considerable less money than when I went up," replied Quincy, seeing that Abner was mystified.

"What?" said Abner. "I mean a real black b'ar, one of those big, shaggy fellers sech as you meet in the woods down in Maine."

"Oh," said Quincy, "I was talking about an open bar, such as you find in bar-rooms and hotels."

This time the laugh was on Abner, and he was considerably nettled by it.

"Go on, Abner, go on!" came from several voices, and thus reassured, he continued:

"Wall, as I wuz goin' to say, I was out partridge shooting down in Maine several years ago, and all I had with me was a fowlin' piece and a pouch of bird shot. In fact, I didn't have any shot left, for I'd killed 'bout forty partridges. I had a piece of strong twine with me, so I tied their legs together and slung 'em over my shoulder. I was jest goin' to start for hum when I heerd the boughs crackin' behind me, and turnin' 'round I saw—Geewhilli-kins!—a big black b'ar not more'n ten feet from me. I had nothin' to shoot him with, and knew that the only way to save my life wuz to run for it. I jest bent over and threw the partridges on the ground, thinkin' as I did so that perhaps the b'ar would stop to eat them, and I could git away. I started to run, but caught my toe in some underbrush and went down ker-slap. I said all the prayers I knew in 'bout eight seconds, then got up, and started to run ag'in. Like Lot's wife, I couldn't help lookin' back, and there wuz the b'ar flat on his back. I went up to him kinder cautious, for I didn't know but he might be sham-min', them black b'ars are mighty cute; but, no, he wuz deader'n a door nail. I took the partridges back to town, and then a party on us came back and toted the b'ar home."

Every one sat quietly for a moment, then Quincy asked with a sober face, "What caused the bear's death; was it heart disease?"

"No," said Abner, "'twas some sort of brain trouble. Yer see, when I threw those partridges onter the ground it brought a purty powerful strain onto my galluses. When we cut the b'ar up we found one of my pants buttons right in the centre of his brain."

Abner's story was greeted with those signs of approval that were so dear to his heart, and Quincy, realizing that when you are in Rome you must do as the Romans do, was not backward in his applause.

All eyes were now turned to the Professor.

"I don't think," said he, "that I can make up a lie to match with those that have jist been told, but if any of you are enough interested in the truth to want to listen to a true story, I kin tell you one that came under my observa-tion a few days ago."

All looked inquiringly at Strout, but none spoke.

"Wall," said he, "I s'pose I must consider as how silence means consent, and go ahead. Wall" he continued, "you all know, or most all on yer do, old Bill Tompkins, that lives out on the road to Montrose. This occurrence took place early las' summer. Old Bill hisself is too close-mouthed to let on about it, but when I was over there the other day, arter givin' Lizzy Tompkins her music-lesson, I got talkin' with her mother, and one thing led to another, and finally I got the whole story outer her. Old Bill had a cow that they called 'Old Jinnie.' She was always mis-cheevous, but last year she'd been wusser'n ever. She'd git out of the barn nights, and knock down fences, and tramp down flower gardens, and everybody said she wuz a pesky noosance. One night old Bill and his family wuz seated 'round the centre table in the sittin'-room. There wuz Mary, his wife; and George, his oldest boy, a young fellow about eighteen; Tommy, who is a ten-year-older, and little Lizzy, who is about eight. George wuz readin' somethin' out of a paper to 'em, when they heerd a-runnin' and a-jumpin', and old Bill said, 'That varmint's got out of the barn and is rampagin' 'round agin.' The winder curt'ins wuz up, and old Jinnie must 'a' seed the light, for she run pell-mell agin the house, and drove her horns through the winder, smashin' four panes. Old Bill and George managed to git her back inter the barn and tied her up.

"As they wuz walking back to the house, old Bill said, 'Consarn her picter, I'll make beef o' her to-morrer or my name ain't Bill Tompkins.' When they got back to the settin'-room, George said, 'How be yer goin' ter do it, dad?' 'Why, cut her throat,' said Bill. 'You can't do it,' said George, 'the law sez yer must shoot her fust in the temple.' 'All right,' said old Bill, 'you shoot and I'll carve.' So next mornin' they led old Jinnie out with her head p'inted towards the barn. George had loaded up the old musket, and stood 'bout thirty feet off. George didn't know just edzactly where the cow's temple wuz, but he imagined it must be somewhere atween her eyes, so he fired and hit her squar' in the forehead. That was enough for old Jinnie, she jist ducked her head, and with a roar like the bull of Bashan she put for George. He dropped the musket and went up the ladder inter the haymow livelier'n he ever did before, you kin bet. Old Jinnie struck the ladder and knocked it galley-west. Old Jinnie then turned 'round and spied little Tommy. He put, and she put arter him. There wasn't nothin' else to do, so Tommy took a high jump and landed in the pig-sty. Old Bill is kinder deef in one ear, and he didn't notice much what wuz goin' on on that side of him. He was runnin' the grindstone and puttin' a good sharp edge on his butcher knife, when he happened to look up and seed old Jinnie comin' head on. He dropped the knife and started for the house, thinkin' he'd dodge in the front door. Over went the grindstone and old Jinnie, too, but she wuz up on her feet ag'in quicker'n scat. She seemed to scent the old man, for when she got to the front door she turned in and then bolted right into the parlor. Old Bill heerd her comin', and he went head fust through the open winder, and landed in the orchard. He got up and run for a big apple-tree that stood out near the road, and never stopped till he'd clumb nearly to the top. Little Lizzie gave a yell like a catamount and ran behind the pianner, which was sot out a little from the wall. Old Jinnie went bunt inter the pianner and made a sandwich of Lizzie, who wuz behind it. Mis' Tompkins heard Lizzie scream, and come to see what the matter was. When she see Jinnie she jist made strides for the wood-shed, and old Jinnie sashayed arter her. Mis' Tompkins went skitin' through the wood-shed. There wuz a pair of steps that led up inter the corn barn, and Mis' Tompkins got up there jist as old Jinnie walked off with the steps. Then old Jinnie took a walk outside and looked 'round as unconsarned as though nothin' had happened. Jist about this time one of them tin peddlers come along that druv one of them red carts with pots, and pans, and kittles, and brooms, and brushes, and mops hung all over it. He spied old Bill up in the tree, and sez he, 'What be yar doin', Farmer Tomp-kins?' 'Pickin' apples,' said old Bill. He don't waste words on nobody. 'Ain't it rather early for apples?' in-quired the peddler. 'These are some I forgot to pick last fall,' replied old Bill. 'Anythin' in my line?' said the ped-dler. 'Ain't got no money,' said Bill. 'Hain't you got something you want to trade?' asked the peddler. 'Yes,' said Bill, 'I'll swap that cow over yonder; you kin have her for fifteen dollars, an' I'll take it all in trade.' 'Good milker?' said the man. 'Fust-class butter,' said old Bill. 'What do you want in trade?' said the man. 'Suit yerself,' said Bill, 'chuck it down side of the road there.' This was soon done, and the peddler druv up front of old Jinnie and went to git her, so as to tie her behind his waggin. She didn't stop to be led. Down went her head agin and she made for the peddler. He got the other side of his team jist as old Jinnie druv her horns 'tween the spokes of the forrard wheel. Down come the pots, and pans, and kittles, in ev'ry direction. A clotheshorse fell on the horse's back and off he started on a dead run, and that wuz the end of poor Jinnie. Before she could pull back her horns, round went the wheel and broke her neck. The peddler pulled up his horse and went back to see old Bill, who was climbin' down from the apple tree. 'What am I goin' to do about this?' said the peddler. 'I wuz countin' on drivin' her over to the next town and sellin' her or tradin' her off, but I hain't got no use for fresh beef.' 'Wall,' said old Bill, 'con-sidering circumstances we'll call the trade off. You kin keep your stuff and I'll keep my beef.' The peddler loaded up and druv off. Then old Bill went in and pulled Lizzie out

from behind the pianner, and put up the steps so Mrs.
Tompkins could come down from the corn barn, and fished
Tommy out of the pig-sty, and threw a bucket of water
over him, and put up the ladder so George could git down
from the haymow, and they all got round poor old Jinnie
and stood as hard as they could and laughed." Here Professor Strout pushed back his chair and rose to his feet.
"That's how old Bill Tompkins got his beef."

There was a general laugh and a pushing back of chairs,
and the whole company arose and went in various directions to their afternoon work. Professor Strout went into
the front entry, for he always entered and left the house by
the front door. Quincy followed him, and closing the door
that led into the dining-room, said, "Mr. Strout, I would
like to see you in my room for half an hour on important
business."

"I guess 'tain't as important as some business of my own
I've got to attend to this arternoon. I'm goin' over to the
Centre to fix up my accounts as tax collector with the town
treasurer."

"I think my business is fully as important as that," said
Quincy, "it relates to your appointment as postmaster."

"Oh, you've got a hand in that, have yer?" asked Strout,
an angry flush suffusing his face.

"I have both hands in it," replied Quincy imperturbably,
"and it rests with you entirely whether I keep hold or let
go."

"Wall," said Strout, looking at his watch, "I kin spare
you half an hour, if it will be as great an accommodation
to yer as yer seem to think it will."

And he followed Quincy upstairs to the latter's room.

CHAPTER XXX.

WHEN they entered the room Quincy motioned Strout to a chair, which he took. He then closed the door and, taking a cigar case from his pocket, offered a cigar to Strout, which the latter refused. Quincy then lighted a cigar and, throwing himself into an armchair in a comfortable position, looked straight at the Professor, who returned his gaze defiantly, and said:

"Mr. Strout, there is an open account of some two month's standing between us, and I have asked you to come up here to-day, because I think it is time for a settlement"

"I don't owe you nuthin'," said Strout, doggedly.

"I think you owe me better treatment than you have given me the past two months," remarked Quincy, "but we'll settle that point later."

"I guess I've treated you as well as you have me," retorted Strout, with a sneer.

"But you began it," said Quincy, "and had it all your own way for two months; I waited patiently for you to stop, but you wouldn't, so the last week I've been squaring up matters, and there is only one point that hasn't been settled. From what I have heard," continued Quincy, "I am satisfied that Miss Mason has received full reparation for any slanderous remarks that may have been started or circulated by you concerning herself."

The Professor attentively regarded the pattern of the carpet on the floor.

Quincy continued, "Miss Lindy Putnam has repeated to

me what she told Mr. Stiles about her visit to Boston, and attributed the distorted and untrue form in which it reached the inhabitants of this town to your well-known powers of invention. Am I right?"

The Professor looked up. "I'll have somethin' to say when you git through," he replied.

"I expect and ask no apology or reparation for what you've said about me," remarked Quincy. "You made your boast that one of us had got to leave town, and it wouldn't be you. When I heard that I determined to stay at what-ever cost, and we'll settle this afternoon which one of us is going to change his residence."

"I don't think you kin run me out o' town," said Strout, savagely.

"Well, I don't know," rejoined Quincy. "Let us see what I have done in a week. You insulted Mr. Pettengill and his sister by not inviting them to the surprise party. I know it was done to insult me rather than them, but you will remember that we three were present, and had a very pleasant time. I was the lawyer that advised Deacon Mason not to loan that five hundred dollars to pay down on the store. I told the Deacon I would loan him five hundred dollars if the store was knocked down to you, but I would have had that store if it had cost me ten thousand dollars instead of three. I was the one who put your war record in the hands of Mr. Tobias Smith, and I was the one that prepared the statement which showed how negligent you had been in attending to your duties as tax collector."

"Payin' so much attention to other people's business must have made yer forget yer own," said Strout, shutting his teeth together with a snap.

"Oh, no," remarked Quincy, with a laugh; "I had plenty of time left to take a hand in village politics, and my friend Mr. Stackpole was elected by a very handsome vote, as you have no doubt heard." Strout dug his heel into the carpet, but said nothing.

"Now," continued Quincy, "I've had your appointment as postmaster held up till you and I come to terms."

"You're takin' a lot of trouble for nothin'," said Strout. "I can't be postmaster unless I have a store. I guess I kin manage to live with my music teachin' and organ playin' at the church."

"I've thought of that," said Quincy. "I don't wish to go to extremes, but I will if it is necessary. Before you leave this room, Mr. Strout, you must decide whether you will work with me or against me in the future."

"S'posin' I decide to work agin yer?" asked Strout; "what then?"

"Well," said Quincy sternly, "if you drive me to it, I'll bring down a couple of good music teachers from Boston. They'll teach music for nothing, and I'll pay them good salaries. The church needs a new organ, and I'll make them a present of one, on condition that they get a new organist."

Strout looked down reflectively for a few minutes, then he glanced up and a queer smile passed over his face. "S'posin' I switch 'round," said he, "and say I'll work with yer?"

"If you say it and mean it, Mr. Strout," replied Quincy, rising from his chair, "I'll cross off the old score and start fresh from to-day. I'm no Indian, and have no vindictive feelings. You and I have been playing against each other and you've lost every trick. Now, if you say so, we'll play as partners. I'll give you a third interest in the grocery store for a thousand dollars. The firm name shall be Strout & Maxwell. I'll put in another thousand dollars to buy a couple of horses and wagons, and we'll take orders and deliver goods free to any family within five miles of the store. Maxwell will have a third, and I'll have a third as silent

partner, and I'll see that you get your appointment as
postmaster."

Quincy looked at Strout expectantly, awaiting his answer. Finally it came.

"Considerin' as how you put it," said Strout, "I don't
think you and me will clash in the futur'."

Quincy extended his hand, which Strout took, and the
men shook hands.

"That settles it," said Quincy.

"Just half an hour!" exclaimed Strout, looking at his
watch.

A loud knock was heard on the door.

"I guess Abner has got tired o' waitin' and has come
arter me," remarked Strout.

Quincy opened the door and Mr. Stiles stood revealed.

"Is Professor Strout here?" asked he.

"Yes," said Quincy; "come in."

"I guess I'll see him out here," continued Abner. "What
I've got to say may be kinder private."

"Come in, Abner," cried Strout, "and let's hear what's
on your mind."

"Wall," said Abner, looking askance at Quincy, "if yer
satisfied, I am. Hiram Maxwell's jest come down from
Mis' Putnam's, and Mis' Heppy Putnam's dead,"—
Quincy started on hearing this,—"and Samanthy Green is
at her wits' end, 'cause she never was alone in the house
with a dead pusson afore, an' Hiram's goin' to take Betsy
Green back to stay with her sister, and then he's goin' to
take Miss Alice Pettengill down home, cuz Miss Pettengill's most tired out; cuz, you see, she's been there since
eight o'clock this mornin', and Mis' Putnam didn't die till
about one o'clock, and Samanthy says Mis' Putnam took
on awful, so you could hear her all over the house, and
Miss Lindy Putnam, she's goin' to take the next train to
Bosting—she's goin', bag and baggage—and I've got to

drive her over to the station, and Bob Wood, he's comin'
along with a waggin to carry her trunks and bandboxes
and sich, and so I've come to tell yer, Professor, that I
can't take yer over to the Centre this arternoon, no how."

"That's all right, Abner," said Strout; "considerin' as
how things has gone, to-morrow will do just as well, but I
wish you'd drop in and tell the town treasurer that I'm
goin' into business with Mr. Maxwell and Mr. Sawyer
here,"—Abner's eyes dilated,—"under the firm name of
Strout, Maxwell, & Co."

"No!" interrupted Quincy, "let the sign read, Strout &
Maxwell."

"And," continued Mr. Strout, "Mr. Sawyer here is goin'
to push through my app'intment as postmaster."

By this time Abner's mouth was wide open. Quincy saw
it, and imagined the conflict going on in poor Abner's
mind.

"What Mr. Strout says is correct," remarked Quincy,
"but you have no time to lose now. Perhaps to-night Mr.
Strout will explain the matter more fully to you."

Abner turned, without a word, and left the room.

"Mr. Stiles is a faithful friend of yours," said Quincy,
turning to the Professor.

"Yes," assented Strout; "Abner's a very good shaft
horse, but he wouldn't be of much vally as a lead."

Quincy again extended his cigar case. This time the
Professor did not refuse, but took two. Holding up one
of them between his fingers, he said, "This is the one I
didn't take when I came in."

"I will have the partnership papers drawn up in a few
days, Mr. Strout, ready for signature, and I will write at
once to my friends in Washington, and urge them to see
the Postmaster General, and have your appointment made
as soon as possible."

"Yer don't let no grass grow under yer feet, do yer?" said Strout.

Quincy was a little taken aback by this remark, for he had not anticipated a compliment from the Professor. He turned to him and said, "Until you forfeit my esteem, we are friends, and it is always a pleasure to me to help my friends."

The men shook hands again, and the Professor left the room.

"Not a bad man at heart," soliloquized Quincy. "I am glad the affair has had such a pleasant termination. Poor Alice! What a time she must have had with Mrs. Putnam, and so Lindy is going to keep her word, and not stay to the funeral. Well, knowing what I do, I don't blame her. Perhaps Mrs. Putnam told Alice that Lindy was not her own child, for Alice would not accept the fortune, I know, if she thought she was wronging Lindy by doing so. I'll go home,"—he smiled as he said this,—"and probably Alice will tell me all about it."

He went down stairs, and not seeing Mrs. Hawkins in the dining-room, walked out into the kitchen, where she was hard at work washing the dinner dishes.

"Law, Mr. Sawyer, why didn't you holler for me ef you wanted anything?"

"I don't wish for anything particularly," said Quincy, "but I do wish to compliment you on your chicken salad; it was as fine as any I ever ate at Young's, or Parker's, in Boston, and," continued he, "here are twelve dollars." He held out the money to her, she wiped her hands on her apron.

"What's that fur?" she asked. "I've got six dollars of your money now."

"That's for Mandy," said Quincy; "and this," pressing the money into her hand, "is for four weeks' room rent; I am liable to come here any time during the next month. I

am going into business with Mr. Strout and Mr. Maxwell
—we're going to run the grocery store over here, and it
will be very handy to be so near to the store until we get
the business established. Good afternoon, Mrs. Hawkins,"
and he took her hand, which was still wet, in his, and shook
it warmly.

He turned to leave the house by the kitchen door, but
Mrs. Hawkins interposed.

"You better go out the front way," said she, and she ran
before him and opened the door leading to the front entry,
and then the front door. As he passed out, she said, "I
wish you success, Mr. Sawyer, and we'll gin you all our
trade."

"Thank you!" said Quincy. He walked down the path,
opened the front gate, and as he closed it raised his hat to
Mrs. Hawkins, who stood in the front doorway, her thin,
angular face wreathed in smiles.

"Wall," said she, as she closed the front door and walked
back into the kitchen, "what lies some folks tell. Now, that
Professor Strout has allus said that Mr. Sawyer was so
stuck up that he wouldn't speak to common folks. Wall, I
think he's a real gentleman. 'Twon't do for any one to run
him down to me arter this."

Here she thought of her money, and, spreading out the
three bills in her hand, she opened the kitchen door and
screamed at the top of her voice, "Jonas! Jonas!! Jonas!!!"
There were no signs of Jonas. "Where is that man? He's
never 'round when he's wanted."

"What is it, Marthy?" said a voice behind her. Turning,
she saw her husband puffing away at his brierwood pipe.

"I thought you went out to the barn," said she, "to help
Abner hitch up?"

"Wall, I did," he replied; "but it didn't take two on us
long to do that. I eat so much chicken salad that it laid
kinder heavy on my stummick, so I went out in the wood-

shed to have a smoke. But where did you git all that money?"

"Mr. Sawyer took the front room for two weeks and paid for it ahead, and do you know he said my chicken salad was jist as good as Mrs. Young and Mrs. Parker makes down to Bosting."

"I don't know Mrs. Young nor Mrs. Parker," said Jonas, "but on makin' chicken salad I'll match Mrs. Hawkins agin 'em any day;" and he went out in the wood-shed to finish his smoke.

As Quincy walked down the road towards the Pettengill house his mind was busy with his thoughts.

"To think," said he to himself, "that while I was listening to those stories, to call them by no worse name, at the dinner table, the woman I love was witnessing the death agony and listening to the last words of a dear friend—the woman who's going to leave her a fortune. Now that she knows that she's an heiress, I can speak; she never would have listened to me, knowing that she was poor and I was rich, and I never could have spoken to her with that secret in my mind that Mrs. Putnam told me—that she was going to leave her all her money. I am so glad for Alice's sake, even if she does not love me. She can have the best medical attendance now, and she will be able to give all her time to her literary work, for which she has a decided genius. Won't she be delighted when I tell her that Leopold has placed all her stories and wants her to write a book?"

As he reached the front gate he saw Hiram driving up the road and Alice was with him. As Hiram stopped, Quincy stepped forward and took Alice's hand to assist her in alighting from the buggy.

"Oh, Mr. Sawyer," said she, "have you heard that Mrs. Putnam is dead, and I've had such a terrible day with her?"

Her nervous system had been wrought to its highest

tension by what she had undergone during the past six hours. She burst into a flood of tears. Then she tottered and would have fallen if Quincy had not grasped her.

"Can you walk?" he asked.

She took a step forward, but he saw at a glance that she had not sufficient strength to reach her room.

"Open the gate, Hiram. Then give the door-bell a good sharp ring, so that Mandy will come quickly."

He took her in his arms and went up the path, by the astonished Mandy, and upstairs to Alice's room, where he laid her tenderly upon her bed. Turning to Mandy, who had followed close at his heels, he said:

"She is not sick, only nervous and worn out. If you need me, call me."

He went into his own room and thanked Heaven that he had been at hand to render her the service that she so much needed. When he went down to supper Mandy told him that Miss Alice was asleep, and she guessed she'd be all right in the morning.

CHAPTER XXXI.

QUINCY reached his room at Mrs. Hawkins's board-ing house about midnight of the day of the town meeting. About the same hour Mrs. Heppy Putnam awoke from a troubled sleep and felt a pain, like the thrust of a knife blade, through her left side. The room was dark and cold, the wood fire in the open grate having died out a couple of hours before, while a cool wind was blowing with great force outside.

Mrs. Putnam came of the old stock which considered it a virtue to suffer and be silent, rather than call out and be saved. So she lay for five long hours suffering intense pain, but declaring to herself, with all the sturdiness of an old Roman warrior or an Indian chief, that she would not ask for any assistance "till it wuz time for folks to git up."

This delay was fatal, or was destined to become so, but she did not know it; she had had colds before, and she had always got well. Why should'nt she now? It is a strange vagary of old people to consider themselves just as young as they used to be, notwithstanding their advanced years. To the majority of the old people, the idea of death is not so appalling as the inability to work and the incapacity to enjoy the customary pleasures of life.

Mrs. Putnam had always been an active, energetic woman until she had lost her power to walk as the result of rheumatic fever; in fact, it was always acknowledged and said by the country folk that she was the better half of the matrimonial firm of Silas and Hepsibeth Putnam. Since her husband's failure to mount to Heaven on the day fixed for the Second Advent she had had entire control of the family finances. Her investments, many of which had been suggested by her deceased son, J. Jones Putnam, had been very profitable.

She owned the house in which she lived, which was the largest, best finished, and best furnished one in the town of Eastborough. It occupied a commanding position on the top of a hill, and from its upper windows could be obtained a fine view of the surrounding country. The soil at Mason's Corner was particularly fertile, and this fact had led to the rapid growth of the village, which was three miles from the business centre of Eastborough, and only a mile from the similar part of the adjoining town of Montrose.

Back of the Putnam homestead were the best barns, carriage houses, sheds and other outbuildings to be found in the town, but for years they had been destitute of horses, cattle, and other domestic animals.

Mr. Putnam had disliked dogs because they killed sheep, and Mrs. Putnam detested cats. For years no chanticleer had awakened echoes during the morning hours, and no hens or chickens wandered over the neglected farm. The trees in the large orchard had not been pruned for a long time, and the large vegetable garden was overrun with grass and weeds.

Back of the orchard and the vegetable garden, and to the right and left of the homestead, were about a hundred and sixty acres of arable pasture and wood-land, the whole forming what could be easily made the finest farm in the town.

The farm had been neglected simply because the income from her investments was more than sufficient for the support of the family. The unexpended income had been added to the principal, until Mrs. Putnam's private fortune now amounted to fully fifty thousand dollars, invested in good securities, together with the house and farm, which were free from mortgage.

When the first streaks of morning reached the room in which Mrs. Putnam lay upon her bed of pain, she seized one of her crutches, and pounded vigorously upon the floor. In a short time Samanthy Green entered the room. She was buttoning up her dress as she came in, and her hair was in a dishevelled condition.

"Why, what on earth's the matter? You wheeze like our old pump out in the barn. You do look real sick, to be sure."

"Wall, if you don't like the looks of me," said Mrs. Putnam sharply, "don't look at me."

"But didn't you pound?" asked Samanthy. "Don't you want me to go for the doctor?"

"No," replied Mrs. Putnam, "I don't want no doctor. The fust thing that I want you to do is to go and comb that frowzy pate of yourn, and when you git that done I want yer to make me a mustard plaster 'bout as big as that;" and she held up her hands about a foot apart. "Now go, and don't stand and look at me as though I wuz a circus waggin."

Samanthy left the room quickly, but she had no sooner closed the door when Mrs. Putnam called out her name in a loud voice, and Samanthy opened the door and looked in.

"Did you call, marm?" she asked.

"Of course I did," said Mrs. Putnam testily. "I guess ye wouldn't have come back if yer hadn't known I did."

Mrs. Putnam was evidently in a bad temper, and Samanthy had learned by years of experience to keep a close mouth under such circumstances, so she waited for Mrs. Putnam's next words without replying. Finally Mrs Putnam spoke. "I wish you'd bring up some wood and start a fire, the room's kinder cold."

When Samanthy reached the kitchen she found Lindy there.

"Why, Miss Lindy," said she, "what are you up so early for?"

"I heard mother pounding and I thought she might be sick."

"She is awful sick," rejoined Samanthy; "I never saw her look so poorly afore; she seems to be all choked up. She wants a big mustard plaster and a fire up in her room, and I don't know which to do fust. Oh!" she cried, "I must comb my hair before I go back;" and she wet a brush and commenced brushing out her long brown hair, which, with her rosy cheeks, formed her two principal claims to good looks.

"Sit down," said Lindy, "and I'll fix your hair up much quicker than you can do it yourself."

"And much better, too," added Samanthy thankfully.

"While you're building the fire," continued Lindy, "I'll mix up the mustard plaster."

When Samanthy entered the chamber with the materials for the fire, Mrs. Putnam opened her eyes and said sharply, "Did yer bring that plaster?"

"No," said Samanthy, "I thought I would build the fire fust."

"Wall," said Mrs. Putnam, "I want the plaster fust, and you go right down stairs and mix it up quick."

When Samanthy returned to the kitchen she found that Lindy had the plaster all ready. Samanthy took it, and started upstairs.

Lindy said to her, "Don't tell her that I made it." As she said this she stepped back into the kitchen and closed the door.

As Samanthy approached the bedside with the plaster, Mrs. Putnam looked up and asked, "Did you make that plaster, Samanthy?"

"Yes'm," replied Samanthy.

"You're lyin', Samanthy Green, and you know yer are. You can't fool me. Didn't I hear yer talkin' to somebody in the kitchen?"

"Yes'm," assented Samanthy.

"Wall," rejoined Mrs. Putnam, "of course I know who it wuz yer wuz talkin' to. Did she make the plaster?"

"Yes'm," again assented Samanthy.

"Give it to me," said Mrs. Putnam.

Samanthy passed it to her, and the old lady crumpled it in her hands and threw it across the room. "Now go down stairs, Samanthy Green, and make me a mustard plaster, as I told yer to, and when I git up outer this I'll see if I can't git somebody to wait on me that kin tell the truth 'thout my havin' to help 'em."

In the course of half an hour the new plaster was made and applied, and a bright fire was shedding its warmth into the room.

"Go down stairs and git yer breakfast," said Mrs. Putnam. " 'Tis a trifle early, but I hearn tell that lyin' makes people hungry."

As Samanthy gave her an inquiring look, Mrs. Putnam said, "No, I don't want nothin' to eat or drink nuther, but when yer git the dishes washed I want yer ter go on an errand for me."

It was half past six when Samanthy Green again stood in Mrs. Putnam's room.

"I want yer to go right down to Zeke Pettengill's and tell his sister Alice that I want her to come right up here. Tell her it's my las' sickness, and I won't take 'no' for an answer. Be sure you put it to her jest as I do; and Samanthy," as Samanthy opened the door and was leaving the room, "say, Samanthy, don't git anybody to do the errand for you."

About ten minutes after Samanthy left the house, Lindy Putnam entered the sick room. Mrs. Putnam's pain had been relieved somewhat by the mustard, and this relief restored, to a great extent, her usual vigor of mind.

"What are you up here for?" cried Mrs. Putnam, a look of displeasure clouding her face.

"I knew Samanthy had gone out, and so I came up to see if I could do anything for you, mother."

"Don't mother me. I ain't your mother, and I mean ev'rybody shall know it soon's I'm dead."

"I've had to say mother before other people," explained Lindy, "and that's why I forgot myself then. Pray excuse me."

"Oh, don't put on yer citified airs when yer talkin' to me. Ain't yer glad I'm goin' ter die?"

"I hope you will get better, Mrs. Putnam," answered Lindy.

"You know better," rejoined Mrs. Putnam. "You'll be glad when I'm gone, for then you kin go gallivantin' 'round and spend the money that my son worked hard fur."

"I've used very little of it," said Lindy; "less than the interest; I have never touched the principal."

Lindy still remained standing at the foot of the bed.

"Didn't yer hear me say I didn't want nuthin'?" asked Mrs. Putnam.

"I will leave the room then," replied Lindy quietly.

"I wish you would," said Mrs. Putnam, "and you'll do me a favor if you'll pack yer duds as quick as yer can and git out of the house and never come back agin."

"I will leave the room, but I cannot leave the house while you are alive," remarked Lindy firmly.

"Why not?" said Mrs. Putnam. "I want to die in peace, and I shall go much easier if I know I haven't got to set my eyes on your face agin."

"I promised Jones," said Lindy, "that I would never leave you while you were alive."

"Oh, you promised Jones, did yer?" cried Mrs. Putnam

with a sneer. "Wall, Jones will let you off on yer promise jest to 'blige me, so yer needn't stay any longer."

As Lindy walked towards the door, Mrs. Putnam spoke again.

"Did yer ever tell anybody I wasn't yer mother?" Lindy hesitated. "Why don't you out with it," said Mrs. Putnam, "and say no, no matter if it is a lie? Samanthy can lie faster'n a horse can trot, and I know you put her up to it."

"I have been impudent and disrespectful to you many times, Mrs. Putnam, when you were cross to me, but I never told you a deliberate lie in my life. I have told one person that you were not my mother."

"What did yer do it fur?" asked Mrs. Putnam.

"I wished to retain his good opinion," replied Lindy.

"Who was it?" inquired Mrs. Putnam eagerly. Lindy did not answer. "Oh, you won't tell!" said Mrs. Putnam. "Wall, I bet I can guess; it's that feller that's boardin' over to Pettingill's."

Mrs. Putnam saw the blood rise in Lindy's face, and she chuckled to herself.

"What reason have you for forming such an opinion?" asked Lindy.

"Wall, I can kinder put two and two together," said Mrs. Putnam. "The day Alice Pettengill came over here with him you two wuz down in the parlor together, and I had to pound on the floor three times afore I could make him hear. I knew you must be either spoonin' or abusin' me."

It was with difficulty that Lindy kept back the words which rose to her lips, but she said nothing.

"Did yer tell him that I wuz goin' to leave my money to some one else?"

"It wasn't necessary," said Lindy, "I judged from some things that he said that you had told him yourself."

"Did he tell you who it wuz?" persisted Mrs. Putnam.

"No," said Lindy. "I did my best to find out, but he wouldn't tell me."

"Good for him," cried Mrs. Putnam. "Then ye don't know?"

"I can put two and two together," replied Lindy.

"But where'd yer git the two and two?" asked Mrs. Putnam.

"Oh, I have surmised for a long time," continued Lindy. "This morning I asked Samanthy where she was going, and she said down to Pettengill's. Then I knew."

"I told her not to tell," said Mrs. Putnam, "the lyin' jade. If I git up off this bed she'll git her walkin' ticket."

"She's ready to go," said Lindy; "she told me this morning that she'd wait until you got a new girl."

Mrs. Putnam closed her eyes and placed both of her hands over her heart. Despite her fortitude the intense pain wrung a groan from her.

Lindy rushed forward and dropped on her knees beside the bed. "Forgive me, Mrs. Putnam," said she, "but you spoke such cruel words to me that I could not help answering you in the same way. I am so sorry. I loved your son with all my heart, and I had no right to speak so to his mother, no matter what she said to me."

The paroxysm of pain had passed, and Mrs. Putnam was her old self again. Looking at the girl who was kneeling with her head bowed down she said, "I guess both of us talked about as we felt; as for loving my son, yer had no right to, and he had no right to love you."

"But we were brother and sister," cried Lindy, looking up.

" 'Twould have been all right if he'd let it stop there," replied Mrs. Putnam. "Who put it into his head that there was no law agin a man marryin' his adopted sister? You wuz a woman grown of eighteen, and he wuz only a young boy of sixteen, and you made him love yer and turn agin his mother, and then we had ter send him away from home ter keep yer apart, and then you ran after him, and then he died, and it broke my heart. You wuz the cause of it, but for yer he would be livin' now, a comfort to his poor old mother. I hated yer then for what yer did. Ev'ry time I look at yer I think of the happiness you stole from me, an' I hate yer wusser'n ever."

"Oh, mother, mother!" sobbed Lindy.

"I'm not your mother," screamed Mrs. Putnam. "I s'pose you must have had one, but you'll never know who she wuz; she didn't care nuthin' fer yer, for she left yer in the road, and Silas was fool enough to pick yer up and bring yer home. What yer right name is nobody knows, and mebbe yer ain't got none."

At this taunt Lindy arose to her feet and looked defiantly at Mrs. Putnam. "You are not telling the truth, Mrs. Putnam," said the girl; "you know who my parents were, but you will not tell me."

"That's right," said Mrs. Putnam, "git mad and show yer temper; that's better than sheddin' crocodile's tears, as yer've been doin'; yer've been a curse to me from the day I fust set eyes on yer. I've said I hate yer, and I do, an' I'll never forgive yer fer what yer've done to me."

Lindy saw that words were useless. Perhaps Mrs. Putnam might recover, and if she did not provoke her too far she might relent some day and tell her what she knew about her parents; so she walked to the door and opened it. Then she turned and said, "Good-by, Mrs. Putnam, I truly hope that you will recover."

"Wall, I sha'n't," said Mrs. Putnam. "I'm goin' to die, I want ter die. I want ter see Jones; I want ter talk ter him; I want ter tell him how much I loved him—how much I've suffered through yer. I'm goin' ter tell him how I've hated yer and what fer, and when I git through talkin' to him, I'll guarantee he'll be my way o' thinkin'."

As the old woman said this, with an almost superhuman

effort she raised herself to a sitting posture, pointed her finger at Lindy, and gave utterances to a wild, hysterical laugh that almost froze the blood in the poor girl's veins.

Lindy slammed the door behind her, rushed to her own room, locked the door, and threw herself face downward upon the bed. Should she ever forget those last fearful words, that vengeful face, that taunting finger, or that mocking laugh?

Samanthy took Alice up to Mrs. Putnam's room about eight o'clock. Alice knelt by the bedside. She could not see the old lady's face, but she took her withered hands in hers, and caressed them lovingly, saying, "Aunt Heppy, I am sorry you are so sick. Have you had the doctor?"

The old lady drew the young girl's head down close to her and kissed her upon the cheek. "The docter kin do me no good. I've sent fer yer becuz I know yer love me, and I wanted to know that one person would be sorry when I wuz gone."

"I'm so sorry," said Alice, "that I cannot see to help you, but you are not going to die; you must have the doctor at once."

"No," said Mrs. Putnam, "I want to die, I want to see my boy. I sent for you becuz I wanted to tell you that I am goin' to leave this house and farm and all my money to you."

"To me!" cried Alice, astonished. "Why, how can you talk so, Aunt Heppy? You have a daughter, who is your legal heir; how could you ever think of robbing your own flesh and blood of her inheritance?"

"She's no flesh and blood of mine!"

"What!" cried Alice, "isn't Lindy your own child?"

"No," said Mrs. Putnam savagely. "Silas and me didn't think we'd have any children, so we 'dopted her jest afore we moved down from New Hampshire and settled in this town."

"Do you know who her parents were?" inquired Alice.

"Alice, what did you do with that letter I gave you the las' time you were here?"

"It is locked up in my writing desk at home," answered Alice.

"What did yer promise to do with it?" said Mrs. Putnam.

"I promised," replied Alice, "not to let any one see it, and to destroy it within twenty-four hours after your death."

"And you will keep yer promise?" asked the old woman.

"My word is sacred," said Alice solemnly.

"Alice Pettengill," cried Mrs. Putnam, "if you break your word to me I shall be sorry that I ever loved you; I shall repent that I made you my heiress." And her voice rose to a sharp, shrill tone. "I'll haunt you as long as you live."

The girl shrank back from her.

"Don't mind a poor old woman whose hours are numbered, but you'll keep yer promise, won't yer, Alice?" And she grasped both Alice's hands convulsively.

"Aunt Heppy," said Alice, "I've given you my promise, and I'll keep my word whatever happens. So don't worry any more about it, Auntie."

For a few moments Mrs. Putnam remained quiet; then she spoke in clear, even tones. Not a word was lost upon Alice. "This adopted daughter of mine has been a curse to me ever since I knew her. She was two years older than Jones. They grew up together as brother and sister, but she wasn't satisfied with that, she fell in love with my son, and she made him love her. She turned him agin his mother. She found out that there wuz no law agin a man's marryin' his adopted sister. We had to send him away from home, but she followed him. She wuz goin' to elope with him, but I got wind of it, and I stopped that; then Jones died away from home and left her all his money. He wuz so bitter agin me that he put in his will that she

was not to touch a dollar of my money, but better that than
to have her marry him. I stopped that!" and the old
woman chuckled to herself. Then her mood changed.
"Such a marriage would 'a' been a sin agin God and man,"
she said sternly. "She robbed me of my son, my only
boy, but I'll git even with her. She asked me this mornin'
if I knew who her parents wuz. I told her no, that she
was a waif picked up in a New Hampshire road, but I lied
to her. I had to."

"But do you know who they were?" said Alice.

"Certainly I do," said Mrs. Putnam; "that letter you've
got, and that yer promised to destroy, tells all about 'em,
but she shall never see it. Never! Never!! Never!!!"

Again she rose to a sitting posture, and again that wild,
mocking laugh rang through the house. Lindy, still lying
upon her bed in her room, heard it, shuddered, and covered
her ears with her hands to shut out the terrible sound.
Samanthy, in the kitchen, heard it, and saying to herself,
"Mrs. Putnam has gone crazy, and only that blind girl
with her," ran upstairs.

When Mrs. Putnam uttered that wild laugh, Alice started
from her chair with beating heart and a frightened look
upon her face. As the door opened and Samanthy entered,
Alice stepped forward. She could not see who it was, but
supposing it was Lindy, she cried out, "Oh, Lindy, I'm so
glad you've come!"

Mrs. Putnam had fallen back exhausted upon her pillow; when she heard the name Lindy she tried to rise
again, but could not. But her indomitable spirit still sur-
vived.

"So you've come back, have you?" she shrieked. "Yer
couldn't let me die in peace. You want to hear more, do
you? Well, I'll tell you the truth. I know who your parents are, but I destroyed the letter; it's burned. That's
what I had the fire built for this mornin'. You robbed me
of my son and I've got even with yer." The old woman

pointed her finger at poor Samanthy, who stood petrified
in the doorway, and shrieked again, "Go!" and she pointed
her withered finger toward the door, "and hunt for your
parents."

The astonished Samanthy finally plucked up courage to
close the door; she ran to Lindy's room and pounded upon
the door until Lindy was forced to admit her; then the
frightened girl told Lindy what she had heard, and again
the worse than orphan threw herself upon her bed and
prayed that she, too, might die.

Alice did not swoon, but she sank upon the floor, overcome by the horror of the scene. No sound came from
the bed. Was she dead? Alice groped her way back to
the chair in which she had previously sat; she leaned over
and listened. Mrs. Putnam was breathing still—faint,
short breaths. Alice took one of her hands in hers and
prayed for her. Then she prayed for the unhappy girl.
Then she thought of the letter and the promise she had
made. Should she keep her promises to the dying woman, and thus be a party to the wronging of this poor girl?

"Mrs. Putnam! Mrs. Putnam!! Aunt Heppy!!!" she
cried; "take back your fortune, I do not want it; only release me from my oath. Oh, that I could send for that
letter and put it back into her hands before she dies! If
Mr. Sawyer were only here; but I do not know where to
find him."

For hours, it seemed ages to Alice, she remained by the
bedside of the dying woman, seeing nothing, but listening
intently, and hoping that she would revive, hear her words,
and release her from that horrid oath.

Suddenly, Alice started; the poor old wrinkled, wasted
hand that she held in hers, was cold—so cold—she leaned
over and put her ear above the old woman's lips. There
was no sound of breathing. She pulled down the bed-
clothes and placed her hand upon her heart. It was still.

Mrs. Putnam had gone to meet the boy she had loved and lost.

Feeling her way along the wall, she reached the door. Flinging it wide open, she cried, "Samantha! Lindy!"

Samanthy came to the foot of the stairs.

"What is it, Miss Pettengill?" asked she.

"She's dead," said Alice, and she sank down upon the stairway.

Samanthy ran quickly upstairs. She went first to Miss Lindy's room and told her that all was over; then she came back, went into Mrs. Putnam's room, pulled down the curtains, went to the bed and laid the sheet over Mrs. Putnam's face. She looked at the fire to see that it was safe, came out and closed the door. Then she helped Alice down stairs, led her into the parlor and seated her in an easy-chair.

"I'll bring you a nice cup of hot tea," said she; "I've just made some for dinner."

Lindy came down stairs and went to the front door. Hiram was there, smoking a cigar, and beating his arms to keep warm. He had been waiting outside for a couple of hours, and he was nearly frozen.

"Mr. Maxwell," said Lindy; and Hiram came up the steps. "Mrs. Putnam is dead," said she. "She expired just a few moments ago, about one o'clock," she continued, looking at her watch. "I want you to go right down to Mrs. Hawkins's and bring Betsy Green back to stay with her sister; then tell Mr. Stiles to come up at once with the buggy and a wagon to carry my trunks to the station. Tell Mr. Stiles I am going to Boston on the next train. When you come back you can take Miss Pettengill home. She will be through her lunch by the time you get back. After you've taken her home, I want you to go and get Mrs. Pinkham, the nurse; tell her Mrs. Putnam is dead, and that I want her to come and lay her out. Then drive over to Montrose and tell Mr. Tilton, the undertaker, that I

want him to make all the arrangements for the funeral
And take this for your trouble," said she, as she passed
him a five dollar bill.

"Oh, that's too much," cried Hiram, drawing back.

"Take it," said Lindy, with a smile; "I have plenty more
—more than I need—more than I know what to do with."

As Hiram drove off he said to himself, "Lucky girl; she's
mighty putty, too. I wonder that city feller didn't shine
up to her. I s'pose she's comin' back to the funeral."

As Lindy turned to go upstairs she looked into the parlor, and saw Alice sitting with her head bowed upon her
hand. Her first impulse was to go in and try to justify herself in the eyes of this girl, with whom she knew that Mr.
Sawyer was in love; but no, she was but a waif, with no
name, no birthright, no heritage; that woman had cut her
off from her people. Truly, she had avenged her fancied
wrongs.

So Lindy went upstairs to her room, and remained there
until after Alice went home.

When Abner Stiles returned from Eastborough, after
having seen Lindy Putnam and all her belongings safe on
board the Boston train, he stopped at the Putnam house
to see if he could be of any further service. Mrs. Pinkham had arrived some time before, and had attended to
those duties which she had performed for many years for
both the young and old of Mason's Corner, who had been
called to their long home. Mr. Tilton, the undertaker
from Montrose, had come over immediately, and had given
the necessary professional service which such sad occasions demand. Mrs. Pinkham called to Mr. Tilton, and
he came to the door.

"No; there is really nothing you can do, Mr. Stiles, unless you will be so kind as to drive around to Deacon
Mason's, Mr. Pettengill's, and Mrs. Hawkins's, and inform
them that the funeral will be from the church, at two

o'clock Friday afternoon. I will see that you are paid for your services."

Undertakers are naturally polite and courteous men. They step softly, speak low, and are even-tempered. Their patrons do not worry them with questions, nor antagonize their views of the fitness of things.

When Abner reached his boarding house, after making his numerous calls, it was about five o'clock; as he went up-stairs he noticed that the door of Strout's room was ajar. In response to his knock, the Professor said, "Come in."

"Wall, how do find things?" said Abner, as he entered the room.

"By lookin' for 'em," said the Professor, with a jaunty air.

"Oh, yer know what I **mean,**" said Abner, throwing himself into a chair and looking inquiringly at Strout. "What was goin' on this noon 'tween you and that city feller?"

"Well, you see," continued Strout, "Mr. Sawyer and me have been at swords' points the las' two months over some pussonal matters. Well, he kinder wanted to fix up things, but he knew I wouldn't consent to let up on him 'less he treated me square; so I gets a third interest in the grocery store, the firm name is to be Strout & Maxwell, and I'm to be postmaster; so, you see, I got the best end after all, jest as I meant to from the fust. But, see here, Stiles, Mr. Sawyer and I have agreed to keep our business and our pussonal matters strictly private in the futer, and you mustn't drop a word of what I've told yer to any livin' soul."

"I've carried a good many of yer secrets 'round with me," responded Abner, "and never dropped one of 'em, as far as I know."

"Oh, yer all right, old man," said the Professor; "but, yer know, for the last two months our game has been to keep talkin'; now it will pay us best to keep our mouths shet."

"Mine's shut," said Abner; "now, what do I git? That job in the grocery store that you promised me?"

"Well, you see," said Strout, "when I made yer that promise, I expected to own the whole store, but now, yer see, Maxwell will want ter pick one of the men."

"Yis, I see," said Abner; "but that leaves one fer you to pick, and I'm ready to be picked."

"Yes, I know," answered Strout; "but the work is goin' to be very hard, liftin' barrels and big boxes, and I'm afraid you couldn't stand it very long."

A disappointed look came over Abner's face; he mused for a moment, then he broke out, "Yes, I see; I'm all right for light work, sech as tellin' lies 'bout people and spyin' out their actions, and makin' believe I've seen things that I never heard of, and hearin' things that were never said; but when it comes to good, clean, honest work, like liftin' barrels and rollin' hogsheads, the other feller gets the job. All right, Professor!" said he, getting up and walking towards the door; "when you want anythin' in my line, let me know." And he went out and slammed the door behind him.

As he went upstairs to his room, he said to himself, "I have sorter got the opinion that the Professor took what wuz given him, instid of gittin' what he asked fer. I kinder guess that it'll pay me to be much more partickler about number one in the futer than I've been."

CHAPTER XXXII.

DEACON MASON had an early caller Wednesday morning. He was out in the barn polishing up his silver-plated harness, for he was going to the funeral on Friday with his family. Hiram had given him notice that he would have to go up to the store at once. The Deacon didn't have anybody in mind to take Hiram's place, and thought he might as well get used to doing his own work until he came across the right party.

He heard a voice. It said, "Good mornin', Deacon Mason;" and, looking up, he saw Abner Stiles standing before him.

"Good mornin', Abner," answered the Deacon, pleasantly; "what does the Professor want?"

"I don't know," said Abner; "I heerd that Hiram was goin' to leave yer, so I came 'round to see if yer wanted ter hire a man."

"Do yer know of one?" asked the Deacon with a smile.

"That's all right, Deacon," said Abner. "I don't blame yer fer havin' yer little joke. I've worked so long fer the Professor that I expect to have it flung up at me. But I've renounced the Evil One and all his wicked ways, and I want to be taken into a good Christian home, and eventooally jine the church."

> "While the lamp holds out to burn,
> The vilest sinner may return,"

quoted the Deacon, as he hung up one piece of harness and took down another.

"That's true as Gospel," said Abner; "and I hope you'll see it's your duty, as I've heerd Parson Howe say, to save the brand from the burnin'."

"Well, you go in and talk to Mrs. Mason," said the Deacon; "she's the one that wants the work done, and if she's satisfied to give yer a trial, it's all the same to me."

"Thank yer, Deacon," answered Abner. "There's one p'int in my favor, Deacon; I hain't got no girl, and I sha'n't take any of your time to go courtin';" and with this sly dig at Hiram, he went in to settle his fate with the Deacon's wife.

On that same Wednesday morning all of the Pettengill family were together at the breakfast table. The conversation naturally turned to Mrs. Putnam's death, and Ezekiel remarked "that she was a nice old lady, and that she and his mother were great friends. It beats all," continued he, "the way Lindy has acted. Abner Stiles told me that she took the half-past three train to Boston, and he said Bob Wood took over an express wagon full of trunks. Samanthy Green told Stiles that Lindy hadn't left a single thing in the house that belonged to her, and it don't look as though she was comin' back to the funeral."

During this recital, Alice listened intently. She flushed then grew pale, and finally burst into tears. All present, of course, attributed her agitation to her well known love for Mrs. Putnam.

"Shall I go upstairs with you, Sis?" asked Ezekiel.

"No," said Alice, drying her eyes, "I'm going into the parlor. I told Mandy to build a fire there, and I want you and Uncle Ike and Mr. Sawyer to come with me."

When they were gathered in the parlor, Alice began her story. Every word said by the dead woman had burned itself deep into her memory, and from the time she entered the sick room until she fell exhausted upon the stairway, after calling loudly for Samanthy and Lindy, not a word was missing from the thrilling narrative. Her audience, including even Quincy, listened intently to the dramatically told story, and they could almost see the frenzied face, the pointed finger, and hear the wild, mocking laugh.

For a few moments nothing was said. Finally, Ezekiel broke the silence.

"Well, I guess," said he, "that will of her'n will stand, all right. Lindy's got enough of her own; she won't be likely to interfere; and I never he'rd of their havin' any other relatives."

Then Uncle Ike spoke up. "I shall go to the funeral, of course, next Friday, and I shall expect to hear the Rev. Mr. Howe stand up in his pulpit and tell us what a good Christian woman Hepsy was; she was so kind and so benevolent, and so regardful of the feelings of others, and it wouldn't make a bit of difference if you went and told him what you've told us, Alice; he'd say just the same thing."

"Oh, hush! Uncle Ike," cried Alice, pleadingly; "she was a good woman, excepting on that one point, and you must own that she had some provocation. Let me ask you a question, Uncle Ike. How far should promises made to the dead be kept?"

"Just so far," replied Uncle Ike, "as they do not interfere with the just rights of the living. Where is that letter that she wanted you to destroy?" he asked.

"Here it is," said Alice, and she took it from the bosom of her dress.

"Well," said Uncle Ike, "if I were in your place I'd open that letter, read it, and if it was likely to be of any value to Miss Putnam in finding her parents or relatives, I'd hunt her up and give it to her. Mrs. Putnam owned up that she lied about it, and the whole thing, any way, may be a bluff. Perhaps it's only blank paper, after all."

"No," said Alice, "I could never open it or read it. I laid awake all night, thinking about my promise, and I finally made up my mind that I would go to see Lindy this morning, and let her read it; but now she has gone away,

and we do not know where to find her. What shall I do
with this dreadful thing?" she cried, as she held the letter
up in her hand.

Quincy felt called upon to speak.

"Miss Pettengill," said he, "I think I could find Miss
Putnam for you." A slight flush arose to Alice's cheek
which did not escape Quincy's notice. He continued,
"When I went to Boston, last Saturday, I happened to
meet her on the train. She told me then something of her
story, and said she was going to leave the house forever, as
soon as Mrs. Putnam died. She also told me that if I ever
learned anything about her parents I could reach her by
advertising in the Personal Column of the New York
'Herald,' addressing 'Linda,' and signing it 'Eastborough.' "

"And will you do this at once for me?" cried Alice,
eagerly. "I am so thankful; you have taken such a load
from my mind, Mr. Sawyer. How fortunate it was that you
met her as you did!"

"I think Mr. Sawyer is about as lucky as they make
'em," remarked Uncle Ike, with a laugh.

"Kind fortune owes me one or two favors yet before I
shall be entirely satisfied," said Quincy. "Now, Miss Pettengill, will you allow me to make a suggestion that will
free you from the further care of this document?"

"I don't care what is done with it," said Alice; "but no
one but Lindy must read it."

"That is my idea exactly," assented Quincy. "I will go
to Boston on the noon train and send that advertisement
to the New York 'Herald.' With your permission, I will
turn that document over to a legal friend of mine. He will
put it in an envelope and seal it up. He will write on the
outside, "To be delivered only to Miss Putnam, on the
written order of Miss Alice Pettengill,' and it will repose
quietly in his big safe until Miss Putnam is found."

"That will do splendidly!" said Alice, with animation.

"What magicians you lawyers are! You discover a way out of every difficulty."

"Wait until you get one of those lawyers working against you," remarked Uncle Ike, "then you'll change your mind. Well, I s'pose now this matter's settled, I can go upstairs and have my morning smoke."

"And I've got to go to the store," said Ezekiel to Uncle Ike, "and get some corn, or those chickens of your'n will swaller the hen coop." And both men left the room together.

"If you can give me a little of your time, Miss Petten- gill," said Quincy, "I have some news for you that I think will please you very much."

"About my stories?" cried Alice.

"Yes," replied Quincy. "Just before I went to Boston last Saturday I got a letter from Leopold, asking me to call on him as soon as convenient. I found him at home Sun- day evening, and this is what he said. The New York house has accepted your series of eight detective stories, and will pay you twenty-five dollars for each of them. The house will send you a check from time to time, as they pub- lish them. Leopold has accepted your long story for the magazine published by the house for which he is reader. He says Jameson will get your other story into one of the Sunday papers, and he will have his dramatic version ready for production next fall. He can't tell how much you will make out of these just yet; the magazine pays by the page and the newspaper by the column, and, of course, Jame- son will give you part of his royalty, if he gets the play on."

"Why, Mr. Sawyer, you are showering wealth upon me like another Count of Monte Cristo."

"But you have not heard all," continued Quincy. "Leo- pold has placed your two songs with a music publishing house, and you will get a royalty on them in time. He says they don't pay any royalty on the first three hundred copies, and perhaps they won't sell; the public taste on sheet music is very fickle. Then, that composer, I can never remember his name, is at work on your poem, 'The Lord of the Sea.' He told Leopold he was going to make it his *opus vitæ*, the work of his life, you know, and he is talking it up to the director of the Handel and Haydn Society."

"How true it is," said Alice, "that gladness quickly follows sadness! I was so unhappy this morning, but now the world never looked so bright to me. You have brushed away all my sorrows, Mr. Sawyer, and I am really very happy to hear the good news that you have told me."

"There is one sorrow that I have not yet relieved you of," continued Quincy.

"And that?" asked Alice, brushing back the wavy golden hair from her forehead, and looking up at him with her bright blue eyes, which bore no outward sign of the dark cloud that dimmed their vision,—"and that is?"—she repeated.

"That letter," taking the hand that held it in both of his own. "If I am to get that noon train I have no time to lose."

"Before you take it," said Alice, "you must promise me that it shall not be opened, and no eye but Lindy's must ever rest upon it."

"You have my word," he replied.

"Then take it," said she; and she released her hold upon it.

He took the letter with one hand, his other hand still retaining its grasp upon hers.

"I go," said Quincy, assuming a bantering tone, "upon your quest, fair lady. If I return victorious, what shall be my reward?"

"Gallant knights," said Alice, as she withdrew her hand from his, "do not bargain for their reward until they have fulfilled their trust."

"I accept the reproof," said Quincy gravely.

"It was not so intended, Sir Knight," responded Alice brightly; "so I will make amends by answering your query. If you return successful, tell me what you would prize the most, and even if it be half my kingdom, it shall be yours."

"I am content, but modern locomotives do not wait even for gallant knights of old. So adieu."

He quitted the room, and Alice stood where he had left her until she heard the rumble of wheels as he drove off for the station; then she found her way to her chair before the fire, and her mind wove the outline of a romantic story, in which there was a gallant knight and a lovely maiden. But in her story the prize that the knight asked when he returned successful from his quest was the heart and hand of the lovely maiden.

Jim Cobb went over to Eastborough Centre, so as to drive the team back. Before going to the station, Quincy stepped into the post office and found a letter addressed to him in a peculiar, but familiar, handwriting.

"From Aunt Ella," he said. "I will read it after I get on the train."

Quincy's Aunt Ella was Mrs. Robert Chessman, his mother's widowed sister.

As soon as the train started Quincy opened his letter. It was short and to the point.

"My DEAR QUINCY:—Maude gave me your address. What are you doing in a miserable, little country town in the winter? They are bad enough in the summer, but in March!—Bah! Come and see me at once, you naughty boy!   AUNT ELLA."

"Dated yesterday," said Quincy; "how fortunate. I will go up to Mt. Vernon Street to-morrow noon and take lunch with her."

When Quincy reached Boston he went directly to his

father's office. The Hon. Mr. Sawyer was not present, but his partners, Mr. Franklin Crowninshield and Mr. Atherton Lawrence, were busily engaged. Quincy took a seat at the desk which he had occupied before going to Eastborough, and wrote out his advertisement for the New York "Herald." It read as follows: "Linda. Important paper discovered; communicate at once with Q. A. S., Eastborough."

He enclosed a check to cover a fortnight's insertion; then walked down State Street to the post office to mail his letter. When he returned, Mr. Lawrence informed him that his father was in his private office. His father greeted him pleasantly, but not effusively; in fact, any marked exhibition of approval or disapproval was foreign to the Sawyer character, while the Quincys were equally notable for their reticence and imperturbability.

"When shall we have the pleasure of your continued presence at home?" asked the father.

"To-night," replied Quincy, with a smile, "I shall be with you at dinner, stay all night, and take breakfast with you."

"I trust your long visit will not oblige you to neglect other more important matters," said the father.

"Oh, no!" answered Quincy. "I have looked out for that."

"And when do you think your health will allow you to resume your position in the office?" inquired the Hon. Nathaniel.

"That is very uncertain," replied Quincy.

"If you do not intend to come back at all," continued the father, "that would simplify matters. I could then make room for a Harvard graduate to study with us."

Quincy reflected. He had been taught by his father not to give a positive answer to any question on the spur of the moment, if more time could be taken, as well as not, for consideration. So, after a few moments of thought, Quincy

said, "I will write you in the course of ten days or a fortnight, and give you a positive answer."

"That will be entirely satisfactory," answered his father.
"As you are going out, will you kindly tell Mr. Crowninshield that I wish to consult with him?"

Quincy knew that the interview had expired by limita-
tion. He went home, but found that his mother and sisters
were out riding.

"They will return in time for dinner," said Delia, the
parlor maid.

Quincy went into the parlor and opened the grand piano.
He sat down before it, touched a few of the keys casually,
then sang, with great expression, the song by J. R. Thomas
entitled "Pleasant Memories." He next wandered into the
library, and took down and glanced at several books that
he had devoured with avidity when a boy of sixteen. Then
he went upstairs to his own room, which he had occupied
since he was eight years old. It looked familiar, everything was in its accustomed place; still, the room did not
look homelike. Strange as it may seem, Quincy had been
happier in the large west chamber, with its old-fashioned
bureau and carpet and bed, than he had ever been in this
handsomely furnished apartment in the Beacon Street
mansion. There was no wide fireplace here, with ruddy
embers, into whose burning face he could look and weave
fanciful dreams of the fortune and happiness to be his in
the future.

He spent a pleasant evening with the family. His father
was present, but passed the time in reading the newspapers
and a legal brief that he wished to more closely examine.
His mother was engrossed in a new novel, but no approving
smile or sympathetic tear demonstrated any particular interest in the fates of the struggling hero or suffering
heroine.

Florence sat at the piano, and, in response to Quincy's
request that she would give him some music, played over

some chromatic scales and arpeggios. He declared that
they reminded him of grand opera, which remark sent
Maude into a fit of satirical laughter, and Florence up to
her room in a pout.

Then Maude fell to asking Quincy questions about himself, to which he returned evasive and untruthful answers,
until she was, as she said, completely disgusted. Then she
dropped her head upon his shoulder, and with the arms of
the brother whom she dearly loved clasped around her, she
went to sleep. He looked at the sweet girlish face and
thought, not of her, but of Alice.

Next morning he was up early, for he knew that a busy
day was before him. The last thing before retiring, and
the first thing upon getting up, he examined his inside
vest pocket, to see if that precious letter, that priceless trust
that he had given his knightly word to deliver, was safe.

He breakfasted early, and eight o'clock found him in
Bowdoin Square, at the corner of Green and Chardon
Streets. His first visit was to a safe manufactory, a few
doors from the corner, where he purchased one for the
firm of Strout & Maxwell.

After traversing both sides of Friend Street, he finally
settled upon two horses, stout country roadsters, and left
an order for their shipment to Eastborough Centre, when
they were notified that the wagons were ready. He bought
the wagons in Sudbury Street. They had red bodies and
yellow wheels, and the words, "Strout & Maxwell, Mason's
Corner, Mass.," were to be placed on them in gold letters.

These tasks completed, Quincy walked up Tremont Row
by Scollay's Building. Crossing Pemberton Square, he
continued up Tremont Street until he came to the building
in which was the law office of Curtis Carter, one of his law
school chums.

"Hello, Curt!" said he, as he entered the somewhat dingy
office.

"Well, 'pon honor, Quincy," cried Curtis, "the sight of

you is good for sore eyes, and I've got such a beastly cold that I can't see with one eye and can't read with the other."

"Well," said Quincy, "I came in here intending to consult you professionally, but I don't think a blind lawyer will answer my purpose."

"Oh, I shall be all right in a few minutes," replied Curtis. "I dropped into Young's as I came up and took an eye-opener. What's the matter, old fellow, breach of promise?"

Quincy took a seat near Curtis's desk.

"No," said he, "it's a case of animosity carried beyond the grave."

"Oh! I see," said Curtis, "party cut off with a shilling, going to try and break the will?"

"Have a cigar?" asked Quincy. "While you are lighting it and getting it under way I may slide in and get a chance to state my business."

"Oh! you want to do the talking?" said Curtis good humoredly. "Well, go ahead, old man;" and he leaned back and smoked complacently.

Quincy then related as much as he thought necessary of the story of the sealed letter, and as he concluded he took the package from his pocket and placed it on the corner of the lawyer's desk.

"You are doing just right," said Curtis; "the probate judges nowadays are looking more carefully at wills, especially when their provisions indicate that the signer was more red Indian than white Christian. I understand you perfectly," he continued; "what you wish me to do is to put this letter in an envelope, seal it securely, and endorse upon it these words, 'To be delivered only to Miss Lindy Putnam upon the written order of Miss Alice Pettengill.'"

"That's it exactly," said Quincy; "only I wish a receipt from you for the document."

"Certainly," replied Curtis. As he raised the lid of his old-fashioned desk the letter fell to the floor. The envelope had received rough treatment in its progress from hand to hand, and it was not strange that when it struck the floor one corner was split open by the fall.

As Quincy stooped to pick it up, he noticed that something that resembled a small piece of white cloth dropped from the broken corner of the envelope. When he picked it up to replace it, he saw that it was a small piece of white cotton cloth, and his quick eye caught the name "Linda Fernborough" stamped thereon with indelible ink. He said nothing, but replacing the piece of cloth passed the package to Curtis, who enclosed, sealed, and endorsed it, and gave a receipt therefor to Quincy.

"I will put this in my big steel vault," said he, as he went into another room.

Quincy knew that Curtis would accept no fee for such a slight service, so placing a five dollar greenback under a paperweight, he quietly left the office and was out of sight long before Curtis, with the bill in his hand, ran down stairs, bareheaded, and looked up and down the street in search of him.

Five minutes later Quincy reached his aunt's house. A "Buttons," dressed in blue livery, opened the door, and Quincy was ushered into the long parlor, which ran the full depth of the house, some sixty feet, in which he had passed many pleasant evenings. He sent up his card, and in a few moments Buttons returned and delivered the speech which Mrs. Chessman had taught him and which he had learned by heart: "Mrs. Chessman desires that you will come up at once."

Quincy bounded upstairs, to the evident astonishment of Buttons, and made his way to the front chamber, which he knew was his aunt's room. She loved the sunlight, and it was a constant visitor in that room, summer and winter. His aunt did not greet him with a "how do you do?" and a hand-shake. Instead of such a formal reception, she gave him a hearty hug and kissed him three times, once on the forehead, then on the cheek, and finally on the lips, in which latter osculation Quincy took part.

His aunt led him to an easy-chair, then threw herself upon a lounge opposite to him. She eyed him attentively for a moment.

"Quincy," said she, "you are better looking than ever; you're almost as good looking as Robert was, and he was the handsomest man I ever saw. How many different country girls have you kissed since you saw me last?"

"I kept the count," said Quincy, "till I went to a surprise party a week ago Monday, and then I lost it."

"Of all the kisses that you have had, whose do you prize the most?"

"Those from my beloved Aunt Ella," replied Quincy.

Aunt Ella smiled and said, "You know how to keep on the right side of an old woman who has got money."

"I didn't think of that until you called my attention to it," said Quincy gravely.

"And I didn't believe it when I said it," added Aunt Ella. A few moments later she rang and ordered a light lunch. When this was over she went to an old secretary with brass handles, opened a drawer, and took out a cigar box.

"I have a few of Robert's cigars left," she said.

Quincy took one and resumed his seat in the easy-chair.

Aunt Ella opened another drawer in the secretary and took out a pouch of tobacco, a package of rice paper and a box of wax tapers. She put these articles on a small diamond-shaped table and placed the table between Quincy and herself. She handed Quincy the match-box, then deftly rolling a cigarette, she lighted it, leaned back upon the lounge and blew rings of smoke into the air, which she watched until they broke.

"Do you think it's horribly unbecoming for me to smoke?" she asked, looking at Quincy.

"Do you wish me to express my real thoughts?" replied Quincy, "or flatter you because you have money?"

Aunt Ella reddened a little, then said, "A good shot, Quincy, but I deserve it. Go on."

"Well, Aunt Ella," said he, "you are the only woman whom I ever saw smoke who, in my opinion, knew how to do it gracefully."

"I think you are sincere," she rejoined, "and I beg pardon for wounding your feelings as I did before. Give me your hand on it."

They shook hands as two men would have done after settling differences.

Then she said, "Now draw your chair up closer, Quincy, and tell me what you've been doing, and what other people have been doing to you since the day before Christmas, the last time I set eyes on you until to-day. You know I am your mother confessor."

Quincy complied, and in his quiet, concise way gave her a full account of his doings in Eastborough, omitting nothing, concealing nothing. If anything, he gave fuller details of his acquaintance with Huldy, Lindy, and Alice than he did of the other portions of his story. He could not forbear to give at full length the account of his final settlement with the Professor.

Aunt Ella laughed heartily at some parts of the recital, and looked sorrowful and sympathetic when she listened to other portions. She rolled and smoked half a dozen cigarettes during its continuance, and when she saw that Quincy had finished his cigar she placed the remainder of the box before him.

When he closed she said, "Quincy, you're a brick. I haven't enjoyed myself so much for years. I do so love anything that isn't commonplace, and your experience is both novel and interesting. What a dear old man Deacon Mason is, and Ezekiel Pettengill is a fine young fellow, honest and square. That Hiram and Mandy must be a team. Are they going to get married?"

"I think so," said Quincy. "He stammers, you know,

and I think he is afraid he will break down when he tries to propose."

Aunt Ella laughed heartily; then she said, "What a constitutional liar that Stiles must be, and as for the Professor, I would like to have a set-to with him myself."

As she said this she doubled up her fists.

"Oh, he wouldn't meet you that way," said Quincy. "He only fights with a woman's weapon, his tongue;" and he told her of his little boxing match with Robert Wood.

Aunt Ella continued: "I can imagine what a pretty, sweet, little country girl Huldy Mason is. My heart aches for Lindy, her martyrdom has been out of all proportion to her contemplated wrongdoing, if wrongdoing it really was. Had I been in her place I would have married Jones and left my clothes behind; and then," said Aunt Ella, "how my heart goes out to that dear, sweet girl that you call Alice! Do you love her, Quincy?"

"Devotedly," answered Quincy, "I never really loved a woman before."

"Then marry her," cried Aunt Ella decidedly.

"Everybody at home but Maude will object," said Quincy.

"Maude's the best one in the family, next to yourself," snapped Aunt Ella.

"They will bring up Uncle Jim," continued Quincy.

"Nonsense!" replied Aunt Ella. "Uncle Jim was a fool; any man is a fool who thinks he can win the battle of life by making a sot of himself. Bring this girl to me, Quincy. She must be a genius, if she can write as you say she can. Let me care for her and love her and make life pleasant and beautiful for her until you get ready to do it yourself."

"I will, some day, Aunt Ella. You are the best friend I have in the world, and when I have the right to bring Alice to you, I will lose no time in doing so. Thank you for your kind words about her. I shall never forget them, and she shall hear them some day. But I must go now."

They both arose. "Promise that you will come and see me every time you are in Boston, Quincy; if you don't, I shall come down to Eastborough to see you."

She gave him another kiss at parting.

As he left the house he deliberated for a moment as to where he should go next. It was half-past four. He decided to go to Leopold's lodgings in Chestnut Street. He found him at home, but for a wonder he was not working.

"This is an off day with me," he explained; "this is our haying season, and I've been working nights, days, and Sundays for a fortnight."

"I came to express Miss Pettengill's obligations and thanks for your kind and very successful efforts in her behalf."

"Oh! that's all right," said Leopold. "By the way, have you told her she ought to write a book?"

"Not yet," said Quincy; "but I'm going to soon. She has just lost a dear friend; but I won't forget it."

"Don't!" repeated Leopold. "She is a diamond that ought to be dug up, cut, and set in eighteen carat gold. Excuse my apparently brutal language, but you get my meaning."

"Certainly," said Quincy; "and you are not working to-day."

"No," replied Leopold; "loafing and enjoying it, too. I've a good mind to turn vagrant and loaf on, loaf ever."

"Come down to Parker's and have dinner with me."

"Can't do it," replied Leopold; "my stomach is loafing, too. 'Twouldn't be fair to make it work and do nothing myself. Just as much obliged. Some other day. Don't forget the book," he cried, as Quincy left the room.

Quincy took his dinner at Parker's, caught the five minutes past six express, and reached Eastborough Centre at half-past seven. Abbott Smith drove him home to the Pettengill house.

The next day was Friday. Everybody at Mason's Corner, with quite a number from Eastborough and Montrose,
came to Mrs. Putnam's funeral. The little Square in front
of the church, as well as the shed, was filled with teams.
While waiting for the arrival of the body, quite a number
of the male residents of Mason's Corner were gathered
upon the steps of the church.

Strout spied Abner Stiles and approached him. "Bob
Wood has jest told me," said the Professor, "that he has decided not to leave his present place, so I've concluded on
second thoughts to give yer that job at the grocery store."

Abner's eyes twinkled.

"I've had my second thoughts, too," said he, "I've hired
out to Deacon Mason for life, and if I jine the church he
says I can work for him in the next world. So I kinder
guess I shall have to decline yer kind invitation to lift boxes
and roll barrels."

When the services were over every person in the church
passed up the centre aisle to take a last view. Her husband had been buried in the Montrose cemetery, and she
had told Mr. Tilton that she was to be laid by his side. The
Eastborough cemetery was in West Eastborough, and for
that reason many of the late residents of Mason's Corner
slept their last sleep at Montrose.

As they stood by the coffin, Alice said, "How does she
look?"

"Very pleasant," replied Quincy; "there is a sweet smile
upon her face."

"I am so glad," said Alice. She pressed his arm a little
tighter, and looking up to him, she said, "Perhaps she has
met her boy, and that smile is but the earthly reflection of
the heavenly one that rests upon her face in her home
above."

"I hope so," replied Quincy; and they walked slowly out
of church and took their places on the rear seat of the Pettengill carryall, Ezekiel and Uncle Ike sitting in front.

Mandy Skinner and Mrs. Crowley had not gone to the funeral. The latter was busy skimming cream from a dozen large milk pans, while Mandy sat before the kitchen stove, with Swiss by her side. She was thinking of Hiram, and wondering if he really intended to ask her to marry him.

"I don't think he's been foolin' me, but now he's goin' into business I should think it was about time for him to speak up or quit."

Swiss suddenly arose, sniffed and went to the kitchen door. The door was opened softly and some one entered the room. Mandy did not turn her head. Perhaps she guessed who it was. Then some one placed a chair close to Mandy and took a seat beside her.

"Say, M-m-m-m-m-a-andy," said Hiram, "will you please read this to me? It's an important document, and I want to be sure I've got it jest right." As he said this he passed Mandy a folded paper.

She opened it and the following words met her eye: "This is to certify that I, Hiram Maxwell, of Mason's Corner, in the town of Eastborough, county of Normouth, and Commonwealth of Massachusetts, hereby declare my intention to ask Miss Amanda Skinner of the village, town, county, and state aforesaid, to become my lawful wedded wife."

"Oh, you big silly!" cried Mandy, dropping the paper, for she didn't think it necessary to read any further.

"Is it all right?" cried Hiram, "it cost a quarter to git it drawn up. Then I swore to it before old Squire Rundlett over to Montrose, and it ought ter hold water. You'd better keep it, Mandy, then I can't fling it up at yer that I never axed yer to marry me."

"Who told you that?" asked the girl indignantly.

"Ma Hawkins. Well, she didn't exactly say it to me, but she spoke it out so loud to Betsy Green that I heered it

clear out in the wood-shed and I'll tell yer what, Mandy,
it kinder made me mad."

"Well, it's all right now," said Mandy soothingly.

"Is it?" asked Hiram, his face beaming with delight.

The next instant there was a succession of peculiar
sounds heard in the room. As Swiss came back from the
kitchen door but one chair was needed for the happy couple,
and an onlooker would have thought that chair was occupied by one person with a very large head, having light
curly hair on one side and straight dark hair on the other,
no face being visible.

It was upon this picture that Mrs. Crowley looked as she
opened the door leading into the kitchen and started to
come into the room with a large pan full of cream.

Astonished, she stepped backward, forgetting the two
steps that she had just ascended. Flat upon her back she
fell, the pan of cream drenching her from head to foot.

"It's drownded I am! It's drownded I am!" she cried at
the top of her voice.

"What's the matter? How did it happen?" said Mandy,
as she rushed into the room, followed by Swiss.

"Shure it's thinkin' I was," moaned Mrs. Crowley,
"when the milk fell on me."

"Thinkin' of what?" cried Mandy sharply. "You couldn't
have been thinkin' of your business."

"Shure I was thinkin' of the day when Pat Crowley and
I both sat in the same chair, forty years ago," said Mrs.
Crowley, rising to her feet and wiping the cream from her
eyes, and nose, and ears.

During this time Swiss was busily engaged having a rich
feast upon the cream left in the pan. Hiram appeared at
the kitchen door to learn the cause of Mandy's absence.

Raising her hands high in the air, Mrs. Crowley said,
"Bless you, my darlints; may yer live long and may all the
saints pour blessin's on yer hids."

And with this invocation the poor old woman hobbled off to her room in the ell and was not seen again until the next morning.

CHAPTER XXXIII.

THE next day was Saturday. While the Pettengill family was at breakfast, Squire Rundlett arrived. He had driven over from Montrose with the partnership papers for Strout, Hiram, and Quincy to sign and also the will of the late Mrs. Hepsibeth Putnam.

As he came into the kitchen he espied Mandy, and a broad smile spread over his face as he said, "Good morning, Miss Skinner, was that paper all right?" Mandy flushed scarlet but said nothing. "Honestly, Miss Skinner," said the Squire, "I think it was a very sensible act on Hiram's part. If men were obliged to put their proposals in writing there wouldn't be any more breach of promise cases."

"I think he was a big goose," finally ejaculated Mandy, laughing in spite of herself.

"At any rate," continued the Squire, "he knew how to pick out a smart, pretty little woman for a wife;" and he raised his hat politely and passed into the dining-room.

Here he was asked to have some breakfast. He accepted a cup of coffee, and, while drinking it, informed Quincy and Alice of the twofold purpose of his visit.

Quincy led Alice into the parlor, the Squire accompanying them. Quincy then retired, saying he would join the Squire in a short time and ride up to the store with him.

When they were alone, the Squire informed Alice that by the terms of Mrs. Putnam's last will she had been left sole heiress of all the real and personal property of the deceased. The dwelling house and farm were worth fully ten thousand dollars, while the bonds, stocks, and other securities, of which he had had charge for many years, were worth at least forty thousand more. For several years Mrs. Putnam's income had been about twenty-five hundred dollars a year.

"It was very kind of her to leave it to me," said Alice; "I have never done anything to deserve it and I would not take it were it not that I understand there are no near relatives, and that Miss Lindy Putnam was amply provided for by her brother."

There was a knock upon the door, and Quincy looked in.

"Come in, Mr. Sawyer," said the Squire. "I have an important bit of news for you that concerns this young lady."

Quincy did as requested and stood expectantly.

The Squire went on: "Mrs. Putnam's old will, made some six years ago, gave all the property to Miss Pettengill, but provided that its provisions should be kept secret for ninety days. In that will I was named as sole executor."

"Why did she change it?" asked Alice earnestly.

"I don't know," replied the Squire. "About three weeks ago she sent for me and cut out the ninety-day restriction and named our young friend here as co-executor with myself."

Alice remained silent, while a look of astonishment crept into Quincy's face.

"I do not quite comprehend her reason for making this change," remarked Quincy.

"Mrs. Putnam was a very far-seeing lady," said the Squire, with a laugh, looking first at Alice and then at Quincy.

A slight flush mounted to Alice's cheeks, and Quincy said coolly, "I do not perceive the application of your remark."

"Easy enough," said the Squire, seeing that he had put his foot in it, and that it was necessary to explain his false step in some way; "easy enough. I have had sole charge of her property for six years, and she wished some cool-headed business man to go over my accounts and see if I had been honest in my dealings with her."

"That way of stating the case is satisfactory," said Quincy, a little more genially.

"I don't think I am in danger of being robbed with two such trusty guardians," said Alice.

Then all three laughed, and the little rift was closed. But the Squire's words had not been unheeded and two hearts were busily thinking and wondering if he had really meant what he said.

The Squire then turned to Quincy. "If you will name a day we will go over to the county town, present the will for probate, and at any time thereafter my books will be ready for inspection."

Quincy named the following Wednesday, and then both men congratulated Miss Pettengill on her good fortune, bade her good morning, and then started to go to the store.

As they passed through the kitchen Mandy was not in sight. She evidently did not intend to have a second interview with the Squire.

When they reached the store they found Strout and Hiram and Mr. Hill and his son already there. The business with Mr. Hill was soon concluded, and he delivered the keys of the property to Squire Rundlett; then the co-partnership papers were duly signed and witnessed, and then the Squire passed the keys to Mr. Obadiah Strout, the senior partner of the new firm of Strout & Maxwell, who formally took possession of the property in his own name and that of his partners.

Since Abner's curt declination of a position in the store, Strout had been looking around for some one to take his place, and had finally settled upon William Ricker, or, as he was generally called, Billy Ricker, a popular young resident of Montrose, as it was thought he could control a great deal of trade in that town.

For a similar reason, Quincy and Hiram had united in choosing young Abbott Smith, who was known by everybody in Eastborough Centre and West Eastborough. Abbott had grown tired of driving the hotel carriage and wished to engage in some permanent business.

The choice was naturally not particularly palatable to Strout, but he had consented to let bygones be bygones and could offer no valid objection. These two young men were to report for duty that Saturday evening, and the close of that day's business terminated Benoni and Samuel Hill's connection with the grocery store.

Sunday morning all of the Pettengill family went to church and listened to a sermon by Mr. Howe, the minister, from the text, "Blessed are the peacemakers, for they shall inherit the kingdom of Heaven."

As they were driving home, Uncle Ike remarked in his dry, sarcastic way, "I s'pose Mr. Howe was thinkin' of Mrs. Putnam when he was praisin' the peacemakers; it's a fashion in the country, I understand, the Sunday after a funeral to preach in a general way about the departed one."

"Mrs. Putnam has been very kind to me," protested Alice, "and you should forgive her for my sake."

"I'll forgive her," said Uncle Ike, "when the wrong she has done has been righted." He shut his teeth together sharply, faced the horses again, and lapsed into silence.

In the afternoon Quincy joined Alice in the parlor, and they sang some sacred music together.

Quincy picked up a book from the table and said, "Why, Miss Pettengill, by this turned down corner I imagine there are some thirty pages of this very interesting story, 'The Love of a Lifetime,' that I have not read to you. Would you like to have me finish it this afternoon?"

"I have been afraid to hear the last chapter," said Alice. "I fear Herbert and Clarice will both die, and I so hate a book with a sad ending. Why don't authors keep their lovers alive—"

"Marry them off and let them live happily ever afterward," Quincy concluded.

"I don't think I could ever write a book with a sorrowful conclusion," mused Alice.

Quincy saw the opportunity for which he had long waited.

"Why don't you write a book?" asked he earnestly. "My friend Leopold says you ought to; he further said that you were a genius, and if I remember him correctly, compared you to a diamond—"

"In the rough," added Alice quickly.

"That's it," said Quincy; "but Leopold added that rough diamonds should be dug up, cut, and set in a manner worthy of their value."

"I am afraid Mr. Ernst greatly overrates my abilities and my worth," said she, a little constrainedly. "But how unkind and ungrateful I am to you and Mr. Ernst, who have been so kind and have done so much for me. I will promise this much," she continued graciously. "I will think it over, and if my heart does not fail me, I will try."

"I hope your conclusion will be favorable," remarked Quincy. "In a short time you will be financially independent and freed from any necessity of returning to your former vocation. I never knew of an author so completely successful at the start, and I think you have every encouragement to make literature your 'love of a lifetime.'"

"I will try to think so too," replied Alice softly.

Then he took up the book and finished reading it. When he had closed, neither he nor she were thinking of that future world in which Herbert and Clarice had sealed those vows which they had kept so steadfastly and truly during life, but of the present world, bright with promise for each of them, in which there was but one shade of sorrow— that filmy web that shut out the beauties of nature from the sight of that most beautiful of God's creations, a lovely woman.

Monday morning Quincy made another trip to Boston. He had obtained the measurements for a large sign, upon which, on a blue ground, the words "Strout & Maxwell" were to appear in large gold letters. He paid another visit to the carriage factory, and ordered two leather covered wagon tops, to be used in stormy weather, and picked out two sets of harness resplendent with brass buckles and bosses and having "S. & M." in brass letters on the blinders.

He reached Aunt Ella's in time for lunch. He told her of the approaching wedding of Ezekiel and Huldy; then, leaning over, he whispered something in her ear, which made her face beam with delight.

"What a joke it will be," cried she, "and how the country folks will enjoy it. Can't I come down to the wedding, Quincy, and bring my landau, my double span of cream-colored horses, and my driver and footman in the Chessman livery? I'll take you and your lady love to the church."

"Why, certainly," said Quincy. "I'll ask Miss Mason to send you an invitation."

"Let me do something to help," begged the impetuous but good-hearted Aunt Ella. "Bring the girls up some morning early. We will go shopping, then we'll lunch here. We will have to go without our wine and cigars that day, you know, and then we'll go to the modiste's and the milliner's in the afternoon. We'll make a day of it, young man."

Quincy leaned back in his easy-chair and blew a ring of blue smoke from one of Uncle Robert's cigars.

"Excuse me, Aunt Ella," said he, "but do you ever intend to get married again?"

"Quincy Adams Sawyer!" cried Aunt Ella, with an astonished look on her face, "are you joking?"

"Certainly not," replied Quincy. "My question was intended to be a serious and respectful inquiry. You are only forty, fine looking, well educated, well connected and wealthy. Why should you not?"

"I will answer you seriously then, Quincy. I could not marry again. Ten years' life with Robert Chessman was a greater pleasure than a lifetime with an ordinary man. I was twenty-five when I married him; we lived together ten years; he has been dead for five. How often I have wished that Robert had lived to enjoy his fortune with me.

"But he was satisfied," she continued. "'Better be a success at the end,' he used to say, 'than be a success in middle life and fall from your greatness. Look at Wolsey, look at Richelieu, look at Napoleon Bonaparte.' He would often remark: 'Earth has no sadder picture than a broken idol.' He used to consider Abraham Lincoln the most successful man that ever lived, for he died before making a mistake, and when he was strongest in the hearts of the people.

"Your question reminds me," continued Aunt Ella, "of something I had in mind to say to you at some future day, but I may as well say it now. How much money have you, Quincy, and what is your income?"

"Father gave me fifty thousand dollars outright when I was twenty-one; it pays on an average six per cent. Besides this he allows me two thousand a year for supposed professional services rendered in his law office."

"That makes five thousand a year," said Aunt Ella quickly. "Well, I'll allow you five thousand more a year, and the day you are married I'll give you as much outright as your father did. That's unconditional. Now, conditionally, if you bring your wife here and live with me you shall have rooms and board free, and I'll leave you every dollar I possess when I'm through with it. Don't argue with me now," she continued, as Quincy essayed to speak. "Think it over, tell her about it. You will do as you please, of course, but I shall not change my mind on this point."

"Didn't your husband leave any relatives that might turn up and prevent any such disposition of your property?"

"When we married, Robert said he was alone in the world," replied Aunt Ella; "he had no sisters, and only one brother, named Charles. Charles was an artist; he went to Paris to study about thirty-five years ago. From there he went to London. Some thirty years ago Robert got a letter from him in which he said he was going to return to America. Robert waited, but he did not come; then he wrote again to his English address, but the letter was returned with the words 'Gone to America' endorsed thereon."

"Was he married?" inquired Quincy.

"Robert never knew," said Aunt Ella, "but he imagined not, as Charlie, as he called him, never spoke in his letters of being in love, much less of being married."

Quincy caught the three o'clock train to Eastborough Centre, and Ellis Smith, another son of 'Bias Smith, who had taken the hotel carriage in place of his brother Abbott, drove him home.

A few days thereafter invitations to the wedding of Ezekiel Pettengill and Hulda Ann Mason were sent broadcast through Eastborough Centre, West Eastborough, Mason's Corner, and Montrose. Then it was decided by the gossips that Ezekiel was going to have Mr. Sawyer and Hiram Maxwell and Sam Hill to stand up with him, while Huldy Ann was going to have Alice Pettengill, Mandy Skinner, and Tilly James as bridesmaids.

The whole town turned out when the two gaudy wagons, with their handsome horses and fine harness reached Eastborough Centre, and a number of Centre folks followed the unique procession over to Mason's Corner. One of the wagons contained the new sign, which was soon put in place, and was a source of undisguised admiration for a long time.

On the tenth of April, Strout & Maxwell's two heavy teams went over to Eastborough Centre and returned about noon heavily loaded, followed by three other teams from

the Centre equally well filled. Then Mr. Obadiah Strout
could contain himself no longer. He let the cat out of the
bag, and the news spread like wildfire over the village, and
was soon carried to Eastborough Centre and to Montrose.
The Mason's Corner church was to have a new organ, a
present from Mr. Sawyer, and Professor Obadiah Strout
had been engaged to officiate for one year.

The nineteenth of April was fixed for Huldy's wedding
day. The hour was ten in the morning. As early as eight
o'clock teams began to arrive from north, east, south, and
west. Enough invitations had been issued to fill the church,
and by half-past nine every seat was taken.

The little church was profusely decorated with vines,
ferns and potted plants, while a wealth of cut flowers
adorned the altar, the front of the new organ, which rose
towering to the very top of the church, and the pews
reserved for the bridal party.

Outside the edifice hundreds of sightseers, not honored
with invitations, lined both sides of the spacious Square in
front of the church, and occupied positions of vantage on
the steps.

It lacked but ten minutes of ten. The sexton rung a
merry peal from the sweet-toned bell, which was the pride
of the inhabitants of Mason's Corner. Within the church
the ushers, having attended to the seating of the audience,
stood just within the door awaiting the arrival of the bride
and groom. They were in dress suits, with white gloves,
and each had a white rose in his butonhole. Robert Wood
and Cobb's twins had been assigned to the right of the
centre aisle, while Abbott Smith, Benjamin Bates, and
Emmanuel Howe had charge of the left side of the edifice.
If any noticed the absence of Samuel Hill and Hiram Maxwell, it did not provoke general remark, although Mrs.
Hawkins asked Jonas if he'd seen Mandy anywhere, and
Tilly James's school chum, Eliza Allen, managed to occupy
two seats, so as to have one for Tilly when she came.

At exactly five minutes of ten, Professor Strout emerged from the rear of the platform and proceeded towards the new organ. He, like the ushers, was in a dress suit, with a white rose in the lapel of his coat. He was greeted with applause and bowed his acknowledgements. He took his seat at the organ and played a soft prelude, during which the Rev. Caleb Howe entered and advanced to the altar.

Then loud cheers were heard from the assembled crowd outside. The organ stopped and the sexton again filled the air with merry peals. The sight outside was one which those inside could not see, and therefore could not appreciate. What was that coming up the road? Mason's Corner had never seen an equipage like that before. An open carriage, drawn by four cream-colored horses, with white manes and tails and silver-tipped harness. A coachman in livery sat upon the box, while a footman, in similar livery, rode behind. Following behind this were other carriages, containing the other members of the bridal party.

Within the church every eye was turned upon the door through which the party was to come. Professor Strout's sharp eye saw the first couple as they reached the entrance, and the strains of Mendelssohn's Wedding March, that have preceded so many happy bridals, sounded through the church. The party included Ezekiel and Huldy, Deacon Mason and wife, Mr. Sawyer and Miss Alice Pettengill, and a handsome, richly dressed lady unknown to any of the villagers, who was escorted by Mr. Isaac Pettengill.

Ezekiel and Huldy advanced and took their positions before the minister, while the remainder of the party took seats in one of the bridal pews.

When the ceremony was over the audience naturally expected that the wedded couple would leave the church by the right-hand aisle, on both sides of which, from end to end, white silk ribbons had been drawn to keep the passage clear.

But no! Shouts and cheers were again heard from outside the church, again the church bell rang out, and once more the melody of the Wedding March fell upon the ears of the Professor's auditors, while to their astonishment Ezekiel and his wife seated themselves quietly in the front bridal pew. Again every eye was turned, every neck was craned, and Samuel Hill and Tilly James walked down the centre aisle and took their places before the clergyman. Again the solemn words were spoken, and this time the spectators felt sure that the double couple would leave the church by the silken pathway.

But no; again were cheers and shouts from the outside borne to the excited spectators within. Once more the sexton sent out pleasing tones from the church bell; once more the Professor evoked those melodious strains from the sweet-toned organ; and as Samuel Hill and his wife took their seats in the front pew beside Mr. and Mrs. Ezekiel Pettengill, the excitement of the audience could no longer be controlled. It overcame all restraint, and as Hiram Maxwell and Mandy Skinner entered, the people arose to their feet and cheered loudly, as they would have done at a political meeting or a circus.

Again, and for the last time, the Rev. Mr. Howe went through the time-honored ceremony, and at its close Mr. and Mrs. Ezekiel Pettengill, Mr. and Mrs. Samuel Hill, and Mr. and Mrs. Hiram Maxwell left the church by way of the right-hand aisle, preceded by the ushers, who strewed the aisle with white roses as they advanced, and were followed by the occupants of the second bridal pew.

As Quincy rode over to Eastborough Centre with his Aunt Ella, after partaking of the wedding breakfast, which was served in Deacon Mason's dining-room, she remarked to him that the events of the day had been most enjoyable, and that she didn't know, after all, but that she should change her mind about getting married again.

When asked by Quincy if she had seen any one whom

she thought would suit her for a second husband, she replied that "Mr. Isaac Pettengill was a very well-preserved
old gentleman, and the most original man in thought and
speech that she had met since Robert died."

Quincy did not inform her that Uncle Ike had a wife
and two grown-up daughters living, thinking it best to reserve that information for a future occasion.

That night Strout & Maxwell's grocery store was the
centre of attraction. Strout was in his glory, and was, of
course, in his own opinion, the most successful feature of
that eventful day. It was a very common thing to get
married, but it was a most uncommon thing to play on a
new church organ, and play as well as he had done, "for
the first time, too," as he remarked a score of times.

Stepping upon a barrel, the Professor called out in a
loud voice, "Order, please," and in a short time the assembled crowd became quiet.

"Friends and Feller Citizens: I have this day received
my commission as postmaster at Mason's Corner, Mass.
Mail matter will be sorted with celerity and delivered only
to the proper parties, while the firm of Strout & Maxwell
will always keep on hand a full assortment of the best
family groceries at reasonable prices. Soliciting your continued patronage, I remain, yours respectively.

                         OBADIAH STROUT, Postmaster.

As the Professor stepped down from the barrel, Abner
Stiles caught him by the arm and said in a low voice,
"Isn't Deacon Mason one of your bondsmen?"

"Yes," said Strout, somewhat pompously, "but what of
it?"

"Why, yer see," said Abner, "I'm workin' for the Deacon now, and I'm just as devoted to his interests as I used
to be to yourn onct, and with a much better hope of reward,
both on this earth and in Heaven, and if he's got money

put up on yer, of course yer won't object if I drop in onct in a while and kinder keep an eye on yer." And with this parting shot he dashed out a side door and was lost to sight.

CHAPTER XXXIV.

BLENNERHASSETT.

WHEN comparatively great events follow each other in quick succession, those of minor importance are liable to escape mention. It was for this reason, probably, that the second visit of Dr. Tillotson was not spoken of at the time of its occurrence. He examined Alice's eyes and declared that progress towards recovery was being made, slowly but surely. He left a bottle of new medicine, and advised Alice, as an aid to recovery, to take a long walk, or a ride, each pleasant day. This advice he repeated to Uncle Ike, who was waiting for him outside the front door, and to Quincy, who brought him from the station and took him back.

On the day fixed upon, Quincy drove over to Montrose, and accompanied by Squire Rundlett, went to the county town and presented Mrs. Putnam's will for probate. In due time the will was admitted, the executors' bonds were filed and approved, and Quincy, at the age of twenty-three, found himself one of the financial guardians of the young heiress, Mary Alice Pettengill, she being his junior by less than two years.

About ten days after Quincy's interview with his Aunt Ella, in which she had signified her intention of making him an allowance, he received a letter from a Boston banking firm, informing him that by direction of Mrs. Ella Chessman, the sum of five thousand dollars had been placed to his credit, and that a similar sum would be so placed on the first business day of January in each succeeding year. A blank card was enclosed for a copy of his signature, and the statement made that his drafts would be duly honored.

When Quincy and his aunt reached Eastborough Centre, after the trio of weddings, they found that they had a full hour to wait before the arrival of the next ingoing train.

This gave plenty of time for the reloading of the horses and carriage on the special car in which they had been brought from Boston and which had been side-tracked.

Quincy wished to accompany his aunt to Boston and escort her to her home, but she demurred. He insisted, but his aunt replied, "Don't go, please don't, Quincy; they will take me for your mother, and I really am not quite old enough for that."

This argument was unanswerable, and Quincy bade her a laughing good-by as the train sped on towards Boston, the special car in charge of the coachman and footman bringing up the rear.

Thus Aunt Ella's visit to Mason's Corner became an event of the past, but the memory of it remained green for a long time in the minds of those who had witnessed her arrival and departure.

Ellis Smith drove Quincy home to the Pettengill house. It was to be home no longer, for Hiram and Mandy were to have the room that Quincy had occupied so long. His trunk and other belongings he had packed up the night before, and at Quincy's request, Cobb's twins had taken them out to Jacob's Parlor, where he found them. He knew that Mr. and Mrs. Hawkins were to spend the afternoon with their daughter and son-in-law.

Quincy also knew that Uncle Ike and Alice were at Deacon Mason's, where Ezekiel and Huldy were to remain for the coming week.

For the first time since he had been at Mason's Corner, Quincy felt lonesome and deserted. He reflected on his way to Mrs. Hawkins's boarding house that these weddings

were all very nice, to be sure, but they had deprived him,
of the society of many good friends, who were now united
by stronger ties than those of simple, everyday friendship.

He did not care to go to the grocery store, for he felt
that the Professor was entitled to all the credit that he was
likely to get for his day's performance, and he did not wish
to detract from it. So he went directly to his room, and
for the first time felt out of sorts with Eastborough and its
people.

He was not hungry for food, so he did not answer the
call to supper, but sat in the dark and thought. He realized that he was hungry, yes, desperately hungry, for love
—the love of one woman, Alice Pettengill. Why should
he wait longer? Even if his father and mother objected his
Aunt Ella was on his side, and her action had made him
independent. He had felt himself so before, but now there
was no doubt of it.

This determined young man then made up his mind he
would declare ·his love at the first auspicious moment.
Then he would go to his parents and learn their verdict
on his proposed action. Thinking thus he went to bed,
and in his dreams, ushers, and bridesmaids, and cut flowers,
and potted plants, and miles of silken ribbon, and cream-
colored horses, and carriages, and clergymen, and organ-
ists, and big pipe organs were revolving about him and
Alice, as the planets revolve about the sun.

Once more Quincy's breakfast was on the stove being
kept warm, and once more Mrs. Hawkins was waiting impatiently for him to come down.

Betsy Green and she were washing the breakfast dishes.
How happy Eve must have been in Eden, where there was
no china, no knives and forks, and no pots and kettles, and
what an endless burden of commonplace drudgery she en-
tailed upon her fair sisters when she fell from her high
estate. Man's labor is uniformly productive, but woman's,
alas! is still almost as uniformly simply preservative.

"Mr. Sawyer," said Mrs. Hawkins to Betsy Green, "is no doubt a very nice young man, but I shouldn't want him for a steady boarder, 'less he got up on time and eat his meals reg'lar."

"I s'pose he's all tired out," remarked Betsy. "He had a pretty hard day of it yesterday, you know, Mis' Hawkins."

"Wall, I s'pose I ought to be kinder easy on him on that account. I must say he managed things fust rate."

"How did the brides look?" asked Betsy.

Poor girl, she was one of the few who were not able to view the grand sight.

"I can think of no word to express my feelin's," replied Mrs. Hawkins after a pause, "but splendiferous! Huldy's dress was a white satin that would a stood alone. She had a overskirt of netted white silk cord, heavy enough to use for a hammock. You know she's neither light nor dark, kind of a between, but she looked mighty poorty all the same."

"Was Tilly James dressed in white, too?" inquired Betsy.

"No," answered Mrs. Hawkins. "She wore a very light pink silk, with a lace overskirt, and it just matched her black eyes and black hair fine, I can tell yer."

"Mandy must have looked pretty, with her light curly hair and blue eyes, and those rosy cheeks."

"Well," said Mrs. Hawkins reflectively, "I'm her mother, and a course I'm prejoodished, but I honestly think she was the best lookin' one of the three. Of course Hiram is no beauty, and I'm all out of patience when he tries to talk to me. But I know he'll make Mandy a good husband, and that's a tarnal sight better'n good looks."

"What color was Mandy's dress?" persisted Betsy.

"Lord a massy," cried Mrs. Hawkins, "I e'en a'most forgot to tell yer. Her dress was a very light blue silk, with a lace overskirt, 'bout the same as Tilly's. Mr. Sawyer gave her two hundred dollars to buy her things with, 'cause she's been so nice to him since he boarded at Pettengill's."

"Who was that stylish lookin' lady that came in a carriage with the four beautiful horses? I saw her outer the attic winder."

"She was a Mrs. Chessman," replied Mrs. Hawkins. I heern tell she's a widder'd aunt of Mr. Sawyer's, and she's as rich as Creazers."

"How rich is that?" inquired Betsey, with an astonished look.

"Creazers," replied Mrs. Hawkins, with an expression that savored of erudition, "was a man who was so all fired rich that he had to hire folks to spend his money for him."

At that moment a step was heard in the dining-room, and both Mrs. Hawkins and Betsy flew to wait upon the new-comer who proved to be Mr. Quincy Adams Sawyer. As he took his seat at the table the Connecticut clock on the mantelpiece struck ten.

At eleven o'clock that same morning Mr. Sawyer knocked at the front door of Mr. Ezekiel Pettengill's residence. How strange it seemed, how much more home-like it would have been to have entered by the back door and to have come through the kitchen and dining-room, as of old. But no! He was not a regular boarder now, only an occasional visitor.

The door was opened by young Mrs. Maxwell, and her usually rosy cheeks were ruddier than ever when she saw who the caller was.

"Is Miss Pettengill in?" Quincy politely inquired.

"She's in the parlor, sir; won't you walk in?" And she threw open the door of the room in which Alice sat by the fire.

"Do I disturb your dreams, Miss Pettengill?" asked Quincy, as he reached her side.

"I'm so glad you have come, Mr. Sawyer," said Alice, extending her hand. "I never was so lonesome in my life as I have been this morning. The house seems deserted.

Uncle Ike ate too many good things yesterday, and says he is enjoying an attack of indigestion to-day. I had Swiss in here to keep me company, but he wouldn't stay and Mandy had to let him out."

"He came up to Mrs. Hawkins's," said Quincy, as he took his accustomed seat opposite Alice. "He walked down with me, but when he saw me safe on the front door-step he disappeared around the corner."

"I didn't tell him to go after you," said Alice, laughing; "but I am very glad that you have come. I have a very important matter to consult you about. You know you are my business man now."

"I'm always at your service," replied Quincy. "I think I know what you wish to see me about."

"And what do you think it is?" asked Alice, shaking her head negatively.

"Well," said Quincy, "I saw Squire Rundlett the day before the weddings and he thought that you might possibly want some money. He had a thousand dollars in cash belonging to you, and I brought you half of it. If you will kindly sign this receipt," he continued, as he took a small parcel from his pocket, "you will relieve me of further responsibility for its safe keeping."

He moved the little writing table close to her chair, and dipping the pen in the ink he handed it to her, and indicated with his finger the place where she should sign. She wrote as well as ever, though she could see nothing that she penned.

"There are eight fifty-dollar bills, eight tens and four fives," he said, as he passed her the money.

"Which are the fifties?" she asked, as she handled the money nervously with her fingers.

"Here they are," said Quincy, and he separated them from the rest of the bills and placed them in her hands.

"Oh! thank you," said she. She counted out four of the bills and passed them to Quincy. "That settles my money debt to you, does it not?" she inquired; "but nothing can pay the debt of gratitude that I owe you for your many acts of kindness to me, Mr. Sawyer."

"I am fully repaid by that very kind speech of yours," replied Quincy. "But what was the important matter you wished to see me about? I don't think it was the money."

"It was not," said Alice. "I have little use for money just at present. I never had so much before at once in all my life. I shall have to learn to be an heiress."

"It's a lesson that is very easily learned," replied Quincy.

"What I wish to speak about," continued Alice, musingly, "is Mrs. Putnam's house. I could never live in it. I could never go into that room again;" and she shuddered.

"You can sell it," interposed Quincy.

"No," said Alice earnestly, "I am going to give it away. Father just made a living here, and Ezekiel can do no better, but with the Putnam farm, properly stocked, he can in time become a rich man, for he is a good farmer, and he loves his work. I wish," continued Alice, "to give 'Zekiel and Huldy the farm outright, then I would like to loan him enough money to buy live stock and machinery and whatever else he may need, so that he may begin his new life under the most favorable auspices."

"I think your proposed action a most commendable one," remarked Quincy. "I am sure you need anticipate no objections on the part of Squire Rundlett or myself. Our duties are limited to seeing that all the property that was willed to you is properly delivered. It gives us no right to interfere with your wishes or to question your motives. I will see Squire Rundlett at an early day and have the matter put into shape. Does Ezekiel know of this?"

"Not a word," said Alice; "I do not wish to speak to him about it until the matter is all settled and the papers are signed. He is high spirited, and at the first mention I know he would refuse my offer, especially if he thought 'twas only known to us two. But when he learns that the deed is done, and that the Squire and yourself are knowing to it, he will be more tractable."

"Speaking of the Putnam house, or more properly, I suppose, Pettengill house number two—"

"This will always be number one," interposed Alice.

"—reminds me," said Quincy, that my efforts to discover Lindy's whereabouts have so far proved unavailing. The advertisement that I put in for a month has run out and I have received no word."

"Do you think she went to New York, as she promised?" inquired Alice.

"I do not," replied Quincy. "I think she always had an idea that Mrs. Putnam had some letter or document in her possession relating to her parents. I think the poor girl lost hope when she learned that it was destroyed, and I imagine that she has intentionally hidden herself and does not wish to be found. I might, after long search, discover her bankers, but she has probably notified them to keep her address a secret. I do not like to confess," he continued, "to so abject a failure, but I really do not know what to do next."

"We must wait and hope," said Alice. Then looking up at Quincy with an arch smile upon her face, she added, "I will extend your time, Sir Knight. Your gallant efforts have so far been unsuccessful, but I shall pray that you may some day return victorious."

Quincy replied in the same tone of banter: "Knowing that you, fair lady, are ever thinking of me, and that my name is ever upon your fair lips in prayer, will spur me to renewed effort, for surely no cavalier ever had a more lovely mistress or a greater incentive to knightly action."

Although he spoke in a chaffing tone, there was an undercurrent of seriousness in his manner and pathos in his voice that made Alice start and flush visibly.

Fearing that he had gone too far he quickly changed the

subject by asking abruptly, "Have you come to any decision about your book?"

"Yes," replied Alice, "and I am ashamed to say that your friend's suggestion and your warm endorsement of it have so increased my egotism and enlarged my appreciation of my own abilities that I am tempted to try it, especially now, as you inform me I am independent and can do as I please."

"Have you progressed so far as to fix upon a subject?" inquired Quincy.

"Yes, provisionally," replied Alice. "I have always been a great admirer of history, and particularly that of my own country. For the period from 1776, no, from 1607, to the present time I have become conversant with the thoughts and acts of our patriots and public men. One character has always been a mystery to me, and I wish to learn all I can about him."

"And he?" questioned Quincy.

"Is Aaron Burr," said Alice. "How I wish I could learn the truth about the loss of his daughter Theodosia; then the real reasons for his duel with Alexander Hamilton are not fully understood at the present day. Then again, I should enjoy writing about that fine old Irish gentleman and lover of science, Harman Blennerhassett, and his lovely wife, Margaret."

"Have you decided upon the title?" still further questioned Quincy.

"I have thought of two," she replied, " 'Theodosia,' and 'Blennerhassett,' but I strongly incline to the latter."

"So do I," said Quincy, "but you will have to do much more reading, no doubt, before you commence writing. Historical novels are usually savagely attacked by the critics, presumably very often from political motives, and you would have to be very strong in your authorities."

"That is what troubles me," said Alice; "if I only could read—"

"But others can read to you and make such notes as you
esire," remarked Quincy. "I should like nothing better
ıan to help you in such a work, but I have been away from
ome so long that I feel it imperative to resume my busi·
ess duties at an early day."

"I think you ought," said Alice. "I could not presume
ɔ trespass upon your kindness and good nature to such an
xtent. The idea of writing this book has grown very
leasing to me, but I can wait until—" She stopped speak·
ıg and placed both of her hands over her eyes. "I can
ait," she repeated, "until my eyes are better."

"Will you allow me to make a suggestion, Miss Petten-
ill?"

Alice smiled and nodded. "You are my literary as well
 s my financial adviser," said she.

"It will no doubt appear quite an undertaking to you,"
ontinued Quincy, "but I shall be very glad to help you.
Iy plan is to secure a lady who reads well and can write a
ood hand to assist you. Besides this, she must understand
ɔrrecting proof sheets. I think Leopold could easily find
ıch a person for you. Then, again, you know what Dr.
'illotson said about your taking exercise and fresh air.
'he second feature of my plan, and the most important in
ıy mind, is to find some quiet place in the country, or at
ıe beach, where you and your amanuensis can both work
nd play. I can buy for you such books as you need, and
ou can finish the work this summer."

Alice reflected. After a few moments' pause she said,
I like the plan and I thank you very much for speaking of
:; but I prefer the beach. I love the plash and roar and
oom of the water, and it will be a constant inspiration to
ıe. How soon can I go?" she asked, with a look upon her
ıce that a young child might have had in speaking to its
ıther.

This was Alice Pettengill's great charm. She was hon-
st and disingenuous, and was always ready to think that

what others deemed it best for her to do was really so. Imitation may be the sincerest flattery, but appreciation of the advice and counsel of others, combined with gratitude for the friendly spirit that prompts it, makes and holds more friends.

Quincy looked at his watch.

"I can get the afternoon train, I think," said he. "I will see Leopold, and then run up and make Aunt Ella a call. She knows the New England coast from Eastport to Newport. Did she speak to you at the wedding?"

"Some lady with a very pleasant voice asked me if I were Miss Pettengill, while we were in the church," replied Alice. "I said yes, and then she told me that her name was Chessman, adding the information that she was your aunt, and that you could tell me all about her."

"I shall be happy to," said Quincy; "but I can assure you it would be much more enjoyable for you to hear it from herself. I hope you will have that pleasure some day." And again adopting a bantering tone, "I trust, fair lady, I shall not return this time from a bootless errand."

Alice listened again, as she had often done, until she heard the sound of departing wheels, and then she fell to wondering whether her future paths in life would continue to be marked out by this Sir Knight, who was ever at her beck and call, and whether it was her destiny to always tread the paths that he laid out for her.

Quincy was fortunate in finding Leopold at home.

"I'm glad you've come, Quincy," said he; "I was going to write you to-night."

"What's up?" inquired Quincy.

"Please pass me that package of papers on the corner of the table," answered Leopold, being loath to rise from his recumbent position on the lounge.

Quincy did as requested and took a seat beside Leopold.

"These," said Leopold, "are the proofs of the first writings of a to-be-famous American author. Glad she took a man's name, so I don't have to say authoress. Here," he continued, "are the proofs of the story, Was it Signed? Cooper wishes it read and returned immediately. Editors wish everything done immediately. They loaf on their end and expect the poor author to sit up all night and make up for their shortcomings. I'm a sort of editor myself, and I know what I'm talking about. This lot," he continued, "will appear in 'The Sunday Universe' a week from next Sunday. I had a copy made for Jameson to work from. Bruce Douglas owes me four-fifty for expenses, necessary but not authorized."

"I will see that you are reimbursed," said Quincy; "want it now?" and he made a motion to take out his pocketbook.

"No," replied Leopold, "I'm flush to-day; keep it till some time when I'm strapped. Last, and most important of all, here are the proofs of the story that is to appear in our monthly. Now, my advice to you is, Quincy, seek the fair author at once, correct these proofs and have them back to me within three days, or they'll go over and she'll be charged for keeping the type standing, besides having her pay hung up for another week."

"She won't mind that," said Quincy, with a laugh. "She's an heiress now, with real and personal property valued at fifty thousand dollars. But what am I to do?" asked he seriously. "I could read the manuscript, but we have no one at Eastborough who knows how to make those pothooks and scratches that you call 'corrections.'"

"Well, you two young aspirants for literary fame are in a box, are'nt you? I was thinking about that fifty thousand. Perhaps I'd better go home with you and get acquainted with the author," said Leopold with a laugh.

"Well," returned Quincy, "it would be very kind of you in our present emergency, but, strange as it may seem, I came to see you this afternoon about securing a literary assistant for Miss Pettengill. She has decided to write that book."

"Good girl!" cried Leopold, sitting bolt upright upon the lounge. "I mean, good boy, for it was, no doubt, your ac-knowledged powers of argument and gently persuasive ways that have secured this consummation of my desire. Let me think;" and he scratched his head vigorously. "I think I have it," said he, finally. "One of our girls down to the office worked so hard during our late splurge that the doctor told her she must rest this week. She rooms over on Myrtle Street. I happened to be late in getting out one day last week, and we walked together up as far as Chestnut Street. She lives nearly down to the end of Myrtle Street."

"No further explanation or extenuation is necessary," said Quincy. "Is she pretty?"

"You're right, she is," replied Leopold. "She's both pretty and smart. She has a beautiful voice and writes a hand that looks like copperplate. She's a first-class proof reader and a perfect walking dictionary on spelling, defini-tions, and dates. They treat her mighty shabby on pay, though. She's a woman, so they gave her six dollars a week. If she were a man they'd give her twenty, and think themselves lucky. I'll run over and see if she is at home. At what time could she go down with you to-morrow?" he asked.

"I'll come after her at nine o'clock. Tell her Miss Pet-tengill will give her eight dollars a week, with board and lodging free."

"All right," cried Leopold, "that's business. While I'm gone just see how pretty those stories look in cold type. I've been all through them myself just for practice."

Leopold dashed out of the room and Quincy took up the proofs of the story, Was It Signed? He became so ab-sorbed in its perusal that Leopold pulled it out of his hand in order to attract his attention.

"It's all right," he said. "She's delighted at the idea of going. She thinks the change will do her good. She can't build up very fast in a little back room, up three flights."

"What's her name?" asked Quincy.

"Oh! I forgot," replied Leopold. "I'll write her name and address down for you. There it is," said he, as he passed it to Quincy. "Her first name is Rosa, and that's all right. She's of French-Canadian descent, and her last name is one of those jawbreakers that no American can pronounce. It sounded something like Avery, so she called herself at first Rosa Avery; then the two A's caused trouble, for everybody thought she said Rose Avery. Being a proof reader," continued Leopold, "she is very sensitive, so while the name Rosa satisfied her inmost soul, the name Rose jarred upon her sensibilities. Thus another change became necessary, and she is now known, and probably will continue to be known, as Miss Rosa Very, until she makes up her mind to change it again."

"I'm greatly obliged, Leopold," said Quincy, making the proofs into a flat parcel and putting them into his inside overcoat pocket.

"Don't mention it, old fellow," remarked Leopold. "You may be the means of supplying me with an assistant some day. If you should, don't fail to call my attention to it."

Aunt Ella was at dinner when Quincy arrived. She sent word up by Buttons for Quincy to come down to the dining-room at once. She was alone in the room when he entered.

"Just in time," said he, "and I'm hungry as a bear."

"That's a good boy; sit down and help me out," said his aunt. "These extravagant servants of mine cook ten times as much as I can possibly eat."

"I don't imagine it is wasted," replied Quincy.

"I think not," said Aunt Ella, with a laugh; "for, judging from the extra plentiful supply, they probably have a kitchen party in view for this evening. But what keeps you away from Eastborough over night?"

"I thought you couldn't eat and talk at the same time," remarked Quincy.

"I can't," she replied. "I'm through eating and I'm going to sit and listen to you. Go right ahead, the servants won't come in. I won't let them stand and look at me when I'm eating. If I want them I ring for them."

Quincy then briefly related the principal events that had taken place at Mason's Corner since the nineteenth, remarking, incidentally, that he had received no word from Lindy.

"Let her alone, and she'll come home when she gets ready," said Aunt Ella. "As to the best place for your young lady to go, I shall have to think a minute. Old Orchard is my favorite, but I'm afraid it would be too noisy for her there, the hotels are so close to the railroad track. I suppose your family, meaning your mother's, of course, will go to Nahant, as usual. Sarah would have society convulsions at Old Orchard. I should like to see her promenading down in front of the candy stores, shooting for cigars in the shooting gallery, or taking a ride down to Saco Pool on the narrow-gauge; excuse me for speaking so of your mother, Quincy, but I have been acquainted with her much longer than you have." She went on, "Newport is too stylish for comfort. Ah! I have it, Quincy. I was there three years ago, and I know what I'm talking about. Quaint place,—funny looking houses, with little promenades on top,—crooked streets that lead everywhere and nowhere, —very much like Boston,—full of curiosities,—hardy old mariners and peaceable old Quakers,—plenty of nice milk and eggs and fresh fish,—more fish than anything else,— every breeze is a sea breeze, and it is so delightfully quiet that the flies and mosquitoes imitate the inhabitants, and sleep all day and all night."

"Where is this modern Eden, this corner lot in Paradise?" asked Quincy; "it can't be part of the United States."

"Not exactly," replied Aunt Ella; it's off shore, I forget

how many miles, but you can find it swimming around
in the water just south of Cape Cod."

"Oh! you mean Nantucket," cried Quincy.

"That's the place," assented his aunt. "Now, Quincy,
I'll tell you just what I want you to do, and I want you to
promise to do it before I say another word."

"That's a woman's way," remarked Quincy, "of avoid-
ing argument and preventing a free expression of opinion
by interested parties; but I'll consent, only be merciful."

"What I'm going to ask you to do, Quincy Sawyer, is for
your good, and you'll own up that I've been more than a
mother to you before I get through."

"You always have been," said Quincy, seriously. "Of
course, I love my mother in a way, but I'm never exactly
comfortable when I'm with her. But when I'm with you,
Aunt Ella, I'm always contented and feel perfectly at
home."

"Bless you, my dear boy," she said. Then, rising, she
went behind his chair, leaned over and kissed him on the
forehead; then, pulling a chair close to him, she went on:
"I haven't spoken to you of her, Quincy, because I have
had no opportunity until now. I've fallen in love with her
myself. I am a physiognomist as well as a phrenologist.
Robert taught me the principles. She's almost divinely
lovely. I say almost, for, of course, she'll be still lovelier
when she goes to Heaven. Her well-shaped head indicates
a strong, active, inventive mind, while her pure heart and
clean soul are mirrored in her sweet face. She is a good
foil for you, Quincy. You are almost dark enough for a
Spaniard or an Italian, while she is Goethe's ideal Mar-
guerite."

It was not necessary for Quincy to ask to whom she referred, nor to praise her powers of discernment. It was
Aunt Ella's time for talking, and she was not inclined to
brook any interference. So she went on.

"I want you to bring her here to me and have Rosa

What-d'yer-call-her come with her. Here they can work and play until you get the nest ready for her down to Nantucket. You say she plays and sings. I love music passionately, but I can't play a note, even on a jew's-harp; but if she plays a wrong note I shall feel inclined to call her attention to it. When I used to go to the theatre with Robert, I delighted in telling him how badly some of the members of the orchestra were playing, but I repented of it. He got in the habit of going out between the acts to escape the music, he said, and I never could keep him in his seat after that."

Quincy laughed heartily at this. "I see no way of stopping this bad habit that gentlemen have of going out between the acts," said he, "unless you ladies combine, and insist on a higher grade of orchestral excellence."

"I have a large library," continued Aunt Ella, "and she may find many books in it that will be of use to her. Robert spent eighteen thousand dollars on it, and I've bought a couple of thousand dollars' worth more since his death. Now, what do you say, Quincy? You know I will do all in my power to make her comfortable and happy while she is here. If Maude runs up, and she's the only one that is likely to, I will tell her that I have friends here from England. I will keep her out of the way. Will you bring her?"

"If she will come, I will," Quincy replied.

"You will never repent it," said Aunt Ella. "Now let us go upstairs."

When they reached her room the cigars and cigarettes were again in requisition.

"I kept my promise the other day, Quincy," said she, "when the three girls were here. What a sweet, rosy-cheeked, healthy, happy trio they were! I wasn't more than twenty myself that day. I give you my solemn promise, Quincy, that I won't smoke a cigarette nor drink a glass of wine while Alice is here,—until after she goes to bed; and then I'll eat a clove and air the room out thoroughly before I let her in in the morning."

Quincy was up early next morning, and at ten minutes of nine reached the lodging house in Myrtle Street. He had taken a carriage, for he knew Miss Very would have her luggage, probably a trunk. His call at the door was answered by a sharp-eyed, hatchet-faced woman, whose face was red with excitement. To Quincy's inquiry if Miss Very was in, the woman replied, "that she was in and was likely to stay in."

"I trust she is not sick," said Quincy.

"No! she ain't sick," the woman replied, "what you mean by sick; but there's worse things than bein' sick, especially when a poor widder has a big house rent to pay and coal seven dollars and a half a ton."

A small trunk, neatly strapped, stood in the hallway. Glancing into the stuffy little parlor, he saw a woman, apparently young, with her veil down, seated on a sofa, with a large valise on the floor and a hand bag at her side.

Quincy divined the situation at once. Stepping into the hallway, he closed the parlor door, and, turning to the woman, said, "How much?"

"Three dollars," replied the woman, "and it's cheap enough for—"

"A miserable little dark stuffy side room, without any heat, up three flights, back," broke in Quincy, as he passed her the money.

The woman was breathless with astonishment and anger. Taking advantage of this, Quincy opened the parlor door, first beckoning to the coachman to come in and get the trunk.

"Miss Very, I presume?" said Quincy, as he advanced towards the young lady on the sofa.

She arose as he approached, and answered, "Yes, sir."

"Come with me, please," said he, grasping the valise. She hesitated; he understood why. "It's all right," he said, in a low tone. "I've settled with the landlady, and you can settle with me any time."

"Thank you, so much," spoke a sweet voice from underneath the veil, and the owner of it followed close behind him, and he handed her into the carriage. As Quincy pulled the carriage door to, that of the lodging house closed with a report like that of a pistol, and Mrs. Colby went down stairs and told the servant, who was scrubbing the kitchen floor, what had occurred, and added that she "had always had her suspicions of that Miss Very."

While Quincy was talking with Alice the day before, his dinner that Mrs. Hawkins had saved for him was being burned to a crisp in and on the stove. Mrs. Hawkins's attention was finally attracted to it, and, turning to Betsy, she said, "Law sakes, somethin' must be burnin.' " Running to the stove, she soon discovered the cause. "Mercy on me!" she ejaculated. "I left that damper open, and his dinner's burnt to a cinder. Wall, I don't care; he may be a good lodger, an' all that, but he's a mighty poor boarder; and it's no satisfaction gittin' up things for him to eat, and then lettin' them go to waste, even if he does pay for it. Them's my sentiments, and I'll feel better now I've spit it out."

The good woman went to work to clean up her stove, while Betsy kept on with the seemingly endless dish washing. Mrs. Hawkins finished her work, and, going to the sink, began to wipe the accumulated pile of dishes.

"I s'pose everybody in town will go to church next Sunday," said Mrs. Hawkins, "to see them brides."

"Will they look any different than they did the other day?" Betsy innocently inquired.

"Well, I guess," remarked Mrs. Hawkins. "I saw Mandy yesterday and she told me all about her trip to the city. Mrs. Chessman went shoppin' with them, and the way she beat them shopkeepers down was a sight, Mandy says. It beats all how them rich folks can buy things so much cheaper than us poor people can. She took them all home to dinner, and Mandy says she lives in the most beautifulest house she ever saw. Then she went to the dressmakers with them, and she beat them down more'n five dollars on each gown. Then she took 'em to the millinery store, and she bought each one of them a great big handsome hat, with feathers and ribbons and flowers all over 'em. Nobody has seen 'em yet, but all three on 'em are going to wear 'em to church next Sunday, and won't there be a stir? Nobody'll look at the new orgin."

"I wish I could go," said Betsy.

Mrs. Hawkins rattled on: "Mandy says she took 'em all into a jewelry store, and bought each one on 'em a breast-pin, a pair of earrings, and a putty ring, to remember her by. Then she druv 'em down to the deepo in her carriage."

"I wish I could see them with all their fine things on," said Betsy, again.

"Well, you shall, Betsy," said good-hearted Mrs. Hawkins. "I'll make Jonas help me wash the dishes Sunday mornin', and you shall go to church."

Betsy's face was wreathed in smiles.

"You're so good to me, Mrs. Hawkins," she cried.

"Well," answered Mrs. Hawkins, "you've worked like a Trojan the last week, and you deserve it. I guess if I go up in the attic I can git a good look at them as they're walking home from church."

In her excitement the old lady dropped a cup and saucer on the floor, and both mistress and maid went down on their hands and knees to pick up the pieces.

CHAPTER XXXV.

THE carriage containing Quincy and Rosa was driven at a rapid rate toward the station. There was no time to lose, as some had already been lost in the altercation with Mrs. Colby. They had proceeded but a short distance, when Rosa took out a pocketbook, and, lifting her veil, turned her face to Quincy.

What a striking face it was! Large, dark blue eyes, regular features, a light olive complexion, with a strong dash of red in each cheek, full red lips, and hair of almost raven blackness. Like lightning the thought flashed through Quincy's mind, "What a contrast to my Alice!" for he always used the pronoun when he thought of her.

"Allow me to cancel part of my indebtedness to you," said Rosa, in a low, sweet voice, and Quincy again thought how pleasant that voice would be to Alice when Miss Very was reading to her.

As Rosa spoke she handed Quincy a two-dollar bill and seventy-five cents in currency.

"I owe you an explanation," she continued. "Mr. Ernst told me that I must be ready to accompany you the moment you called, so I packed and strapped my trunk last evening. When I returned from breakfast this morning I looked through my pocketbook, and found to my surprise that I lacked a quarter of a dollar of enough to pay for my week's lodging. In my haste I had put my jewel case, which contained the greater part of my money, in my trunk, and I realized that there would not be time to unpack and pack it again before your arrival. I offered Mrs. Colby the two seventy-five, and told her I would send her the balance in a letter as soon as I arrived at my destination. To my astonishment, she refused to take it, saying that she would have the three dollars or nothing."

"If I had known that," said Quincy, "she would have got nothing."

"Oh! it's all right," remarked Rosa, with a smile. "I know the poor woman has hard work to make a living, and I also know that she has lost considerable money from persons failing to pay at all or paying part of their bills and then not sending the balance, as they promised to do."

"And did she get up all that ugliness for a quarter of a dollar?" inquired Quincy.

"Oh! that wasn't the reason at all," replied Rosa; "I've always paid her promptly and in advance. She was mad because I was going away. If she lets the room right off she will get double rent this coming week, for it so happened my week ended last night."

"Lodging-house keepers," said Quincy, "seem to be a class by themselves, and to have peculiar financial and moral codes. Here we are at the station," he added, as the carriage came to a stop.

As Quincy handed Rosa from the carriage, his observant eye noticed that the hand placed in his was small and well-gloved, while the equally small feet were encased in a pair of dainty boots. "She is true to her French origin," he soliloquized, as they entered the station,—"well-booted, well-gloved. I am glad she is a lady."

The train was soon on its way to Eastborough. It was an accommodation, and Quincy had plenty of time to point out the objects of interest on the way. Rosa was not a lover of the country. She acknowledged this to Quincy, saying that she was born and educated in the country, but that she preferred paved streets and brick sidewalks to green lanes and dusty roads.

Alice had not waited for Quincy's return to broach the matter of the gift of the Putnam house to Ezekiel and Huldy. She had simply asked Quincy, so as to assure herself that there was no legal objection or reason why she should not make the transfer.

After breakfast the next morning she told her uncle that she wished to have a talk with him in the parlor, and when they were alone together, she stated her intentions to him, as she had to Quincy. The old gentleman approved of her plan, only suggesting that it should be a swap; that is, that Ezekiel should deed the house in which they were, in which, in fact, she owned a half-interest, to her, so she would be sure of a home in case she lost part of her money, or all of it, or wished to live in the country.

Most opportunely, Ezekiel and Huldy came over that morning to make a call, and the matter was soon under discussion in family conclave.

Ezekiel at first objected strenuously to the gift. He would buy the house, he said, and pay so much a year on it, but both Alice and Uncle Ike protested that it was foolish for a young couple to start in life with such a heavy debt hanging over them.

The only circumstance that led him to change his mind and agree to accept the Putnam homestead as a gift was Uncle Ike's suggestion that he deed the Pettengill homestead to Alice, and pay her all he received for the sale of products from the present Pettengill farm; but 'Zekiel would not accept any loan. He said Deacon Mason had given his daughter five thousand dollars outright, and that would be all the cash they would need to stock and carry on both the farms.

Then 'Zekiel said he might as well settle on who was to live in the two houses. He knew that Cobb's twins would like to stay with him, and he would take them up to the Putnam house with him. Mrs. Pinkham had been hired by the executors to remain with Samanthy until some one came to live in the house. Ezekiel said Samanthy was a good girl, and he and Huldy both liked her, and he felt pretty sure she'd be willing to live with them, because she was used to the house, and as it was the only one she'd ever lived in, it would seem like going away from home if she left there and went somewhere else.

Then 'Zekiel was of the opinion that Abbott Smith and Billy Ricker had better board with Hiram and Mandy, because the grocery teams and horses would have to be kept in the Pettengill barn, as there was no stable to the grocery store. " 'Twon't be stealin' anythin' from Mrs. Hawkins if they don't board with her, cuz none of 'em ever lived with her afore."

"Don't you think, 'Zekiel," asked Huldy, "that Uncle Ike ought to come down stairs and have a better room? It will be awful hot up there in the summer. Alice and I used to play up there, and in July and August it was hot enough to roast eggs, wasn't it, Alice?"

Alice, thus appealed to, said it might have been hot enough, but she was positive that they never did roast any up there, although she remembered setting the attic floor on fire one day with a burning glass. 'Zekiel remembered that, too, and how they had to put new ceilings on two rooms, because he used so much water to put the fire out.

When Uncle Ike got a chance to speak, he said to Huldy, "Thank you, my dear Mrs. Pettengill," with a strong accent on the Mrs., which made Huldy blush a rosy red, "but I wouldn't swap my old attic for all the rest of the rooms in the house. My old blood requires warmth, and I can stand ninety-six without asking for a fan. When I come up to see you, you can put me in one of your big square rooms, but I sha'n't stay long, because I don't like them."

The noise of wheels was heard, and Huldy ran to the window to look out.

"Oh, it's Mr. Sawyer," said she; "and he's got a young

lady with him, and she's got a trunk. I wonder who she is? Do you know, Alice?"

"I don't know who she is," replied Alice; "but I can imagine what she's here for."

"Is it a secret?" asked Huldy.

"No, not exactly a secret," replied Alice. "It's a business matter. I have a great many things to be read over to me, and considerable writing to do, and as Mr. Sawyer is going away, I was obliged to have some one to help me."

"Well!" said Huldy, "you'll miss Mr. Sawyer when he goes away; I did. Now you mustn't get jealous, Mr. Pettengill," she said to 'Zekiel; "you know Mr. Sawyer and I were never in love with each other. That was all village gossip, started by, you know who, and as for Mr. Sawyer liking Lindy Putnam, or she liking him, I know better. She's never got over the loss of her brother Jones, who, it seems, wasn't her real brother, after all; and Samanthy Green told me the other day that Lindy wanted to marry him."

"I think matters are getting rather too personal for me," said Uncle Ike, rising. "I may get drawn into it if I stay any longer. I always liked Lindy Putnam myself." And the old gentleman laughed heartily as he left the room.

"Well, I guess you and me'd better be goin', if we want to be home at dinner time," said 'Zekiel to Huldy. Then, going to his sister, he took her in his arms and kissed her on the cheek. "You know, Alice," said he, "that I ain't much of a talker, but I shall never forget how good you've been to me and Huldy, and if the old house burns down or you get lonesome, you'll always find the latchstring out up to the new house, an' there'll be a room, an' board, an' good care for you as long as you want to stay. Eh, Huldy?" said 'Zekiel, turning to his wife.

"You know, 'Zekiel," replied the impulsive Huldy, "I've

said a dozen times that I wished Alice would come and live with us. Won't you, Alice?" she added. "I never had a sister, and I think it would be delightful to have one all to myself, especially," she added archly, "when I have her brother, too."

"I could never live in that house," said Alice, with a slight shudder; "besides, I think my future path in life is being marked out for me by the hand of Fate, which I am powerless to resist. I am afraid that it will take me away from you, my dear ones; but if it does, I shall always love you both, and pray for your happiness and success."

At the front door 'Zekiel and Huldy met Quincy. The latter had turned Miss Very over to the care of Mrs. Maxwell, and had got one of the twins to carry the young lady's trunk to her room, which was the one formerly occupied by Mandy. He had then driven the carryall around to the barn and was returning, anxious to bear his tidings of success to Alice, when he met the departing couple.

"I hear you are going to leave us," said Huldy.

"Who told you?" inquired Quincy.

"Alice," replied Huldy; "and I told her she'd miss you very much when you were gone."

"I am afraid," replied Quincy, "that any service that I have rendered Miss Pettengill has not been of so important a nature that it would be greatly missed. I am glad that I have succeeded in securing her a companion and assistant of her own sex, which will much more than compensate for the loss of my feeble services."

"That's what I don't like about city folks," said Huldy Pettengill, as she walked along the path, hanging on her husband's arm.

"What's that?" asked 'Zekiel bluntly.

"Because," continued Huldy, "they use such big words to cover up their real feelings. Of course, he wouldn't let on to us, but any one with half an eye could see that he's head over heels in love with your sister Alice, and he'd stand on his head if she told him to."

"Well, Alice is too sensible a girl to ask him to do that sort of thing," said 'Zekiel frankly. "Any way, I don't believe she's in love with him."

" 'Twould be a great match for her," said Huldy.

"I don't know 'bout that. On general principles, I don't believe in country girls marryin' city fellers."

"I know you don't," said Huldy, and she gave his arm a little squeeze.

"But," continued 'Zekiel, "Alice is different from most country girls. Besides, she's lived in the city and knows city ways. Anyway, I sha'n't interfere; I know Mr. Sawyer is a respectable young man, and, by George! when he wants to do anything, don't he jest put it through. The way he sarcumvented that Strout was as good as a circus."

"I think I sarcumvented that Strout, too," said Huldy, as they reached the corner of Deacon Mason's front fence.

"You've been quite a little flirt in your day," remarked 'Zekiel, "but it's all over now;" and he squeezed the little hand that stole confidingly into his big, brawny one.

Quincy at once entered the parlor and found Alice seated in her accustomed easy-chair.

"You have returned, Sir Knight," was the remark with which Alice greeted him.

"I have, fair lady," replied Quincy, in the same vein; "I have captured one of the enemy and brought her as a prisoner to your castle. Here are some documents," he continued, as he placed the proofs in Alice's hands, "that contain valuable secrets, and they will, no doubt, furnish strong evidence against the prisoner."

"What is it?" asked Alice, holding up the package.

"They are the proofs of three of your stories," replied Quincy, relapsing into commonplace; "and Leopold says they must be read and corrected at once. If we can attend to this during the afternoon and evening, I will go up to

Boston again to-morrow morning." Quincy then told Alice about Rosa and the terms that he had made with her, and Alice expressed herself as greatly pleased with the arrangement. "You will find Miss Very a perfect lady," said Quincy, "with a low, melodious voice that will not jar upon your ears, as mine, no doubt, has often done."

"You are unfair to yourself, when you say that," remarked Alice earnestly. "Your voice has never jarred upon my ears, and I have always been pleased to listen to you."

Whether Quincy's voice would have grown softer and sweeter and his words more impassioned if the interview had continued, cannot be divined, for Mrs. Maxwell at that moment opened the parlor door and called out, "Dinner's ready," just as Mandy Skinner used to do in the days gone by.

Miss Very was introduced to Alice and the others at the dinner table, and took the seat formerly occupied by 'Zekiel. Quincy consented to remain to dinner, as he knew his services would be required in the proof reading. When Cobb's twins reached the barn, after dinner, Jim said to Bill, "Isn't she a stunner! I couldn't keep my eyes off'n her."

"Neither could I," rejoined Bill. "I tell yer, Jim, style comes nat'ral to city folks. I'll be durned if I know whether I had chicken or codfish for dinner."

After the noonday meal the three zealous toilers in the paths of literature began work. Quincy read from the manuscript, Rosa held the proofs, while Alice listened intently, and from time to time made changes in punctuation or slight alterations in the language. No sentence had to be rewritten, and when the reading of the story, Was It Signed? was finished, Rosa said, "A remarkably clean set of proofs; only a few changes, and those slight ones. In the case of very few authors are their original ideas and second thoughts so harmonious. How do you manage it, Miss Pettengill?"

"Oh, I don't know," replied Alice, with a smile, "unless it is that I keep my original ideas in my mind until they reach the stage of second thoughts, and then I have them written down."

"You will find Miss Pettengill very exact in dictation," said Quincy to Rosa. "I took that long story there down in pencil, and I don't think I was obliged to change a dozen words."

"To work with Miss Pettengill," remarked Rosa, "will be more of a pleasure than a task."

This idea was re-echoed in Quincy's mind, and for a moment he had a feeling of positive envy towards Miss Very. Then he thought that hers was paid service, while his had been a labor—of love. Yes, it might as well be put that way.

The sun had sunk quite low in the west when the second story, Her Native Land, was completed. "How dramatic!" cried Rosa; "the endings of those chapters are as strong as stage tableaus."

"It is being dramatized by Jameson of the 'Daily Universe,'" said Quincy.

"I am well acquainted with Mr. Jameson," remarked Rosa; "I belong to a social club of which he is the president. He is a very talented young man and a great worker. He once told me that when he began newspaper work he wrote eighteen hours out of twenty-four for a month, and nearly every night he woke up and made notes that he wrote out in the morning. Do you believe in unconscious mental cerebration, Mr. Sawyer?"

"I'm afraid not," replied Quincy, laughing; "I never had ideas enough to keep my brain busy all day, much less supply it with work at night."

"Mr. Sawyer is always unfair to himself," remarked Alice to Miss Very. "As for myself, I will answer your question in the affirmative. I have often gone to bed with only the general idea of a story in my mind, and have awakened with the details all thought out and properly placed."

"1 think it best to postpone the reading of the last story until after supper," said Quincy.

Alice assented, and, turning to Rosa, asked, "Do you like the country, Miss Very?"

"To speak honestly," replied Rosa, "I do not. I told Mr. Sawyer so on the train. It is hotter in the country than it is in the city. I can't bear the ticking of a clock in my room, and I think crickets and owls are more nerve-destroy-ing than clocks, and I positively detest anything that buzzes and stings, like bees, and wasps, and hornets."

"But don't you like cows, and sheep, and horses?" asked Alice; "I love them."

"And I don't," said Rosa frankly. "I like beefsteak and roast lamb, but I never saw a cow that didn't have a fero-cious glare in its eye when it looked at me." Both Quincy and Alice laughed heartily. "As for horses," continued Rosa, "I never drive alone. When I'm with some one I alternate between hope and fear until I reach my destina-tion."

"I trust you were more hopeful than fearful on your way from Eastborough Centre," said Quincy.

"Oh! I saw at a glance," remarked Rosa, "that you were a skilful driver, and I trusted you implicitly."

"I have had to rely a great deal upon Mr. Sawyer," re-marked Alice, "and, like yourself, I have always placed the greatest confidence in him. Huldy told me this morning, Mr. Sawyer, that I would miss you very much, and I know I shall."

"But you will have Miss Very with you constantly," said Quincy.

"Oh! she does not like the country," continued Alice, "and she will get homesick in a little while."

"One's likes and one's duties often conflict," said Rosa;

and a grave look settled upon her face. "But how can you write your book down here, Miss Pettengill? You will have to consult hundreds of books, if you intend to write an historical novel, as Mr. Sawyer told me you did. You ought to have access to the big libraries in Boston, and, besides, in the second-hand bookstores you can buy such treasures for a mere song, if you will only spend the time to hunt for them."

"That reminds me," broke in Quincy, "that my aunt, Mrs. Chessman,—she is my mother's only sister, who lives on Mt. Vernon Street,—wished me to extend a cordial invitation to you two young ladies to visit her, while I am getting your summer home ready for you. She suggests Nantucket as the best place for work, but with every opportunity for enjoyment, when work becomes a burden."

"Oh, that will be delightful," cried Rosa. "I love the sea, and there we shall have it all around us; and at night, the great dome of Heaven, studded with stars, will reach down to the sea on every side, and they say at 'Sconset, on the east end of the island, that when the breakers come in the sight is truly magnificent."

Quincy was inwardly amused at Rosa's enthusiasm, but it served his purpose to encourage it, so he said, "I wish Aunt Ella were her to join forces with Miss Very. You would find it hard work to resist both of them, Miss Pettengill."

"You mean all three of you," said Alice, with a smile.

"If we go to Nantucket," added Rosa, "I shall have to spend a week in the city, and perhaps more. I have no dresses suitable for so long a residence at the beach."

"Neither have I," coincided Alice, with a laugh.

There the matter was dropped. Quincy knew too much to press the question to a decision that evening. He had learned by experience that Alice never said yes or no until her mind was made up, and he knew that the answer was more likely to be favorable if he gave her plenty of time for reflection; besides, he thought that Alice might wish to know more particularly what his aunt said, for she would be likely to consider that his aunt must have some reason for giving such an invitation to two persons who were virtually strangers to her.

After supper, the third story, How He Lost Both Name and Fortune, was read and corrected, and it was the unusually late hour of eleven o'clock before the lights in the Pettengill house were extinguished. It was past midnight when Quincy sought his room at Mrs. Hawkins's boarding house, and the picture of Alice Pettengill, that he had purloined so long ago, stood on a little table at the head of his bed, leaning against a large family Bible, which he found in the room.

The next morning he was up early, and visited the grocery store. Mr. Strout and Hiram both assured him that business had picked up amazingly, and was really "splendid." The new wagons were building up trade very fast. Billy Ricker went over to Montrose for orders Monday, Wednesday, and Friday mornings, and delivered them in the afternoons. This gave Abbott Smith a chance to post up the books on those days, for he had been made bookkeeper. He went to Eastborough Centre and Westvale, the new name given to West Eastborough at the last town meeting, Tuesday, Thursday, and Saturday mornings. He delivered goods on the afternoons of those days, which gave him an opportunity to spend Sunday at home with his father and his family.

When Quincy reached the Pettengill house, Mrs. Maxwell informed him that Miss Pettengill was in the parlor alone. After greeting Alice, Quincy asked, "But where is Miss Very?"

"I told her I should not need her services until after I had seen you," she replied. "I have a question to ask you, Mr. Sawyer, and I know you will give me a truthful answer. What led your aunt to invite me to come and visit her?"

Quincy knew that Alice had been considering the matter, and this one simple question, to which she expected a truthful answer, was the crucial test.

He did not hesitate in replying. If he did, he knew the result would be fatal to his hopes.

"Only the promptings of her own good nature. She is one of the warmest-hearted women in the world," continued Quincy. "I will tell you just how it happened. I told her I had found an assistant to help you in your work, and that the next thing was to fix upon a place for a summer residence. I asked her opinion, and after considering the advantages and disadvantages of a score of places, she finally settled upon Nantucket as being the most desirable. Then she said, 'While you are finding a place and getting it ready for them, ask Miss Pettengill to come and visit me and bring her friend. Tell her that I am rich, as far as money goes, but poor in love and companionship. Tell them both that I shall love to have them come and will do everything I can to make their visit a pleasant one.' Those were her words as nearly as I can remember them;" and Quincy waited silently for the decision.

It soon came. Alice went to him and extended her hand, which Quincy took.

"Tell her," said Alice in her quiet way, "that I thank her very much and that we will come."

"How soon?" inquired Quincy anxiously and rather abruptly.

"In a few days," replied Alice. "I can get ready much sooner with Miss Very to help me."

She withdrew the hand, which she had unconsciously allowed to remain in his so long, and a slight flush mounted to her cheek, for Quincy had equally unconsciously given it a gentle pressure as he relinquished it.

"I must do up these proofs," said he, going to the table.

"I will get the next train to Boston. I will be back to-morrow noon, and in the afternoon I will drive over to Montrose about that deed of the Putnam house. I know Aunt Ella will be delighted to hear that you are coming." But he said nothing about his own delight at being the bearer of the tidings.

When he had gone, Alice sat in her chair as she had many a time before and thought. As she sat there she realized more strongly than she had ever done that if Fate was marking out her course for her, it had certainly chosen as its chief instrument the masterful young man who had just left her.

The remainder of that day and the morning of the next Alice spent in dictating to Rosa a crude general outline of Blennerhassett. During the work she was obliged, naturally, to address Rosa many times, and uniformly called her Miss Very. Finally Rosa said, "Wouldn't you just as soon call me Rosa? Miss Very seems so stiff and formal."

"I hope you will not consider me uncompanionable or set in my ways," remarked Alice. "We are working, you know, and not playing," she continued with a sweet smile. "I have no doubt you are worthy of both my esteem and love, but I have known you less than a day and such things come slowly with me. Let me call you Miss Very, because you are that to me now. When the time comes, as I feel it will, to call you Rosa, it shall come from a full heart. When I call you Rosa, it will be because I love you, and, after that, nothing will ever change my feelings towards you."

"I understand you," replied Rosa. "I will work and wait."

Quincy arrived at about the same time of day that he did when he came with Rosa. Miss Very had gone to her room, so that he saw Alice alone. He told her that his aunt was greatly pleased at her acceptance and would be ready to receive her at any time that it was convenient for her to

come. He proffered his services to aid her in getting ready
for the journey, but she told him that with Miss Very's help
she would need no other assistance.

"I have another matter of business to speak about," continued she, "and if you will kindly attend to that, when you
go to Montrose, it will oblige me very much. You are always doing something to make me your debtor," she added
with a smile.

"I would do more if you would allow me," replied
Quincy.

"The fact is," said Alice, "'Zekiel does not wish to borrow any money, nor would he accept the gift of the Putnam homestead unless he, in turn, deeded this house and
farm to me. He is going to run this farm and pay me what
he gets from the sale of products. If you will have Squire
Rundlett draw up both deeds and the agreement, the whole
matter can be fixed before I go away."

Quincy promised to give his attention to the matter that
afternoon. He drove up to his boarding house and hitched
his horse at the front door. Mrs. Hawkins saw him enter
and take his seat at the dinner table. "There's that Mr.
Sawyer; he's slept in this house just one night and eaten
just one meal up to this noon for nigh on a week. Them
city folks must have Injun rubber stummicks and cast iron
backs or they couldn't eat in so many different places and
sleep in so many different beds. Why, if I go away and
stay over night, when I git home I'm allus sicker'n a horse
and tired enough to drop."

Quincy went to Montrose that afternoon and saw Squire
Rundlett. The latter promised to make the papers out the
next day, and said he would bring them over for signing
the following morning. Quincy drove down to Deacon
Mason's and told 'Zekiel when to be on hand, and after
leaving the team in the Pettengill barn, saw Alice and informed her of the Squire's proposed visit. He told her

that he would come down that morning to act as a witness,
if his services were required.

He spent the next day at the grocery store, going over
the stock with Strout and Abbott Smith, and had a list
made of articles that they thought it would be advisable to
carry in the future. He told Strout that he would visit
some wholesale grocery houses in Boston and have sam-
ples sent down.

"Mr. Sawyer is improvin'," said Mrs. Hawkins to Betsy
the next morning after breakfast. "He's slept in his bed
two nights runnin', and he's eat four square meals, and
seemed to enjoy them, too. I guess he didn't git much
when he was jumpin' 'round so from one place to another."

Squire Rundlett kept his word, and the legal documents
were duly signed and executed. Alice told the Squire that
she was going away for several months, and that she would
undoubtedly send to him from time to time.

"My dear Miss Pettengill," replied the gallant Squire,
"you shall have all you ask for if I have to sell my best
horse and mortgage my house. But I don't think it will
be necessary," he added. "Some more dividends and interest have come in and I have more than a thousand dollars to your credit now."

After the Squire had left, Alice told Quincy that her
preparations were all made, and that she would be ready
to go to Boston the next day. The mid-day train was fixed
upon. After dinner that day, Quincy informed Mrs. Hawkins that he wished to pay his bill in full, as he should
leave for good the next day.

Holding the money in her hand, Mrs. Hawkins entered
the kitchen and addressed Betsy.

"Just what I expected," said she; "jest as that Mr. Sawyer got to stayin' home nights and eating his meals like a
Christian, he ups an' gits. I guess it'll be a dry summer.
I kinder thought them two boys over to the grocery would
come here, but I understand they're goin' down to Petten-

gill's, and somebody told me that Strout goes over to Eastborough Centre every Sunday now. I s'pose he's tryin'
to shine up again to that Bessie Chisholm, that he used to
be sweet on. When he goes to keepin' house there'll be
another boarder gone;" and the poor woman, having bor-
rowed enough trouble, sat down and wiped a supposed tear
out of each eye with her greasy apron.

Quincy reached Aunt Ella's residence with the young
ladies about noon. Aunt Ella gave the three travellers a
hearty welcome, and the young ladies were shown at once
to their rooms, which were on the third floor at the front of
the house. They were connected, so that Rosa could be
close at hand in case Alice should need assistance.

While the footman and Buttons were taking the trunks
upstairs, Quincy asked his aunt if he could leave his trunk
there for a short time. "I do not wish to take it home,"
he said, "until after I have the ladies settled at Nantucket.
The carriage is waiting outside and I am going to get the
one o'clock train."

"I will take good care of your trunk," said Aunt Ella,
"and you, too, if you will come and live with me. But
can't you stop to lunch with us?" she asked. But Quincy
declined, and requesting his aunt to say good-by to the
young ladies for him, he entered the carriage and was
driven off.

After luncheon, which was served in the dining-room,
General Chessman and Aides-de-Camp Pettengill and Very
held a counsel of war in the General's private tent. It was
decided that the mornings should be devoted, for a while,
at least, to shopping and visiting modistes and milliners.
Miss Very was also to give some of her time to visits to the
libraries and the second-hand bookstores looking for books
that would be of value to Alice in her work. The afternoons
were to be passed in conversation and in listening to Miss
Very's reading from the books that she had purchased or
taken from the libraries. The evenings were to be filled up

with music, and the first one disclosed the pleasing fact that Miss Very had a rich, full contralto voice that had been well cultivated and that she could play Beethoven or the songs of the day with equal facility.

While the feminine trio were thus enjoying themselves in Boston with an admixture of work and play, Quincy was busily engaged at Nantucket in building a nest for them, as he called it.

He had found a large, old-fashioned house on the bluff at the north shore, overlooking the harbor, owned by Mrs. Gibson. She was a widow with two children, one a boy of about nineteen, named Thomas, and the other a girl of twelve, named Dorothy, but generally designated as Tommy and Dolly.

Mrs. Gibson consented to let her second floor for a period of four months, and to supply them with meals. The price was fixed upon, and Quincy knew he had been unusually lucky in securing so desirable a location at such a reasonable price.

There were three rooms, one a large front room, with a view of the harbor, and back of it two sleeping rooms, looking out upon a large garden at the rear of the house. Quincy mentally surveyed the large room and marked the places with a piece of chalk upon the carpet where the piano and the bookcase were to go. Then he decided that the room needed a lounge and a desk with all necessary fixtures and stationery for Rosa to work at. There were some stiff-backed chairs in the room, but he concluded that a low easy-chair, like the one Alice had at home, and a couple of wicker rocking chairs, which would be cool and comfortable during the hot summer days, were absolutely essential.

He then returned to Boston, hired an upright piano and purchased the other articles, including a comfortable office-chair to go with the desk. He was so afraid that he would forget some article of stationery that he made a list and checked it off. But this did not satisfy him. He spent a whole morning in different stationery stores looking over their stocks to make sure that he had omitted nothing. The goods were packed and shipped by express to Mrs. Thomas Gibson, Nantucket, Mass. Then, and not till then, did Quincy seek his aunt's residence with the intelligence that the nest was builded and ready for the birds. When he informed the ladies that everything was ready for their reception at their summer home, Aunt Ella said that their departure would have to be delayed for a few days, as the delinquent dressmakers had failed to deliver certain articles of wearing apparel. This argument was, of course, unanswerable, and Quincy devoted the time to visiting the wholesale grocers, as he had promised Strout that he would do, and to buying and shipping a long list of books that Miss Very informed him Miss Pettengill needed for her work. He learned that during his absence the proofs of The Man Without a Tongue had been brought over by Mr. Ernst and read and corrected, Aunt Ella taking Quincy's place as reader.

At last all was ready, and on the tenth of May a party of three ladies and one gentleman was driven to the station in time for the one o'clock train. They had lunched early and the whole party was healthy, happy, and in the best of spirits. Then came the leave-takings. The two young ladies and the gentleman sped away upon the train, while the middle-aged lady started for home in her carriage, telling herself a dozen times on the way that she knew she would be lonesomer than ever when she got there.

The trip by train and boat was uneventful. Alice sat quietly and enjoyed the salt sea breeze, while both Quincy and Rosa entertained her with descriptions of the bits of land and various kinds of sailing craft that came in sight. It was nearly seven o'clock when the steamer rounded Brant Point. In a short time it was moored to the wharf, and the party, with their baggage, were conveyed swiftly to Mrs. Gibson's, that lady having been notified by Quincy to expect them at any moment. He did not enter the house. He told Miss Very to address him care of his aunt if they needed anything, and that Mr. Ernst and himself would come down when Miss Pettengill had completed two or three chapters of her book. Quincy then bade them good-by and was driven to a modest hotel close to the steamboat wharf. He took the morning boat to Boston, and that afternoon informed Aunt Ella of the safe arrival of his fair charges.

"What are you going to do now?" asked Aunt Ella.

"I'm going to find my father," replied Quincy, "and through him secure introductions to the other members of my family."

"Good-by," said Aunt Ella; "if they don't treat you well come and stay with me and we will go to Old Orchard together about the first of June. I never skip out the last of April, because I always enjoy having a talk with the assessor when he comes around in May."

When Rosa took her seat at the new desk next morning, she exclaimed with delight, "What a nice husband Mr. Sawyer would make!"

"What makes you think so?" inquired Alice gravely.

"Because he'd be such a good hand to go shopping," Rosa answered. "I've been all over this desk twice and I don't believe he has forgotten a single thing that we are likely to need."

"Good work requires good tools," remarked Alice.

"And a good workman," interposed Rosa.

"Then we have every adjunct for success," said Alice, "and we will commence just where we left off at Mrs. Chessman's."

The work on the book progressed famously. Alice was in fine mental condition and Rosa seemingly took as much interest in its progress as did her employer. In three weeks the three opening chapters had been written. "I

wonder what Mr. Sawyer and Mr. Ernst will think of that?"
said Alice, as Rosa wrote the last line of the third chapter.

"I am going to write to Mr. Sawyer to-day. We must
have those books before we can go much farther. Would
it not be well to tell him that we are ready for our audience?"

Alice assented, and the letter reached Quincy one Friday evening, it being his last call on his aunt before her
departure for Old Orchard. "Give my love to both of
them," said Aunt Ella, "and tell Alice I send her a kiss. I
won't tell you how to deliver it; you will probably find some
way before you come back."

Quincy protested that he could not undertake to deliver
it, but his aunt only laughed, kissed him, bade him good-by,
and told him to be sure and come down to Maine to see
her.

Quincy and Leopold took the Saturday afternoon boat
and arrived, as usual, about seven o'clock. They both repaired to the hotel previously patronized by Quincy, having decided to defer their call upon the young ladies until
Sunday morning. It was a bright, beautiful day, not a
cloud was to be seen in the broad, blue expanse above them.
A cool breeze was blowing steadily from the southwest,
and as the young men walked down Centre Street towards
the Cliff, Leopold remarked that he did not wonder that the
Nantucketers loved their "tight little isle" and were sorry
to leave it. "One seems to be nearer Heaven here than he
does in a crowded city, don't he, Quincy?" Quincy thought
to himself that his Heaven was in Nantucket, and that he
was very near to it, but he did not choose to utter these
feelings to his friend, so he merely remarked that the sky
did seem much nearer.

They soon reached Mrs. Gibson's and were shown directly to the young ladies' parlor and library, for it answered both purposes. They were attired in two creations
of Mrs. Chessman's dressmaker, Aunt Ella having selected

the materials and designed the costumes, for which art
she had a great talent. Rosa's dress was of a dark rose tint,
with revers and a V-shaped neck, filled in with tulle of a
dark green hue. The only other trimming on the dress was
a green silk cord that bordered the edges of the revers and
the bottom of the waist. As Quincy looked at her, for she
sat nearest to the door, she reminded him of a beautiful
red rose, and the green leaves which enhanced its beauty.
Then his eyes turned quickly to Alice, who sat in her easy-
chair, near the window. Her dress was of light blue, with
square-cut neck, filled in with creamy white lace. In her
hair nestled a flower, light pink in color, and as Quincy
looked at her he thought of the little blue flower called
forget-me-not, and recalled the fact that wandering one
day in the country, during his last year at college, he had
come upon a little brook, both sides of which, for hundreds
of feet, were lined with masses of this modest little flower.
Ah! but this one forget-me-not was more to him than all
the world beside.

The greetings were soon over, and Quincy was assured
by both young ladies that they were happy and contented,
and that every requisite for their comfort had been supplied
by Mrs. Gibson.

The reading then began. Rosa possessed a full, flexible,
dramatic voice, and the strong passages were delivered with
great fervor, while the sad or sentimental ones were tinged
with a tone of deep pathos.

At the conclusion Alice said, "I wish Miss Very could
read my book to the publishers."

"You forget," remarked Leopold, with a laugh, "that
reading it to me will probably amount to the same thing."

A merry party gathered about Mrs. Gibson's table at
dinner, after which they went for a drive through the
streets of the quaint old town. Quincy had, as the phre-
nologists say, a great bump for locality. Besides, he had
studied a map of the town while coming down, and, as he

remarked, they couldn't get lost for any great length of time, as Nantucket was an island, and the water supplied a natural boundary to prevent their getting too far out of their way.

While Dolly Gibson was helping her mother by wiping the dinner dishes, she said, with that air of judicial conviction that is shown by some children, that she guessed that the lady in the red dress was Mr. Leopold's girl, and that the blind lady in the blue dress was Mr. Quincy's.

After a light supper they again gathered in the parlor and an hour was devoted to music. Leopold neither played nor sang, but he was an attentive and critical listener. It was a beautiful moonlight night, and Leopold asked Rosa if she would not like to take a walk up on the Cliff. She readily consented, but Alice pleasantly declined Quincy's invitation to accompany them, and for the first time since the old days at Mason's Corner, he and she were alone together.

They talked of Eastborough and Mason's Corner and Aunt Ella for a while. Then conversation lagged and they sat for a time in a satisfied, peaceful silence.

Suddenly Quincy spoke. "I had almost forgotten, Miss Pettengill, I bought a new song yesterday morning, and I brought it with me. If you have no objection I will try it over."

"I always enjoy your singing," she replied.

He ran down stairs and soon returned with the music. He seated himself at the piano and played the piece through with great expression.

"It is a beautiful melody," remarked Alice. "What is it?"

"It is a German song," replied Quincy, "by Reichardt. It is called 'Love's Request.' I will sing it this time."

And he did sing it with all the force and fervor of a noble, manly nature, speaking out his love covertly in the words of another, but hoping in his heart that the beautiful girl who listened to him would forget the author and think only of the singer. How many times young lovers have tried this artful trick, and in what proportion it has been successful only Heaven knows.

"The words are very pretty, are they not?" said Alice. "I was listening so closely to the melody that I did not catch them all."

"I will read them to you," rejoined Quincy, and going to the window, where the light was still bright enough, he read the words of the song in a low, impassioned voice:

"Now the day is slowly waning,
   Evening breezes softly, softly moan;
Wilt thou ne'er heed my complaining,
   Canst thou leave me thus alone?
Stay with me, my darling, stay!
   And, like a dream, thy life shall pass away,
   Like a dream shall pass away.

"Canst thou thus unmoved behold me,
   Still untouched by love, by love so deep?
Nay, thine arms more closely fold me,
   And thine eyes begin to weep!
Stay with me, my darling, stay!
   And, like a dream, thy life shall pass away,
   Like a dream shall pass away.

"No regret shall e'er attend thee,
   Ne'er shall sorrow dim thine eyes;
'Gainst the world's alarms to 'fend thee,
   Gladly, proudly, would I die!
Stay with me, my darling, stay!
   And, like a dream, thy life shall pass away,
   Shall pass away."

As Quincy finished reading, Leopold and Rosa came suddenly into the room.

"We were not eavesdropping," explained Leopold, "but just as we were going to enter the room we heard your voice and knew that you were either reading or speaking a piece, so we waited until you had finished."

"I was only reading the words of a new song that I brought down to Miss Pettengill," said Quincy; "she liked the melody and I thought she would appreciate it still more if she knew the words."

"Exactly," said Leopold; "that's the reason I don't like opera, I mean the singing part. All that I can ever make out sounds like oh! ah! ow! and when I try to read the book in English and listen to the singers at the same time I am lost in a hopeless maze."

The young gentlemen were soon on their way to their hotel, and the next afternoon found them again in Boston.

The month of June was a busy, but very enjoyable one, for both Alice and Rosa. They were up early in the morning and were at work before breakfast. They ate heartily and slept soundly. Every pleasant afternoon, when tea was over, they went riding. Tommy Gibson held the reins, and although Dolly was not yet in her teens, she knew every nook and corner, and object of interest on the island, and she took a child's delight in pointing them out, and telling the stories that she had heard about them. The books that Quincy brought on his last visit were utilized, and Miss Very made up another list to be sent to him before his next visit.

The proofs of three more stories Mr. Ernst sent down by mail, and after correction, they were returned to him in a similar manner. Little Dolly Gibson was impressed into service as a reader, for Rosa could not read and correct at the same time, and there was no obliging Mr. Sawyer near at hand. As Huldy had said, Alice did miss him. It must be said, in all truthfulness, not so much for himself, but for the services he had rendered. As yet, Alice's heart was untouched.

When Dolly Gibson showed her mother the money that Miss Very had given her, at Alice's direction, she was told to take it right back at once, but Dolly protested that she had earned it, and when her mother asked her to tell how, the child, whose memory was phenomenal, sat down and made her mother's hair stand almost on end and her blood almost run cold with her recitals of the Eight of Spades, The Exit of Mrs. Delmonnay, and He Thought He Was Dead.

"They are immense," cried Dolly, "they beat all the fairy stories I ever read!"

In due time another letter was sent to Mr. Sawyer, informing him that more books were needed, and that more chapters were ready, and on the morning of the last Sunday in June the young ladies were awaiting the arrival of Mr. Sawyer and Mr. Ernst.

The morning had opened with a heavy shower and the sky was still overcast with angry-looking, threatening rain clouds. Within the little parlor all was bright and cheerful.

Familiar voices were heard greeting Mrs. Gibson and the children, and men's footsteps soon sounded upon the stairs. Leopold entered first, and, advancing to Rosa, handed her a large bouquet of beautiful red roses.

"Sweets to the sweet, roses to Miss Rosa," said he, as he bowed and presented them.

"They are beautiful," she exclaimed.

"All roses are considered so," he remarked with a smile.

While this little byplay was going on, Quincy had approached Alice, who, as usual, was sitting by the window, and placed in her hand a small bunch of flowers. As he did so he said in a low voice, "They are forget-me-nots. There is a German song about them, of which I remember a little," and he hummed a few measures.

"Oh! thank you," cried Alice, as she held the flowers before her eyes in a vain effort to see them. "The music is pretty. Can't you remember any of the words?"

"Only a few," replied Quincy. Then he repeated in a low, but clear voice:

> "There is the sweet flower
> They call forget-me-not;
> That flower place on thy breast,
> And think of me."

"Say, Quincy, can't you come over here and recite a little poem about roses to Miss Very, just to help me out?" cried Leopold. "All I can think of is:

> "The rose is red,
> The violet's blue—"

"Stop where you are," said Rosa laughingly, "for that will do."

Alice dropped the forget-me-nots in her lap. The illusion was dispelled.

The newly-completed chapters were next read, and quite a spirited discussion took place in regard to the political features introduced in one of them. Dinner intervened and then the discussion was resumed.

Alice maintained that to write about Aaron Burr and omit politics would be the play of "Hamlet," with Hamlet left out; and her auditors were charmed and yet somewhat startled at the impassioned and eloquent manner in which she defended Burr's political principles.

When she finished Leopold said, "Miss Pettengill, if you will put in your book the energetic defence that you have just made, I will withdraw my objections."

"You will find that and more in the next chapter," Alice replied.

And the reading was resumed.

The angry, threatening clouds had massed themselves once more; the thunder roared; the lightning flashed and the rain fell in torrents.

Leopold walked to the window and looked out. "Walking is out of the question," said he; "will you come for a sail?"

Music filled the evening, and during a lull in the storm the young men reached their lodgings.

Another month had nearly passed. The weather was much warmer, but there was a great incentive to hard work —the book was nearly finished. Quincy had sent down a package of books soon after his return home, and Alice and Rosa had worked even harder than in June.

Another letter went from Miss Very to Mr. Sawyer. It contained but a few words: "The book is done. Miss Pettengill herself wrote the words, 'The end,' on the last page, signed her name, and dated it 'July 30, 186—.' She awaits your verdict."

The first Sunday in August found the young ladies again expectant. Once more they sat on a Sunday morning awaiting the advent of their gentlemen friends. The day was pleasant, but warm. Soon a voice was heard at the front door. Both ladies listened intently; but one person, evidently, was coming upstairs. Alice thought it must be Mr. Sawyer, while Rosa said to herself, "I think it must be Mr. Ernst."

A light knock, the door was opened and Quincy entered. Rosa looked up inquiringly.

"Mr. Ernst," said Quincy, "wished me to present his regrets at not being able to accompany me. The fact is he will be very busy this coming week. He is going to try to close up his work, so that he can come down next Saturday. He intends to take a month's vacation. I shall come with him, and we will endeavor to have a fitting celebration of the completion of your book, Miss Pettengill.

You young ladies look very cool and comfortable this hot day."

They were both dressed in white, Alice with a sash of blue, while Rosa wore one of pink.

"Then we shall have no reading till next Sunday," remarked Rosa.

"Yes," said Quincy, seating himself in one of the willow rockers; "we have decided upon the following programme, if it meets with Miss Pettengill's approval. I am to listen to the remainder of the book to-day. I will hand the complete manuscript over to him to-morrow afternoon. He will then finish the chapters that he has not read and turn the work over to his firm, with his approval, before he comes down for his rest. If the work is accepted, Mr. Morton, one of the firm, will write him to that effect."

"The plan is certainly satisfactory to me," said Alice, "and Miss Very and I will be delighted to contribute our aid to the proposed celebration."

Rosa then resumed her reading. But dinner time came before it was completed. At that meal they were all introduced to Captain Henry Marble.

"My only brother," Mrs. Gibson said, by way of introduction. "He's just home from a cruise. His ship is at New Bedford. He is going to take the children out late this afternoon for a sail in the harbor. He always does when he comes here. Wouldn't you ladies and Mr. Sawyer like to go with him?"

Captain Marble repeated the invitation, adding that he was an old sailor, that he had a large sailboat, and that they were "only going to Wauwinet, not out to sea, you know, but only up the inner harbor, which is just like a pond, you know."

Rosa thought it would be delightful, but such a trip had no attractions for Alice, and it was finally decided that Rosa should go, while Alice and Mr. Sawyer would remain at home.

The reading of the remaining chapters of Blennerhassett was completed by three o'clock, and at quarter of four, Miss Very, attired in a natty yachting costume, which formed part of her summer outfit, was ready to accompany Captain Marble and the children on their trip.

When they were alone Quincy turned to Alice and said, "I bought another song yesterday morning, which I thought you might like to hear."

"Is it another German song?" asked Alice.

"No," replied Quincy, as he took a roll from the piano and opened it. "It is a duet; the music is by Bosco, but you can tell nothing by that. The composer's real name may be Jones or Smith."

He seated himself at the piano and played it through, as he had done with that other song two long months before.

"I think it more beautiful than the other," said Alice. "Are the words as sweet as those in that other song?"

"Then you have not forgotten the other one," said Quincy, earnestly.

"How could I forget it?" answered Alice. "Rosa has sung it to me several times, but it did not sound to me as it did when you sang it."

"I will sing this one to you," said he; and Alice came and stood by his side at the piano.

Quincy felt that the time to which he had looked forward so long had come at last. He could restrain the promptings of his heart no longer. He loved this woman, and she must know it; even if she rejected that love, he must tell her.

"It is called 'The Bird of Love,'" he said. Then he played the prelude to the song. He sang as he had never sung before; all the power and pathos and love that in him lay were breathed forth in the words and music of that song.

With his voice lingering upon the last word, he turned and looked up at Alice. Upon her face there was a startled, almost frightened look.

"Shall I read the words to you, Miss Pettengill?"
There was almost a command in the way he said it. His
love had o'ermastered his politeness.

Alice said nothing, but bowed her head.

Then Quincy recited the words of the song. He had no
need to read them, for he knew them by heart. It seemed
to him that he had written the words himself. He did not
even remember the author's name, and Alice stood with
bowed head and closed eyes and drank in these words as
they fell from his lips:

> In this heart of mine the bird of love
> Has built a nest,
> Has built a nest.
> And so she has in mine!

Response:

> And so she has in mine!

> And she toils both day and night, no thought
> Of food or rest
> Of food or rest,
> And sings this song divine.

Response:

> And sings this song divine.

Duet:

> All the day long,
> Such a sweet song,
> Teaching love true,
> I love! Do you?

When Quincy came to the last line, instead of reading it
he turned to the piano and sang it with even more passion
in his voice than at first.

"Will you try it over with me?" he said. And without
waiting for her reply he dashed off the prelude.

Their voices rang out together until they reached the
line, "And so she has in mine." As Alice sang these words
she opened her eyes and looked upward. A smile of su-

preme joy spread over and irradiated her face. Her voice
faltered; she stopped, then she caught at the piano with her
right hand. She tottered and would have fallen if Quincy
had not sprung up and taken her in his arms.

"Is it true, Alice?" cried he; "is it so? Can you truly
say, 'And so she has in mine?'"

And Alice looked up at him with that glorious smile still
upon her face and softly whispered, "'And so she has in
mine,' Quincy."

Quincy led her to the lounge by the window, through
which the cool evening breeze was blowing, and they sat
down side by side. It has been truly said that the conversations of lovers are more appreciated by themselves than
by anybody else, and it is equally true that at the most ten-
der moment, in such conversations, intensely disagreeable
interruptions are likely to occur.

Sometimes it is the well-meaning but unthinking father;
again it is the solicitous but inquisitive mother; but more
often it is the unregenerate and disrespectful young brother
or sister. In this case it was Miss Rosa Very, who burst
into the room, bright and rosy, after her trip upon the
water. As she entered she cried out, "Oh! you don't know
what you missed. I had a most delightful—" She stopped
short, the truth flashed upon her that there were other delightful ways of passing the time than in a sailboat. She
was in a dilemma.

Quincy solved the problem. He simply said, "Good-by,
Alice, for one short week."

He turned, expecting to see Miss Very, but she had van-
ished. He clasped Alice in his arms, and kissed her, for
the first time, then he led her to her easy-chair and left
her there.

As he quitted the room and closed the door he met Miss
Rosa Very in the entry.

"I did not know," said she, "but I am so glad to know it.
She is the sweetest, purest, loveliest woman I have ever

known, and your love is what she needed to complete her happiness. She will be a saint now. I will take good care of her, Mr. Sawyer, until you come again, for I love her, too."

Quincy pressed her hand warmly, and the next moment was in the little street. He was a rich man, as the world judges riches, but to him his greatest treasure was Alice's first kiss, still warm upon his lips.

CHAPTER XXXVI.

WHEN he bade Alice good-by for a week, Quincy was keeping a promise he had made to his father. The second evening before he had spent with his family at Nahant, and while he was smoking an after-dinner cigar upon the veranda, the Hon. Nathaniel had joined him.

"Quincy," said the latter, "I must ask you when you intend to resume your professional duties. You are now restored to health, and it is my desire that you do so at once."

"While I would not wilfully show disrespect to your wishes, father," said Quincy, calmly, "I must say frankly that I do not care to go back to the office. The study of law is repugnant to me, and its practice would be a daily martyrdom."

"What!" cried the Hon. Nathaniel, starting in his chair. "Perhaps, sir, you have fixed upon a calling that is more elevated and ennobling than the law."

"One more congenial, at any rate," remarked Quincy.

"Then you have chosen a profession," said his father with some eagerness. "May I inquire what it is?"

"It can hardly be called a profession," he answered. "I've bought a third interest in a country grocery store."

If the Hon. Nathaniel started before, this last piece of information fairly brought him to his feet. "And may I inquire, sir," he thundered, "if this special partnership in a country grocery store is the summit of your ambitions? I suppose I shall hear next that you are engaged to some farmer's daughter, and propose to marry her, regardless

of the wishes of your family, and despite the terrible example supplied by your Uncle James."

"It hasn't come to that yet," remarked Quincy, calmly,
"but it may if I find a farmer's daughter who comes up to
my ideal of a wife and to whom I can give an honest love."

The Hon. Nathaniel sank back in his chair. Quincy
continued, "I will not try to answer your sarcastic reference to the grocery store. It is a good investment and an
honorable business, fully as honorable as cheating the
prison or the gallows of what is due them; but the summit
of my ambition is by no means reached. I am young yet
and have plenty of time to study the ground before ex-
panding my career, but I will tell you, privately and confidentially, that my friends have asked me to run for the
General Court, and I have about decided to stand as a candidate for nomination as representative from our district."

"I am glad to hear you say that, Quincy," said his father,
somewhat mollified, and he edged his arm-chair a little
closer to his son, despite the heavy clouds of smoke emitted
from Quincy's cigar. "If you get the regular nomination
in our district it's tantamount to an election. I need
scarcely say that whatever influence I may possess will be
exerted in your favor."

"Thank you," said Quincy; "I mean to stump the district, anyway. If I lose the regular nomination I shall take
an independent one. I had rather fight my way in than be
pushed in."

His father smiled and patted him on the arm. Then they
rose from their chairs, Quincy observing that as he was
going away early in the morning he would immediately
retire.

"That reminds me," said his father. "I have a favor to
ask of you, Quincy. It is this, Lord Algernon Hastings,
heir to the earldom of Sussex, and his sister, Lady Elfrida,
are now in Boston, and bring letters from the Lord High
Chancellor, with whom I became acquainted when I was

in England, two years ago. I have invited them to visit us here next week, and my wish is that you will spend as much of your time at home as possible and assist me in entertaining them—I mean the son, of course, particularly."

Quincy's thoughts flew quickly to Nantucket and back. Had he foreseen what was to happen on his coming visit, he would have hesitated still longer, but thinking that, after all, next Sunday's journey might not end any more conclusively than the previous one, he presently turned to his father and answered:

"I will do so. I must go to-morrow, but I will return early on Monday, and will stay at home the entire week."

"I thank you very much, Quincy," said the Hon. Nathaniel, and he laid his hand on his son's shoulder as affectionately as he was capable of doing, when they entered the house.

Lady Elfrida Hastings and her brother, Lord Algernon, arrived in due season, and Quincy was there to assist at their reception. The former was tall, and dark, and stately; her features were cast in a classic mould, but the look in her eye was cold and distant, and the face, though having all the requirements of beauty, yet lacked it. To Mrs. Sawyer and her daughter, Florence, the Lady Elfrida was a revelation, and they yearned to acquire that statuesque repose that comes so natural to the daughter of an earl. But Maude told her brother that evening that the Lady Elfrida was a "prunes and prisms," and was sure to die an old maid.

Lord Algernon was tall and finely built; he had a profusion of light brown curly hair, and a pair of large blue eyes that so reminded Quincy of Alice that he took to the young lord at once. They rode, played billiards, bowled, and smoked together.

One afternoon while they were enjoying a sail in the bay, Quincy inquired of his guest how he liked America.

" 'Pon honor, my dear fellow, I don't know," replied Lord Algernon. "I came here for a certain purpose, and have failed miserably. I am going to sail for home in a week, if my sister will go."

"Then you didn't come to enjoy the pleasures of travel?" remarked Quincy, interrogatively.

"No! By Jove, I didn't. My sister did, and she supposes I did. I'm going to tell you the truth, Mr. Sawyer. I know you will respect my confidence." Quincy nodded.

"The fact is," Lord Algernon continued, "I came over here to find a girl that I'm in love with, but who ran away from me as soon as I told her of it."

"But why?" asked Quincy, not knowing what else to say.

"That's the deuce of it," replied Lord Algernon; "I sha'n't know till I find her and ask her. I met her at Nice, in France; she was with her mother, a Mdme. Archimbault; the daughter's name was Celeste—Celeste Archimbault. They said they were not French, they were French Canadians; came from America, you know. I was traveling as plain Algernon Hastings, and I don't think she ever suspected I was the son of an earl. I proposed one evening. She said she must speak to her mother, and if I would come the next evening about seven o'clock, she would give me her answer, and I thought by the look in her eye that she herself was willing to say 'Yes' then. But when I called the next evening they had both gone, no one knew where."

"You are sure she was not an adventuress?" inquired Quincy. "Excuse the question, my lord, but you really knew nothing about her?"

"I knew that I loved her," said Lord Algernon, bluntly, "and I would give half of my fortune to find her. I know she was a true, pure, beautiful girl, and her mother was as honest an old lady as you could find in the world."

"I wish I could help you," remarked Quincy.

"Thank you," said Lord Algernon; "perhaps you may be able to some day. Don't forget her name, Celeste Archimbault; she is slight in figure, graceful in her carriage, lady-like in her manners. She has dark hair, large, dreamy black eyes, with a hidden sorrow in them; in fact, a very handsome brunette. Here is my card, Mr. Sawyer. I will write my London address on it, and if you ever hear of her, cable me at once and I'll take the next steamer for America."

Quincy said that he would, and put the card in his card-case.

He excused himself to Lord Algernon and his sister that evening; a prior engagement made it necessary for him to leave for Boston early next morning, and the farewells were then spoken. Lord Algernon's last words to Quincy were whispered in his ear, "Don't forget her name—Celeste Archimbault!"

The next Sunday morning Quincy and Leopold, as they approached Mrs. Gibson's house on the Cliff, found Rosa Very standing at the little gate. She had on the white dress that she had worn the Sunday before, but which Leopold had not seen. Upon her head was a wide-brimmed straw hat, decked with ribbons and flowers, which intensified the darkness of her hair and eyes."

"Don't forget her name—Celeste Archimbault," came into Quincy's mind, but he said, "Nonsense," to himself, and dismissed the thought.

"All ready for a walk on the Cliff?" asked Leopold, as he raised his hat and extended his hand to Rosa. She shook hands with him and then with Quincy. She opened the little gate, placed her hand on Leopold's arm and they walked on up the Cliff Road.

As Quincy entered the little parlor, Alice sprang toward him with a cry of joy. He caught her in his arms, and this time one kiss did not suffice, for a dozen were pressed on hair and brow and cheek and lips.

"It is so long since you went away," said Alice.

"Only one short week," replied Quincy.

"Short! Those six days have seemed longer than all the time we were together at Eastborough. I cannot let you go away from me again," she cried.

"Stay with Me, My Darling, Stay," sang Quincy, in a low voice, and Alice tried to hide her blushing face upon his shoulder.

Then they sat down and talked the matter over. "I must leave you," said Quincy, "and only see you occasionally, and then usually in the presence of others, unless—"

"Unless what?" cried Alice, and a sort of frightened look came into her face.

"Unless you marry me at once," said Quincy. "I don't mean this minute; say Wednesday of this coming week. I have a license with me I got in Boston yesterday morning. We'll be married quietly in this little room, in which you first told me that you loved me. We could be married in a big church in Boston, with bridesmaids, and groomsmen, and music on a big organ. We could make as big a day of it as they did down to Eastborough."

"Oh, no!" said Alice; "I could n t go through that. I cannot see well enough, and I might make some terrible blunder. I might trip an ! fall, and then I should be so nervous and ashamed."

"I will not ask you to go through such an ordeal, my dearest. I know that we could have all these grand things, and for that reason, if for no better one, I'm perfectly willing to go without them. No, Alice, we will be married here in this room. We will deck it with flowers," continued Quincy. "Leopold will go to Boston to-morrow and get them. Rosamond's Bower was not sweeter nor more lovely than we will make this little room. I will get an old clergyman; I don't like young ones; Leopold shall be my best man and Rosa shall be your bridesmaid. Mrs. Gibson and her brother, who I see is still here, shall be our witnesses, and we will have Tommy and Dolly for ushers."

Both laughed aloud in their childish glee at the picture

that Quincy had painted. "I could ask for nothing better,"
said Alice; "the ceremony will be modest, artistic, and
idyllic."

"And economical, too," Quincy added with a laugh.

And so it came to pass! They were married, and the
transformation in the little room, that Quincy and Alice
had seen in their mind's eye, was realized to the letter.
Flowers, best man, bridesmaid, witnesses, ushers, and the
aged clergyman, with whitened locks, who called them his
children, and blessed them and wished them long life and
happiness, hoped that they would meet and know each
other some day in the infinite—all were there.

This was on Wednesday. On Thursday came a letter
from Aunt Ella. It contained the most kindly congratulations, and a neat little wedding present of a check for fifty
thousand dollars. She wrote further that she was lonesome
and wanted somebody to read to her, and talk to her, and
sing to her. If the book was done, would not Miss Very
come to spend the remainder of the season with her, and if
Mr. Ernst was there could he not spare time to escort Miss
Very.

That same evening Leopold received a letter from Mr.
Morton. It simply read, "Blennerhassett accepted; will
be put in type at once and issued by the first of November,
perhaps sooner."

The next morning Leopold and Rosa started for Old
Orchard, and the lovers were left alone to pass their honey-
moon, with the blue sea about them, the blue sky above
them, and a love within their hearts which grew stronger
day by day.

CHAPTER XXXVII.

FOR Quincy and Alice, day after day, and week after week, found them in a state of complete happiness. The little island floating in the azure sea was their world, and for the time, no thought of any other intruded upon their delightful Eden. It seemed to Quincy all a blissful dream of love, and everything he looked upon was wreathed in flowers and golden sunshine.

But lotus land is not so far distant from the abodes of mortal man but that his emissaries may reach it. The first jarring note in the sweet harmony of their married life came in the form of a letter from Dr. Culver, who wrote to remind Quincy that it would soon be time to start in ploughing the political field. Quincy's reply was brief and to the point.

"MY DEAR CULVER:—I will see you in Boston on the tenth of September.   Q. A. S."

When Aunt Ella learned that her nephew was going to town, she made hurried preparations for her departure from Old Orchard, and wrote to him insisting that he and Alice should come and stay with her. This invitation they gladly accepted, Quincy arranging in his mind to explain matters to his family by saying that, as he had now entered politics and would necessarily have a great many callers to entertain, he thought it best to make his headquarters with Aunt Ella until the campaign was over.

Accordingly, the ninth of September saw them located at Mt. Vernon Street. On the very day of their arrival, proof of the remaining stories and a large instalment of Blennerhassett reached them, with a note from Ernst: "Please rush. Press is waiting."

Miss Very's assistance was now absolutely necessary, but when Quincy asked Leopold for her address, he was surprised at the reply he received.

"I haven't seen her," said Leopold, "since we came back from Old Orchard together. In fact, since that time, our relations, for some reason or other, have undergone a great change. However, I think I can help you out. I don't believe in keeping a good friend like you, Quincy, in suspense, so I will tell you the truth. I am married. My wife is fully as competent to assist Mrs. Sawyer as Miss Very would have been. She is in the library now at work. I will go and ask her."

He entered the room, closing the door behind him. Quincy threw himself rather discontentedly into a chair. He fancied he heard laughing in the next room, but he knew Alice would be disappointed, and he himself felt in no mood for laughter.

Leopold opened the library door. "Quincy, I've induced her to undertake the task," he said. "Do spare a moment from your work, Mrs. Ernst; I wish to introduce to you Mr. Quincy Adams Sawyer, the husband of the author of that coming literary sensation, Blennerhassett. Mr. Sawyer," he continued, "allow me to present you to my wife, Mrs. Rosa Ernst." And as he said this, Leopold and Rosa stood side by side in the doorway.

"When did you do it?" finally ejaculated Quincy, rushing forward and grasping each by the hand. "Leopold, I owe you one." And then they all laughed together.

By some means, Dr. Culver said by the liberal use of money, Barker Dalton secured the regular nomination from Quincy's party. The latter kept his word and entered the field as an independent candidate. A hot contest followed. The papers were full of the

speeches of the opposing candidates, and incidents connected with their lives. But in none relating to Quincy
was a word said about his marriage, and the fact
was evidently unknown, except to a limited few. When
the polls closed on election day and the vote was
declared, it was found that Sawyer had a plurality of two
hundred and twenty-eight and a clear majority of twenty-
two over both Dalton and Burke, the opposing candidates.
Then the papers were full of compliments for Mr. Sawyer,
who had so successfully fought corruption and bribery in
his own party, and won such a glorious victory.

But Quincy never knew that the Hon. Nathaniel Adams
Sawyer had used all his influence to secure his son's elec-
tion, and for every dollar expended by Dalton, the Hon.
Nathaniel had covered it with a two or five if necessary.

The publication of Blennerhassett had been heralded by
advance notices that appeared in the press during the month
of October.

These notices had been adroitly written. Political prejudices, one notice said, would no doubt be aroused by state-
ments made in the book, and one newspaper went so far
as to publish a double-leaded editorial protesting against
the revival of party animosities buried more than two generations ago. The leaven worked, and when the book was
placed in the stores on the eleventh of November, the demand for it was unparalleled. Orders came for it from all
parts of the country, particularly from the State of New
York, and the resources of the great publishing house of
Hinckley, Morton, & Co. were taxed to the utmost to meet
the demand.

While Quincy was fighting Dalton in the political field,
another campaign was being planned in the clever diplo-
matic brain of Aunt Ella. It related to the introduction of
Alice, the "farmer's daughter," to the proud patrician family of Sawyer, as Quincy's wife—no easy matter to accom-
plish satisfactorily, as all agreed.

The initial step was taken a couple of weeks after Thanksgiving, when a daintily-engraved card was issued from Mt. Vernon Street, which read:

"Your company is respectfully requested on the evening of the tenth of December at a reception to be given to Bruce Douglas, the author of Blennerhassett."

One evening, Quincy ran up the steps of the Mt. Vernon Street house. He opened the door and started to run up the stairs to his wife's room, as was his custom, when he came into collision with a young lady, who, upon closer inspection, he found to be his sister Maude.

"Come in here," she said. She grasped him by the arm, and, dragging him into the parlor, she closed the door behind him.

"Oh, Mr. Man!" she cried, "I've found you out, but horses sha'n't drag it out of me. No, Quincy, you're always right, and I won't peach. But 'twas mean not to tell me."

Quincy looked at her in voiceless astonishment. "What do you mean, Maude, and where did you gather up all that slang?"

"I might ask you," said Maude, "where you found your wife. I've been talking to her upstairs. She must have thought that papa and mamma knew all about it, for she told me who she was, just as easy. Who is she, Quincy?"

He drew his sister down beside him on a sofa. "She was Miss Mary Alice Pettengill. She is now known to a limited few, of which you, sister Maude, are one, as Mrs. Mary Alice Sawyer; but she is known to a wide circle of readers as Bruce Douglas, the author of many popular stories, as also of that celebrated book entitled Blennerhassett."

"Is that so?" cried Maude; "why, papa is wild over that book. He's been reading it aloud to us evenings, and he said last night that that young man—you hear, Quincy?—

that young man, had brought the truth to the surface at last."

"Now, Maude," said Quincy, "you go right home and keep your mouth shut a little while longer, and when you are sixteen"—"the ninth of next January," broke in Maude—"I'll give you a handsome gold watch, with my picture in it."

"I don't have to be paid to keep your secrets, Quincy," replied Maude archly, as Quincy kissed her.

"I know it, dear," said Quincy; "I'll give you the watch, not as pay, but to show my gratitude."

Quincy took an early opportunity to explain to his wife his remissness in not informing his parents of his marriage, and disclosed to her Aunt Ella's plan.

On the tenth, Mrs. Chessman's spacious parlor was thronged from nine till eleven o'clock with bright and shining lights, representing the musical, artistic, literary, and social culture of Boston. Among the guests were the Hon. Nathaniel Adams Sawyer, his wife, and his daughters, Florence and Maude. The surprise of the visitors at the discovery that Bruce Douglas was a young woman was followed by one of great pleasure at finding her beautiful and affable.

The reception and entertainment were acknowledged on all sides to have been most successful, and a thoroughly pleased and satisfied company had spoken their farewells to author and hostess by quarter-past eleven. So, when Quincy came up Walnut Street and glanced across at his aunt's house, a little before twelve, he found the windows dark and the occupants, presumably, in their beds.

As part of her plan, Quincy had been advised by Aunt Ella to stay away from the reception, to spend the night at his father's house, and to be sure and take breakfast with them, so as to hear what was said about the previous evening.

As soon as the morning meal was over, Quincy ran quickly upstairs, seized his hand-bag, which he always kept packed, ready for an emergency, and in a very short space of time, reached Mt. Vernon Street. He found his wife and aunt in the den. The latter was reading a manuscript to Alice.

As soon as the greetings were over, and a little time given to discussing the reception, Quincy asked: "Who is this Mr. Fernborough that Maude told me about this morning?"

"He is an English gentleman," explained Alice, "who has come to this country to see if he can find any trace of an only daughter, who ran away from home with an American more than thirty years ago, and who, he thinks, came to this country with her husband. His wife is dead, he is alone in the world, and he is ready to forgive her and care for her, if she needs it."

"He hasn't hurried himself about it, has he?" said Quincy; "but why did he come to you?"

"That's the strange part of it," Alice replied. "He said he thoughtlessly picked up a magazine at a hotel where he was staying, and his eye fell upon my story, How He Lost Both Name and Fortune. He read it, and sought me out, to ask if it were fiction, or whether it was founded on some true incident. He was quite disappointed when I told him it was entirely a work of the imagination."

"Did he say what hotel?" asked Quincy.

"No," replied Alice; "but why are you so interested in a total stranger?"

Then Quincy told the story of the broken envelope— the little piece of cloth—and the name, Linda Fernborough.

"I must find him at once," said he, "for I have an impression that his daughter must have been Lindy Putnam's real mother. You gave me my reward, Alice, before my quest was successful, but I gave my word to find her for

you, and I shall not consider myself fully worthy of you
till that word is kept."

"But what did your father and mother say?" broke in
Aunt Ella.

"My father took me to task," began Quincy, "for not
being present at the reception, but I told him I had to see
Culver on some political business. Then he remarked that
I missed a very pleasant evening. He complimented Aunt
Ella, here, for her skill as an entertainer, and expressed
his surprise that Bruce Douglas, instead of being a young
man, was a young and very beautiful woman. Yes, Aunt
Ella, he actually called my wife here a very beautiful young
woman."

"That is a capital beginning!" cried Aunt Ella. "Go on,
Quincy."

"In order to continue the conversation, I ventured the
remark that Bruce Douglas came from an ordinary country
family and one not very well off; for which aspersion, I
humbly ask your pardon, Mrs. Sawyer. Father replied
that he thought that I must have been misinformed; that
Bruce Douglas was worth fifty thousand dollars in her own
right, and he added that she would become a very wealthy
woman if she kept up her literary activity."

"What did sister Sarah say?" asked Aunt Ella.

"Well," said Quincy, "I resolved to do something des-
perate, so I asked: 'Doesn't she look countrified?' again
asking your pardon, Mrs. Sawyer."

"No," said mother, "she has the repose of a Lady Clara
Vere de Vere, and is as correct in her speech as was the
Lady Elfrida Hastings."

"It will come out all right," cried Aunt Ella; and Quincy,
kissing his aunt and wife, and promising to write or telegraph every day, caught up his hand-bag and started forth
in search of the Hon. Stuart Fernborough, M. P.

When Quincy left his aunt's house he had not the slightest idea which way would be the best to turn his footsteps.

He commenced his search, however, at the Revere House, then he tried the American House, but at neither place was Mr. Fernborough a guest.

At the Quincy House the clerk was busy with a number of new arrivals. He had just opened a new hotel register, and the old one lay upon the counter. Quincy took it up, and turning over the leaves, glanced up and down its pages. Suddenly he started back; then, holding the book closer to his eyes he read it again. There it was, under the date of September 10, "Mdme. Rose Archimbault and daughter." The residence given in the proper column was "New York." Quincy kept the book open at the place where he found this entry until the clerk was at leisure. He remembered Mdme. Archimbault and daughter in a general way. He was sure that they arrived from Europe the day that they came to the hotel, and he was equally sure that they went to New York when they left. What made him positive was that he remembered asking the young lady when she wrote New York in the register if she had not just returned from Europe. She said yes, but that her home residence was in New York.

Quincy thanked the clerk, and started forth again in search of the elusive Mr. Fernborough. A visit to Young's, Parker's, and the Tremont furnished no clue, and Quincy was wondering whether his search, after all, was destined to be fruitless, when he thought of a small hotel in Central Court, which led from Washington Street, a little south of Summer Street.

It was noted for its English roast beef, Yorkshire mutton chops, and musty ale, and might be just the sort of place that an English gentleman would put up at, provided he had been informed of its whereabouts.

On his way Quincy dropped into the Marlborough, but Mr. Fernborough had not been there, and Quincy imagined that the little hotel in Central Court was his last hope.

His persistence was rewarded. Mr. Fernborough was

not only a guest, but he was in his room. Quincy sent up his card, and in a very short time was shown into the pres· ence of a courtly gentleman, between sixty and seventy years of age. His face was smooth shaven, and had a firm but not hard expression. His eyes, however, showed that he was weighed down by some sorrow, which the unyield· ing expression of his face indicated that he would bear in silence rather than seek sympathy from others.

Quincy's story was soon told. The old gentleman lis· tened with breathless interest, and when at the close Quincy said, "What do you think?" Mr. Fernborough cried, "It must be she, my daughter's child. There are no other Fernboroughs in England, and Linda has been a family name for generations. Heaven bless you, young man, for your kindly interest, and take me to my grandchild at once. She is the only tie that binds me to earth. All the others are dead and gone."

The old gentleman broke down completely, and for sev· eral minutes was unable to speak.

Quincy waited until his emotion had somewhat subsided. Then he said, "I am at your service, sir; we will do our best to find her. I have a feeling that she is in New York, but not a single fact to prove it. We can take the one o'clock train, if you desire."

The old gentleman began at once to prepare for the jour· ney. Quincy told him he would meet him at the hotel office, and from there he sent a note to Aunt Ella inform· ing her of his intended departure.

Arriving in New York they were driven at once to the Fifth Avenue Hotel. Quincy prevailed upon Sir Stuart to retire at once, telling him that he would prepare an ad· vertisement and have it in the next morning's issue of the "New York Herald."

Quincy wrote out two advertisements and sent them by special messenger to the newspaper office. The first one read: "Linda: important paper not destroyed, as suspected. Communicate at once with Eastborough, 'Herald' office." The second was worded as follows: "Celeste A———t: an American friend has a message for you from me. Send your address at once to Eastborough, 'Herald' office. ALGERNON H."

Then began the days of weary waiting; the careful examination of the "Herald" each morning, to be sure that the advertisements were in, for both had been paid for a week in advance. The request for mail made every morning at the "Herald" office received a stereotyped "no" for answer; then he vowed that he would advertise no more, but would enlist other aids in the search.

On the morning of the eighth day Quincy stood upon the steps of the Fifth Avenue Hotel. He was undecided which way to go. It is in such cases of absolute uncertainty that unseen powers should give their aid, if they ever do, for then it is most needed. He did not hear any angels' voices, but he crossed over Broadway and started up town on the right-hand side of that great thoroughfare. As he walked on he glanced at the shop windows, for they were resplendent with holiday gifts, for Christmas was only one short week away.

Just beyond the corner of Broadway and Twenty-ninth Street his attention was attracted by a wax figure in a milliner's window. The face and golden hair reminded him of his wife, and he thought how pretty Alice would look in the hat that was upon the head of the figure. His first inclination was to go in and buy it, then he thought that it would make an unhandy package to carry with him, and besides his taste might not be appreciated.

"Thinking, however, that he might return and purchase it, he glanced up at the sign. One look and he gave a sudden start backward, coming violently in contact with a gentleman who was passing. Quincy's apology was accepted and the gentleman passed on, giving his right shoulder an occasional pressure to make sure that it was not dislocated. Then Quincy took another look at the sign to make sure that he had not been mistaken. On it he read, in large golden letters, "Mdme. Archimbault."

It was but the work of an instant for Quincy to enter the store and approach the only attendant, who was behind the counter nearest the door.

"Could I see Mdme. Archimbault?" he inquired in the politest possible manner.

"Ze madame eez seeck zis morning, monsieur, mais ze Mademoiselle Celeste eez in ze boudoir."

As she said this she pointed to a partition with windows of ground glass, which extended across the farther end of the store, evidently forming a private department for trying on hats and bonnets. Quincy said nothing, but taking out his cardcase passed one to the attendant.

The girl walked towards the boudoir, opened the door and entered. Quincy followed her, and was but a few feet from the door when it was closed. He heard a woman's voice say, "What is it, Hortense?" And the girl's reply was distinctly audible. This is what she said, "A veezitor, mademoiselle."

An instant's silence, followed by a smothered cry of astonishment, evidently from mademoiselle. Then ensued a short conversation, carried on in whispers. Then Hortense emerged from the boudoir, and facing Quincy said, "Ze mademoiselle weel not zee you. She has no desire to continue ze acquaintance."

As she said this she stepped behind the counter, evidently thinking that Quincy would accept the rebuff and depart. Instead of doing this he took a step forward, which brought him between Hortense and the door of the boudoir. Turning to the girl he said in a low tone, "There must be some mistake. I have never met Mademoiselle Archimbault. I will go in and explain the purpose of my visit." And before Hortense could prevent him, Quincy

"ALICE RECOVERS HER SIGHT." (ACT IV.)

had entered the boudoir and closed the door behind him.

In the centre of the room stood a beautifully carved and inlaid table. Before it sat an elegantly-dressed woman, whose hair, artistically arranged, was of the darkest shade of brown—almost black. Her arms were crossed upon the table, her face was buried in them, and from her came a succession of convulsive sobs, that indicated she was in great physical or mental distress.

Quincy felt that she knew he was there, but he did not speak.

Finally she said, and there was a tone of deep suffering · in her voice: "Oh! Algernon, why have you followed me? I can never, never marry you. If it had been possible I would have met you that evening, as I promised."

The thought flashed across Quincy's mind, "This is the girl that ran away from Lord Hastings. But why did she call me Algernon?" Then he spoke for the first time. "Mademoiselle, there is some misunderstanding; my name is not Algernon. I am not Lord Hastings."

As he spoke he looked at the woman seated at the table. She looked up; there was an instantaneous, mutual recognition. In her astonishment she cried out, "Mr. Sawyer!"

As these words fell from her lips, Quincy said to himself, "Thank God! she's found at last." But the only words that he spoke aloud were, "Lindy Putnam!"

"Why do I find you here," asked Quincy, "and under this name? Why have you not answered my advertisements in the 'Herald?'" And he sank into a chair on the ·other side of the little table.

The revulsion of feeling was so great at his double discovery that he came nearer being unmanned than ever before in his life.

"How did you come by this card!" asked Mademoiselle Archimbault in a broken voice. "When you have explained, I will answer your questions."

Quincy took the card from her hand and glanced at it.

"What a big blunder I made and yet what a fortunate one,"
cried he, for he now saw that he had sent in Lord Hastings's card bearing the London address. "Lord Hastings
himself gave it to me," he continued. "He was a guest at
my father's cottage at Nahant last summer. He came to
America and spent three months vainly searching for you.
He loves you devotedly, and made me promise that if I
ever found you I would cable at once to the address on
that card, and he said he would come to America on the
next steamer. Of course when I made that promise I did
not know that Lindy Putnam and Celeste Archimbault
were one and the same person."

"But knowing it as you now do, Mr. Sawyer, you will
not send him any word. Give me your solemn promise
you will not. I cannot marry him. You know I cannot.
There is no Lindy Putnam, and Celeste Archimbault has
no right to the name she bears."

"Did you come to New York when you left Eastborough,
as you promised you would?" inquired Quincy.

"No, I did not, Mr. Sawyer," said she. "Forgive me,
but I could not. I was distracted, almost heartbroken
when I reached Boston the day she died. She had robbed
me of all hope of ever finding my relatives, and but for
my hatred of her I believe I would have had brain fever.
One thing I could not do, I would not do. I would not
remain in America. I was rich, I would travel and try to
drown my sorrow and my hatred. I did not go to a hotel,
for I did not wish any one to find me. What good could
it do? I looked in the 'Transcript' and found a boarding
place. There I met Mdme. Archimbault, a widow, a
French-Canadian lady, who had come to Boston in search
of a niece who had left her home in Canada some five years
before. Mdme. Archimbault had spent all the money she
had in her unavailing search for her relative, and she told
me, with tears in her eyes and expressive French gestures,
that she would have to sell her jewelry to pay her board,

as she had no way of making a living in a foreign land. Then I told her part of my story. She was sure her niece was dead, and so I asked her to be my mother, to let me take her name and be known as her daughter. I told her I was rich and that I would care for her as long as our compact was kept and the real truth not known. My visit to Nice and my meeting with Algernon Hastings, he has no doubt told you. I did not know he was a lord, but I suspected it. So much the more reason why he should not marry a nameless waif, a poor girl with no father or mother and all hope lost of ever finding them. I came back to America with Mdme. Archimbault, covering my tracks by cross journeys and waits which he could not anticipate. We landed in Boston."

"I found your names in the Quincy House register," remarked Quincy.

"I don't think I could escape from you as easily as I did from him," she said, the first faint sign of a smile showing itself upon her face. "I went to my bankers in Boston and told them that I had been adopted by a wealthy French lady named Archimbault. I informed them that we were going to return to France at once. They made up my account, and I found I was worth nearly one hundred and forty thousand dollars. I took my fortune in New York drafts, explaining that madame wished to visit relatives in New York, and that we should sail for France from that port. I did this so my bankers could not disclose my whereabouts to any one. We came here, but I could not remain idle. I always had a natural taste for millinery work, so I proposed to madame that we should open a store under her name. We did this late in September, and have had great success since our opening day. Now you know all about me, Mr. Sawyer. Give me your promise that you will not tell Lord Hastings where I am."

"Then," said Quincy, "you do not know why I am here."

"To keep your word to Lord Hastings, I presume.
What other reason could you have?"

"Then you have not read the Personal Column in the
'New York Herald?' " Quincy inquired.

"No," said she. "Why should I?"

Quincy took a copy of the paper from his pocket, laid it
upon the table and pointed with his finger to the word
"Linda." She read the advertisement, then looked up to
him with distended eyes, full of questioning.

"What does the paper say? It could not have disclosed
much or you would not have waited so long to tell me."

Then Quincy related the story of the sealed package,
how it had been given to Alice Pettengill long before Mrs.
Putnam died; how Miss Pettengill had sworn to destroy it,
but would not when she learned that it might possibly contain information relating to her parents. He told her that
Miss Pettengill would not allow any one to read it but herself; and how he had promised to search for her until he
found her. Then he related the incident at the lawyer's
office and the piece of cloth bearing the name, "Linda Fernborough," "which," said Quincy, "I think must have been
your mother's maiden name." He did not tell her of the
old gentleman only five blocks away, ready and willing to
claim her as his granddaughter without further proof than
that little piece of cloth.

Quincy looked at his watch. "I have just time," said
he, "to get the one o'clock train for Boston. I will obtain
the papers to-morrow morning, and be in New York again
to-morrow night. The next morning early I will be at
your residence with the papers, and let us hope that they
will contain such information as will disclose your parentage and give you a name that you can rightfully bear."

She wrote her home address on a card and passed it to
him.

He gave her hand a quick, firm pressure and left the
store, not even glancing at Hortense, who gazed at him

with wonderment. He hailed a hack and was driven to
the hotel. He found Sir Stuart and told him that he had
found his supposed granddaughter, but that he must wait
until he returned from Boston with the papers, that his
wife's feelings must be respected, and that the document
could only be opened and read by the person who had been
known to her as Lindy Putnam.

Quincy reached Mt. Vernon Street about eight o'clock
that evening. His wife and aunt listened eagerly to the
graphic recital of his search. He pictured the somewhat
sensational episode in the boudoir in the most expressive
language, and Alice remarked that Quincy was fast gather-
ing the materials for a most exciting romance; while Aunt
Ella declared that the disclosure of the dual personality of
Linda and Celeste would form a most striking theatrical
tableau.

Aunt Ella informed him that she had been requested by
Mr. and Mrs. Nathaniel Adams Sawyer to extend an invitation to Miss Bruce Douglas to dine with them on any
day that might be convenient for her. "I was included in
the invitation, of course," Aunt Ella added. "What day
had we better fix, Quincy?" she inquired.

"Make it Christmas," replied Quincy. "Tell them Miss
Bruce Douglas has invitations for every other day but
that for a month to come. What a precious gift I shall
present to my father," said he, caressing his wife, who laid
her fair head upon his shoulder.

"Do you think he will be pleased?" asked Alice.

"I don't know which will please him most," replied
Quincy, "the fact that such a talented addition has been
made to the family, or the knowledge, which will surely
surprise him, that his son was smart enough to win such a
prize."

The next morning Quincy arose early and was at Curtis
Carter's office as soon as it was opened. Alice had signed
an order for the delivery of the package to him and he pre-

sented it to Mr. Carter's clerk, to whom he was well known.
The ponderous doors of the big safe were thrown open and
the precious document was produced. When the clerk
passed the package to him and took Alice's order therefor,
Quincy noticed that a five-dollar bill was pinned to the envelope; a card was also attached to the bill, upon which was
written: "This money belongs to Mr. Quincy Sawyer; he
dropped it the last time he was in the office."

Quincy would not trust the package to his hand-bag, but
placed it in an inside pocket of his coat, which he tightly
buttoned. After leaving the lawyer's office he dropped
into Grodjinski's, and purchased a box of fine cigars. He
had the clerk tack one of his cards on the top of the box.
On this he wrote:

"MY DEAR CURTIS:—Keep the ashes for me; they make
good tooth powder.   QUINCY."

The box was then done up and addressed to Curtis Carter, Esq., the clerk promising to have it delivered at once.

Quincy had found a letter at his aunt's from Mr. Strout,
asking him to buy a line of fancy groceries and confec-
tionery for Christmas trade, and it was noon before he had
attended to the matter to his complete satisfaction. A
hasty lunch and he was once more on his way to New York,
and during the trip his hand sought the inside pocket of his
coat a score of times, that he might feel assured that the
precious document was still there.

Arriving, Quincy proceeded at once to the Fifth Avenue
Hotel. Sir Stuart was eagerly awaiting his arrival, and
his first question was, "Have you the papers?"

Quincy took the package from his pocket and placed it
on the table before him, remarking as he did so, "It must
not be opened until to-morrow morning, and then by the
young lady herself."

The old man pushed the package away from him and

turned a stern face toward Quincy. "I yield obedience," said he, "to your wife's command, but if one man or two stood now between me and my darling's child, I would have their lives, if they tried to keep her from my arms for one instant even."

After a little reflection he apologized for his vehement language, and sought his room to think, and hope, and wait —but not to sleep.

The next morning, a little before nine o'clock, a carriage containing two gentlemen stopped before a modest brick dwelling in West Forty-first Street. A servant admitted them and showed them into the little parlor. The room was empty. Quincy pointed to a sofa at the farther end of the room, and Sir Stuart took a seat thereon. Quincy stepped into the entry and greeted Celeste, who was just descending the stairs.

"Sir Stuart Fernborough is in your parlor," said he; "he may be, and I hope to Heaven he is, your grandfather, but you must control your feelings until you know the truth. Come and sit by me, near the window, and read what is written in this package, so loud that he can hear every word." As he said this he placed the package, which might or might not prove her honorable heritage, in her hands.

They entered the room and took seats near the window. Celeste opened the package with trembling fingers. As she did so that little telltale piece of cloth, bearing the name "Linda Fernborough," once more fell upon the floor. Quincy picked it up, and held it during the reading of the letter, for a letter it proved to be.

It had no envelope, but was folded in the old-fashioned way, so as to leave a blank space on the back of the last sheet for the address. The address was, "Mr. Silas Putnam, Hanover, New Hampshire."

Celeste began to read in a clear voice: "Dear brother Silas."

"Is there no date?" asked Quincy.

"Oh, yes," replied Celeste, "March 18, 183—."
"Thirty years ago," said Quincy.
Celeste read on:

"DEAR BROTHER SILAS:—You will, no doubt, be surprised
to find I am in this town when I usually go to Gloucester
or Boston, but the truth is I had a strange adventure during my last fishing trip on the Polly Sanders, and I thought
I would come into port as close to you as I could. About
ten days ago I had a good catch on the Banks and sailed
for home, bound for Boston. A heavy fog came up, and
we lay to for more than twenty-four hours. During the
night, heard cries, and my mate, Jim Brown, stuck to it
that some ship must have run ashore; and he was right,
for when the fog lifted we saw the masts of a three-master
sticking out of water, close on shore, and about a mile
from where we lay. We up sail and ran down as close as
we dared to see if there was anybody living on the wreck.
We couldn't see anybody, but I sent out Jim Brown with
a boat to make a thorough search. In about an hour he
came back, bringing a half-drowned woman and just the
nicest, chubbiest, little black-eyed girl baby that you ever
saw in your life. Jim said the woman was lashed to a spar,
and when he first saw her, there was a man in the water
swimming and trying to push the spar towards the land,
but before he reached him the man sunk and he didn't get
another sight of him."

"Oh, my poor father!" cried Celeste. The letter dropped
from her hands and the tears rushed into her eyes.
"Shall I finish reading it?" asked Quincy, picking up the
letter.
Celeste nodded, and he read on:

"I gave the woman some brandy and she came to long
enough to tell me who she was. She said her name was

Linda Chester or Chessman, I couldn't tell just which. Her
husband's name was Charles, and he was an artist. He
had a brother in Boston named Robert, and they were on
their way to that city. The wrecked ship was the Cana-
dian Belle, bound from Liverpool to Boston. I didn't tell
her her husband was drowned. I gave her some more
brandy and she came to again and said her husband left a
lot of pictures in London with Roper & Son, on Ludgate
Hill. I asked her where she came from and she said from
Heathfield, in Sussex. She said no more and we couldn't
bring her to again. She died in about an hour and we buried her at sea. I noticed that her nightdress had a name
stamped on it different from what she gave me, and so I
cut it out and send it in this letter. Now, I've heard you
and Heppy say that if you could find a nice little girl baby
that you would adopt her and bring her up. I sold out my
cargo at Portland, and so I've put in here, and I'll stay
till you and Heppy have time to drive down here and make
up your minds whether you'll take this handsome little baby
off my hands. Come right along, quick, for I must be off
to the Banks again soon. From your brother,

OBED PUTNAM,

Captain of the Polly Sanders.

"Portsmouth Harbor, N. H.

"P. S. The baby was a year old the eighth of last January. Its name is Linda Fernborough Chessman."

The tears had welled up again in the young girl's eyes,
when Quincy read of the death of her mother and her
burial at sea. His own hand trembled perceptibly when
he realized that the young woman before him, though not
his cousin, was yet connected by indisputable ties of relationship to his own aunt, Mrs. Ella Chessman. Following
his usual habit of reticence he kept silence, thinking that it

• would be inappropriate to detract in any way from the happy reunion of grandfather and granddaughter.

Sir Stuart had scarcely moved during the reading of the letter. He had sat with his right hand covering his eyes, but yet evidently listening attentively to each word as it fell from the reader's lips. As Quincy folded up the letter and passed it back to Linda, Sir Stuart arose and came forward to the front part of the room. Quincy took Linda's hand and led her towards Mr. Fernborough. Then he said, "Sir Stuart, I think this letter proves conclusively that this young lady's real name is Linda Fernborough Chessman. I knew personally Mr. Silas Putnam, mentioned in the letter, and scores of others can bear testimony that she has lived nearly all her life with this Silas Putnam, and has been known to all as his adopted daughter. There is no doubt but that the Linda Fernborough who was buried at sea was her mother. If you are satisfied that Mrs. Charles Chessman was your daughter, it follows that this young lady must be your granddaughter."

"There is no doubt of it in my mind," said Sir Stuart, taking both of Linda's hands in his. "I live at Fernborough Hall, which is located in Heathfield, in the county of Sussex. But, my dear, I did not know until to-day that my poor daughter had a child, and it will take me just a little time to get accustomed to the fact. Old men's brains do not act as quickly as my young friend's here." As he said this he looked towards Quincy. "But I am sure that we both of us owe to him a debt of gratitude that it will be difficult for us ever to repay."

The old gentleman drew Linda towards him and folded her tenderly in his arms. "Come, rest here, my dear one," said he; "your doubts and hopes, your troubles and trials, and your wanderings are over." He kissed her on the forehead, and Linda put her arms about his neck and laid her head upon his breast.

"You are the only one united to me by near ties of blood

in the world," Sir Stuart continued, and he laid his hand on Linda's head and turned her face towards him. "You have your mother's eyes," he said. "We will go back to England, and Fernborough Hall will have a mistress once more. You are English born, and have a right to sit in that seat which might have been your mother's but for the pride and prejudice which thirty years ago ruled both your grandmother and myself."

Leaving them to talk over future plans, Quincy went back to the hotel and wrote two letters. The first was addressed to Lord Algernon Hastings in London. The other was a brief note to Aunt Ella, informing her that a party of four would start for Boston on the morning train and that she might expect them about four o'clock in the afternoon.

It lacked but five minutes of that hour when a carriage, containing the party from New York, stopped before the Mt. Vernon Street house. It suited Quincy's purpose that his companions should first meet his wife, although the fact that she was his wife was as yet unknown to them.

The meeting between Alice and Linda was friendly, but not effusive. They had been ordinary acquaintances in the old days at Eastborough, but now a mutual satisfaction and pleasure drew them more closely together.

"I have come," said Linda, "to thank you, Miss Pettengill, for your kindness and justice to me. Few women would have disregarded the solemn oath that Mrs. Putnam forced you to take, but by doing so you have given me a lawful name and a life of happiness for the future. May every blessing that Heaven can send to you be yours."

"All the credit should not be given to me," replied Alice. "The morning after Mrs. Putnam's death I was undecided in my mind which course to follow, whether to destroy the paper or to keep it. It was a few words from my Uncle Isaac that enabled me to decide the matter. He told me that a promise made to the dead should not be carried out if it interfered with the just rights of the living. So I decided to keep the paper, but how? It was then that Mr. Sawyer came to the rescue and pointed out to me the line of action, which I am truly happy to learn has ended so pleasantly."

"Grandpa and I have both thanked Mr. Sawyer so much," said Linda, "that he will not listen to us any more, but I will write to Uncle Ike, for I used to call him by that name, and show him that I am not ungrateful. I have lost all my politeness, I am so happy," continued Linda; "I believe you have met grandpa."

Sir Stuart came forward, and, in courtly but concise language, expressed his sincere appreciation of the kind service that Miss Pettengill had rendered his granddaughter.

Then Linda introduced Mdme. Archimbault as one who had been a true friend and almost a mother to her in the hours of her deepest sorrow and distress.

"Now, my friends," said Quincy, "I have a little surprise for you myself. I believe it my duty to state the situation frankly to you. My father is a very wealthy man—a millionaire. He is proud of his wealth and still more proud of the honored names of Quincy and Adams, which he conferred upon me. Like all such fathers and mothers, my parents have undoubtedly had bright dreams as to the future of their only son. One of their dreams has, no doubt, been my marriage to some young lady of honored name and great wealth. In such a matter, however, my own mind must decide. I have acted without their knowledge, as I resolved to deprive them of the pleasure of my wife's acquaintance until Christmas day."

Stepping up to Alice, Quincy took her hand and led her forward, facing their guests. "I take great pleasure, my friends, in introducing to you my wife, Mrs. Quincy Adams Sawyer."

There came an exclamation of pleased surprise from Linda, followed by congratulations from all, and while

these were being extended, Aunt Ella entered the room.
She advanced to meet Sir Stuart, who had been present at
Alice's reception. Quincy introduced Mdme. Archimbault,
and then Aunt Ella turned towards Linda. "This is the
young lady, I believe," said she, "who has just found a
long-lost relative, or rather, has been found by him. You
must be very happy, my dear, and it makes me very happy
to know that my nephew and niece, who are so dear to me,
have been instrumental in bringing this pleasure to you.
But have you been able to learn your mother's name?
Quincy did not mention that in his letter."

"Yes," said Quincy, stepping forward, "the letter contained that information, but I thought I would rather tell
you about it than write it. My dear aunt, allow me to introduce to you Miss Linda Fernborough Chessman."

"What!" cried Aunt Ella, starting back in astonishment.

"Listen to me, Aunt Ella;" and taking her hand in his
he drew her towards him. "Your husband had a brother,
Charles Chessman; he was an artist and lived in England;
while there he married; he wrote your husband some thirty
years ago that he was going to return to America, but
Uncle Robert, you told me, never heard from him again
after receiving the letter."

"Yes, yes!" assented Aunt Ella; "I have the letter. But
what is the mystery, Quincy? You know I can bear anything but suspense."

"There is no mystery, auntie, now; it is all cleared up.
Uncle Robert's brother Charles married Linda Fernborough, Sir Stuart's daughter. The vessel in which father,
mother, and child sailed for America was wrecked. Father
and mother were lost, but the child was rescued. This is
the child. Aunt Ella, Linda Chessman is your niece, but
unfortunately I am unable to call her cousin."

Aunt Ella embraced Linda and talked to her as a mother
might talk to her daughter. Her delight at finding this
relative of the husband whom she had loved so well and

mourned so sincerely, showed itself in face, and voice, and action. Her hospitality knew no bounds. Linda must stay with her a month at least, so must Sir Stuart and Mdme. Archimbault. It was the holiday season, and they must all feast and be merry over this happy, unexpected return.

It was a joyous party that gathered in the dining-room at Aunt Ella's house that evening. She said that such an occasion could not be fitly celebrated with plain cold water, so a bottle of choice old port was served to Sir Stuart, and toasts to Mrs. Sawyer and Miss Chessman were drunk from glasses filled with foaming champagne.

Then all adjourned to Aunt Ella's room and Uncle Robert's prime cigars were offered to Sir Stuart and Quincy. But Aunt Ella had too much to say to think of her cigarette. For an hour conversation was general; everybody took part in it. The events of the past year, which were of so great interest to all present, were gone over, and when conversation lagged it was because everybody knew everything that everybody else knew.

Quincy spent that night at his father's house. The next morning his mother told him that the author had selected Christmas day on which to be received by them at dinner, and that she was making unusual preparations for that event.

"I wish I could invite a few friends to meet her that day," said Quincy.

"You may invite as many as you choose, Quincy, if you will promise to be here yourself. You have been away from home so much the past year I hardly anticipate the pleasure of your company on that day."

"Have no fear, mother," Quincy said. "I wish very much to meet the author that father and you are so greatly pleased with. Of course Aunt Ella is coming?"

"Certainly," answered his mother. "I understand that the author has been stopping with her since the reception."

"I shall invite five friends," said Quincy, "and you may depend upon me."

To his mother's surprise he gave her a slight embrace, a light kiss upon her cheek, and was gone.

The sun showed its cheerful face on Christmas morning. The snow that fell a fortnight previous had been washed away by continued heavy rains. A cold wind, biting, but healthful, quickened the pulse and brought roses to the cheeks of holiday pedestrians.

The programme for the meals on Christmas day had been arranged by Mrs. Sawyer as follows: Breakfast at nine, dinner at one, and a light supper at six. It had always been the rule in the Sawyer family to exchange Christmas gifts at the breakfast hour. Quincy was present, and his father, mother, and sisters thanked him for the valuable presents that bore his card. Father, mother, and sisters, on their part, had not forgotten Quincy, and the reunited family had the most enjoyable time that they had experienced for a year.

As Quincy rose to leave the table, he said to his mother, "I have another gift for father and you, but it has not yet arrived. I am going to see about it this morning."

"You will be sure to come to dinner, Quincy," fell from his mother's lips.

"I promise you, mother," he replied. "I would not miss it for anything."

A little after noontime, the Chessman carriage arrived at the Beacon Street mansion of the Hon. Nathaniel Adams Sawyer, and a moment later Mrs. Ella Chessman and the young author, Bruce Douglas, were ushered into the spacious and elegant parlor. They were received by Mr. and Mrs. Sawyer and their daughter Florence.

Twenty minutes later a carriage arrived before the same mansion. Its occupants were Sir Stuart Fernborough, his granddaughter, and Mdme. Archimbault. A few minutes later Mr. and Mrs. Leopold Ernst appeared, having walked the short distance from their rooms on Chestnut Street. The new arrivals were presented to Mr. and Mrs. Sawyer by Mrs. Chessman, and a pleasant ante-prandial conversation was soon under way.

From behind the curtains of a second-story window of the mansion, a young miss had watched the arrival and departure of the carriages. As the second one drove away she exclaimed, "Oh! what a lark! Those last folks came in Aunt Ella's carriage, too. I bet Quincy and auntie have put up some sort of a game on pa and ma. I won't go down stairs till Quincy comes, for I want to give my new sister a hug and a squeeze and a kiss, and I sha'n't dare to do it till Quincy has introduced her to pa and ma."

At that moment the young man, faultlessly attired, came down stairs from the third story, and Maude sprang out from her doorway on the second floor and said in a whisper, "How long have you been home, Quincy?"

"I came in about half-past eleven," he replied.

"Oh, you rogue," cried Maude. "I have been watching out the window for an hour. I see it all now, you don't mean to give pa and ma a chance to say boo until after dinner. Let me go down first, Quincy."

Maude went down stairs and was duly presented to the assembled guests as the youngest scion of the house of Sawyer.

At exactly five minutes of one Quincy entered the parlor through the rear door. Aunt Ella and Alice were seated side by side between the two front windows. As Quincy advanced he exchanged the compliments of the season with the guests. Finally the Hon. Nathaniel and his son Quincy stood facing Aunt Ella and Alice.

"Quincy," said his father, in slow, measured tones, "it gives me great pleasure to present you to the celebrated young author, Bruce Douglas."

Quincy bent low, and Alice inclined her head in acknowledgment. He reached forward, clasped her hand in his and

took his place by her side. "Father, mother, and sisters,"
he cried, and there was a proud tone in his clear, ringing
voice, "there is still another presentation to be made—that
Christmas gift of which I spoke this morning at breakfast.
You see I hold this lady by the hand, which proves that
we are friends and not strangers. To her friends in the
town of Eastborough, where she was born, the daughter of
an honest farmer, who made a frugal living and no more,
she was known by the name of Mary Alice Pettengill. To
the story and book-reading public of the United States, she
is known as Bruce Douglas, but to me she is known by the
sacred name of wife. I present to you as a Christmas gift,
a daughter and a sister."

There was a moment of suspense, and all eyes were fixed
upon the parents so dramatically apprised of their son'o
marriage. The Hon. Nathaniel cleared his throat, and advancing slowly, took Alice's hand in his and said, "It gives
me great pleasure to welcome as a daughter one so highly
favored by nature with intellectual powers and such marked
endowments for a famous literary career. I am confident
that the reputation of our family will gain rather than lose
by such an alliance."

"He thinks her books are going to sell," remarked Leopold to his wife.

Mrs. Nathaniel Adams Sawyer took Alice's hand in hers
and kissed her upon the cheek. "You will always be welcome, my daughter, at our home. I know we shall learn
to love you in time."

It was Florence's turn now. Like her mother, she took
her new sister's hand and gave her a society kiss on the
cheek. Then she spoke: "As mother said, I know I shall
learn to love you, sister, in time."

A slight form dashed through the front parlor door, and
throwing her arms about Alice's neck, gave her a hearty
kiss upon the lips. "My sweet sister, Alice, I love you now,
and I always shall love you, and I think my brother Quincy

is just the luckiest man in the world to get such a nice wife."

Then abashed at her own vehemance, she got behind Aunt Ella, who said to herself, "Maude has got some heart."

Dinner was announced. The Hon. Nathaniel Adams Sawyer offered his arm to Mrs. Quincy Adams Sawyer, and they led the holiday procession. Sir Stuart Fernborough, M. P., escorted Mrs. Sarah Quincy Sawyer; next came Mr. Leopold Ernst and Miss Linda Fernborough Chessman, followed by Mr. Quincy Adams Sawyer and Mrs. Leopold Ernst; behind them walked, arm in arm, Mrs. Ella Quincy Chessman and Mdme. Rose Archimbault; while bringing up the rear came the Misses Florence Estelle and Maude Gertrude Sawyer. Maude had politely offered her arm to Florence, but the latter had firmly declined to accept it. In this order they entered the gorgeous dining-room and took their places at a table bearing evidences of the greatest wealth, if not the greatest refinement, to partake of their Christmas dinner.

CHAPTER XXXVIII.

FIVE years passed away, years of not unmixed happiness for any of those with whom this story has made us acquainted. Quincy and Alice had undergone a severe trial in the loss of two of the three little ones that had been born to them; the remaining child was a fair little boy, another Quincy, and upon him the bereaved parents lavished all the wealth of their tenderness and affection.

In his political life, however, Quincy had found only smooth and pleasant sailing, and thanks to his bright and energetic nature, and not a little, perhaps, to his father's name and influence, he had risen rapidly from place to place and honor to honor. One of his earliest political moves had been the introduction of a bill into the House for the separation of Mason's Corner and Eastbrough into individual communities.

Soon after the incorporation of the former town under its new name of Fernborough, Abbot Smith, at Quincy's suggestion, had started the Fernborough Improvement Association, and now after these few years, the result of its labors was plainly and agreeably apparent. The ruins of Uncle Ike's chicken coop had been removed, and grass covered its former site. Shade trees had been planted along all the principal streets, for the new town had streets instead of roads. The three-mile road to Eastborough Centre had been christened Mason Street, and the square before Strout & Maxwell's store had been named Mason Square. Mrs. Hawkins's boarding house had become a hotel, and was known as the Hawkins House. The square

before the church was called Howe's Square, in honor of
the aged minister. The old Montrose road was now dignified by the appellation of Montrose Avenue. The upper
road to Eastborough Centre that led by the old Putnam
house was named Pettengill Street, although Ezekiel protested that it was a "mighty poor name for a street, even
if it did answer all right for a man." The great square
facing Montrose Avenue, upon which the Town Hall and
the Chessman Free Public Library had been built, was
called Putnam Square. On three sides of it, wide streets
had been laid out, on which many pretty houses had been
erected. These three streets had been named Quincy
Street, Adams Street, and Sawyer Street.

It was the morning of the fifteenth of June, a gala day in
the history of the town. The fifth anniversary of the laying
of the corner stone of the Town Hall and the library was
to be commemorated by a grand banquet given in the Town
Hall, and was to be graced by many distinguished guests,
among them the Hon. Quincy Adams Sawyer and wife,
and Mrs. Ella Chessman. After the banquet, which was to
take place in the evening, there was to be an open-air concert given, followed by a grand display of fireworks. During the feast, the citizens were to be admitted to the galleries, so that they could see the guests and listen to the
speeches.

About ten o'clock the visiting party started off to view
the sights of the town. Under the leadership of the town
officers they turned their steps first towards the new library. On entering this handsome building, they observed
hung over the balcony, facing them, a large oil painting of
a beautiful dark-haired, dark-eyed woman, dressed in satin
and velvet and ermine, and having a coronet upon her
head. Underneath was a tablet bearing an inscription.

"An admirable portrait," said Quincy to his wife. "Can
you read the tablet, dear? I fear I shall really have to see
Dr. Tillotson about my eyes."

Alice smiled at the allusion, and directing her gaze upon it, read without the slightest hesitation: "Linda Putnam, once a resident of this town, now Countess of Sussex, and donor of this library building, which is named in honor of her father, Charles Chessman, only brother of Robert Chessman."

During the evening festivities the Town Hall was brilliantly lighted, and every seat in the galleries and coigns of vantage were occupied. The guests at the banquet numbered fully sixty. A Boston caterer, with a corps of trained waiters, had charge of the dinner. During its progress the Cottonton Brass Band performed at intervals. They were stationed in Putnam Square, and the music was not an oppressive and disturbing element, as it often is at close range on such occasions.

When coffee was served, Toastmaster Obadiah Strout, Esq., arose, and the eyes of banqueters and sightseers were turned toward him.

"This is a glorious day in the history of our town," the toastmaster began. "The pleasant duty has fallen to me of proposing the toasts to which we shall drink, and of introducing our honored guests one by one. I know that words of advice and encouragement will come from them. But before I perform the duties that have been allotted to me, it is my privilege to make a short address. Instead of doing so, I shall tell you a little story, and it will be a different kind of a story from what I have been in the habit of telling."

This remark caused an audible titter to arise from some of the auditors in the galleries, and Abner Stiles, who was sitting behind Mrs. Hawkins, leaned over and said to her, "I guess he's goin' to tell a true story."

The toastmaster continued: "More than six years ago a young man from the city arrived in this town. It was given out that he came down here for his health, but he wasn't so sick but that he could begin to take an active part in town affairs as soon as he got here. They say confession is good for the soul, and I'm goin' to confess that I didn't take to this young man. I thought he was a city swell, who had come down here to show off, and in company with several friends, who looked at his visit down here about the same as I did, we did all we could for a couple of months to try and drive him out of town. Now I am comin' to the point that I want to make. If we had let him alone the chances are that he wouldn't have stayed here more than a month any way. Now, s'posen he had gone home at the end of the month; in that case he never would have met the lady who sits by his side to-night, and who by her marriage has added new lustre to her native town. If he had not remained, she never would have written those stories which are known the world over, and I tell you, fellow-citizens, that in writing Blennerhassett, An American Countess, The Majesty of the Law, and The Street Boy, she has done more to make this town famous than all the men who were ever born in it."

The speaker paused and drank a glass of water, while cheers and applause came from all parts of the gallery. Abner Stiles apparently forgot his surroundings, and, thinking probably that it was a political rally, called out, "Three cheers for Alice Pettengill"! which were given with a will, much to his delight, and the surprise of the banqueters.

The toastmaster resumed: "If he had gone away disgusted with the town and its people, he never would have found out who Linda Putnam really was, and she, consequently, would never have been what she is to-day, a peeress of England and the great benefactress of this town, a lady who will always have our deepest affection and most sincere gratitude."

Again the orator paused, and the audience arose to its feet. Applause, cheers, and the waving of handkerchiefs attested that the speaker's words had voiced the popular feeling. Once more Abner Stiles's voice rose above the din, and three cheers for "Lindy Putnam, Countess of Sussex," were given with such a will that the band outside caught the enthusiasm and played "God Save the Queen," which most of the audience supposed was "America."

"In conclusion," said the orator, "I have one more point to make, and that is a purely personal one. Some writer has said the end justifies the means, and another writer puts it this way, 'Do evil that good may come.' In these two sayin's lies all the justification for many sayin's and doin's that can be found; and if I were a conceited man or one inclined to praise my own actions, I should say that the good fortune of many of our distinguished guests this evening, and the handsome financial backin' that this town has received, are due principally to my personal exertions."

Here the speaker paused again and wiped his forehead, which was bedewed with perspiration.

"Good Lord!" said Mrs. Hawkins to Olive Green, who sat next to her, "to hear that man talk anybuddy would think that nobuddy else in the town ever did anything."

"To conclude," said the speaker, "I don't wish, fellercitizens, to have you understand that I am defendin' my actions. They were mean in spirit and mean in the way in which they were done, but the one against whom they were directed returned good for evil, and heaped coals of fire on my head. At a time when events made me think he was my greatest enemy, he became my greatest friend. It is to his assistance, advice, and influence that I owe the present honorable position that I hold in this town, and here tonight, in his presence, and in the presence of you all, I have made this confession to show that I am truly repentant for the past. At the same time, I cannot help rejoicing in the good fortune that those misdeeds were the means of securin' for us all."

As the speaker sat down, overcome with emotion, he was greeted with applause, which was redoubled when Mr. Sawyer arose in his seat. But when Quincy leaned forward and extended his hand to Strout, which the latter took, the excitement rose to fever heat, and cheers for Quincy Adams Sawyer and Obadiah Strout resounded throughout the hall and fell upon the evening air. This time the band played "The Star Spangled Banner."

Again the toastmaster arose and said, "Ladies and gentlemen, the first toast that I am going to propose to-night is a double one, because, for obvious reasons, it must include not only the State, but its chief representative, who is with us here to-night. Ladies and gentlemen, let us drink to the Old Bay State, and may each loyal heart say within itself, 'God save the Commonwealth of Massachusetts!'" The guests touched their lips to their glasses. "And now," continued the toastmaster, "to his Excellency QUINCY ADAMS SAWYER, Governor of the Commonwealth, whom I have the honor of introducing to you."

The Governor arose amid wild applause and loud acclamations, while the band played "Hail to the Chief!"

THE END.